GRIDLINKED

Neal Asher was born in Billericay, Essex, and still lives nearby. His love of the strange began on hearing *The Hobbit* as a child, and he started writing SF and fantasy at the age of sixteen, perhaps motivated by a compliment from his English teacher for a story written after an overdose of E. C. Tubb books. After leaving school he worked in a firm which made steel furniture, ran a card school in which the main prerequisite was an ability to make tea . . . and produced a fantasy novel that is still gathering dust among his files.

Some years later he began seriously to write short stories. He now has an open-air job that helps keep his mind clear for writing, and has had many stories published by British small-press SF and fantasy magazines. Also previously published have been his novellas *Mindgames: Fool's Mate*, *The Parasite* and, most recently, *The Engineer*, as well as short-story collections, *Runcible Tales*, and *Mason's Rats*. His next full-length novel, *The Skinner*, will also be published by Macmillan and Pan.

Also by Neal Asher

The Parasite
Runcible Tales
The Engineer
Mindgames: Fool's Mate

GRIDLINKED

Neal Asher

PAN BOOKS

First published 2001 by Macmillan

This edition published 2002 by Pan Books
an imprint of Macmillan Publishers Ltd
20 New Wharf Road, London N1 9RR
Basingstoke and Oxford
Associated companies throughout the world
www.panmacmillan.com

ISBN 0 330 48433 8

1 3 5 7 9 8 6 4 2

A CIP catalogue record for this book is available
from the British Library.

Typeset by Intype London Ltd
Printed and bound in Great Britain by
Mackays of Chatham plc, Chatham, Kent

To my family for keeping my feet on the
ground while allowing my head to stay in the clouds.
What a stretch.

Acknowledgements

Thanks, firstly, to 'technical support' in the form of my brother Martin and, secondly, to all those people who have helped or tolerated my struggle up the writing ladder. To my parents for their editing, criticism, and for not telling me to get a proper winter job, and to Caroline for her unflinching support, and to those independent press publishers who believed in me: Anthony Barker (Tanjen), Geoff Lynas (Threads), Tony Lee (Pigasus Press), Graeme Hurry (Kimota), Elizabeth Counihan (Scheherazade), Alf Tyson (Piper's Ash), David Logan (Grotesque), Pam Creais (Dementia 13), Andy Cox (TTA), Chris Reed (BBR) and many others. Also to Simon Kavanagh for his intelligent appraisal of the original manuscript, and to Peter Lavery of Pan Macmillan for spotting a good bet without the intercession of an agent.

Prologue

(Solstan 2432)

A blue snow was falling on the roof of the embarkation lounge, where it melted and snaked across the glass in inky rivulets. Freeman put his coffee on the table, then slumped in the form chair. He winced at the sudden increased throbbing behind his eyes, then turned his watery gaze on the other travellers hurrying across the mosaic floor, their obedient hover-luggage at heel behind them, and with thoughts like grey slugs he tried to remember exactly what had happened last night. He distinctly remembered a half-catadapt woman undressing him in the middle of the dance floor, but beyond that everything was a blur. A deep feeling of guilty depression settled on him and he tried to distract himself by reading the brochure entry in his note screen. It took him two attempts to turn it on.

The Samarkand buffers are galactic upside, which means more energy comes in than is taken out. This is why the way-station runcible is here rather than on Minostra. Minostra is only capable of supporting a runcible for local transport; that is, under 100 light-years. There, the heat pollution of a galactic runcible would have caused an ecological disaster, whereas on Samarkand the energy, as heat, is used as the impetus—

'This your first time?'

Freeman glanced across at the apprehensive individual who took a seat next to him. Typical well-hugger trying to look like a member of the runcible culture, he thought. The vogue slick-pants and corsair shirt told him all he needed to know. The Sensic augmentation behind the man's left ear told him things he did not want to know. Unlike those who lived for the thrill of new worlds and new experiences, this guy's dress was inappropriate and his augmentation a cheap copy likely to scramble his brains within a month. But then who was Freeman to judge? He managed to scramble his brains without mechanical aid.

'No, been through a few times.' Freeman returned his attention to his note screen. Right at that moment he did not feel in a conversational mood. Vaguely he recalled sweaty nakedness, and wondered if he had screwed her there on the dance floor. Shit.

—for a terraforming project. It has been argued that this—

'Makes me nervous.'

'What? Sorry?'

'Makes me nervous. Never understood Skaidon technology, even when I was plugged in.'

Freeman tried to dispel the laughing face of the cat-woman from his mind.

'Well, Skaidon was a clever git even before he hooked up with the Craystein computer.'

—cold world should be—

'We should be able to understand it, unaugmented.'

2

Freeman took a couple of detox tablets from the half-used strip in his top pocket. You weren't supposed to take more than one at a time, but right then he needed them. The pills went down with a gulp of scalding coffee. He coughed, wiped tears from his eyes.

'No human understands Skaidon tech, even with augmentation. I work on the damned things, and half the time I don't know what I'm doing.'

On reflection it was not the best thing to say to someone nervous of using a runcible.

The man stared at him while Freeman finished his coffee and looked yearningly back at the dispensing machine. There might just be time for another one before his slot.

'It's my slot shortly. I'm off. Don't worry, it's perfectly safe. Runcibles hardly ever go wrong.'

Shit – did it again.

As he moved off across the mosaic floor Freeman felt his head lightening as the black cloud of extreme hangover lifted. He regretted that he had not put that guy's fears to rest, but then nothing but a number of further trips through the gate would do that. With runcible transmissions of quince, i.e. mitter travellers, amounting to somewhere in the billions for every hour solstan, and only the minutest fraction of one per cent of them coming to harm in transit, it was more dangerous crossing this floor.

At the far end of the lounge were the gates to the runcibles, and near them was a vending machine. Freeman saw there were three people waiting before Gate Two: one catadapt and two human normals. The catadapt was using the coffee machine. He felt a horrible sinking sensation: half-catadapt. It was her; the orange and pink fur in a V down her back was very distinctive, as was the plait from her hair woven down the middle of it. Instead of going over to his gate, he halted by a pillar and studied the news-screen mounted there. The usual media pap, but at least he did not have to speak to it. From the corner of his eye he saw her drinking her coffee as if she really needed it, gulping it down. She then ran to the gate and through, discarding her cup on the floor. Was she suffering too? Wouldn't it be the limit if she had been going to Samarkand? The other two people also went through. They must have been heading for the same place, or else resetting would have taken longer. He headed over to the gate, pausing for only a moment as the black horseshoe-crab of a cleaning robot hummed past trailing the acrid odour of strong carpet cleaner. He had a flash of memory. There had definitely been a carpet. He felt a further lifting of the cloud. There had been no carpets on the dance floor.

By the departure gate Freeman pressed his hand to a plate on the log-on column. His identity, credit rating and destination appeared on a screen to the left of his hand. He pressed again to confirm. The door before him opened and he stepped through onto a moving walkway. This took him through a long corridor, ribbed like the gullet of some reptile, then to a door leading to the runcible chamber.

The chamber was a thirty-metre sphere of mirrored glass floored with black glass. The runcible itself stood at the centre of this, mounted on a stepped pedestal. It might have been the altar to some cybernetic god of technology. Nacreous ten-metre-long incurving bull's horns jutted up from the pedestal. Between them shimmered the cusp of a Skaidon warp, or the 'spoon' as it was now called, hence the weird nomenclature Skaidon technology had acquired.

Five-dimensional singularity mechanics. Skaidon warp. Skaidon technology . . .

Much as he hated to admit it, Freeman preferred the runcible spoons and quince of Edward Lear's nonsense poem. He did not like the bit about quince being *sliced*, since quince was the collective noun for those who travelled using the runcibles. Most people knew the ancient poem now, and Freeman wondered what Lear would think of this novel use of his words. He walked up to the pedestal, mounted the steps to the cusp, stepped through, and was gone.

Shoved into underspace, dragged between shadow stars, Freeman travelled, thumbing his nose at relativity, in the cusp of a technology his unaugmented mind could not comprehend. Between runcibles he ceased to exist in the Einsteinian universe. He was beyond an event horizon, stretched to an infinite surface with no thickness, travelling between stars as billions of those called 'quince' had done before him.

Done, in that instant when time is divided by infinity and brought to a standstill.

Done, in the eternal moment.

Freeman passed by 253 light-years. The second runcible caught him, dragged him back over the horizon and channelled the vast build-up of energy he was carrying . . . only . . . only this time something went wrong. Freeman passed through the cusp still holding his charge. The Einsteinian universe took hold of him and ruthlessly applied its laws, and in that immeasurable instant he appeared at his destination, travelling the smallest fraction possible below the speed of light.

On the planet Samarkand, in the Andellan system, Freeman supplied the energy for a thirty-megaton nuclear explosion; the atoms of his body yielding up much of their substance as energy. Eight thousand people died in the explosion. Another 2000 died of radiation sickness in the weeks that followed. A few hundred survived even this, but, without the energy tap from the runcible buffers and with most installations knocked out, the cold returned to Samarkand and they froze to death. Two survived, but they were not human, and it was open to conjecture that they were even alive. His family and friends mourned Freeman when they discovered what had happened to him, and sometimes, when she was in a good mood, a half-catadapt woman smiled at a memory; other times she winced.

Like a discarded child-god's building block, the two-kilometre cube of ceramal which was the headquarters of Earth Central Security rested on the shore of Lake Geneva. There were no windows or doors in this structure and, for the 50,000 people that worked there, the only ingress was via runcible. They came in naked and left naked, and were scrutinized molecule by molecule each way, yet even they had no idea what information was gathered, what decisions were reached, and what orders given. Each time they left, they left part of their minds inside, downloaded into another mind that knew it all.

Some comedian, at the inception of the project, had christened him Hal, after the computer in an ancient classic, but that was now classified information. Earth Central was an AI, and an exceptionally large AI for a time when a planetary co-ordinator could be lost in an ashtray. Earth Central was the size of a tennis ball, but then terabytes of information were processed in its etched-atom circuits in picoseconds; information received, collated, acted upon. Orders given. The ruler of the human polity was not human.

Unbuffered jump to Samarkand – confirmed.
Major buffer failure – confirmed.
– Analysis Of Cyclic Rebellion by Edward Landel –
ORDER: AGENT 2XG4112039768 ON RUNCIBLE TRACE.
Possible alien involvement – unconfirmed.
Trace to second quadrant.
– Terrorism In The Twentieth Century –
ORDER: CANCELLED.
All human life on Samarkand extinguished –
projection.
– Sea Of Death (Hood) –
ORDER: AGENT PRIME CAUSE TO CHEYNE III.
'What's the problem, Hal?'
QUESTION: HOW DO YOU DO THAT?
Laughter.

It all took less than a second. The laughter faded as the strange old Oriental disappeared from the chamber. Earth Central experienced chagrin, or a near emulation, then turned to other matters. As it continued to collate extant information and give orders, it continued to absorb the vast body of human knowledge in the infinitesimally small fractions of seconds between. Hundreds of light-years away, its decisions were acted upon.

1

*Of course you can't understand it. You're used to
thinking in a linear manner, that's evolution for you.
Do you know what infinity and eternity are? That
space is a curved sheet over nothing and that if you
travel in a straight line for long enough you'll end up
where you started? Even explained in its simplest
terms it makes no sense: one dimension is line, two
dimensions are area, three are space and four are
space through time. Where we are. All these sit on top
of the nullity, nil-space, or underspace as it has come
to be called. There's no time there, no distance,
nothing. From there all runcibles are in the same place
and at the same time. Shove a human in and he
doesn't cease to exist because there is no time for him to
do so. Pull him out. Easy. How do the runcible AIs
know when, who and where? The information is
shoved in with the human. The AI doesn't have to
know before because there is no time where the spoon
is. Simple, isn't it . . .?*

From *How It Is* by Gordon

Angelina Pelter gazed out across a seascape as colour-

9

drained as a charcoal drawing and felt her purpose harden: this was her home, this was the place she must defend against the silicon autocrat Earth Central and all its agents. She looked up at the sky with its scud of oily clouds. It had the appearance of a soot-smeared sheet, pulled taut from the horizon. The sun was a hazy disc imbedded there. She lowered her gaze to where waves the colour of iron lapped against the plascrete slabs on the side of the sea wall. The day reflected her mood.

'Doesn't it get to you?' she asked him.

He looked at her blankly. Probably searching his data-bank for a suitable response, she thought. He was playing the part of a man romantically involved; in love. She wondered just how difficult it had been for him last night, when he had been inside her – if he had felt anything. She shuddered and pushed her hand deeper into her pocket, clasped the comforting warm metal there. How had she been fooled? He was handsome, yes; his hair short-cropped and a sort of silver colour, his skin that bland olive of the bulk of extraterrestrial humanity, his features sharp, striking – so much so that they belied the dead flatness of his grey eyes. But he was not so handsome, so perfect, as to give away what he was. He had faults, scars, the habit of picking his toenails in bed, a tendency not to suffer fools. All emulation, wasn't it?

'The dark otters are swarming,' he stated.

It was a concise observation. He probably knew their number and deviation from standard size. Angelina felt slightly sick and hardly heard his next words.

'An interesting sight . . . This is what we have come here to see?'

Not good enough.

Arian had been right from the start: he was a plant. She had to do it. She had to do it now. But it was difficult – so very hard to kill someone she had actually allowed through her defences, allowed to make love to her . . . have sex with her . . . emulate the actions of mating.

He stepped away from her, nearer to the edge, and looked down. The sea roiled, as viscid as oil against the sea wall. Below the surface, dark otters were shooting back and forth as they hunted adapted whitebait introduced two centuries before, still to learn that Earth flesh tasted foul and gave no nutrition. Angelina pulled out the weapon it had cost them so much to obtain. Money, and more than one life.

'Sometimes I think,' he said, turning to her with his face twisted in a parody of understanding, 'that the—'

He saw the weapon.

'You made love like a machine,' Angelina said as she levelled the gun at him. The gun was matt black, and had the shape of an old projectile gun, but with LCD displays on its side and a barrel that was an open cube with a polished interior. It was what some called an antiphoton weapon, yet what it projected was not antiphotons, merely field-accelerated protons. It had been a necessary lie, once. Separatists had developed it, and now a Separatist would use it. Angelina had never seen one before, let alone used one. Necessary again. She watched him for a reaction. For a moment he appeared to be listening to something distant, then he slumped in defeat.

'How long have you known?' he asked, turning his

11

shoulder to her and looking inland to the floodplain and neat fields of adapted papyrus.

Angelina lied. 'We had you figured out shortly after you arrived. Our scans showed you were human, but we know about chameleonware. You fooled us for a short while with your devil's advocate bit, but you screwed up by knowing too much. You're a fucking emulation. I made love to an android.'

'So last night meant nothing to you?' he asked.

'Nothing,' she replied. She would have to do it now, before the tears spilled.

'Hence the proscribed weapon,' he said, his face blank. He was talking to stay alive.

'There'll be nothing left of you, you bastard!'

'Yes, I can see you—'

He moved, and the movement was almost too swift for Angelina to follow. She saw something glittery shooting towards her face. He was gone. Her finger closed on the touch-plate. She was knocked backwards. There was a brief pain. Blackness.

Cormac hit the ground as the air shrieked. The shot cut past him with a violet flash, and then splashed to the ground as Angelina fell. Damp soil exploded. Violet fire flared for a moment and was extinguished. He rolled to his feet as the shuriken came in for its second strike, its chainglass blades extending as it whirred. He hit the recall on its holster and it halted in midair. It returned to him with a vicious reluctance, shaking away blood and pieces of bone. Its auxiliary blades retracted. He watched a runnel the shape of a question mark, which her weapon had cut into the ground, as it glowed a laval red that slowly faded. He held out his arm like a falconer awaiting the return of his bird. After the shuriken had snicked itself away in its metal holster on his forearm, he squatted down by Angelina. There was a lot of blood. Her head was attached by only skin and muscle the width of his finger. He reached out and grasped her hand, as if giving comfort, while final nervous reactions shivered and flexed the body that had clung to him the night before. In a moment the shivering and jerking ceased.

The AI had, superfluously, told him he was permitted to use maximum sanction. That had always been a favourite AI euphemism for murder. That permission had been implicit the moment she had drawn the weapon. Coldly, Cormac considered his options. The AI had already instructed him that the part he was playing here must be closed down immediately. Well, this effectively did just that. He could not see the rest of the cell welcoming him back after killing their leader's sister.

Angelina dead. Instructions?

The delay was not so long this time. He reckoned the moon had moved above the horizon and he was now in line of direct contact.

Destroy weapon and any pertinent evidence. When you have done this you must return to the runcible. You will receive further instructions while in transit.

Runcible AI, why so fast?

You have your instructions, Ian Cormac.

Cormac reached down and pulled the gun from

Angelina's knotted fingers. He weighed it in his hand and wondered who was supplying the Cheyne III Separatists with such items. Before this emergency recall it had been his intention to find out. No chance now. As he studied the weapon he felt a momentary flush of annoyance. He had blown it. The recall had come at an opportune moment. What the hell had he been thinking? He stared at the weapon introspectively and it took him a moment to register that all its displays had dropped to zero. It started to vibrate and emit a high-voltage whine. He shook his head. Bad enough that they were obtaining weapons with this destructive potential, but weapons that were keyed as well? From where he was kneeling, he tossed the proton gun out to sea. The whine it was emitting passed out of audio range, and it hit the water like a piece of hot iron. He watched its glow sink into the depths and disappear. Shortly after, there was a brief copper-green flash, and bubbles of steam foamed to the surface as the weapon dumped its load. Cormac watched as the bodies of whitebait floated to the surface.

Cormac?

Cormac gazed beyond to where waves were breaking over a just-submerged reef, then he slowly stood. The breeze from the sea was cold and quickly penetrated his legs. Glancing down he saw that he had been kneeling in Angelina's blood.

Cormac? I've had an energy spike from your location.

Beyond the reef something large was cutting through the waves. A fluke the size of a man turned in the air, throwing up spray, and a wide black body submerged. Cormac gave a nod and looked down at the body of the woman he had made love to.

Weapon was palm-keyed to Angelina. It self-destructed.

Are you injured?

All systems are functional.

I asked if you were injured.

Cormac inspected himself. 'I am unhurt,' he said, out loud.

A sea breeze was carrying with it a burnt-wood smell. On the landward side of the sea wall the papyrus was all papery whispering and seed heads nodding knowingly. Here, blue herons hunted for whitebait and flounders in the straight channels between the rows of plants, and juvenile dark otters hunted the blue herons. Those otters that caught a heron only did so once; the adapted meat of this Earth-originated bird was poison to a native of Cheyne III. Cormac stared at a heron as it pulled from the grey water a flounder seemingly too large for it to swallow. With an instruction that was almost without language, he accessed wildlife information and statistics. In one corner of his visual cortex he fast-forwarded pictures of the changes terraforming had wrought here. He speed-read and downloaded a file on the introduction of the blue heron, while a commentary mumbled subliminally in the background.

The heron, oblivious to this attention to it, flipped and turned its prey into position, and eventually gulped it down. The flounder struggled in its baggy neck as the bird moved on after other prey, dark shadows following close behind it. Cormac blinked and shook his head. He dispelled the mumbles and the access he couldn't quite remember requesting. His arms were burning with the weight he carried. He looked down, then, after a further pause, he placed Angelina's headless body in the passenger seat of his open-topped antigravity car. Then he turned round and went back for her head.

I should feel something.

What was there to feel? She had been a terrorist, and it was his duty to protect the citizens of the Polity from her like. To his knowledge she had been personally and directly responsible for three deaths. Indirectly, with her brother Arian, she had been involved with Separatist outrages that had left hundreds of Polity citizens dead or maimed. Cormac knew all about them; the statistics scrolled at the edge of his vision as he stopped by Angelina's head, then stooped and picked it up by its long blonde hair.

Angelina's face was without expression, utterly relaxed in death. A shudder went through him. He felt something almost like a cringe of embarrassment. Holding her head like some grotesque handbag, he returned to the car. He opened the driver's door and reached across to put the head in the body's lap before he got in. Once he was in, he secured her belt before his own. He did not want her falling across the control console; she was making enough mess as it was. He had considered leaving her, but it would be better if she disappeared completely, and he knew how to achieve that; it had been one of the first things he had learnt from the Cheyne III Separatists. Cormac grimaced to himself, then pulled up on the joystick. The car rose ten metres and halted. He turned it out towards the sea and shoved the stick as far forward as it would go. This detour, to where the ocean-going dark otters swam, wouldn't take long. It never did.

Three minutes and he was out over water as black as oil. He looked for a sign, and soon saw a huge swirl 100 metres from him; it was an egg-carrier, and a big one. Once above it, he opened the passenger door, unclipped Angelina's belt, and shoved her out. The carrier turned on her. A toothless mouth, as of a huge carp's, opened and closed with a foaming splash, then the dark otter dived, its wide sleek back like a glimpse of the turning of some immense tyre.

Cormac shook his head. Something was tense and clenched round his insides. He blinked as if in the expectation of tears. And then he surprised himself by feeling regret. He regretted that her sodium-salt-filled body might poison the dark otter. Grudgingly he acknowledged to himself that it was precisely this lack of involvement that had betrayed him. He closed the passenger door and frowned at the pool of blood on the seat. The rental company would not be happy, he thought, with a kind of tart indifference. He turned the AGC and headed at full speed for Gordonstone.

The system of papyrus fields, protective breakwaters, sluices and tidal channels occupied a band four kilometres wide and 140 kilometres long. Cormac glanced down as the AGC sped above a robot harvester. The machine had the appearance of a giant chrome scorpion devoid of tail and legs, and driven along by riverboat wheels. He watched it feeding papyrus into its grinding maw with its five-metre mandibles, and noted the cubic turds of compressed papyrus it left behind. He accessed and quickly learnt that the harvester was a Ferguson Multiprocessor F230 and was about twenty solstan years old. The ultra-fine fibres from the gene-spliced plant the machine harvested made a much sought-after kind of silk. It was Cheyne III's only large export and source of foreign wealth. Of course, sources of wealth were the reason the Separatists had managed to recruit so well here.

The seas of Cheyne III swarmed with dark otters. They were thriving despite centuries of human colonization of the land, as well as colonization of the sea by the adapted Earth lifeforms. Many colonists felt that they occupied space that could be utilized for highly commercial industrialized sea farming. It had been suggested that perhaps there could be a few less dark otters. A customized virus would do the trick. But the Polity had come down hard on that: it was against conservation strictures agreed to when Cheyne III had first been colonized. If any such virus was released, the entire population of Cheyne III would be subject to a fine which in turn would be used to fund a repopulation project. The Polity had samples of all known dark otter genes. This lack of understanding of the hardships faced by the citizens of Cheyne III had caused much resentment.

Cormac looked beyond the papyrus fields to forested areas thinly scattered with villas and repromansions. It was the people who lived here who had been most resentful. They had stood to make an awful lot of money from the exploitation of the seas. The people of Gordonstone, which reared from the haze like a tiara of silver monoliths, had been resentful only when told, by those who lived in mansions and villas, what they were losing out on. The whole farrago offended Cormac deeply. He could not forgive avoidable ignorance.

At city limits Cormac applied for computer guidance, received it, then punched in his destination on the control console. As soon as the city AI took over, he released the stick and leant back. The AGC climbed half a kilometre and accelerated past its manual governor. At this speed the city rapidly drew close, and he soon saw sprawling ground-level arcologies below the plascrete towers. These shining buildings cloaked the ground like the etchings of an integrated circuit. From this height only a green blur could be seen between the buildings, but Cormac knew that there lay endless beautiful gardens and parks, greenhouses and warm lakes, playing fields and orchards. The towers that punched up from this Eden at regular intervals rose for hundreds of storeys into the sky and contained apartments for those who preferred a less bucolic lifestyle. Every tower was an object of beauty, with its projecting balconies and conservatories and its distinctive AI-designed architecture. Strangely enough, by Earth standards, this city was not particularly well-to-do. Even so, its citizens enjoyed a lifestyle that in another age would have been viewed as nothing short of numinous.

Under city control the AGC decelerated as the Trust House Tower came in sight. Here was the kind of building common to Earth. It stood half a kilometre high and was in effect a self-contained city. The city AI put Cormac's craft in a stacking pattern with all the others that were spiralling down to the fifty hectares of rooftop landing pads. It did not take long for the AI to bring him to the pad above one of the hotel complexes. The AGC was dropped neatly in a row of five similar vehicles enclosed by a privet box hedge. Cormac climbed out and sauntered easily to the nearby drop-shaft. Chipped amethyst crunched underfoot, and somewhere a thrush was singing its heart out.

Cormac smiled at the first person he saw: a woman in a cat-suit and spring heels. He smiled because this should have been expected; it was a lovely day. People smile on lovely days. The woman studied him dubiously with slitted cat's eyes. Must be back in, he thought irrelevantly, and considered, then rejected, accessing information on the latest fashions. It was only as he drew abreast of the woman that he noticed she was looking at the front of his shirt. He returned her gaze levelly, and once past her he glanced down.

Idiot!

The blood spattered there was not exactly a fashion accessory. He hurried to the cowled entrance of the drop-shaft, quickly hit his floor-level plate, and stepped out into open air. The irised antigravity field closed around him and controlled his descent. As floor after floor sped by him he removed his shirt and rolled it up. He had it tucked under his arm as he slowed to a halt at his own floor, and stepped out onto the sea-fibre carpeting. In moments he reached the door to his room and hit the palm-lock. It was with chagrin that he noted the bloody smear he left there as he entered. Before closing the door he wiped the smear away with his shirt.

'Messages,' he said, tossing his shirt on the floor and kicking off his shoes.

'Arian Pelter commed you at 20:17, but left no message,' the sexy voice of the Trust House AI told him. He grimaced to himself as he stripped off his trousers. It was now 20:35. Of course he did not need to see the clock to find this out. He always knew the time, to the second.

'Did he leave any provisos with his message?' Cormac asked.

'Only that he be informed when you return,' the AI replied.

'Oh good,' said Cormac.

'There is a problem?' the AI asked him.

'None at all,' said Cormac as he rolled up his discarded clothes and took them to the disposal chute in the kitchen area. He tossed the clothing in, cycled it, and quickly headed for his bathroom. The shower he turned on full and as hot as he could stand. He had the strongest soap on the list mixed into the water and the sonic cleaner going as well. It had always been his experience that blood was a complete bastard to remove.

'Ian Cormac, please respond?' the Trust House AI urged. Cormac supposed it must have been its second or third request for his attention. He shook soap from his ears and clicked the control of the shower to pure cold water. When he had taken as much of that as he could stand, he stepped from the stall and took up his towel. He did not have time to luxuriate in the warm air blast.

'Yes, I'm here.'

'John Stanton and Arian Pelter wish to see you. They are verified. Shall I allow them access?'

'No. I do not wish to see them.'

'Will there be any further message?'

'No further message.'

Cormac quickly pulled on Earth army trousers, desert boots, a hardwearing monofilament shirt and sleeveless utility jacket. This clothing was more to his liking than his dress of the last few months. He looked around and took in the comfortable form chairs and thick carpeting. That wonderful shower, a jacuzzi bath, and a bed that he had thought might be intent on eating him when he first lay on it. He suspected he would not be enjoying such comforts again for a little while. He considered the belongings he had installed here: the designer clothing dispenser, the brandy collection, the antique weapons. They were all cover; aimed to present him as a weapons merchant prepared to sell to terrorists. There was nothing much here he really wanted. From his grip he removed a small toylike gun, which he tucked into one pocket of his jacket, and a chip card, which he tucked into the other.

'Ian Cormac, my apology for this interruption, but Mr Pelter is most insistent. He informs me that he wishes to see you on a matter of great importance and urgency,' said the House AI.

'I bet he does,' said Cormac. Of course Angelina's brother wanted to have words with him. He had not expected him ever to return. 'Tell me, where is he at the moment?'

'He is at the inner-street level of this complex. Do you have any messages for him?'

'Yes, tell him I'll come down to him shortly.'

'Message relayed,' the AI replied, but by then Cormac was through the door.

Cormac hit the pad for the floor immediately below the roofport and stepped into the drop-shaft. As he ascended he looked down. Pelter was supposedly twenty floors below him, but Cormac had never put much faith in what low-level AIs told him; they were too easily fooled. He stepped out into the penthouse area of the House. Here the apartments were spread out like bungalows, with glass-roofed gardens in between. He knew that the roofport was directly above him, and supposed that light was refracted in from the side of the building to the gardens. It produced an interesting effect, but not one he wanted to ponder for too long. He quickly headed to the nearest stairwell to the roof, pulled out his thin-gun, and ascended very quietly.

John Stanton was a bruiser with a surprising intellect. He appeared a complete thug, with his boosted musculature, reinforced skeleton and red-fuzzed neckless dome of a head. However, apart from the man's mercenary approach to life, Cormac liked him. He also found it easy to recognize him from behind, and John was unfortunate in choosing the top of that particular stairwell for cover.

Cormac kept his gun zeroed on the red dome of Stanton's head as he climbed the stairs with utter control, and in utter silence. Stanton did not react until Cormac was only a pace away from him. Then he turned, saw Cormac and, because he had no weapon immediately to hand, launched a heel-of-the-hand strike. Cormac pulled back, looped his own arms round Stanton's arm, his gun hand above and his other arm below, twisted his body and scissored his arms. The bones of Stanton's arm broke with a loud crack. He had no time to yell as, off-balance, he slammed headfirst into the side of the stairwell. Stanton went down, tried to rise. Cormac smashed the heel of his left hand down and Stanton went down again and stayed down, his breathing laboured. Cormac stepped back and pointed his weapon at Stanton's head. He thought about Angelina, then turned the gun aside. The Separatist movement could recruit the likes of Stanton whenever they wanted. He convinced himself he let the man live for purely logical reasons.

From the vantage point of the stairwell there was no sign of any suspicious characters, though there were plenty of people wandering to and from the many AGCs ranged along the roof. Cormac turned back to Stanton and pulled open his coat. He raised an eyebrow at the nasty-looking pulse-gun concealed there. It was large for such a weapon, and had been moulded in the shape of a Luger. He took it out and removed its charge: double canister. This was the kind of weapon that fired pulses of ionized aluminium dust. Good for close work. He tossed both the charge and gun itself down the stairwell before searching the man again. The comunit he had expected to find was half the size of a chip card. It was also DNA locked. Cormac swore quietly and tossed it to one side, and then he looked back out towards the roofport. Still no sign of Pelter. Cormac moved out of cover and walked casually over to the nearest AGC.

'That's about as far as you go, Agent.'

Cormac threw himself forward, firing off one shot towards the voice as he hit the ground. A double flash exploded amethyst chips just fractionally behind him. He came up in a crouch and fired at a ducking figure, then dived behind a Ford Macrojet. Another flash and the vehicle's boot blew open. Cormac realized he'd backed himself into a corner, and immediately jumped onto the roof of the Ford, then over the adjacent hedge. More flashes – and the smell of burning wood.

'What did you do with her, fucker?'

Amateur.

He zeroed on the voice with a speed-accessed auditory program. Pelter was crouching behind a D-Bird four cars along that same row. Cormac stood up, aimed his thin-gun and just walked towards the car itself. When Pelter stood up too, he was surprised to see Cormac out in the open, and had no time to aim the pulse-rifle he held. Three sharp cracks and Pelter spun, his rifle bouncing off the cowling of the D-Bird. Cormac rounded the vehicle and looked down at him. Pelter was still alive, though those three impacts on his armour vest had probably cracked a few ribs. He glared back at Cormac with complete hatred. Cormac studied him appraisingly: so like his sister with his long blond hair, perfect features and startling violet eyes. In fact he was almost too much like her, as if he'd arranged deliberate alteration. In a purely superficial way, he was beautiful. But his vanity was a standing joke amongst the members of the Separatist cell here on Cheyne III, though not a joke they would dare to share with him

'What have you done with her? Where *is* she?'

'Probably just starting to work her way through an egg-carrier's digestive tract,' Cormac replied as he stepped in close and aimed the thin-gun straight at Pelter's forehead. He watched the man's expression as a look of loss, which wasn't quite grief, battled with fear for predominance. Cormac thought about all the things this man had done and did not feel the same restraint he had felt with Stanton. He saw Pelter recognize this reaction in him, and saw fear winning the battle.

'Please no,' Pelter begged, then winced as Cormac adjusted his aim slightly. 'No . . . don't kill me.' Pelter's voice had a whining edge to it that Cormac had never heard before. He made up his mind.

A squeeze of the trigger brought an entirely unexpected result, when one of the turbines of the D-Bird flashed purple and blew with a numbing detonation. Cormac hit the ground hard and did not have much chance to roll out of the fall. He staggered upright as an AGC roared into view. A quick glance to one side showed him that Pelter was gone. Shit. Cormac ran for the nearest roofless AGC as the one directly above screamed into a steep turn. He dived into it just as the air shrieked, and plascrete erupted in a purple flash behind him. He slammed his chip card into its slot in the onboard computer and an emergency message lit the screen: *Manual governors offline. City control offline. Do not proceed. Do not—* The computer moaned to itself and a wisp of smoke rose out of the console. Cormac yanked up on the stick just as purple fire flared off metal to his right. The car shot up into the sky like a dustbin lid off a stick of dynamite.

Up and running. Am pursued by hostile. Request laser strike.

The acceleration thrust him back into his seat. He slammed the stick over to avoid another AGC coming in to land. The one he occupied slid sideways past it, and he caught a glimpse of the driver mouthing something uncomplimentary. Cormac eased the stick down and pushed it forward. The turbines whined, then screamed, as he shot out across the roofports, then over the city.

Request denied. Cannot initiate strike over city.

Cormac swore to himself, and then started weaving his car from side to side, as the other car shot up behind and above him and tried to match his course.

Request strike when I reach city limits.

The air took on a purplish tinge to his left and he jerked the stick to the right.

I will do what I can, Ian.

Cormac pulled his gun and snapped a couple of shots at his pursuers. The gun made no audible sound over the roar of turbines, but actinic flashes surrounded his pursuer's car and he saw pieces falling from it. He had time only to grin to himself before the seat beside him burst into flame. He jerked the stick back and the car decelerated fast. His head struck the console as the other car shot above him. As it turned, he yanked an extinguisher from under the console and directed a spray of cold-foam at the burning seat. Then he rammed the stick forward again. The two cars passed each other separated by only a few metres. Cormac's ears crackled as he was nearly dragged from his seat, but he was soon able to regain control.

Runcible AI, I am in an extremely life-threatening situation. How much longer on this course will take me past city limits?

There was a long delay as if the AI was chewing over the question. Cormac saw his pursuers coming up behind and above him again. Behind their car he saw a bladelike flame blink out. They had boosters so he had no chance of escaping them. He began to weave again.

On a straight course you will reach city limits in one minute. I cannot initiate strike until four minutes after that.

'What!' Cormac yelled.

The situation is serious?

'Too fucking right it is!'

Another purple flash burnt the paint off the rear of his AGC, and set the rear seats smoking.

It is good that you have retained the ability for at least some emotional response.

'What the hell are you talking about?'

Cormac took another couple of snap shots at his pursuers. Missed completely.

This.

The pursuing car glowed red, became an expanding cloud of smoke and debris cut through with a bar of light. The shockwave hit a moment later. Cormac turned aside to avoid flying debris, then throttled down.

'What the hell are you playing at?'

I was instructed by Earth Central to test you. This will be discussed further after you arrive.

Cormac closed his eyes and took a slow breath. It annoyed him that he had lapsed into verbalization.

I wish to discuss this now.

There was no reply from the runcible AI.

The two analgesic patches slapped directly onto his carotid were enough to make the pain bearable, but Arian Pelter did not yet feel able to walk. He had been reluctant to use the patches, as the pain was clean, and it helped shut out his self-disgust. He'd *begged* . . . no, no, he'd only begged to give himself time. Yeah, that was it. With his legs against the parapet wall he felt his right eye fill with tears. Nothing in his left eye – he didn't like to think about that. He shook his head, and then regretted it as fluid ran down over his face and neck. He lifted a hand to wipe the fluid away, then desisted. It was bad. He dared not touch it. Perhaps this was what he deserved for such weakness. He closed his working eye and thought about his sister. It was easier to be angry at her, to have that anger displace any other emotions. Why the fuck had he let her persuade him? Why had he so seriously underestimated this dealer character? He looked at the comunit he'd placed on the low wall. It was fizzing, as it had done since those last fateful words.

'*We got him Arian! We're gonna take him down!*'

The flash . . . that flash in the sky the moment the

comunit had beeped and started fizzing. It had to have been a satellite laser. OK, fine, that made the bastard ECS, but what kind of ECS Monitor had the pull to order a satellite strike? Pelter heard somebody approaching behind him. He locked his jaw against the pain, picked his pulse-rifle off the wall and turned with it held out one-handed. It was only Stanton, cradling his arm.

'I thought you were boosted, John,' said Pelter, his pulse-rifle still pointed at Stanton's gut.

'I'm sorry, Arian. He just went through me. He got away?'

Pelter saw the momentary expression of horror on Stanton's face, though it was quickly shielded. He went on. 'We know he wasn't boosted, John. We scanned him. He had a little cerebral wiring left over from on old aug fitting, that was all.'

Stanton shook his head. He appeared tired and frightened, and he could not take his eyes from Pelter's face. 'He just went through me, Arian. He had to be ECS. Had to be.'

Arian thought about how easily he had been taken. The fucker had just walked right over like he was out for a casual stroll. He lowered his rifle to his side, clamped his mouth against the rising sickness inside him and pushed himself away from the wall. He was still unsteady, but he could stand.

'We need to go, Arian. Police'll be here soon. No way they can ignore this. We have to get you to Dr Carl,' said Stanton, then added, after glancing round, 'Where are the boys?'

'They didn't make it. He pulled a laser strike down on the car.'

Pelter closed his eye. Shit, the pain was coming back already.

Stanton stared at Pelter for a long moment. How the hell was he even standing? Pelter's left eye was gone, just melted out. The area around it was as badly burned, and Stanton could see his cheekbone. They had to get out of here fast. He glanced around, then walked over to the nearest AGC. Christ, his arm hurt. He carefully manoeuvred it so he could put the hand of that same arm into his pocket, to give it some support, then he pulled his pulse-gun. Now for the tricky bit. He put his gun between his teeth, groped around in his pocket for the charge it had just taken him vital minutes to find in the stairwell, and pushed it into place. *Are we dangerous or what?* he thought, before he blew out the AGC's lock.

'We got a car now, Arian. Best we get out of here,' he said.

Arian took a long slow breath and began to walk over. Stanton considered helping him, but rejected the idea. He knew Arian Pelter well: like this he was dangerous, a cornered rat.

'Hey! What the hell you! . . . oh.'

The man was an ophidapt with an augmented physique, so perhaps he'd thought he could handle a couple of AGC boosters. He stood two metres tall, his skin was finely scaled, and fangs overhung his narrow bottom lip. He blinked snake eyes and halted when Pelter turned to him, pointing the pulse-rifle. Stanton glanced at the ophidapt, then at Pelter. His remaining violet eye seemed almost to be glowing.

'Come on, we have to go,' said Stanton. But it was a desultory attempt to forestall what was certain now. He got into the driver's seat of the car.

The ophidapt held up his hands and started backing away.

'This the hell I,' said Pelter, and shot him in the stomach. The ophidapt went down, clutching at his smoking torso, but in panic he struggled back onto one knee as Pelter, stiff-legged and appearing ready to collapse himself, walked over to him.

'See what it's like? See?' said Pelter, stabbing the barrel of his weapon in the ophidapt's face. The man nodded, tears in his snake eyes.

'Arian, we haven't got time for this,' said Stanton. He deliberately paid no attention to what was going on. Instead, he took out a chip card very like Cormac's and shoved it into the slot of the onboard computer. Often, the likes of Pelter did not bother to continue once they were without an audience, he had found.

Pelter lowered his weapon, and turned to walk back toward the AGC. The ophidapt already looked relieved. But that look of relief lasted only so long as it took Pelter to turn and shoot him in the throat. The ophidapt went over backward, hissing like the creature he had adapted to.

'The bastard,' Pelter said.

Stanton knew he was not referring to the ophidapt.

2

> ***Cosmetics:*** *We are allowed to alter ourselves cos-*
> *metically as much as we want, and can afford, and*
> *because of this humanity has now acquired such rich*
> *variety. Genetic adaptations are allowable in limited*
> *circumstances, hence seadapts who can work easily on*
> *ocean farms, heavy-G adaptations for obvious*
> *reasons, and the Outlinkers who are adapted for*
> *working in vacuum. Some confusion exists about the*
> *purpose of catadapts and ophidapts. Please, please,*
> *readers, be aware that these two terms are misnomers.*
> *These are not adaptations. They are cosmetic alter-*
> *ations. Catadapts do not have nine lives nor require a*
> *litter tray rather than a toilet, and ophidapts do not*
> *have poisoned fangs nor do they swallow their dinner*
> *whole!*
>
> From *New Vogue*

Strobing red and green lights came in from every direction. A police cruiser with its external impact cushions
inflated, and its retinue droids zipping along behind it
like a scattering of large silver bubbles, shot past them to
the right. The two officers inside the cruiser glanced

across, but kept going. Stanton guessed they were reacting, but had no idea yet what they were reacting to. Jesus, gunfights on roofports and satellite strikes. A real secret and undercover cell this one. It had to be blown here.

'We'll dump this and get another, then I'll get us to Dr Carl,' he said, and did not expect a reply. Pelter had another two patches on his neck, so had to be out of it. The one patch he had on for his arm was already making things a bit hazy for him.

'We go to the Norver Bank,' said Pelter, and turned to look at Stanton.

'Arian, you're in a bad way. You need to get fixed up.'

'We go to the Norver Bank, then we go to Sylac.'

'Arian . . .'

'If . . . they don't know who we are now, they will soon enough. ECS will tell them and there'll be warrants out for us. We go to the Norver Bank first.'

Stanton absorbed that as, one-handed, he guided the AGC down to one of the arcology ports. There he knew he would be able to find a less easily traceable AGC. It took him another second to take in something else Pelter had said.

'Sylac! Are you crazy?'

He instantly regretted saying that when Pelter turned to him again. It was that dead look. He had seen it many times before, and always prior to a killing.

He quickly went on. 'Why Sylac? You know what he's into. That cyber shit will fuck you up bad, Arian.'

Pelter stared through the side window as Stanton brought the AGC in to land. He sounded tired when he spoke next, which was a better sign. 'When I want your opinion I'll ask for it, John. Just do what I pay you for and get me there,' he said.

Stanton could not help adding, 'You can bet he's being watched. ECS barely tolerates him. You wanted him hit a year back.'

'Nevertheless – Sylac.'

Stanton switched off the AGC and climbed out, as the single turbine wound down. He glanced around. This carport was positioned between the side of a five-storey arcology and a forested playground. Below the black oaks and spliced fruit trees he could see kids roaring about on AG scooters. The vehicles here were not so new as those on the Trust House Tower. Many of them, even though they retained the city-control option and were entirely legal, were unregistered. He saw a likely choice close by. This AGC was under a roofed-over section of the port, and 100 metres in, which was precisely what he wanted. It had gang colours painted over corrosion, stubby glide wings and a turbine that obviously did not belong to it. It was the same on many other worlds where the Polity was not well liked. People wanted to retain as much independence as they could, but it made them an easy mark. Cradling his arm, Stanton nodded to himself and moved round to the passenger side as Arian popped his door. Arian refused his offer of assistance. There was fluid pouring from the burn on his face and he looked hideous.

'This should give us an hour, maybe more. I blew the onboard comp, so they'll have to use a satellite trace if there's one available,' said Stanton, then pointed to his choice of AGC. 'They won't know we took that one until it's reported.'

Pelter said nothing. He just began walking in the direction indicated. Stanton walked at his side in readiness. It was only when they were under the roofing that Pelter staggered and nearly collapsed. Stanton supported him with his good arm, letting his broken one hang at his side. It was swollen to twice its normal size, and despite the patch it hurt like hell. But if Pelter could take what had happened to him . . . When they reached the second car, Stanton did not need to shoot out the lock nor use his chip card. They were lucky in this. He wondered if they had been lucky in all else. It wouldn't appear so, but they were alive.

Cormac did not see the strange looks he was getting as he walked up the boarding ramp of the delta-wing shuttle. Yes, he was sweat-stained and a little frayed about the edges, but many of them were of a considerably weirder appearance. Perhaps it was his fixed and utterly emotionless expression; a rigidity of control that appeared dangerously fragile. Many would have been interested to hear his internal monologue.

Runcible AI, I am at the shuttle.

Still there was no reply. Cormac tried a non-verbal access direct to the AI and it was blocked. This puzzled him. It was almost as if the AI was behaving irrationally, which was, of course, impossible.

I need to know to what your inference pertained . . . Why was it necessary for me to have an emotional response? I do not understand.

He halted at the small queue waiting at the head of the ramp and gazed out across the acres of plascrete on which stood hundreds of different ships. The AI was just not going to speak to him. Very well, who was he to judge it? There had to be reasons. This was not a gland-oriented human he was dealing with here. He shut down on that line of action and concentrated on the ships he was looking at.

The designs of these vessels were weird and various, with often no concessions made to wind resistance. It was one of these that had been bringing in weapons for the Cheyne III Separatists, and now he would probably never know which one. It wouldn't be any of the small insystem ships, but it had to be something with under-space engines that could get it Out-Polity, where such weapons could be easily purchased. And what weapons, too. The Cheyne III Separatists were the best armed of their sort he had come across in twenty years. They were rumoured to have obtained something *really* special, something almost unthinkable. What could possibly be more important than tracking—

'Sir . . . Sir?'

Cormac blinked and turned his attention to the stewardess. With a surge of irritation he pressed his hand down on the palm-reader she was holding. How inefficient human beings were. Whose ridiculous idea was it to staff the shuttles with them? Angelina had mistaken him for an android. He considered that a compliment. Machines always had perfectly logical reasons for doing the things they did.

'Ah yes, Ian Cormac, I am afraid there has been an error concerning your seat booking.'

Cormac stared at her bland smile and chromed teeth, trying to connect what she had just said to any kind of reality he knew. He quickly accessed bookings and

37

speed-read down the passenger manifest. There was his name, in the wrong place. He replayed, word for word, the request he had routed through the city AI, as the runcible AI had not been speaking to him. There could be no error.

'What do you mean?' he asked, when he could think of nothing else appropriate.

'You requested a privacy seat. Unfortunately you were assigned to a public section. Your seat is D16.'

Runcible AI, there is some problem with my seat booking.

No reply. He tried elsewhere.

City AI, there is some problem with my seat booking.

Again there was no reply.

'Yes . . .' said Cormac to the stewardess. He took his card and was taken to his seat by a grinning steward. Was this some kind of joke?

'Here you are, sir.'

Cormac sat down.

The city AI made a mistake?

He looked around. Sitting right next to him was a grey-haired old man in wrinkled businesswear. Some people considered it dignified to appear old; Cormac had never understood why. The man had narrow eyes and a look Cormac felt he ought to recognize. He accessed and bounced. No connection. He tried again and this time got a download before even posing his question:

The look is Japanese for the moment.

'Heading for Cereb?'

Cormac stared at the old man as he tried to figure out what the hell was happening with his link. Had he damaged it? How was that possible? It was inside his skull and he would need to suffer something of an order of magnitude greater than concussion to damage it. He continued staring at the old man. What had he said? Cereb? He could think of no suitable reply. The shuttle was going to Cereb, the moon with the runcible installation. It did not go anywhere else.

The old man leant forward. 'I said, y'heading for Cereb?'

He said it very loudly. Other passengers turned to see what the commotion was.

'Yes,' said Cormac acidly. 'I am heading for Cereb.'

He felt ridiculous.

'Don't like the place myself. Damned AIs – a man needs to think for himself.'

Cormac turned away from him. A finger like an iron bar prodded him in the ribs.

'What y'think?'

Cormac snapped, 'AIs are efficient. Without them we would—'

'Belt.'

'I beg your pardon?'

The old man pointed down at Cormac's seat belt. Cormac fastened it across. You did not need belts in executive class; shockfields did that job. You did not have to put up with obnoxious old men either. He lay back and breathed a controlling breath, tried access again and got a sluggish response. Schematics of some sort of engine flashed up in his visual cortex. He had not asked for that. He opened his eyes again when he felt the distinctive twisting in his inner ear as the AG of the delta-wing engaged and it lifted from the ground. He listened to the rushing of wind as the wing shot forwards and immediately began to tilt up. Through the elliptical portal on the front surface of the wing, before their seating section, he saw grey cloud coming at them like a falling wall. Viewed through the portal behind, control towers dropped away as the wing turned up to forty-five degrees. AG re-aligned and the acceleration increased. The shuttle punched through the wall of cloud.

'Now this is what I call technology!'

Cormac glanced at the old man, hoping he was not being addressed this time.

'Better than a bunch of moronic nanocircuits!'

Cormac closed his eyes.

Runcible AI. I am in transit. Please reply.

There was that inexplicable delay, but this time he received his reply.

Horace Blegg will brief you once the shuttle is out of the well. He will contact you.

Cormac kept his eyes closed. He did not want to open them. Horace Blegg: the prime human agent of Earth Central, AI and government. He was called 'Prime Cause', and he only turned up when something critical was happening. Cormac clicked a few key facts together. Blegg was reputed to be Japanese. There were not many of them to be seen since the great 'quakes had sunk the islands. The story went that Blegg was a naturally occurring immortal from the pre-space age, that he was apparently the survivor of one of the first fission explosions on Earth. Rumour and fantasy stuck to the man like burrs to a dog. He was a legend.

Cormac opened his eyes and glanced at the old man. The old man winked at him.

With one hand shoved in his pocket and his damaged arm held as steady as possible, Stanton walked through the sliding glass doors into the medshop. To his left a number of motorized trolleys had been abandoned and had yet to take themselves off to their various niches in the wall behind. Each trolley was wheeled – AG was perhaps too expensive for this shop – and had a basket at waist height and a control box on the back that some advertising executive must have thought amusing to devise in the shape of an old-fashioned tin first-aid kit. Stanton ignored the credit-card slot in the top of his box; instead he dropped a handful of New Carth shillings into the tray below it. The tray tilted and the box swallowed his money. A read-out next to the card slot flickered up to show him his credit. As he walked on down the aisles of the shop, the trolley followed like a pet dog.

The shop offered everything an injured man might want, from aspirin and synthiskin sprays up to cell-welding units. Far at the back he could even see the chromed glitter of racked surgical robots. Stanton made his selection of temporary dressings and bandages, synthiskin and some long plastic spatulas he could use as splints, a drug injector and drugs that carried all sorts of warnings and disclaimers, as well as a couple of saline kits. As he tossed them into the trolley, the read-out quickly dropped towards zero. Glancing round he noticed that most of the people here were probably not Cheyne III residents. The people who bought such supplies were either seasoned runcible travellers or the crews or single owners of spaceships. When he had finished he hurriedly left the shop. The trolley went with him.

Outside the shop was an arcade with walled flower-beds running down its middle. The perfume issuing from the blooms was almost sickly in its intensity. Above, the street was roofed over, from the tops of the arcology buildings on either side, with hexagons of pink glass. Below this hung globular security drones on thick power cables. None of these seemed to be paying him attention. As he walked to the end of the arcade, past the many shops, cafés and arched entrances to leisure complexes, Stanton kept a wary eye out for other watchers. He saw none, however. The people here were oblivious to him, so intent were they on hedonistic pursuits. Soon he stepped from the arcology onto a ground-level AGC park. Amethyst gravel crunched underfoot and numerous AGCs were parked in single bays in a labyrinth bounded by squat conifer hedges with foliage more blue than green. When he reached their stolen AGC Stanton peered inside. Pelter was still unconscious, the drug patches and his injuries having finally taken their toll. Stanton opened the driver's door and quickly tossed his purchases onto the seat. The trolley spat his change into its tray, and waited.

'Keep it,' Stanton said, and the trolley rolled off almost jauntily.

First his own injury. Inside the car Stanton loaded the injector, rolled up his sleeve, and applied the device to his forearm. In seconds that arm was just a cold, numb lump. With his other hand he pulled it from his pocket and laboriously splinted it. For good measure he slapped another patch on the bicep. Once he was sure that broken bone could not move, he reached across and turned Pelter's head towards him. He hissed between his teeth at what he was seeing, and reached for the can of synthiskin. When he finished covering that side of the Separatist's head, he pulled the patches from the man's neck and applied a stick-on dressing over the whole mess. Nothing more he could do about it, really. Pelter needed some serious reconstruction. This done, Stanton stabbed the tube from one of the saline packets into a vein in Pelter's lower arm, tilted it until the air bubbled up out of the pipe to the surface of the saline, and then squeezed the packet to inject the liquid. When that packet was empty he stuck the other one to the roof of the AGC, connected up a long tube and stabbed that in too. He shot a cocktail of drugs the manufacturers would have warned against directly into Pelter's throat. Within a minute the man gasped, opened his eyes and sat forwards.

'How long?' he croaked.

'About an hour,' Stanton told him.

'Well, get moving. We may already be too late.'

Pelter studied the drip and the tube, and anger flashed across his features. He seemed about to tear the tube out, but then the anger faded and he sat back.

'That was risky, John,' he said.

Stanton nodded as he engaged power, then lifted the cup control of the car. With a deep hum it rose into the air. He thumbed the guide ball in the cup and the vehicle slid forwards over the park. Pelter was silent for a moment. When he spoke again it was through gritted teeth.

'We'll have to be ready to move quick. Even if the

withdrawal isn't refused, a Polity AI'll be on it soon after,' he said

Stanton nodded again. The pain was returning to his arm and he wanted it bone-welded sooner rather than later. He thumbed the ball further forward and swung the AGC fast round the edge of the arcology. *Here*. The arcade was just a side-shoot from the main complex. He brought the car down to a second park at the centre of a complex of singular buildings. Here the wealthier corporations had their bases built specifically for them. They did not need to rent space from the arcology.

'If an AI is on it now, we won't get out of here,' he said.

Without replying Pelter opened the door and got out. He was still angry at Stanton's disobedience, but was moving OK now. The saline infusion and the drugs had given him an energy Stanton knew Pelter would pay for later. Stanton got out and followed him.

The booth for auto transactions protruded from the side of the Norver Bank building like a Victorian conservatory. The building itself was a domed affair, much like a mosque, at the edge of one of the arcology parks. Pelter walked through the sliding door and straight up to one of the cash machines. Stanton stayed by the entrance and watched as Pelter placed his hand on the palm-reader and put his remaining eye up against the retinal scanner.

'Identified. What do you require, Arian Pelter?' the machine asked him in its silky voice.

'I wish to make a cash withdrawal,' Pelter replied.

Stanton noted other customers casting glances in

both his and Pelter's directions. It didn't surprise him. He would have noticed the pair of them too.

'Please key in the required amount and confirm,' the machine instructed.

Pelter tapped away for a moment, then placed his palm and his eye again. A low note sounded in the air, and Stanton could see Pelter speaking, but could not hear him. A soundfield had come on and the bank machine was no doubt asking Pelter if he required the services of bank security. Stanton looked up and saw the eye in the ceiling swivelling to observe him. He heard the door lock itself behind him. Pelter continued talking. After a moment the door lock clicked off again. Pelter stepped back as a hatch slid open in the base of the cash machine. He reached in and took up the briefcase the bank had provided him for his withdrawal, probably at no extra charge. Pelter and Stanton quickly exited the building.

'How much?' Stanton asked once they were airborne again. Pelter opened the briefcase and exposed its contents. Stanton whistled at the little eyes that glittered back at him from black velvet.

'That's four million New Carth shillings in a hundred thousand units,' said Pelter.

'What kind?'

'Etched sapphires, scan-enabled. They're redeemable anywhere, even Out-Polity. Stay with me, John, and ten of them are yours. Try to take them from me and I'll kill you.'

'I don't work like that,' said Stanton. 'You know that.'

'Yes . . . now get us to Sylac.'

'As you say, Arian.'

45

Sylac was a surgeon of a kind that was frowned on in the Polity. There was not much that humans could do to themselves that was disallowed, including cosmetic alteration, genetic adaptation and cyber-implants and alterations. What the Polity did frown upon was people who carried out the aforementioned without sufficient qualification, or those who liked experimenting, and for whom the human body was a testing ground, even a playground. But so long as no one complained there was nothing that could be done about these people. No one complained about what Sylac did to them. In nearly every case they came to him for something other, more reputable surgeons would refuse to handle.

Stanton neither liked nor trusted the man, and he could not understand Arian wanting to be here. He studied his surroundings. The operating theatre was cutting edge, in more ways than the metaphorical. A surgical robot, looking something like a giant chrome cockroach, was crouched over the operating table. The devices lining one wall had labels on them like 'Bone-weld Inc.', 'Cell Fuser' and 'Nervectonic'. Below these, in row upon row of cryogenic cylinders, were things he knew he would not really want to study too closely. Spares or leftovers, probably.

A long workbench on the other side of the theatre was strewn with devices of which Stanton had only scant recognition. There he saw selections of cerebral augmentations, booster-joint motors, nerve links and synaptic plugs, and those were but a small portion of what lay there. Stanton realized that many of these items were intended for those wanting to go further than mere physical boosting or cerebral augmentation. Some people, he knew, actually wanted to lose their humanity and go completely cyborg.

'Well?' said Sylac. He turned around to them and crossed his arms, all four of them.

Sylac was his own advertisement. He was apparently human up to the waist, but thereafter things started to go drastically wrong. From his waistline there protruded two double-jointed arms, which would have looked more suitable on the surgical robot. The extremities of these two arms bore no resemblance to human hands. They were a confetti of blades and esoteric instruments. His torso was keel-shaped so as to support this set of additional appendages. His head, set above perfectly normal shoulders and arms, had a half hemisphere on one side of it, as if a cannonball was in the process of obliterating it.

'Glad you could see us,' said Pelter.

Sylac looked at the both of them. 'Your usual doctor retired?' He smirked.

Pelter walked unsteadily forward to the operating table. Sylac retained his smirk as he watched. Stanton knew the surgeon had every reason to feel confident; neither Separatists nor ECS had been able to do anything about him for some time. His augmentation had taken him not far from the level of a Polity AI, and the technology with which he surrounded himself made it unlikely that anything less than a tactical strike could take him out, and even that . . .

Pelter placed four etched sapphires down on the table.

'Rather excessive for a few repairs,' said Sylac.

Pelter unclipped an object like a small black pebble from his belt, which he placed next to the sapphires.

'Ah,' said Sylac.

'You can do my friend first,' said Pelter. 'What I want is going to take a little longer.'

Stanton hesitated when Pelter looked towards him, then moved further into the theatre. Sylac watched him for a moment, then glanced towards the operating table. At that same glance the surgical robot straightened up and began moving some of its instrument arms in a manner that could only be described as eager. Sylac moved over to the table and swept up the sapphires and the other object Pelter had deposited there. A second after this the table motors hummed gently as it folded in a number of places. In moments it had become a chair with a headrest and arms. Sylac gestured to the chair with one of his metal arms. The gesture was graceful, which made it all the more unnerving. Stanton moved across and sat. He looked at Sylac, but the cybersurgeon had turned away and was walking to his side bench. Instead of Sylac, the robot moved round beside Stanton. A thin arm darted out and sliced cleanly through his sling.

'Wait a minute!' Stanton cried.

Two padded clamps darted out, pulled his arm aside and pinned it to the chair arm. He felt the broken bone grinding inside and yelled more in shock than in pain.

Sylac looked round at him. 'I do have other things to do, man. You only have a broken arm,' he said.

A sharp pain in his shoulder, and Stanton looked around at the disc now pressed there. His arm went completely dead: nerve-blocker. Stanton looked over at

Arian, but the Separatist had his concentration fixed on Sylac, who was inspecting the black device.

'What do you want with this, Pelter?' he asked.

'I want it connected into a military aug, and I want that interfaced with my optic nerve,' said Pelter, and so saying he peeled the dressing from his face.

Sylac looked at the ruin of his face with something like disinterest. 'I'll have to do some grafting there, but your payment covers that,' he said.

Pelter went on. 'I also want my finger and handprints removed and my retinal print changed.'

Fascinated as he was by this exchange, Stanton could not concentrate on it. The robot now removed the splint and bandages from his arm with a scuttling of curved scalpels. This would have been bad enough in a proper hospital, but here? It then split his shirt sleeve and parted it . . . only, Stanton suddenly realized, it wasn't just his shirt that the machine had opened. He looked away quickly from the neatly snapped bone he could see there, and cringed at the sound of small tubes sucking away the blood that started to well up. There was movement next, but no pain, then came the reassuring drone of a bone welder. Stanton could not say he was impressed with Sylac's bedside manner.

'What will you be linking to?' Sylac asked Pelter, the pebble object now held up close to his eye.

'That is my concern.'

Sylac shrugged and held out the object. 'This control unit I can slot inside your skull without creating too much pressure,' he said, then turned and picked up a grey aug from the bench. It was the shape of a kidney bean and about five centimetres long. He continued.

'This is a big ugly piece of hardware, Arian Pelter, and you're not going to look pretty with that optic interface.'

'I don't really care, just make sure it works,' Pelter replied.

Stanton looked at him. This was not the Pelter he knew. Where was his acclaimed vanity? The man had spent a fortune on cosmetic alterations during the time Stanton had known him. He looked to Sylac to find the surgeon gazing back at him. He felt a sudden tug at his shoulder and a deep ache returned to his damaged arm. He glanced down and saw that the wound had now been welded shut.

'I have work to do,' said Sylac, 'so I'd rather you did not sit there all day.'

Keeping a wary eye on the robot, Stanton slid from the chair. He flexed his fingers expecting more pain, but found none. Pelter moved to occupy the chair in his place as Sylac walked over, his cyber-arms opening out, the complex glittering fingers of their hands revolving. Pelter turned to Stanton. 'There's something I need to do, John. Meet you in the Starport Boulevard in two days, at the Saone, usual time. When I meet you there, I'll want to know who he was and where he went,' he added.

So that was it. 'You'll be all right?' asked Stanton.

Pelter just stared at him for a moment, then turned away. Of course he would be all right. If Sylac had wanted them dead, they would never have got this far, and if he had wanted to kill them here, there was nothing John could do to prevent it. He watched for a moment as the robot shoved the nerve-blocker up against Pelter's neck. Then he turned away and got out of there, wishing

he could close his ears to the sounds that then proceeded.

Once free of Cheyne III, the shuttle's antigravity was
displaced by the thrust of ionic boosters. Through the
portals, star-strewn space faded in to replace the last
orange-and-blue phosphorescence of atmosphere.
Cormac felt himself slowly sag into his seat as gravity of
one G was eased on for the benefit of the passengers.

'Come on, get that belt off. Time for a drink.'

Cormac released his belt and woodenly followed
Blegg to the shuttle bar. As he watched the old man
elbow other passengers from his path, he just stood back
and waited. He was finding it difficult to keep himself
under control, for he had suddenly acquired the almost
overpowering urge to ask Blegg why he had such a ridiculous name.

'I'll have a large Scotch,' said Blegg, then, turning to
Cormac, asked, 'You?'

'Albion water, please.'

'Barman! Two large Scotches!'

Cormac shook his head and studied the interior of the
shuttle. The bar stood at the rear of this particular wing.
Ten metres to his left was the bulkhead, behind which
engines purred and the shuttle's AI that controlled the
craft with but a fraction of its ability. Beyond that bulkhead was the other thick-sectioned wing containing
another thousand passengers. Too many lives here to
entrust to a mere human pilot. Cormac returned his
attention to the bar and watched as webbed hands
poured out their drinks. A machine could have done
that so much more efficiently. He took the drink Blegg

handed him, and followed him back to their seats. As they sat down, Blegg gestured to the barman, a seadapt.

'You know, a machine could do that job much more efficiently, but why should the shuttle company pay for the expensive hardware when people like him are prepared to do the job for the fun of it, for the free passage?'

Cormac stared at Blegg with deep suspicion. 'I was told you are to brief me.'

'Your arse is so tight I'm surprised you bother eating.'

Cormac sipped some of his Scotch to stifle his desire to reply.

'Briefing,' said Blegg.

Cormac looked at him and suddenly found himself gazing into eyes resembling nailheads. Suddenly the sounds all around him receded, and something cold touched his spine. A new voice then spoke in his mind.

There has been a buffer failure at the Samarkand runcible facility.

Cormac drank more of his Scotch.

Is that you?

'Of course it was me,' said Blegg. 'Did it sound like the usual silicon moron? Now think about what I just told you.'

Cormac immediately accessed a runcible tech site and began downloading figures. Something black encroached at the edges of his vision, and everything he had been pulling in was corrupted. He saw files just fading out and draining away. Then something thumped inside his head, and the connection was gone. He experienced an hallucination, part visual and part tactile. A twisted illusion. He was groping about inside his own head, lost and panicking. A hand slapped on his shoulder and pulled him back.

'I said,' said Blegg, 'think about what I just told you. Think.'

Cormac stared again into those eyes. He felt the tug of power there and he made an effort of will.

Stupid to panic. Use your mind.

He did as Blegg suggested, and applied the simple mental calculating techniques he'd been taught longer ago than he cared to remember. Figures started to come up and, after rechecking, he started to put together a nightmare scenario. And somehow, because he had worked this out for himself, it all seemed more real.

'Anyone coming through would have done so at near light speed,' he said, and in his mind's eye – that facet he normally used for downloaded images – he saw what must have happened.

It is called imagination, Ian Cormac.

Cormac looked at Blegg, but Blegg had turned away from him, watching as one of the other passengers walked by. As he began his reply, he slowly swung his gaze back to Cormac.

'Before it was destroyed, the Samarkand runcible AI managed to transmit for point three seconds. Major structural breakdown, not detected in time to prevent reception. A runcible technician by the name of Freeman came through. He most certainly would have known nothing about it. Thirty megatons, conservative.'

'Sabotage?' said Cormac, as those nailhead eyes locked on him.

'It seems likely. You're aware of runcible safety parameters?'

Cormac nodded, then asked, 'Are we talking mega-death here?'

'No, the Samarkand runcible was upside and located on a cold world.'

'What sort of figures?'

'There were ten thousand nine hundred and five people on Samarkand, including AIs. The few Golem androids there would have been close to the explosion, and would almost certainly have been destroyed along with the runcible AI. As for the rest . . . the world was being terraformed by bleed-off from the runcible buffers. It will almost have returned to its original state by the time you get there.'

Cormac nodded and absorbed that information. There might be survivors. There *might*. 'Did Samarkand serve a colonized world?'

'Not really. The nearest colonized world is the planet Minostra: twelve light-years away, with its own planet-based runcible. Samarkand is a way-station world for the influx to the centre of the Polity. We were lucky in that, if in little else.'

'My mission?'

'One of investigation. You'll travel from Minostra on a starship that has the unfortunate name *Hubris*. It's going there to set up a stage-one runcible to bring the rest of the runcibles through, and to search for survivors, though it's unlikely there'll be any. We have to know what happened there. I don't have to tell you how important this is.'

'I know. If someone has found a way to sabotage runcibles . . . Could it be Separatists?'

'There's that possibility.'

Cormac leant back in his seat, sipped at his Scotch, but found he had finished it. Blegg took his glass.

'No, I . . .'

'Ian Cormac, it is time you learnt what it is to be human again.'

Blegg went to the bar and Cormac turned to watch him. The seadapt barman served him immediately, even though there was a crowd waiting. Blegg said something to him and the barman laughed, the gill slits on each side of his neck opening and closing as he did so. Blegg shortly returned with two fresh drinks. Cormac took his and stared into it doubtfully.

'It's said you do not have internal augmentation – that you link with AIs in some other manner,' he said, without looking up.

Horace Blegg chuckled. 'A lot is said about me, but don't concern yourself. Your primary concern is this mission. For its duration you'll be without direct information access.'

Cormac felt something lurch inside him. It was a confirmation of something he had been expecting, something that was overdue, yet it was something he could not visualize at this moment.

'Why . . . surely there will be a transmitter on the ship?' he said, perhaps trying to delay the inevitable.

Blegg shook his head. 'In the service of Earth and the Human Polity you have been gridlinked for thirty years now. Studies show that nearer twenty years is the safe limit psychologically. Your ability to comprehend the spectrum of human emotion has been impaired, and it is imperative that it should not be. Without it, your usefulness becomes . . . less.'

'I am becoming dehumanized, is that what you're telling me?'

'Your recent mission has shown this.'

Cormac considered his complete misjudgement of the situation with Angelina. He reached almost instinctively for access. It flooded through the wiring in his skull, with all its reassuring excess of information.

'I see,' he said, suddenly feeling more confident. 'But by taking away my information access, do you not impair my efficiency another way?'

'It's our opinion we're removing an impairment.'

'Wouldn't someone else be better?'

Blegg smiled. 'You're just right for this mission.'

Cormac sat back in his seat and studied the man. It was said he was immortal, a telepath, and that he could wear any guise. Cormac was completely aware that he was being manipulated, but *how* he just could not see. He reckoned that when he did find out, the surprise would be a nasty one. That was how it usually went. He closed his eyes and tried to bring some stillness to himself, before asking his next question.

'Sleep,' said Blegg, almost as if reading his mind. 'These shuttles run slowly for our purposes, but at least there will be time for you to rest, and to consider.'

Who the hell are you telling to sleep?

He managed to ask that one question before blackness came down on him like a falling wall.

3

Dark Otter: amphibious lifeform found on the planet Cheyne III in the Aldour belt. Gordon gave these creatures this name because of their similarity to the otter (lutra) family of Earth (for more information on the otter, refer to 'Earth', subsection 'Extinct Species', heading 'Carnivores', reference 1163), though this similarity is superficial, and only noticeable in the creature's juvenile form. Physiologically they are closer to the Terran amphibians and go through a similar, though inverted, metamorphosis. Its juvenile stage ranges in size from one centimetre to three metres. It then changes into the limbless pelagic adult. There are three sexes: male, female, and egg-carrier. Egg-carriers up to fifty metres in length are reported to exist, which is something of an anomaly because they are supposed not to survive the hatching of the eggs inside them. A more definitive study than the one in Gordon's memoirs is required.

From *Quince Guide*, compiled by humans

The Meercat was too heavy for the AG units it was carrying, but that made for an exhilarating ride. The catamaran smacked wave-tops and left a scudding machine-gun wake as the shuttle turbine mounted between the hulls got it up to speed. The cabin, mounted just above and ahead of this ancient engine, was an elongated ellipse secured by struts made of the same carbon fibre as the hulls and the rest of the structure. The bottom half of it was opaque and the top half a dome of welded-together panes of chainglass. Overall the vessel was the same dull grey as the waves it sped over, a deliberate effect created by the photoactive paint smeared thickly on every surface. It was a cheaper alternative to chameleonware, and the choice of many who did not want their activities scrutinized.

Inside the cabin there was a distinctly unpleasant atmosphere. Arian Pelter was a both depressing and threatening presence seated in one of the acceleration chairs. Captain Veltz would have rather not taken on this job, but he knew what happened to people who refused the likes of the Separatist leader. He had often enough found their remains inside the dark otters he caught.

'This should be the area,' he said with a glance at Geneve. He hoped to Christ she'd keep her mouth shut now. She'd already pissed Pelter off by asking too much about the source of the transponder signal and he now looked ready to kill.

'I still have no signal,' Pelter said through gritted teeth.

Veltz shut down the throttle, then eased off the AG – no point in wasting power. It would be a waiting game for a little while yet. He turned and looked at Pelter, trying again not to show any reaction to what he was seeing.

A square-section pipe protruded from Pelter's left eye, curved round back on itself to lie along the side of his head, above his ear, where it connected to an ugly grey aug, anchored behind the ear itself. Around that eye the skin was pink and new and obviously a graft. His eyelids were sealed round the pipe

'As I said,' said Veltz, after clearing his throat, 'those egg-bearers go deep, and can stay down for half a day or more. We just have to wait. You won't get the transponder signal at that depth, and even if you did we wouldn't be able to do anything about it.'

Pelter looked at him with his remaining violet eye. Veltz wondered just what sort of mill he had been put through. Pelter was scarcely the kind to get into anything dangerous without a train of his thugs to back him up. Maybe there was a power struggle going on amongst the Separatists. Maybe Veltz was making a bad move here by helping Pelter out. It had just seemed a good idea not to refuse at the time.

'How do you know it's still in this area?' asked Pelter.

'They're territorial. They always stay put,' replied Veltz.

'Unless they're driven off by a younger contender,' interjected Geneve.

Pelter turned and glared at her. 'I'm speaking to Veltz. When I want your opinion I'll ask for it, otherwise keep your mouth shut or you will find yourself wearing a very special smile. Is that clear?'

Geneve seemed set to rebel until Veltz gave her a panicky warning look. She subsided and he quickly began speaking to fill the uncomfortable silence.

'That doesn't happen very often. Only when the egg-carriers are getting old. This one here is in its prime, as far as I can recollect.'

He had actually no idea what the egg-carrier in this area was like, as he concentrated his hunting activities further out to sea. He just kept envisioning that 'smile' Pelter had referred to. It was what they normally did to traitors: cut away their lips and cheeks, before bringing them out here to throw them alive into the sea. Again, Veltz had seen the evidence.

'Let's hope your recollection is not in error,' warned Pelter.

Veltz turned back to his controls, re-engaged AG, and turned on the turbine. It was more for something to do than to serve any purpose. Sod the power wastage. He could understand how Geneve wanted to join in, sitting there with her thumb up her arse, and eager to use the sophisticated targeting equipment run by the console in front of her. Abruptly she stood up.

'I'll make us some coffee,' she said, and ducked through the bulkhead door into the rear half of the cabin. Pelter watched her go with that dead expression on his face. Veltz could feel sweat pricking his forehead. He almost cried out with relief when the device Pelter clutched let out a beep and drew the Separatist's attention to its narrow screen.

'East,' he said, 'about two kilometres.'

'Geneve! Get back in here!' Veltz bellowed as he wound the turbine up to full power. The catamaran slammed forward with enough force to press Veltz and Pelter back into their chairs. In the galley Geneve swore, and there was a clattering sound. Veltz eased off on the acceleration when the catamaran was at a speed he felt comfortable with. He had never found the top speed. Just as the AG was insufficient for the Meercat, the turbine was far too much. Two such turbines had been capable of boosting into orbit a shuttle weighing ten times as much as the catamaran.

Geneve hurried back into the cabin, all thoughts of coffee forgotten. She plumped down in her chair and fixed her lap strap across, before hinging a targeting mask across her face. She took hold of the control handle on her console. A low droning came from below the cabin as the harpoon gun lowered. Cable-feed motors quickly cycled up to speed.

'You should be getting sight of it shortly,' she said.

Veltz could see the ribbed wake of the carrier. He too secured his lap strap, then looked at Pelter until he had his attention before nodding towards the distant disturbance. Pelter got out of his seat and walked up to stand behind the two of them.

'I see it,' he said. 'Just don't miss.'

Veltz decelerated as they closed on the visible signs of the egg-carrier. Pelter stumbled, then quickly got back into his own seat and strapped himself in. Veltz made sure the Separatist did not see the satisfied grin he allowed himself at that moment.

'Go port and past,' said Geneve.

Veltz eased the Meercat over and followed her instructions. He reduced AG so the water acted as a brake. The harpoon whined and thumped as Geneve moved the control handle.

'No good. Come back on the other side,' she said.

Pelter glared out at the monstrous creature as it breasted the swell in what seemed the slow-motion leaps of a giant slug. The core of hate and explosive anger in him seemed to be reaching a nexus. He would have some satisfaction here with at least some kind of kill, some kind of pain, in recompense for the pain he felt. Here he would find something to damp out the image, which kept replaying in his mind, of the narrow barrel of that thin-gun only centimetres from his face.

'All slow. Locked in!'

Veltz slammed back on the turbine and the AG controls. There came a crump from underneath the cabin, and a black line cut from there, across waves like translucent iron, to the apex of an arch of flesh. The cable motor shrieked as their brakes went on, and a vague smell of something burning permeated the cabin. Pelter watched the cable go slack, then tighten again, as the motor went into reverse and that arch folded down. A great froglike head broke the surface and its black maw opened and bellowed. The egg-carrier thrashed and stirred up a bluish spume. Each time it thrashed, the cable motors whined as they gave or took accordingly. The catamaran was tugged sideways across the swell, waves beating flat against it till it seemed the boat might break. Veltz studied Pelter, expecting him to ask if the craft could take this sort of pounding. Inexperienced people usually did, yet Pelter did not. Instead, he stared at the thrashing of the dark otter, and the spreading stain of its inky blood, with a horrible avidity.

'It's slowing now,' said Geneve.

Veltz nodded and flipped over a heavy antique switch on his console. Under the floor of the cabin there came another sound that started low and quickly cycled up to a high pitch, then apparently moved beyond human audio range. Veltz watched the antique dial next to the switch climbing slowly. He heard Pelter's belt unclip and glanced round, always nervous whenever the Separatist was moving about. Pelter then pushed himself from his chair and stepped across. Geneve disconnected her targeting grid and swung it aside. She watched Pelter warily.

'That's an old U-charger cycling up,' he said. 'Where the hell did you get allotropic uranium?'

'Came with the junked shuttle I bought. U-chargers were more efficient than a fusion lump then. It comes in handy,' said Veltz and, so saying, reached for the button next to the switch. Pelter's hand snapped forward and closed on Veltz's wrist. Veltz was riveted by that single violet eye. He could smell antiseptic strong over a faint whiff of corruption.

'Let me,' said Pelter, and then slowly released his wrist. Veltz drew his hand back and placed it back on the steering column. With venom Pelter slammed his hand down on the button and watched the effects.

The line from the vessel to the struggling dark otter momentarily glowed a dull red. The otter exploded from the water, then crashed down again, small lightnings webbing across its smooth black skin. After it hit the water, it sank, then bobbed to the surface once more, completely inert. Pelter sighed, and Veltz saw the expression on his face go from avidity to disappointment.

'What now?' he asked.

'Now we tow it to the Banks. They should be exposed now, and should remain exposed for the next eight hours,' Veltz replied.

'How long till we get there?'

'An hour, give or take.'

Pelter nodded and returned to his chair. Veltz turned away from him and hit controls on the more modern touch console. The cabin, on gimbals at the ends of its support struts, silently turned until it was facing the other way. Now they could see the turbine ahead of and below them, between the hulls. The line to the dark otter had remained in place as Veltz slowly applied thrust. It was a careful acceleration this time; he did not want to tear the harpoon out of their prize.

Cormac had a brief view of Cheyne III through the elliptical portal as the shuttle decelerated and banked. Like any living world seen from this distance, it was a jewel pinned to the blackness of space and bore no hint of the flaws to be found on a closer inspection. Opalescent clouds swirled over blue sea, and partially concealed a continent mottled brown and purple, which he had always felt resembled a man stooping to do up his shoelace. Soon the planet slid from view and the shuttle was coming in over a plain of rock formations that resembled the surface of a human brain. He understood why the first settlers had named Cheyne III's largest moon Cereb.

'I'm not going to shut down your link,' Blegg said.

Cormac nodded as the runcible installation came into view. He noted the sudden surge of excited talk from the other passengers. There, on the plain of rock, stood a city of glass and light. On clear nights it was something you could actually see from the surface of the planet. He drew his eyes away from the vision only when a soft chime announced a message.

'Please fasten your seat belts,' said the soft voice of the shuttle AI. Cormac did as instructed. The message was very different in executive class.

'Who will shut it down, then?' he asked.

'Any runcible AI will do so when you request it to,' Blegg replied.

Retros fired and the gravity inside the shuttle was slowly adjusted to that of Cereb's. Cormac felt his weight decreasing, but that gave him no lift.

'Am I ordered to disconnect?' he asked.

Something roared and the shuttle vibrated. It dipped down towards the shuttleport on the outskirts of the installation. Here was a webwork of glowing lines, almost like some huge circuit diagram, which painted the artificially levelled rock. The shuttle decelerated on retros and clawing AG fields. It tilted and sank down towards a boxed area beside a cluster of towers like perspex cigars. As it descended, Cormac caught a glimpse of the walkway snaking out across the rock.

'You are not *ordered* to disconnect. We do not order people to desist from actions that are killing them, just so long as they know it, and harm no one else,' Blegg replied.

'The link is killing me?'

'I did not say that. It would kill you if you were to continue in your present line of work. *You* have to decide if you want to continue.'

Cormac got the picture. He grimaced as he listened to the shuttle's skids extend and crunch on stone. While passengers were unclipping their belts and grabbing up for their hand luggage in a manner unchanged in centuries, he considered his options. He had been gridlinked for thirty years. He had been with ECS for ten years longer than that. Perhaps it *was* time for a change. He thought about the things he had seen and the things he had done. Many of the latter were not admirable, but they had been necessary. Perhaps it was time for him to retire, buy a nice little residence beside a sea on some nice peaceful planet? He unclipped his belt and stood. Time for a change? Like hell it was.

Runcible AI.

Yes, Ian Cormac.

I wish you to disconnect and completely shut down my gridlink.

You wish me to do this now?

Yes.

Goodbye to you, Ian Cormac.

Cormac lurched where he stood, felt a hand seemingly made of iron grip his arm and steady him. He felt a hundred connections shutting down one by one. Huge frames of reference dragged themselves from his skull down to infinitesimal dots and just blinked out. A deep ache dug its claws into the base of his skull and suddenly, all around his head, there was only empty air.

'You do not delay once you have made a decision,' said Blegg. 'It is why we are glad to have you working for us, Agent Cormac.'

A voice, just a spoken voice: soundwaves vibrating hair-cells in his auditory canal. How the hell could he manage with such an inefficient system? As he disembarked and walked into the connecting tunnel, Blegg silent at his side, Cormac had never felt so empty.

The Banks, two of them exposed by the receding tide like giant beached flounders, consisted of heaped penny oysters and trumpet shells. The former were an adaptation that had taken to the Cheyne III environment with alacrity, but only after an unexpected mutation. Though elsewhere they were appreciated for their distinctive, nutty taste, here they were noted only for their lethality. The latter was a native mollusc that grew up to a metre long and had an appearance much as its name implied. They were also poisonous to humans, but had been the dark otters' main food source. It had come as a surprise to ecologists to discover that penny oysters had also become a favourite.

'OK, Geneve, wind it out,' said Veltz, more for Pelter's benefit than hers; she knew what she was doing.

The cable motor went into reverse, so the dead egg-carrier remained where it was as Veltz turned his vessel to come athwart one of the banks.

'That should do us,' said Veltz.

The motor brake squeaked on and Veltz watched the cable as it dragged up the slope of the bank. He kept going until the Meercat was on one side of the bank and the corpse on the other, then he slewed the boat round to face the bank itself.

'Wind it in,' he said.

The motors came on again, drawing the cable taut and pulling both otter and vessel in towards the bank. Eventually the Meercat grounded and, a moment after that, so did the corpse. Veltz eased up the thrust on the turbine as the motor continued to whine, keeping the Meercat in position. The dark otter slowly slid up the bank, ripping its skin on the sharp edges of the penny oysters and breaking the trumpet shells off at their stems. Soon it was clear of the water and draped over the central ridge formed of shellfish.

'OK, that's enough. Close off the barbs and get our knife back,' said Veltz.

Geneve hit another control, then increased the speed on the cable motor. The ceramal harpoon was pulled from the body of the dark otter, leaving a wound like obscene blue lips. It clanged to the ground and the motor rapidly wound it in.

Pelter stood. 'Let us take a look then,' he said.

Veltz and Geneve unclipped their belts and also stood up. Geneve strapped the sheath of a long chainglass boning knife across her back. Veltz took a similar instrument from his seat and strapped it on. Pelter looked at both of them for a moment, then turned his back and stepped through the bulkhead door. Veltz saw Geneve's questioning expression and shook his head. Not a good move. They both wanted to get out of this alive.

Pelter lowered a metal roll-ladder from the hatch in the floor of the galley section of the cabin. He was first down to the mollusc-bound island. Geneve followed, then Veltz.

'This is where you always bring them?' asked Pelter.

'Yeah,' Veltz replied. 'Every high tide their kin dispose of the evidence. The bones would be indigestible, but, of course, there are never any left.'

Pelter nodded. 'Otter bone still gets a good price?' he asked.

Veltz studied the mounded corpse. It was over six metres long and two wide. There had to be a good ton of hard copper-impregnated bone under that slick black skin. The price would have been something just over 10,000 New Carth shillings. *Would* have been. Veltz doubted Pelter would allow them time to proceed with their butchery. This corpse would be lost in the next tide. He looked at Pelter and wondered what the hell the Separatist was delaying for. Pelter returned his look for a moment, then turned away.

'OK,' he said. 'Cut it open.'

Geneve drew her chainglass blade and held it up in the watery sunlight for a moment. She then stepped up onto the ridge and walked to where the otter's huge and eyeless frog head lay sideways on the ground, its maw agape. She drove the tip of her knife into its baggy throat, then, taking the handle in both her hands, she walked backwards and drew the blade down the length of the creature's body. The body unzipped with the pressure of its bulk, spilling blue and purple offal down the ridge and across the bank. The offal did not steam, as Pelter had expected it to. He turned and looked at Veltz. Without a word the captain drew his own knife and joined Geneve. He began sorting the offal with the blade of his knife, then swore quietly. He had to ask, so he turned to Pelter.

'We really need to know what we're looking for,' he said.

'Who, not "what".'

It was all the reply Veltz needed and he continued

his search. After a moment he said, 'This is the main intestine. Similar set-up to an Earth mammal.' Pelter just stared, only displaying any reaction when Veltz split the intestine and spilled its contents. Masses of bile-bound shellfish spilled across the bank. From these there rose a little steam into the air, and a coppery tang of decay.

'Not there,' said Veltz. 'Have to try its stomach.' He and Geneve pulled a long-veined sack the size of a sleeping bag from the offal spread at the head end of the creature. Geneve stabbed her knife into one end of this sack.

'Careful!' Pelter shouted.

They both turned towards him, then Geneve looked to Veltz.

'Not so deep,' he advised.

Geneve pulled her knife out so that only the tip was inserted into the skin of the stomach. She drew it down, then across in an L. Veltz stood on one side of the stomach to press its contents out of the slice. More shellfish squeezed out across the bank. Then the head-less body of Angelina Pelter tumbled out with them. Her brother, his face seeming dead round its mutilation, stepped up onto the ridge and gazed down at her.

'Where's her head?' he asked.

Veltz and Geneve looked at each other.

'Was the transponder in her head?' Veltz asked hesi-tantly.

Pelter said nothing for a long moment as he stared at what remained of his sister. When he looked up, his expression was puzzled and vulnerable. 'I asked you where her head is,' he said.

'How the fucking hell are we supposed to know?' Geneve snapped. 'It could be at the bottom of the ocean, in another otter. Whoever killed her could have taken it as a trophy!'

Pelter's hand snapped out and Geneve screamed. Her boning knife spun through the air and she staggered back with both hands to a face now pouring blood. She slipped on intestines and fell. Pelter turned on Veltz.

'Where's her head?' he shouted. He had a short, wide blade in his right hand. Yellowish fluid was seeping out round his optic link. Veltz moved back, though careful where he stepped, his boning knife held ready at his side.

'You didn't have to do that. Why'd you do that?' he said, ashamed of the whine that was coming into his voice.

'Her head!' Pelter yelled, and he waved his right arm almost in dismissal. Veltz buckled. It felt like he had been punched in the stomach. Pelter's knife was imbedded up to its hilt in his guts. His legs went weak and he went down on his knees.

'You took her fucking head!' Pelter raged at the sky. When he looked down again his expression had regained its avidity. Veltz tried to stand, but couldn't. He watched Pelter kicking at the spread offal, then striding over to pick up Geneve's boning knife. That Veltz knew what to expect was no comfort. The next high tide would take away what Pelter left there.

As he carried the body of his sister to the Meercat Pelter looked up again. 'You're dead. You're a walking dead man.'

His expression was flat and blank, and now the fluid

ran clear from where his left eyelid was sealed to metal. Perhaps the fluid was tears.

The Cereb runcible installation had, over a period of sixty years, turned into a small city. Originally there had been only the runcible itself, sitting inside a fifty-metre sphere of mirrored metal, which in turn was clamped between the curved grey monoliths of the runcible buffers and sealed under an airtight dome a quarter of a kilometre across. These constructions remained unchanged at the heart of the city. The city itself had grown up to cater for the huge transient populations of travellers. As a consequence of this, it mainly consisted of hotels, hypermarts and leisure facilities. There was little in the way of residential building. All of these buildings had at first been linked together with tunnels; now the areas between them were roofed over. The main building material used for this roofing was chain-glass, so to any visitor it appeared they had walked into a giant conservatory.

Cormac stepped through the shimmer-shield airlock into a reception area hundreds of metres wide and floored with the cut stone of the moon. Walled off in the centre of this area were small groves of palm trees and other more exotic tropical plants. All around were shops, restaurants and more dubious leisure facilities. Some of the buildings were only a couple of storeys high. Those any higher than four storeys penetrated the diamond-patterned roof through which the Cheyne III sun glared down.

'You will of course need to register your testimony,' said Blegg, as they set out across the stone floor.

Cormac observed the slightly amused expression on Blegg's face. He considered commenting on the obvious implication, rejected it for a moment, then decided, What the hell?

'Would this be because there's a chance I might not be coming back?' he asked.

'That is a possibility, though I was thinking it would be an idea for the local police to deal with the cell here before it goes to ground.'

'Very neat,' said Cormac. 'Best I pay a visit to the local constabulary.' He altered his course across the stone floor to a gap between buildings, and to a moving walkway beyond, but Blegg clamped a hand on his shoulder to stop him. Cormac turned and looked at him. Blegg seemed to have changed. He no longer appeared so old and he now had a distracted air about him.

'I will leave you now, and you will make your way with suitable efficiency and logic.'

'Going inscrutable on me again, are you?' Cormac asked.

'Do not accept things as they appear to be, Ian Cormac.'

'Have I ever?' Cormac asked.

'Yes, you *are* right for this.'

It was a parting statement. Blegg turned and walked away across the stone floor. Cormac watched him for a moment, then he sighed and rubbed at his weary eyes. When he looked again Blegg was gone. He swore to himself and set off again. It was all so bloody typical of him. Why couldn't he have just said goodbye and walked away normally?

*

The lading docks cut a swathe through the band of papyrus fields. Here the bales of compressed plant matter were loaded onto robot barges and sent inland by canal to the processing plants. Doug Pench had worked on Dock A for most of his life. He enjoyed it there. He earned enough to pay for his big apartment on the edge of the South Arcology of Gordonstone, and enough to run a Model T replica AGC and a cabin cruiser, for which, incidentally, he had a free mooring. He also did not have to put up with too much lip from his workforce, that workforce being a crew of five ancient auto handlers.

He was working on Handler Three again when he first heard it. He had the handler's casing open and was keying in, by hand, a control code, the original of which had corrupted. Fifth time that week. If it happened again he swore he would kick the thing into the sea and let it join the bales it had taken to tossing there as if intent on loading an invisible barge. The sound was a vaguely irritating buzz. He looked up and saw only the four bales that were now floating out to sea, swore, and returned to his task. The sound grew and became even more irritating.

Pench stood and stretched, walked to the edge of the compacted papyrus jetty and tilted his head. The sound was like that of one of the old shuttles taking off. After a moment he nodded to himself. Of course: Veltz's boat. Sounded like he was thrashing it. Perhaps one of those bastard ECS Monitors was onto his operation.

He squinted out to sea and scratched at his bushy beard. Nothing in sight yet. He walked to the end of his dock and looked back down the swathe of other docks. Parel had walked out on Dock B to see what was going on as well.

'Thrashing it a bit, ain't he?' Parel shouted.

'Monitor after him, guaranteed,' Pench shouted back, and then turned to squint out to sea again.

The drone was deep, with an undertone that told him something was working at its limit. Pench could only pick out the Meercat because of the flashes of white water behind it. It was really moving. It wasn't properly a boat, but a very low-flying aircraft, and it was now coming straight at him. Pench glanced along the cluttered dock, then back at the rapidly approaching catamaran. He should dive into the water and get down as deep as he could. That was his only chance, but somehow he just couldn't get his legs moving. Paralysed, he stared straight into the blurred eye of the turbine and knew it was just going to eat him up. His gaze flicked up to the cabin, and he knew for a moment that feeling of displacement that comes with nightmares. The Meercat, ten metres from Dock A, hit a floating papyrus bale and cartwheeled. Pench watched it scream above him and felt the draught of the turbine intake tugging at his overalls. He watched it take out Docks B to F as it disintegrated, and he watched the turbine, free at last, leap into the sky and arc out over the papyrus fields.

Pench walked back down his own dock, his legs weak, and a strange taste in his mouth. He went into his little hut and called in an emergency. The police and various members of the emergency services that turned up ten minutes later found him sitting on his dock with his back against Auto Handler Three. None of them believed his story about the headless woman driving Veltz's boat, but it would become an oft-repeated legend.

4

Pulse-gun: To call a weapon this is comparable to
describing the wide range of pre-runcible weapons as
'bullet guns'. The name is inadequate and misleading.
There are many kinds of pulse-gun. A laser could well
be described as such because it fires rapid pulses of
lased light. The pulse in all cases describes the packet,
and not the form of the energy itself. Ionized gas or
aluminium dust pulses are usually confined to
handguns, and electromagnetic pulses – because of size
constraints – to larger weapons. Some more esoteric
weapons do fire microwave and ultrasound pulses. It is
worth remembering that within these parameters there
is huge variation in effect, ranging from level of stun to
the size of the hole.

From *The Weapons Directory*

Cormac assumed that the Cereb police station was a
small affair because here so much was visible to the
omnipresent runcible AI, and crime was, mostly, not an
option. A portico, with a hemispherical roof of ribbed
ceramal, protruded from a building little different from
those surrounding it, all with their mirror-glass windows

76

and false-brick or stone façades. The portico was supported by pillars and completely open. Inside it, against the pillars, stood service consoles for those who did not want to take their problem as far as a human officer. As he stepped inside, Cormac noted telltale signs in the construction of the roof. There were armoured shutters up there, ready to slam down at any moment. Maybe small did not necessarily mean inefficient or unready; Cheyne III was, after all, a world that had seen a lot of Separatist activity. He walked to the mirrored door of the station and slapped his hand against it once.

'ECS agent Ian Cormac. Scan me and get confirmation from the runcible AI,' he said. It was only after he said it that it hit him: had he still been linked, this door would have been already open and everything would be ready for him. But this was how it would be from now on. Could he take it? He was glad when the door slid open almost immediately.

Cormac walked into a foyer tiled with a local marble he had noticed before. It struck him as unfortunate that it was white with blood-red swirls across it. Along two walls were rows of decidedly uncomfortable looking chairs, and on the walls behind these chairs were active and inactive posters showing still and moving pictures of criminals, recorded crime scenes, proscribed weapons and, for some reason he could not fathom, some rather strange adaptations. At the back of the foyer was a large, apparently wooden, panel door. Cormac knew that the wood was probably a skin over case-hardened ceramal.

'Scan confirms that you are carrying a thin-gun and an active attack weapon. Please remove these items, place them on the floor, and move back four paces,' said a rather hoarse female voice. Cormac looked up at the ceiling and observed a curious light fitting. It was a bulbous disc with a half-metre diameter and flat edges on which complex patterns and small lights flickered. Swivelling underneath it was a short chrome cylinder with cooling fins all around it. The disc was attached to the ceiling by a thick rod of ceramal, and down this rod ran ominously thick cables.

'I take it you haven't had confirmation of my identity from the runcible AI yet,' he said.

'Place your weapons on the floor and move back four paces,' the security drone replied.

'I presume,' said Cormac, wincing slightly at the sound of security shutters closing behind him, 'that you wish me to place my weapons on the floor so you can make them safe – that is, melt them into slag?'

'This is my third request. Place your weapons on the floor and move back four paces,' said the drone.

Cormac clicked a button on his shuriken holster. No doubt the drone saw this, because it began to emit an AC hum. Cormac wondered just what its reaction speed was. He knew it would go for the shuriken in the first instance, and that would be its mistake. As he readied himself, the AC hum abruptly cut off. Behind him the shutters clicked open.

'Agent Cormac, welcome to Cereb police station,' said the drone, and the wood-skinned door opened before him. He looked towards the bulky, uniformed woman who came through.

'You were taking a little bit of a risk there, weren't you?' she asked him. Her voice was similar to the drone's, but not quite identical. He studied her. Because her uniform, with its impact-absorbing layers and buried mesh, effectively concealed her physique, she appeared fat. By the heavy muscles that he could see supporting her head, and by the shape of her hands, Cormac guessed her to be a heavy-G adaptation.

'Who might I be addressing?' he asked.

'First Constable Melassan, and you are the famous Ian Cormac of ECS, or should that be notorious? Aren't you getting a little too high-profile for undercover work?'

Cormac smiled to himself and paused for a moment before replying. 'Let me answer your first question first: I was taking a calculated risk,' he said.

'No, you'd have been stunned,' said Melassan.

'And I must say *no* to you. I would have launched my . . . attack weapon, and your drone here would have focused on it, assuming it to be the greatest threat. It would then have been locked into destroying something very reflective moving at the speed of sound. And while it was working that one out, I would have killed it with this.' Cormac removed his thin-gun and held it out to her.

She took it and inspected it. 'ECS issue. Very neat,' she said and made to hand it back.

'No, keep it,' he said. 'I won't be able to take it through the runcible.'

She nodded and pocketed the weapon. 'I still don't understand why,' she said.

He looked down at her and became suddenly quite aware that, though she was two heads shorter than himself, she did possess the capability of snapping him in half if she allowed her to get hold of him. He held up his arm and pulled down his sleeve to expose the shuriken holster.

'This is a Tenkian. It is worth a great deal of money, it has sentimental value, and it has saved my life on many occasions. I would not have it casually destroyed because of an identification error. I owe it at least that,' he said.

'AI?' she asked him.

'Borderline. There has been dispute about the issue. What kind of Turing test do you use on a throwing star that does not speak?'

She watched his arm as he lowered it, then returned her attention to his face. She gestured with her thumb, then turned and walked through the door. Cormac followed her into an open office laid out with desks for three occupants. She headed for the one nearest the window, but rather than seek sanctuary behind it, as he had expected, she sat on it and faced him with her arms crossed.

'Well, what can we do for you, Agent Cormac?' she asked.

Cormac pulled round a swivel chair from one of the other desks and sat astride it. 'It is more a case of what I can do for you. I have come here to register my testimony with the Cheyne III police and make available to you certain . . . closed ECS files.'

'Concerning?'

'The Separatist cell on Cheyne III that has been responsible for just about every . . . incident here for the last five years, and, as I recollect, such incidents would include the flame-bombing of the Eriston police station two years ago. It is of course the case that Separatists consider anyone other than themselves to be collaborators. As for police who enforce Polity law . . .'

'No need to labour the point,' said Melassan. She pushed herself up from her desk and went round to sit behind it. As Cormac pulled his chair over, she activated a console to her left. In front of him a section of the desk turned over to show a plate with the impression of a human hand in it. From beside this an arm rose out of the desk with something like a pair of binoculars at its end. Cormac placed one hand in the impression, and with his other hand pulled the binoculars up to his eyes.

'Confirmed retinal scan, palm print, and DNA profile. Testimony of Ian Cormac, Agent 1X1G of Earth Central Security, Cereb runcible AI is online, First Constable Melassan witnessing.'

After that single statement Melassan nodded to Cormac, and he began, 'This is the sworn testimony of Ian Cormac, Agent 1X1G of Earth Central Security. Prior to this testimony, and taken in conjunction with it, I release ECS evidence files Cheyne III Sep. twelve to fifty-four, and all my files pertaining to Angelina Pelter. Now, I think that for this testimony it would be best for me to begin with Angelina's brother, one Arian Pelter . . .'

Pelter wore the grey businesswear of one of the millions of faceless executives who travel from system to system with bland indifference. He carried his bank-supplied briefcase like many of said executives. But he had his blond hair tied back in a ponytail so that his augmentation and optic link were exposed for all to see. His appearance was not any more unusual than that of many people around him, some of whom looked positively weird. Yet people avoided him, stepping from his path and looking back once they were past him. Something about getting anywhere *near* this individual made them uncomfortable.

Pelter stopped at the Café Saone, at the furthest end of this boulevard that teemed below an illusory sky. He sat on a hard stool, placed his case on the glass-topped bar, and thought again about the killer of his sister. Why was it that an image of the man holding that thin-gun to Pelter's face seemed to be permanently imprinted on the vision of his missing eye? He could not shake this illusory presence, and it made Pelter constantly angry. Where was the bastard now, he wondered. The runcible on Cereb was working continuously, and hundreds passed through it every solstan day. Was he already gone?

'Coffee,' he said indifferently, and without looking round. A three-fingered chrome hand placed a cup of coffee next to him and snatched up the shilling he tossed on the glass. Stanton, who had seen Pelter arrive and was coming towards him, saw the aug and optic link and nearly turned away, but his own particular honour, combined with the promise of a million New Carth shillings, kept him walking.

'Executives don't pay with cash,' he said, taking the stool beside Pelter. 'What have you had done, Arian?'

'Who the fuck is he, John?' Pelter asked, his voice flat and without acknowledgement of Stanton's question.

Stanton surveyed the area, then glanced at the met-alled android that was frying burgers only a couple of paces away from them, behind the counter.

'Not here. I've got a room,' he said.

Pelter was off his stool in a second and walking from the café. Stanton took up the case he had abandoned and quickly went after him. The android cleared the untouched coffee, and wondered if it would ever understand humans: always in such a hurry.

Cormac leant back for a moment and looked across the desk at Melassan. At first she had found it difficult to hide her joy at all the wonderful evidence revealed by the files he opened for her and for all the Cheyne III police on the planet below. As that evidence had mounted up, with its descriptions of punishment killings, of the 'disappeared', and the sadisms for which there was simply no excuse, that joy was replaced by a kind of grim determination.

Cormac sipped some of the water she had provided. 'After their fiasco of an attempt to wipe out the dark otters, Sayber, Tenel and Pelter made the decision to call in some professional help. That help came first in the form of an Out-Polity mercenary called John Stanton. Of Stanton's past I know very little, other than to say he appears to have worked for many Separatist groups and was just not around when said groups were brought down. He has no Separatist leanings himself. He is simply as I described him: a mercenary. His lack of fanaticism makes him less dangerous than the likes of Pelter, even though he is boosted and quite capable of murder. His professionalism makes him more dangerous in that he can guide the likes of Pelter into more effective actions.'

'I had to call in a lot of favours on this one, and it took money, real money, Arian,' said Stanton, wearily lowering himself into a director's chair and rubbing at his itching arm. You expected that itch if you went to a cheap bone-welder, but cheap was not a word he would have applied to Sylac. He tolerated it and hoped that that was all it was: an itch. He watched Pelter pacing up and down. He noted that the Separatist had his hair tied back as if he was proud of his facial mutilation.

'I don't care how much it cost so long as we got answers,' Pelter spat.

'He's top-line: a fully gridlinked ECS agent by the name of Ian Cormac. I guess you could say that leaves our pride intact.'

Pelter turned on him and grabbed the front of his jacket. He pushed his head in so close they were nearly nose to nose. Stanton smelt something slightly putrid and pulled his face back.

'Pride! You think I care about pride! He cut her head off, John! He cut her fucking head off!'

Stanton waited until Pelter released him and returned to his pacing before wiping the spittle from his face. Pelter had not cared that much for his sister. They had been alike in that: too self-involved for such emotion. Stanton wondered what it was that was really bugging the man.

'Do you recognize the name?' he asked.

Pelter stopped pacing and looked at him. There was nothing in his expression for a moment, then realization dawned. 'Aster Colora . . . Shit! He's the one who went to Aster Colora. That Dragon thing! He took out our entire network there. Well, that seals it: he dies, and I see him die.'

To emphasize his point Pelter kicked over a small coffee table before slumping into the short sofa next to it. He put his hands behind his head and interlaced his fingers there.

'Crane will be with me – and some of the boys. We'll find the fucker,' he said.

Stanton looked askance at him. 'Crane's dangerous, you know that,' he said. The single eye fixed on him in reply. Stanton felt compelled to go on. 'I don't think it's too much of a problem working out where Cormac's going. The problem will be getting to him,' he said.

'Go on,' said Pelter.

'You haven't heard? It's on all the news channels,' said Stanton.

'I'm getting impatient, John.'

Stanton stood and walked over to the wallscreen. He expertly tapped the small touch-console below it and stepped back. A headline flashed up as the news story he wanted came online.

SAMARKAND RUNCIBLE DISASTER

Stanton watched Pelter as the story unfolded with its ersatz graphics and scenarios. No one yet knew how bad it was, they reported, but it was definitely bad. Pelter's expression was avid. Stanton knew that he wished this could be put down as a Separatist action; personally he doubted that possibility. Separatist organizations just did not have the clout to cause something as devastating as this. The highest they usually achieved was the detonation of a tactical atomic in a city, and after that ECS would come in and wipe them out, every last one of them. Stanton would take their pay up to the point when they started planning something like that, then he would make himself scarce. As the news story closed he wondered if he might be getting near to one of those points now.

'You think he'll go there?' Pelter asked.

'He went straight out on the first shuttle to Cereb, so he's on his way there. I'd say he must have been recalled, else he would still be here mopping up the mess.' Pelter fixed him with that look again.

Stanton quickly went on. 'The nearest runcible to Samarkand is on Minostra. That's where any rescue or clear-up operation will be run from. We should easily be able to confirm that he went there. Just a little money in the right pocket.'

'Very well,' Pelter said. 'We need something more than a few handguns and explosives.'

'Anything more would be expensive, and difficult to bring here,' said Stanton.

'I don't want them here. Where's our usual supplier?'

'Huma – and he's one of many there.'

'Very well, that's where we go. Contact Dusache, Menneken, Corlackis and Svent, and have them meet us there. Promise them double the usual. We also get Mr Crane because, unless I miss my bet, friend Ian Cormac is going to have Golem backup.'

Yeah, thought Stanton, the point where he moved on was arriving. Maybe a million shillings was not enough.

'Where is Mr Crane?' he asked.

'At the residence. He's hidden there.'

Stanton shook his head. 'Risky. Local police will be all

over the place by now. You know that. ECS will realize we'll be on the lookout for another plant, like Cormac, and they won't bother. There's also no advantage to them to let us continue operating. They'll hand all their evidence over to the locals and there'll be warrants out for everyone in your cell.'

Pelter pressed his hand to his augmentation and appeared confused for a moment. As that confusion passed, he pulled his hand away and clenched it into a fist.

'Which is why we need Mr Crane. We have to tidy up here first. There are three people who know just a little too much about off-planet operations. They get picked up and the entire cause will be in trouble. So I can't allow them to be picked up,' he said.

Stanton kept his mouth shut. On the one hand, Pelter wanted to go after Cormac, which was a dubious operation at best. Yes, it would mean getting rid of a dangerous enemy to the Separatist cause, but, in reality, their resources would be better spent elsewhere. His real reason was plain vengeance. On the other hand, Pelter was considering a ruthless action for the Separatist cause, an action that, although preventing other operations being discovered, would certainly make him – or the cause – no friends.

Pelter stood. 'We do it *now*. We get Mr Crane,' he said.

'As you say, Arian.'

Stanton stood up as well, telling himself to focus on the main issue here: a million New Carth shillings. After he had obtained that payment, he could retire and leave this lunatic to his self-destruction.

'Why are you leaving it now?' Melassan asked as she banged away at her touch-console, before sealing the testimony and transmitting copies down to Cheyne III.

'I've been called in – something else ECS wants me to deal with,' Cormac replied.

'That Samarkand thing?'

'Yes, that is somewhat more serious.'

'What I don't understand,' said Melassan, turning from her console, 'is why you were called in here at all. Surely a cell like this is beneath your notice?'

Cormac grimaced and wondered if he would have noticed that same edge of sarcasm a few hours ago. 'It's about the hardware,' he said. 'In that one year with them I've seen them using pulse-guns easily as effective as anything ECS possesses, some very high-quality planar explosives, and more recently a proton gun. I also heard rumours of an android, maybe a Golem, broken to psychotic, and used for select hits. I'd like very much to know where they got hold of such a monster, if it really exists.'

'If it exists,' Melassan repeated.

'There is always a chance that it does, and such a chance cannot be ignored. Can you imagine the mayhem such a creature could do with the right programming?'

'You tell me. You're the expert.'

Cormac let that go and replied, 'Assassination, anywhere. With an android like that you have a weapon you can take through any runcible because it would not be recognized as a weapon. Such an android might, just might, get through quite sophisticated defences, even those round one of the big AIs, maybe a runcible AI or

a planetary governor and, once there, take control . . .
Just imagine a psycho in control of a planetary defence
grid.'

'That bad?'

'Possibly that bad. The kind of possibility we cannot
allow.'

'It's probably not true. Probably just propaganda.'

'Yes, let us hope so.'

5

Money: People need a form of currency that is not just registered somewhere in a silicon brain. Human corporations like Cybercorp, System Metals and JMCC tried, in the early centuries of the millennium, to ban cash money, but they failed. The resultant black economies in the end produced an entirely new currency. The New Yen we know today was that currency, though it can hardly be described as 'new' anymore. Since its inception it has had many contenders. The greatest of these is the comparatively recent 'New Carth Shilling'. It is the case that so long as there are things of value to be exchanged, there will be money. Without it someone, at some point, will write an IOU, and in reality that's how it all started.

From *How It Is* by Gordon

The Pelter residence was large, and set in its own grounds outside the city. In Stanton's experience it was always the wealthy ones who bemoaned Polity takeover, because it prevented them getting even wealthier at other people's expense. The residence itself had something of the appearance of a Roman villa, but with decorations somewhat more baroque. It was surrounded by orchards of self-pruning pig-apple trees. The trees produced apples the size of human heads. They were never picked and at certain times of the year, effectively the twin summers experienced on Cheyne III, the orchards often swarmed with fruit wasps and small blade beetles. This was now one of those times, but the *worrying* swarms were not in the orchards. The swarms that there were, which they saw during a fly-by, were around the residence itself, and were of a distinctly uniformed variety.

'They may have found him by now,' Stanton observed, secretly hoping that was true.

'They are searching the house and I have no doubt they will find a lot that is of interest, but they will not find Mr Crane there,' Pelter replied. 'Anyway, they have not yet come anywhere near him. He would have heard them.'

That was it. Stanton gazed at Pelter and understood now what the aug, control unit and optic link were all about. Great: a human lunatic linked to an artificial one. Pelter had his own personal gridlink.

'Can't you just tell him to come out to us?' he asked.

Pelter twisted his face into what might be described as a smile. 'So you understand, John?'

'Let's say, I know what you're doing . . . Right, where do you want me to bring us down?'

Pelter pointed out beyond the orchards. 'Bring us down in Tenel's orchard. We'll walk in for Crane, then maybe go and visit Tenel afterwards, if he's in.'

'They'll have him by now,' Stanton said.

'Not for long,' Pelter replied. 'Not for very long at all.'

With an almost vicious twist of the joystick Stanton brought their latest stolen AGC down low, and without lights. He landed it between the rows of plum and cherry trees that Tenel favoured on his property. Stanton waited a moment for his vision enhancement to kick in before he climbed from the vehicle. It surprised him how well Pelter coped in the dark, despite having only one eye. Then again, perhaps Sylac had made some other alterations he did not know about. As he followed the Separatist leader down between the rows of trees, he wondered if even Pelter knew what those alterations were.

In minutes they came to a broken-down chainlink fence. In the pig-apple trees beyond this, blade beetles were rattling their razor wing-cases. The sound made Stanton's arm itch even more than it already did. At least the wasps were somnolent at night.

'If one of them hits you, be very certain you do not yell out,' Pelter said.

Stanton remembered the last time such a beetle had hit him in the face. He had required the services of a cell-welder then, too. He folded up his collar as high as he could and ducked his head into it. These insects could kill people, not deliberately, but with the accidental brush of a wing across a vein when medical help was far away. In some areas a kind of armour had to be worn for fruit picking.

'How far is it?' he asked. It seemed to him that they must be getting a bit too close to the residence and the flashing lights. Knowing the beetles liked light, he hoped the cops were having a bad time of it.

'No further,' muttered Pelter, and pointed ahead.

A few metres ahead of them stood the statue of a bearded gentleman clad in impact armour and holding some weapon horizontally across his stomach.

'My grandfather. He served in the Prador war,' he explained.

'Here?' asked Stanton.

'Earth, I think. He left here a century ago.'

So saying, Pelter turned back towards the statue and pressed one hand to the side of his head. It was obvious that he was new to using augs and internal control mechanisms. Stanton shook his head and thought he might tell him about it – sometime.

Somewhere an engine started, and with a low grating noise the statue slid to one side. Exposed now was a square entrance and steps leading down. Pelter gestured and Stanton followed him below. It was dark, even for enhanced vision, especially when the statue slid back into place. Once it had stopped sliding, a greenish light flickered on. They were in what appeared to be a small wine cellar bounded by three walls racked with wine bottles and one wall of stone inset with an armoured door.

'I didn't answer your question about getting him to come out to us,' said Pelter.

'Are you going to answer it now?' Stanton asked.

'Yes.' Pelter walked to one wall of wine bottles. He studied it for a moment, then stepped aside as a vertical section, four bottles wide, slid out. In a moment a set of shelves was revealed. From one shelf he removed two slim square cases. He ignored the various weapons and makings of explosive devices that occupied the other shelves, and held up just the pair of cases.

'We had to come here for our new identities,' he explained.

He lowered the cases and nodded towards the armoured door. This action initiated four loud thumps as locks disengaged. The door opened silently. Stanton thought it would be more appropriate for the door to creak.

'Even Crane would have a problem with that door,' Pelter commented.

Stanton looked inside the room beyond and wondered just how true that statement was.

They called him Crane because he was so very tall. They called him *Mr* Crane because he was so very prone to dismembering people. However, even politeness did not work. Mr Crane would kill people as ordered by the holder of his control module, though occasionally he killed people for reasons that were inscrutably his own. John Stanton stared at him and felt the urge to just turn and go. Mr Crane was two and a half metres tall, so appeared slightly ridiculous sitting in a normal-sized camp chair. He was also utterly still. Over his attenuated frame he wore a coat that stretched right down to his much-patched, beloved lace-up boots. A hat with a wide droopy brim hid his features. Stanton noticed there was mould on the brim of that hat, just as there was on Mr Crane's overcoat. Not surprising, as it was damp down here.

'How long's he been here?' he whispered.

'Two years,' Pelter replied, and his hand moved up to the metal on the side of his head. This gesture now

confirmed for Stanton the antecedents of the module
Pelter had caused Sylac to implant in his skull.

'It was that hit out on the island, wasn't it? You sent
him there to kill one man . . . and how many was it he
killed in the end?' he asked.

Pelter said, 'Don't push it, John. You're a lot more
dispensable than he is.'

Stanton bit off any more comments and just watched
them. What were they saying to each other, he wondered. What did their little electrical conversation
entail?

'Come on, Crane. Time to wake up,' Pelter said,
aloud.

Mr Crane stood up in one abrupt movement. Stanton
took in the black glitter of eyes now open below the brim
of the hat. Crane's head turned toward Pelter, and he
took one long pace forward. Pelter stepped back, his
hand pressing harder against the side of his head, and an
expression of intense concentration on his face. Crane
did not move further; instead he reached up and
removed his hat to expose a totally bald head, a thin-
featured face and those completely black eyes.

'That's better,' said Pelter.

Stanton reflected how Crane's artificial skin looked
just that: *artificial*. It had been previously suggested that
his skin should be changed, but no one ever wanted to
get that close. Stanton supposed the skin must serve the
purpose of preventing blood getting into Mr Crane's
workings. He made sure he kept well out of reach as
Crane emerged from his prison. Pelter lowered his hand,
then turned for the stairs. Crane walked just a pace
behind him, taking dainty little steps to hold the same

position. Stanton picked up the two cases, followed, and wished he were somewhere else.

Cormac glanced up through the transparent roof, then back at the mirrored containment sphere. It seemed that there was a hand closing tighter in his chest for every moment he went without linking in. Maybe he had made the wrong move? Maybe it would be better to have stayed linked and got out of ECS? Immediately upon thinking these questions, which since leaving the shuttle he had been asking himself with greater regularity, he felt an angry self-contempt.

ECS had been Cormac's life for so very long, and he truly believed in what he was doing. He looked ahead at the short queues before the various embarkation gates. *There* was an example of what he had been defending: those queues never became very long. There were no papers to be handed over, no passports, and no lengthy customs bureaucracy to bypass. Polity citizens travelled in absolute freedom from world to world. The only restriction was on proscribed weaponry, and even that did not prevent travel. If said weaponry was registered and deactivated, you could take it along with you. Even if you did not register it, you could still travel, only the weapon would be dust at your destination; disintegrated by the autoproscription device the runcibles had inbuilt. To travel distances once inconceivable, all you had to do was book your place and pay a fee, register your identity with the runcible AI when you arrived at the sphere, and walk on through. So bloody damned simple. These people here with their daft cosmetic alterations and possibly brain-scrambling augs, they just had no idea, no idea at all.

Cormac stared down at his hands, unclenched them and flexed his fingers. OK – it was going to be OK.

I will remain calm.

He began walking again before people started to wonder why he was standing still in the middle of the embarkation lounge staring up at the sphere. All he needed now was some Samaritan to come up to him and tell him not to be frightened of it. He smiled tightly to himself as he walked along, then, before he reached the row of gates, he turned towards one of the wide and ornately cast synthestone pillars that ostensibly supported the chainglass roof. At one of the four consoles, in the base of the pillar, he halted and slapped his hand down on the reader. He blinked on a momentary flash of red as the reader scanned his retinal pattern.

'Identity confirmed, Ian Cormac,' spoke an androgynous voice.

'I want passage to Minostra as soon as possible,' he said, then he turned his head slightly as all sounds beyond him suddenly cut out. A privacy field that he had not requested had developed. Now a completely different voice, but one he recognized, spoke from the console.

'Would that be executive class or second?' the Cheyne III runcible AI asked him.

Cormac frowned, but felt a kind of joy. This perhaps was the nearest he could come to linking. This privacy, this difference.

'I think there is nothing worse than a runcible AI – an

intelligence responsible for the lives of thousands every day – that likes to make jokes,' he growled.

'Then let us move on to something without humour. Arian Pelter has disappeared. Before doing this, he managed to withdraw Separatist funds as well as his personal fortune in cash. He was also seen visiting Sylac, whom I believe you know. Other events may also be connected. A turbine-powered catamaran was driven into the old lading docks and caused extreme damage. I only mention this because of the rumour that it contained a headless woman.'

'That may have some relevance,' Cormac conceded, immediately shutting down on an emotion he did not want to identify. 'Pelter was always one for melodramatic gestures. Combine something like a Viking funeral with a Separatist blow against the industry the Polity condescends to allow . . . Is that all?'

'I have no more information to pass on to you at present.'

'Will you pass on anymore?'

'If instructed.'

'Who instructed you this time?'

'Horace Blegg . . . Now, if you go to Gate C, your departure time will be in ten minutes.'

'Thank you.'

'Good luck, Ian Cormac.'

Cormac was about to ask if he needed it, when the privacy field suddenly shut off. He turned away and headed for Gate C. As he walked, he pulled up his sleeve and punched in the deactivation sequence on his shuriken holster. Within minutes of leaving the Minostra containment sphere, he would be able to reactivate it. The main reason for the proscription was to prevent a person carrying an active weapon within the sphere itself. All weapons on the proscribed list were of the types capable of being used to damage a runcible; an occurrence that could easily lead to another Samarkand.

First Constable Abram spoke quietly and calmly into his mike as he watched the house through his favoured pair of antique binoculars. It was a small place by the standards of the area: one of those Tundra chalet replicas that had been all the rage half a century back. The roof was red-tiled over a construction of synthetic wood painted a quaint pale blue, which appeared silver in the light of Cereb, and there was a rocking chair on the veranda. Appearances could be deceptive: this did not seem the residence of an arch-criminal. He lowered the viewer and sighed. He would have preferred to bathe the place in searchlights, but blade beetles were rattling in the trees behind him and they would be attracted to the light. Already four of his men had been sent back for cell-welding after that fiasco at the Pelter residence. The men he had with him now had intensifier augs, so didn't need much in the way of light to operate. But things could still be missed.

'Now, I will ask again, because it is of a great deal of interest to me, are you all in position?'

Abram was noted for his relentless sarcasm. Many of his constables found it more frightening to be summoned into his presence than pulled before some of the other more explosive officers. He knew this, but just could not help himself, sometimes wondering if it was a sickness. He nodded to himself as four positive replies came back to him over the radio.

'Now I strongly suggest that when I say the word "Go" – that wasn't it by the way, it will be a moment yet – that you break down a few doors and arrest Alan Tenel for his numerous crimes. Now . . . Go?'

Abram raised his binoculars again and increased the magnification. Those who had braved his sarcasm to ask him why he used such an old instrument always got the same reply: 'Image intensifiers are the product of characterless technology. I will use them only when necessary.' It was perhaps half the truth. He knew it was probably more to do with establishing a kind of individualism: a common pastime in the vast sprawl of humanity.

He watched two of his officers moving onto the veranda. From the back of the house came the sound of breaking glass. There was a flash that momentarily blacked the binoculars' lenses. When the blackness faded, the officers were gone from view, but he could still hear them.

'Alan Tenel, get up and move away from the bed. Hands out in front of you.'

'What? . . . Who the hell do you think you are?'

'I won't ask a second time.'

'This is private property. How dare you!'

'Tenel, you're a Separatist shit and you're under arrest. You can walk out of here fully dressed or I can drag you out by your ankles and focus the lights on you. Plenty of blade beetles waiting out there . . . That's better.'

'Excellent reading of his rights, Pearson. I must

remember that approach line next time I'm lecturing new recruits,' said Abram.

Nothing more than sounds of movement came over the radio for a moment.

'Sorry, sir, but he seemed a bit reluctant to co-operate.'

Abram emerged from the orchard as his constables hauled Tenel out of his house. Pearson, who, like a lot of the older recruits, was a heavy-G adaptation, had one hand clamped on Tenel's upper arm. Abram studied carefully this man they had arrested.

Tenel was small and old, and didn't look as if he could offer any trouble. Pearson and Alex were capable of tearing the man in half between them, and Jack and Solen, walking behind, both towered a head and a half above him. Abram momentarily wondered if the information given them had been mistaken, then dismissed the thought. ECS did not make that kind of error. As Tenel drew closer, Abram began to note a certain weaselly confidence.

'You do know why you've been arrested, I take it?' he asked.

'You've made a mistake, First Constable – one for which you'll pay dearly,' said Tenel.

Abram wondered what that meant: was it the usual bluster of men with a bit more in their bank accounts than the general population, or something more sinister?

'I never pay dearly for my mistakes,' said Abram. 'I'm a policeman.'

'You won't be laughing when they . . .'

Tenel stared beyond Abram and over to the right.

Suddenly his eyes grew wide and his mouth dropped open. He pulled against the grip the two constables held on him – then he pulled harder.

'You have to get me out of here,' he said quickly.

Abram stared at him.

'You have to get me out of here!'

As Tenel struggled harder, there was spittle on his chin. Abram glanced round and saw, standing at the edge of the orchard, a very tall and odd-looking man.

'Ground him,' Abram ordered. 'Pearson, Jack, with me.'

As Pearson released Tenel's arm, Alex tripped the prisoner and forced him face-down on the ground. Solen dropped to a crouch, aiming the stubby laser carbine he was holding. Abram began walking towards the odd man, with Pearson and Jack behind him. He heard the various sliding metallic sounds as laser carbines were brought to bear and primed. Probably OTT again. This individual was more than likely a gardener employed because he was so uncommonly tall and could prune the trees more easily than most.

'No, let me go!' Tenel shouted, then his cries became muffled, no doubt as Alex shoved his face into the dirt. Abram smiled to himself; Alex was not above a little brutality when necessary. He hooked his binoculars on his belt and rested his hand on the butt of his pulse-gun. The tall man stepped further out from the trees, then stopped, very still. Abram felt a momentary nervousness, then told himself not to be ridiculous; he had two of the toughest cops on the force with him.

'Who are you?' he asked when they got closer.

The man started moving towards them, his lanky strides eating up the ground in between.

'I suggest you stop right there.' Abram drew his pulse-gun.

The man just kept on walking.

'I said stop! Stop, damn it! Oh shit!'

Abram fired, all the time thinking: Oh, you poor bloody idiot. There was a thud and a puff of smoke – embers falling from the man's coat. His stride did not diminish at all. Abram fired twice more, to nil effect on the man's progress. There were flames rising from his coat now. With one sharp movement he slapped them out and continued, trailing smoke.

Jack and Pearson opened up with laser carbines, red flashes cutting through the night – and suddenly the strange man was on them. Abram felt something like a piledriver hit his chest. Next thing he knew, he was on his back on the ground, straining for breath as he looked up. Pearson had his carbine right in the man's face, his finger down on the trigger. Smoke was billowing into the night, and sheets of burning skin fell about the man's shoulders. A long arm snapped out and the carbine spun away in pieces, then Pearson was held up high by his biceps, kicking at air. Jack rushed in from the side with a flat dropkick that would have dented steel plate. Abram heard Jack's leg snap and saw him caught in the action of kicking, the man's other hand gripping his ankle. Suddenly he was released, but before he could fall back that same hand had snapped up to his throat. Their attacker brought Jack and Pearson together with sickening force, then discarded them like a couple of food wrappers.

Abram smelt burning plastic, and suddenly knew what they were dealing with. He got breath into his lungs, where it bubbled. Shattered ribs ground together in his chest as he fought to speak into his mike. He looked up as their opponent loomed over him. The hat and all the face covering had been burned away, to expose an underface seemingly made of brass. The hand covering had also been burned away to expose the same metal. Not a man then, only one choice left really. Abram expected this face and hands to be the last he saw, but the face turned away as multiple shots set clothing afire. The attacker moved on.

'Android . . . fucking run . . . let it . . . have him.'

The words cost him, and Abram spat blood as he painfully turned over to face his remaining two officers, and the prone Tenel.

'Run . . . fuck . . . run.'

But it was not they who ran – it was the android, with unhuman acceleration. It had Solen first, just picked him up and threw him. Solen smashed straight through one of the wooden pillars supporting the veranda, then into the front of the house. He hung there for a moment amongst splintered boards before peeling out and thudding down. Alex sensibly tried to escape. He moved only a pace before a flat brass hand punched through his back and out through his chest. He hung there pinioned and squirming for a second before he died, then the android lowered its arm and Alex's corpse slid bonelessly to the ground.

Abram tried reaching up to change the frequency on his radio, aiming to call for backup. But the control was at his shoulder and he just could not raise his arm that far. With dimming vision he saw the android now standing over Tenel. The little man was on his knees as if pleading, but not for long. The thing grabbed his shoulder, then yanked him up and spun him, all in one movement. It next caught his ankle in one hand, and held him there while it gutted him with the other. Abram wished he could turn off his earplug, because the screams now came through multiplied from four different throat mikes. Abram closed his eyes and kept utterly still as the android dropped what was left of Tenel and moved back in his direction. He listened as the heavy footsteps halted right next to him. An android . . . what chance did he have? It would hear his heart beating. He slowly opened his eyes and gazed up at its brass face.

'Go . . . on then,' he managed.

The android squatted beside him with its elbows on its knees, gore dripping from its massive brass hands. In a curiously birdlike way, it tilted its head to one side and studied him, then it reached out one of those hands and plucked his binoculars from his belt. What now? What the hell was it doing, toying with him like this? How the hell had someone made a sadistic android? As Abram watched in puzzlement, it stood up, placed the binoculars in the pocket of its long coat, closed one metal eyelid slowly over one black eye, then walked away. Abram felt sure it had winked at him. But he never told anyone that.

6

In the twenty-first century the 'disposable culture' prevailing on Earth threatened ecological catastrophe. Landfill sites were rapidly filling with disposable nappies and plastic throwaways. The power stations that burnt this plastic waste, as well as the vulcanized rubber tyres of the time, went some way to alleviating the problem. But a solution was not truly found until all the industries concerned were forced to use biodegradable materials. Even then the problem remained, for the power stations were eventually closed down because of their contribution to global warming. Later in that century the problem was again apparently solved by use of a bacterium genetically modified to eat plastic. This solution unfortunately caused its own disaster, when this same bacterium then proceeded to devour other forms of plastic and rubber, and even developed a taste for fossil fuels. The war and the chaos resulting from this crisis is a matter of common record. So, when you have finished drinking this self-heating coffee, please remember that, even though it is made of self-collapsing plastic, this cup still won't look very nice lying on the pavement, so you must dispose of it in a sensible and considerate manner.

From The Coffee Company

This was the area agreed on, but Stanton could see no sign of them on the white sands. The papyrus, then. Here a stand of papyrus, seeded from the beds in the north, protruded like a tongue out into the sea. He slowed and circled the AGC over it. No sign of activity. He had promised himself that at the first sign of the police getting close, he would run. Things were just getting too bloody. He brought the AGC down until it was only a few metres above the sand, then edged it into the papyrus and let it settle there, crushing the thick stalks beneath it. Before getting out he cursed and then grabbed up the parcel he had placed on the passenger seat. Madness, all of it. He stamped through the papyrus to the white sand beyond and surveyed his surroundings.

'Over here.'

Pelter stepped out from the same stand, but further up the beach. He waited until he was sure Stanton saw him, then stepped back in. Stanton followed him along a crushed-down path to a small open area where the plants had been ripped out and neatly stacked to one side. Probably Mr Crane's work – he was good at ripping.

'Well?' said Pelter.

Still clutching the package Stanton glanced at Mr Crane, who was squatting with his back to a wall of papyrus. The android was studying a number of objects lying on the ground in front of him. There was a piece of green crystal that might have been emerald but was more likely beryl, a chainglass blade, an old egg-shaped data unit, a small toy dog made of rubber, and a pair of antique binoculars. Did this monster's insanity have a name, Stanton wondered.

'They're checking every passenger going onto the shuttles, so there's not much chance of getting through with our friend here. Anyway, I'm told the runcible facility is crawling,' he said.

'We knew that would happen,' said Pelter. 'My patience is not endless, John.'

Stanton decided not to point out that Pelter's patience was practically non-existent.

'It cost us five thousand, but I got confirmation. Cormac went to Minostra, where he was taken aboard a delta-class deep-spacer called *Hubris*. *Hubris* went on to Samarkand. My contact has information that the ship's taking a stage-one runcible there, but he can't confirm it.'

'And the other?' asked Pelter.

'Quarter of a million for the three of us. We have to be at the spaceport first thing in the morning, and we have to get in there by ourselves. Jarvellis says that it's then or never, as she's leaving at first light. Apparently it's getting just a bit too hot around the ports. Not only are the police searching for us, but they're following up on Cormac's report about proscribed weapons. ECS monitors down there have been asking pointed questions about why an insystem cargo transport needs underspace engines.'

'Is that all?'

'No, when we get to the *Lyric* the hold doors will be open. Inside she'll provide supplies for insystem, and two cold coffins for when she takes us interstellar. That's all we get. She wants no contact with us,' Stanton said.

Pelter rubbed at his optic link and Stanton noted Mr Crane's head come up.

'That bitch has made a lot of money from us over the years, and she won't let us into the crew quarters!' Pelter started at a whisper and finished on a shout.

Stanton gestured to Mr Crane. 'She knows about him. She brought him here,' he said.

'You told her?' Pelter asked.

Stanton felt sweat breaking out on his forehead. Mr Crane was putting away his toys.

'I had to, Arian,' he said. 'If we'd turned up without letting her know we had him with us, she might well have not opened her ship at all. I couldn't risk that.'

Pelter lowered his hand, then abruptly he squatted. Mr Crane froze.

'Very well,' he said. 'We'll get over there in the night and go on in. I don't think we'll have too much trouble. Now . . . John . . . give Mr Crane his parcel.'

Stanton walked over to the android, dropped the parcel on the ground before him and stepped back. Crane reached out one brass hand and pulled it closer. He tore locally manufactured paper wrapping away and tilted his head at the contents. Then he stood and stripped off his old, burned coat. Stanton observed that very little synthetic skin now clung to Crane's brass body. There was none at all on his arms, or on his face and head. He carefully placed his old coat on the ground and took up the new one. Methodically he buttoned it up, before taking up the wide-brimmed hat that had become slightly crushed in the parcel. He first straightened the hat, then placed it carefully on his head. His toys he removed from the pockets of his old coat and placed in the pockets of his new one. After a pause he squatted back down and started to take them out again, one by one.

'Mr Crane is very pleased,' said Pelter.

'I'm glad to hear that,' Stanton replied.

A white craft, looking like nothing less than a giant cuttlefish bone, rose into the night sky in eerie silence. When it was half a kilometre up, the green light of an ion drive stuttered, and it accelerated away. Stanton watched it for a moment, then focused his attention back down on the fence. More activity than usual; he had expected no less.

Security round the spaceport was heavy, but quite simply less secure than that around the runcible installation. Here a submind of the runcible AI had as its domain the perimeter fence and the two gates, but because cargos could be large, or sealed, or containing items impenetrable to scan and which, under Polity law, could not be unpacked, only scanned, things still got through. Also, because the Polity was supposed to be effectively without borders for its citizens, there were no constant restrictions on their passage. Because ECS would be searching for him and Pelter and Mr Crane, Stanton now expected restrictions. However, he did wonder if the authorities really thought it likely the three of them would just try walking in there.

Proscribed weapons were the only items disallowed. Stanton considered that, with the freedoms the Polity allowed, it had shot itself in the foot as far as rebellion – and the apprehending of criminals – was concerned. The sort of ad hoc operation going on now was full of holes. After searching the length of security fence once again, he lowered his intensifier and turned to Pelter.

'Local cops at both gates, and a couple of ECS Monitors,' he said, and then peered at the glowing face of his watch. 'We've got about an hour.'

Pelter nodded and glanced at their original AGC. Stanton followed his gaze. The two men inside were, of course, utterly still. There was something a bit spooky about seeing them sitting there in Stanton's and Pelter's clothing. The two ECS Monitors had drunk just a little too much in the arcology bar, so had no time to react when Mr Crane stepped out in front of them. Of course, reacting would have done them no good. Mr Crane just slammed their heads together and carried them away. Stanton wished he had not slammed them together quite so hard, as he pulled the collar of the appropriated uniform away from his neck. The blood inside was drying fast and the hardening material scratched against his skin.

'You'd better try and link in,' he added, when Pelter seemed disinclined to move.

Pelter looked at Mr Crane, then at the AGC again.

'There a problem?' Stanton asked.

'Mr Crane will be off the command frequency for the duration, but he is pleased with his coat,' Pelter replied. Stanton translated that as 'off his leash', and wondered if he wanted to take this any further. Was it a calculated risk or suicide?

'We can try ramming the fence,' he suggested.

Pelter stared at him, all indecision wiped from his face. 'We stay with this plan. It gives us all the best chance.' He turned to Mr Crane who was sitting in the back of the Monitors' AGC. Mr Crane took off his hat and dropped down out of sight. Pelter raised a hand to the side of his head, and let out a slow breath as he concentrated. While he was doing this Stanton walked over to their original vehicle and opened the door. An arm flopped out and he picked it up and tucked it back into the dead man's lap before taking a chip card from his pocket. He rested it in the slot of the onboard computer and watched Pelter. After a moment Pelter turned towards him.

'Now,' he said.

Stanton pushed the card home, then punched in a code that their cell had bought almost a year ago now.

'City control . . . city control . . . city control,' the computer burbled.

'I have it,' said Pelter, his voice echoed by the computer.

Stanton turned and reached over the dead man's shoulder, gave the tap of the oxygen cylinder there one half turn, and then stepped back and slammed the door of the vehicle. He held up his thumb to Pelter. The vehicle's AG engaged and it lifted from the ground. Above Stanton's head it spun 360 degrees, then tilted from side to side. It then hovered stable where it was.

'Let's do it,' said Pelter, his face creased with concentration and a manic grin. He lowered his hand and turned toward the Monitors' vehicle, climbing in the passenger side. Stanton hesitated to join him. He did not like the fact that Mr Crane was now sitting up again and looking about himself with birdlike interest. When he finally did get in the car, Stanton could feel the skin on his back crawling.

'You can handle the targeting?' Pelter asked him.

Stanton hit the controls on the steering column, then from the roof he dropped down a targeting mask. As he did this, two polished cannons whined out of the bonnet of the car and swivelled from side to side.

'You just handle the target, I'll handle the targeting,' he said.

Pelter gave him a dead look, then returned his attention to the AGC with the corpses in it. It rose higher into the air, its turbines droned and it shot off away from the spaceport. Stanton lifted off and was quickly in behind it. Shortly the arcology came into view, with its great tower blocks looming behind.

'Let's get some attention,' said Stanton, and on the locked onboard computer he manually turned on the radio long enough to shout, 'We've got him! We've got him! It's Arian Pelter! In pursuit of Arian Pelter!' Then he turned it off. 'Now some fireworks,' he said.

Wisps of vapour came off the cannons as they warmed up, and laser light ignited the early morning mist. Pelter swerved the AGC they were apparently chasing, and had it screaming back towards the spaceport.

'A few more like that, I think,' said Pelter, his voice strained.

More laser fire lit the night. The citizens of Gordonstone were treated to the sight of an ECS Monitors' AGC blasting away at a citizen's AGC, and missing time and again. Many citizens cheered on the fugitive as he fled between the city blocks and over the roofs of the arcologies. They were then treated to the sight of more ECS and local police vehicles joining the chase, and speeding out towards the spaceport. It soon became impossible to see which one was the original pursuer . . .

'All warning shots,' said Stanton as he eased back on the control column and let the last of the other pursuers get ahead. 'Why bother shooting someone down who you know has to land and will most certainly be caught?'

Pelter did not answer. Stanton studied him and saw that fluid was seeping out round his optic link again. It was mixing with the sweat on his face.

'We're coming to the spaceport. Time to wrap it up, Arian.'

The AGC reputedly containing the fugitives Arian Pelter and John Stanton attempted a high-speed landing in the spaceport. It clipped the top of the fence and slewed violently to one side. Over the fence it clipped the grab claw of an old cometary mining ship, then went nose-first into the plascrete below an Apollo-replica insystem leisure craft. It somersaulted once, then hit the base of the Apollo and exploded. The criminals had to have been carrying explosives, as there was nothing explosive in the makeup of a normal AGC. Shortly after this explosion, all the pursuing craft came in to land in the spaceport.

Stanton brought the AGC down a good distance back from the flames and the flashing lights. Pelter turned and stared at Mr Crane, and all the bird motions ceased. The android tilted his head to one side, then quite meekly got out of the vehicle. It struck Stanton that he had the appearance of a cartoon businessman, standing there holding Pelter's briefcase, but really there was nothing about him to make children laugh. Stanton got out of the AGC shortly after Pelter, and the three of them moved off between the looming ships.

'It's right over the other side,' said Stanton, and then snorted at the sound of laughter from behind them. 'We should be halfway from the system by the time they find out they've been celebrating the wrong funeral.'

The three of them continued on through the megalithic shadows cast by the early sun breaking over the horizon. Soon they came in sight of the further fence. Stanton pointed to a ship that consisted of three spheres linked by tubes that were a third of their diameter; the triangle this construction formed was 100 metres along the side and enclosed a circular drive plate. The *Lyric* was one of the smaller ships here. Stanton led them to one of the thirty-metre spheres, where a ramp led to an open iris door, beyond which harsh light glared. Pelter halted him with a hand on his shoulder and made a sharp gesture with his other hand. Mr Crane strode on ahead, his heavy boots clunking on the ramp as he entered the ship. Pelter then pressed his hand to his optic link. Stanton wondered when Pelter would get used to it enough to stop doing that.

'OK,' said Pelter after a moment, and they followed the android in.

The hold was a disc cut right through the sphere, its walls the insulated skin of the ship itself. Circular lighting panels were set in, evenly, all around. To one side there were bundles and packages. In the centre of the hold, cylindrical cryopods were secured in an open framework. This framework ran from ceiling to floor and took up most of the space. From each of these pods skeins of optic cable and ribbed tubes ran to junction plugs in the floor. Two separate pods were bolted to the floor at the end of the framework. They too were linked into the ship's systems. On every pod was stencilled the words 'Oceana Foods Stock Item', and a number.

Stanton ignored Pelter's intake of breath and chose not to look at him.

'Fucking animals,' Pelter hissed.

Stanton did not want to correct him. It would perhaps be best if he did not know that this cargo mainly consisted of edible molluscs in cryostasis.

'They'll work for us. They've been adapted,' was all he said.

As soon as they were well into the hold, the ramp retracted behind them. Pelter turned to watch it, but Stanton kept his eye on Crane, who was just returning, having completed a circuit of the cargo framework. When Crane stopped and abruptly squatted down, he turned and watched the door iris shut on the dawn light. As the final dot was extinguished, an intercom crackled.

'You've got sleeping bags, food, water and a toilet,' a woman's voice told them. 'You can't see the toilet – I've linked it into the plumbing on the other side from you. The two cryopods, I suggest you use at the earliest opportunity, as supplies are limited. Now, the matter of payment.'

Pelter gestured to the briefcase Crane was holding. 'I have it here, Jarvellis. Just let me through and we'll complete the transaction,' he said.

'Arian Pelter, if you think I am going to open the bulkhead door with that thing on board, then you are more stupid than I gave you credit for,' said Jarvellis.

116

'There is, just for this kind of eventuality, a hatch in the bulkhead door, to your left.'

Stanton saw frustrated anger twist Pelter's face, then get quickly suppressed. The Separatist looked to Mr Crane, and the android stood up. Just at that moment there was a lurch and Stanton felt his stomach twist. They were up and moving. They'd made it. Crane walked over, his head tilting as if he had an inner-ear problem. He handed the case to Pelter.

'Not yet, Pelter,' said Jarvellis.

'Why not? Don't you want your money?'

There was a surge of acceleration, inadequately compensated for in the hold. Ionic boosters.

'I say not yet because I am not entirely stupid. I open the access hatch and friend Crane there will have enough purchase to rip out the bulkhead door. I won't open the hatch until we're out of atmosphere. Then, if any attempt is made to break through a door, of which – I want you to be aware – there are two, I'll just open the hold to vacuum. Is that perfectly clear?'

'Clear,' said Pelter through gritted teeth.

'That is very unsociable of you, Jarv,' said Stanton.

'Sorry, John. I do like you, but this is business.'

Pelter looked at Stanton, his expression dead.

'Now,' said Jarvellis, 'I have a ship to fly.'

The intercom crackled again.

'You know her well?' Pelter asked.

'She's probably still listening,' Stanton warned. 'All that crackly intercom shit has to be a blind.'

'I asked if you know her well.'

'Yeah, I know her. *You* know her. I've had a few drinks

with her. Don't matter. She opens that door and we're both out of it,' said Stanton.

Mr Crane froze again. Stanton reminded himself that you had to be damned careful around this kind of lunatic, even if you were on his side. Pelter stood as still almost as the android, then he let out a slow whistling breath. Mr Crane squatted and began to take out his toys. Stanton went to the supplies Jarvellis had provided for them, and found a six-pack of coffee. He pulled two off, handed one to Pelter, then went and sat on one of the rolled-up sleeping bags. He pulled the tab on his coffee and held it in his hand while it rapidly heated.

'You know, these edge-of-Polity worlds can get a little rough,' he said.

'I am aware of that,' Pelter replied, then he stared down at the cup he was holding. He had not yet moved, or pulled the tab on it. Stanton wondered when the Separatist had last eaten or drunk anything, for he had not seen him do so. Eventually Pelter moved to the wall and sat down with his back against it. He pulled the tab on his coffee.

'Social order breaks down in the face of dictatorial takeover,' he said, without a great deal of conviction.

'It always seemed to me,' said Stanton, 'that you got whole worlds behaving like naughty children trying to cause as much mayhem in their classroom as possible before the teacher got there.'

'An archaic image . . . The truth is that their behaviour is a result of despair.'

Stanton sipped his coffee rather than disagree. Pelter was a committed Separatist and was blind to the realities. The Polity was something that could be described as a benevolent dictatorship in which all enjoyed their portion of plenty. Separatists were always in the minority, like all terrorists, and were hugely resentful of what they considered the blind complacency of their fellow citizens. So far as he understood it, only two worlds had seceded, both for a period of less than ten solstan years. In both cases the Polity was called in to clear up the mess. In the case of one of those worlds, that mess being large radioactive wastelands. Despair . . . ninety per cent of the population were having a party prior to subsumption.

'Huma can get a bit rough, you know,' he said, labouring to keep a conversation going.

'I do not think I will have a problem with rough,' Pelter replied, giving Mr Crane a meaningful glance.

'Yes . . . but you do realize that there will be weapons there that could destroy even Mr Crane. No Polity weapons proscription on Huma, and some pretty nasty characters.'

'That is why we are going,' said Pelter and sipped his coffee.

Stanton was groping around for something else to say when the intercom crackled.

'Time, I think, to sort out the payment,' said Jarvellis.

Pelter stared into the air for a long time, before he put his coffee to one side and stood. Mr Crane began putting away his toys, until Pelter turned to look at him. The android then retrieved the ones he had put away, and continued sorting them as if playing some strange game of patience. Pelter stepped over to him, squatted by the briefcase, and opened it. From inside he tore a black strip with ten of the etched sapphires embedded in it. Stanton deliberately looked away as Pelter closed the case and stood up again. The Separatist leader was paranoid enough as it was; he didn't need to be made aware of Stanton's interest in etched sapphires.

Pelter took the strip round the racked cargo to the second bulkhead door. In the bottom of the door a circular hatch half a metre across irised open.

'Just toss them in,' said Jarvellis.

Pelter rolled the strip up and tossed it through. The hatch closed with a crack.

'Good to do business with you, Arian Pelter.'

Another crackle signified the exchange was over.

Stanton looked at Pelter and saw the deadness there. He knew this signified a craving to kill. The side-to-side movement of Pelter's head, as he scanned the hold for visible cameras, speakers or microphones, signified that he had not yet found something on which to focus that craving.

Beyond atmosphere, the stuttering of the *Lyric*'s ion engines became a constant glare. Unlike the larger Polity ships it did not have ramscoop capability, and had to accelerate for some time before it reached what was sometimes referred to as 'grip speed'. This speed varied for the size of ship and the efficiency of its underspace engines. For the *Lyric* it was approximately 50,000 kilometres per hour: a speed it took the ship, with its limitations on fuel expenditure, twenty hours to reach. When it did, the underspace engines engaged, fields gripped the very substance of space and ripped something ineffable, and the ship dove into the wound. Stanton woke with a gasp at a sudden feeling of panic and groped for his pulse-gun. He opened his eyes and sat upright.

'This hold is not completely shielded,' said Pelter from where he was sitting cross-legged on a sleeping bag, facing Mr Crane, who was seated the same. He did not look round, but went on. 'A good job there is some shielding, else we both would've been screaming by now. Getting that close can drive a man insane.'

Stanton leant forward. A glimpse of underspace could certainly do that to a normal man. He wondered what it would do to Arian Pelter. Drive him sane?

'We should go under,' he said.

'Yes,' said Pelter. 'I have nearly finished with Mr Crane.'

'Finished what?'

'I do not want anything untoward happening while we are under. Mr Crane will watch for us. He has, after all, got the patience of a machine.'

'I shouldn't think she'd try anything.' Stanton stood up. 'She just doesn't want to get anywhere near him.' He walked over to the pods and stared down at them for a long moment. Abruptly he stooped down and slapped the touch-plate on one of them. The pod split down its length to expose a metal interior impressed with a man's shape. 'Claustrophobic' seemed too weak a term to describe it. Jarvellis had not gone so far as to provide any padding, but then what padding did you need when you were all but dead? Either side of the neck were the junctions for the carotids and jugular arteries. From that point his blood would be replaced with a kind of antifreeze. At the base of the skull impression was a simple circular disc: the nerve-blocker. Inside the rest of both manshapes were pinholes only centimetres apart. Each, Stanton knew, contained a needle. The body had to be saturated with antifreeze to prevent terminal cell damage. Stanton swallowed dryly and began to undress. Shortly Pelter joined him and looked down into the pod.

'I've never done this before,' said Pelter.

'Nothing to it,' Stanton replied. 'Just get undressed and climb inside. The nerve-blocker hits before the lid closes, and that's all you know until you wake.'

Pelter nodded and began to remove his clothes. Before climbing into the pod, Stanton glanced back at Mr Crane. The android was sitting with Pelter's brief-case in its lap: it was sorting its toys again. As Stanton lay down in the cold metal, he wondered if that was all Mr Crane would do throughout the months of their journey.

Then, nothing.

7

A ball flung through a curtain of black cobwebs, the starship *Hubris* entered real space. For an instant, the starship, a kilometre-wide pearl, was poised ahead of spacial distortions like a mutilated finger, then the invisible wings of the ram-fields folded out, and caught-hydrogen phased to red and hid the ship. The pearl was lost in the flaw of some vast jewel, decelerating from dark, down into the system. Then, a pin-wheel of lasers striated a blood-drop of hydrogen and it became a different plasma: a fusion flame like an orange segment cut from a small sun, blasting against the same spacial distortions that collected the hydrogen. Into the gravity well, *Hubris* dropped: three-quarter light, half a light, then speeds measured in a mere few thousands of kilometres per second. The fields weakened as the quantity of hydrogen increased. Finally the hydrogen ceased to phase, and the ship became visible again. The fusion reaction shut down and was gone like a droplet of milk swirled away in water. The pearl that was the ship rolled round the edge of the gravity well: a ball cast into the roulette wheel that was the Andellan system.

*

Cormac stared out onto the cold emptiness, and felt it was mirrored in himself. What was it the shuttle pilot who had taken him from Minostra to the *Hubris* had said?

'You OK? You look half dead.'

Apposite – so very apposite. Cormac couldn't remember what his reply had been, something trivial, something unassured, verbal. There had been other exchanges, each trailing away into banality until he was glad of cold-sleep's oblivion. Now, two hours since thaw-up, feeling was really returning. He looked down at his hands, concentrated until the quiver stilled, and wondered. Was he feeling embarrassment now or some aspect of link withdrawal? Truly, how fucked up was he that he could not identify his own emotions? He lowered his hands to his sides. It was recorded somewhere. It had to be. He turned from the portal and studied the touch-console in the corner of his room. Yes, he did feel embarrassment. He recalled the look Chaline, the science officer in charge of re-establishing the runcible link, had given him when he had asked for instruction on the console's use. For thirty years he had been out of phase. Having instant access to information had stunted his ability to learn. He again lived through her patronizing explanation, then went over and studied the console. The touch-controls were stacked and very complicated, but there was always an easier way for less complex access.

'*Hubris*, display anything you have on gridlink withdrawal . . . please,' he said.

The screen flickered and one word appeared: *Searching . . .*

In a couple of seconds a number of file headings appeared. He sat down at the console and with unpractised fingers began to work through each file. What he read there only confirmed things he already knew: long-term linking was much like drug addiction, and like drug addiction it could be broken with willpower, with inner strength. The situation as it stood was unacceptable, and Cormac intended to rectify it. He sat with his fists clenched until there was a knock at the door. It might have been only a few seconds; it might have been for minutes. He unclenched his fists, wiped the screen and stood.

'Enter,' he said.

The woman who came through was tall and classically beautiful. She had luxuriant black hair, skin that seemed unnaturally white, a ripe and muscular figure only just covered with clinging body suit, thin but perfect features and striking green eyes. Only she was not a human woman.

'You are NG2765?' Cormac asked.

'I am Jane.'

'My apologies, I did not know your name . . . but you are a Golem Twenty-seven?'

Jane smiled evenly, and then looked with a raised eyebrow at the lurid pot plant Cormac had shoved behind the sofa. Cormac swallowed annoyance: the Golem series was too damned good. In a way he preferred the other makes; the ones that appeared less human and less than perfect.

'Yes, I am.'

'I require assistance. It was the science officer's suggestion that you be assigned to me.'

Damn it! Why did he feel so uncomfortable? He had to remember she was an AI-run machine, albeit an extremely sophisticated one.

'What kind of assistance do you require?'

Cormac took a slow breath and wondered if his hands were shaking again. He did not look. 'I wish you to accompany me to the surface. I am without information access and there are many questions . . .' He realized, even as he was saying it, that it was wrong.

'Have you considered an aug? Mika could fit you one.'

Cormac clamped down on a sudden surge of longing. No, an augmentation would be no good. It would be like having alcohol instead of heroin. He had to beat this. 'I will not have an aug,' he said.

Jane nodded thoughtfully, then said, 'You will be going down with the investigative team, I presume?'

'Yes.'

'Well, any questions you may wish to ask me might as easily be addressed to them. Many of them have augs, and Chaline has recently been gridlinked.'

Cormac shook his head. Chaline gridlinked? He did not want to get anywhere near how that made him feel. He focused on the problem at hand. How could he tell this . . . woman that without information access he found it difficult to talk to people? To real live people. He did not feel . . . superior. He had wanted a thinking machine, yet the only ones on the *Hubris* were the ship's AI and the Golem androids. There wasn't a lowly drone robot or metal-skinned android in sight. They were all stored away for emergency use.

'Please, hold yourself in readiness,' he said, his jaw locking up. 'That will be all.'

Jane smiled, nodded, and left him. He stood there feeling gauche and confused. He had expected something else. She was too human.

Beyond the angled windows of the shuttle bay, Samarkand was a yellow onyx marble wrapped in filaments of white cloud and Andellan burned with a distant cold light. Thus would Sol appear from an orbit just beyond Jupiter. Only because this was a very uncrowded area of the galaxy could the sun be distinguished from the other faint stars. This was a remote place: a place where help would always come too late.

Cormac pulled on his coldsuit and wondered if he would find anything unexpected down there. Survivors, for example. Even from here the brownish ring of the ground-zero was visible at the centre of the planet – a cankerous iris – *Hubris* being poised over it, geostationary. He turned as Chaline came up beside him.

'For our initial study we're putting down outside the accident site. There's an undamaged heat-sink station on the edge of New Sea. We might be able to get some information from the submind there, though we get no response from it on the usual channels.'

She looked at him warily with wide green eyes as she tied back her curly black hair. Her features were very fine and her skin black as obsidian. When he first saw her, he thought her black skin a cosmetic effect or alteration. It came as a great surprise for him to discover it was natural, not even an extraterrestrial adaptation. It made a change from the olive-brown of the run of humanity, or the luridly dyed skins of members of the runcible culture, and it was unusual to come across any of the old-Earth racial types this far out. Blegg was an exception, in every area.

'Yes, OK,' he said, his thoughts still on the subject of 'race' and groping after answers from a link that was no longer there.

With the explosion of the human population across the stars, the gene pool had been thoroughly stirred. There had been a song, something about 'chocolate-coloured people by the score'. Really ancient. Cormac had not understood it until he had learnt from his link what a 'score' was, and that chocolate had once come in only one colour. The song had been right in one sense: the 'melting pot' had occurred, but now, with adaptation and alteration, skin colour was spread across the spectrum and was the least of differences between human kinds.

'We can't bring down the runcible until we find out what happened to the one here. Your concern is who. My concern is *how*, as my command area is mostly runcible installation,' she said, studying him dubiously.

'Of course,' he said, and turned back to the window. He sensed her standing at his shoulder for a moment, then turning away to rejoin the others. Was he so short with her because she was linked? Was he that petty? Christ, where was his self-control?

Two of the group behind him were Earth Central soldiers. He could assume command of them whenever he needed, but for the moment he left them to operate independently. They had the training. Crisis would stratify the command structure. He wondered if the set-up had been Blegg's idea: to give him time to readjust. He turned and surveyed them all as they fixed and clipped up their coldsuits, and he noted how the two women avoided his gaze. The soldiers seemed oblivious to his attention.

As the last seal was closed and hoods were pulled up, Jane entered the shuttle bay. She still wore her clinging bodysuit. For a moment Cormac had thought she might not be coming. Then he remembered: what need did she have of thermal protection? He strapped on his face-mask and put up his hood before joining her and the others. He felt more comfortable that way. People, damned people. He noticed Chaline give Jane a strange look.

'We can board now,' said Chaline.

The wing was a small carrier, its span only 150 metres or so. It sat on the polished floor of the bay like a grounded raptor. Once they had entered it and taken their places, Cormac was glad to see Jane move to the fore and take the pilot's chair. He felt foolish in her presence. She left the doors between the cockpit and passenger area open. This gave them all a good view through the chainglass screen. Cormac sat and Chaline sat down next to him. He noted that he was the only one wearing his mask. He removed it and studied the people with him – hardened himself against the urge to just shut them out.

The two soldiers were both big, fit-looking men. Brezhoy Gant, the one who was sitting beside the door, was either completely shaven or just naturally hairless. Cormac noted that his skin had a slightly purple tinge, and wondered if some ancestor had used adaptogens. He felt a return of that empty feeling when he realized that if he wanted to know he would have to ask – politely.

Patran Thorn was an evil-looking man with a Vandyke beard and hooked nose. Cormac thought he had an appearance more suitable to someone wielding a cutlass than the high-tech, cold-adapted weaponry he was carrying. Mika, the other member of the party, was crew. She was a medical and life-sciences officer, and was along in the unlikely event they might find survivors. She was a diminutive woman, who appeared little more than a girl, and was a complete contrast to Chaline. Her hair was pale orange and closely cropped, and her skin was very pale. Her eyes were the demonic red of an albino. She looked fragile, whereas Chaline looked vigorous. But Cormac had seen the tattoo on the palm of her hand and knew that she was Life-coven from Circe. She had his respect, as did all who graduated from that secretive place.

'I wonder why Jane isn't wearing survival gear?' Chaline asked of anyone.

This annoyed Cormac. She had a link; why didn't she use it?

'She has no need of it,' he said.

Chaline looked at him as if he was an idiot. Cormac was about to say more, but closed his mouth before he could cram his other foot in it. Of course, he should have realized. Androids normally tried very hard not to display what they were, so Jane was going down onto the surface dressed as she was, only for his sake – to give him the comfort and crutch of knowing he was with a machine. Cormac felt horribly embarrassed, then in turn extremely angry. It was about time he started thinking for himself, about time he regained some independence. What had he lost? Just a voice in his head that could answer a few questions – information as easily obtainable from any console. He no longer had that facility now, so he would make do with what he did have. He leant back in his seat and strapped himself in. The shuttle shuddered as the gravity in the bay went off, and they all lifted against their straps. Under air-blast impellers, the shuttle began to drift towards the irised door at the end of the bay.

'Chaline.' He turned and faced her directly. No more masks. 'Jane is not wearing survival gear so that I might be more aware of her unhumanity . . .'

Don't overplay it. This woman isn't an idiot.

'I was gridlinked, previously.'

Chaline stared at him for a moment until realization hit her. 'I see . . . Hence the . . . console.'

Mika spoke up then. 'You were linked for a long time.'

It was a statement, not a question. Life-coven did not often need to ask questions.

'How long?' asked Chaline.

'Thirty years. You lose sight of humanity in that time – and certain manual skills.' He tried a tentative smile.

Chaline smiled back and nodded. 'The opinion was that, as an agent of Imperial Earth Central, you were too high and mighty to associate with mere runcible technicians and crew.'

'My apologies,' said Cormac. It was autonomous politeness, and he saw that it was taken as such.

Ahead of the shuttle, the door irised open on a shimmer-shield: a direct offshoot of Skaidon tech. The shuttle passed through it as if through the skin of a bubble.

'Acceleration,' said Jane. If she had listened in on the

conversation, she showed no sign. The conversation had been low, but not beyond her hearing. Few sounds were.

The slight thrust pushed them back into their seats, and Samarkand slid to one side of the front screen. Andellan came into view, tracking a black spot across the screen as the chainglass reacted to blot out damaging UV.

Chaline spoke again, obviously a rehearsed speech. 'As acting science officer I am directing this, and you are along as an advisor, though I know you have veto and can assume command in a crisis. However, I would like to know, do you have any idea as to what we may find?'

Cormac considered for a moment. This was a thought that had been occupying him in those moments when he had not been feeling sorry for himself. He cleared his throat and concentrated on turning his unspoken thoughts into spoken words.

'Well, we might get something from the submind at the heat-sink station, but I doubt it. The destruction of the runcible AI will have . . . damaged it. That's the problem with centralized processing. Any information it might have retained will be badly scrambled. What we need to get a look at is the buffers, if there's anything left of them.'

'Sabotage?' wondered Gant.

Cormac looked across at him. 'That is considered likely.'

Gant nodded ponderously and removed a packet from the top pocket of his coldsuit, and from that a thin white tube that he placed in his mouth. He held a small chrome device up to it and a small flame flickered into life. Cormac realized with a feeling of shock that the tube was a cigarette, and Gant was smoking. He had not seen anyone smoke since he was last on Earth, twelve years ago. It had been all the rage then. He noted that Mika and Chaline were eyeing the soldier with fascination. Gant was aware of them all watching him as he puffed out a fragrant cloud of tobacco smoke.

'Sorry.' He removed the packet and offered it. Mika and Chaline refused, not offensively – there was no social ostracism of those indulging in this now harmless habit – but with surprise. Obviously they had never been to Earth. Cormac accepted both a cigarette and Gant's lighter to light it. It was only another method of communicating.

'Thank you.' He lit the cigarette and drew on it, then in a tight voice went on with, 'You know, out here these things are not often seen?' He held up the cigarette. Gant shrugged and leant back, after retrieving his lighter. The comment did not seem to bother him.

'I take it you come direct from Earth?' said Cormac.

Gant nodded. 'Yeah, Ukraine – fifteen hundred kilometres from the original Samarkand.'

'Fifteen hundred,' Cormac repeated.

'Yeah,' said Gant, studying the tip of his cigarette. 'You know it was established by Uzbeks and was a major stopping point on the Great Silk Road. That's why this place was named after it: it was also a stopping place, a way station. I always wanted to see what it was like.'

Cormac was not sure if he was talking about the ancient city or the planet. He also wondered what was buried underneath that rambling. He left it.

'Your friend?' Cormac looked across at Thorn, who was gazing out a window, his expression pensive.

'English.'

'A long way to come.'

Cormac drew on his cigarette and stifled a cough. A very long way to come. There was something more to these soldiers, if Central was prepared to send them all this way. He entertained a suspicion.

'You're Sparkind.'

Gant grinned at him, and Cormac repressed the urge to swear. Blegg had made this as difficult for him as he could without compromising the mission. It seemed that everything he needed to know he would have to *learn*. He suspected this might be Blegg's idea of a recovery programme from Cormac's gridlinking.

'What are Sparkind?' asked Chaline.

Gant's face fell.

Cormac explained, 'Kind of soldier. They have a certain reputation.'

Mika said, 'They dealt with the situation on Darnis; twelve of them against a unit of cyborgs and a small army. The name is the same as that of an ancient race of fighters.' Her expression was blank.

Gant's smile returned. 'No, *they* were called Spartans – and we don't live like them,' he said.

Mika frowned. She obviously did not like to be found wrong.

'How many of you are there on the *Hubris*?' asked Cormac.

'Just one group,' replied Gant.

Four of them. Not inconsiderable. What was Blegg expecting?

Gant continued. 'The other two are Golem Thirties.' He was still smiling.

Cormac tried not to let his annoyance show. This was information he should have received long ago. Had he been gridlinked, of course, he would have already known. He also reckoned he would have directed things with all the sensitivity he had shown on Cheyne III. Damn Blegg.

Samarkand grew and grew until an arc of it filled the screen; frozen oceans of a sulphurous yellow edged with shores of pure malachite; rolling mountain ranges that seemed made of desert sand. Chaline pointed out a spreading stain of reddish-green across the surface of one ocean. It issued from one point on the shore.

'Heat-sink station,' she said. 'The colouring is from adapted algae. They should survive the freezing process and start oxygenating, once the seas thaw out.'

'That will take a lot of energy,' Cormac observed.

'Well, you've seen how much energy one human body can carry in.'

She looked to the side, where the brown ring at the edge of the blast-site could be seen. It was just coloration to the level ground and over a nearby range of hills, from fallout – from the heat flash. They all knew that nothing could have survived within it. Cormac pursed his lips in thought for a moment, then turned to the two Sparkind.

'What was your brief,' he asked, 'exactly?'

Thorn said, 'Quite simple, my friend, we are here to make sure nothing . . . military gets in the way of re-establishing runcible link. Beyond that, we were told to do whatever you tell us to do. There was a briefing that,

135

for this initial survey, only Gant and I would be needed, and that further orders from you might be . . . lacking.'

He gave a crooked grin, to which Cormac could not help but respond.

'Anything else?' he asked.

'Only that the other two were to hold themselves in readiness. I suppose you don't need the big guns yet. Anyway, they were orders that were surprisingly lacking in detail. I hope that what detail there is doesn't conflict.'

'It won't,' said Cormac, and clamped down on his frustration. He had learnt nothing. Only two for the initial survey. Where or when would all four be needed? Cormac cursed Blegg's reticence. It seemed to him now he had only been sent here to learn something which was probably already known, and to be rehabilitated. He did not like playing this sort of game.

A dull droning sound told them they were entering the thin and frigid atmosphere. The droning grew to a roar as cloud whipped against the shuttle. The shuttle banked and spiralled down towards the planet. This noise precluded speech, but it seemed no time before they were hurtling above a mountain range under a sky the colour of old brass, and before the roar became a dull and distant thunder.

'We'll be approaching the station shortly. The weather is very bad. Ground temperature one-seventy Kelvin. You'll need your suit heaters on, and full seal on your masks,' Jane told them.

'Those are the mountains the runcible energy-surplus used to heat. There was a line of big microwave dishes transmitting the surplus energy,' said Chaline. 'On a busy day the rock used to melt. The heat-sink stations at New Sea were intended for the next stage of terraforming. They had recently come into operation and were melting the seas.'

'It wasn't just algae they introduced. There were moulds, lichens and planktons round the station, and even adapted angel shrimp. Whoever did this wrecked much more than a runcible,' said Mika.

Yes, Cormac realized, what had happened here must seem doubly painful to someone trained on Circe. Not only had there been a huge loss of human life, but also the loss of a nascent ecology. There had probably been many from the Life-coven working here on Samarkand.

Soon the station came into sight. It had the appearance of an iron cathedral on the shore of the frozen sea. It had spires and arches in its makeup, but none of them were for decoration. The arching structures that clawed into the ground and the sea carried heavy-gauge superconductors and the spires and turrets were microwave receivers that employed field technology rather than the bulky dishes used heretofore. Jane guided the shuttle close over the structure itself, then down into the cleared area that ringed it. Here were parked private AGCs, and to one side was the wreck of a carrier. Perhaps it had just been landing or taking off when the blastwave hit. They all saw it, and made no comment. Without a doubt it contained bodies; but a fraction of the total dead.

The shuttle settled a hundred metres from the doors of the station. As the rest of them unstrapped from their seats, Cormac remained where he was and stared thoughtfully at the carrier. It occurred to him then that the cold would not have returned here immediately. When Jane came up beside him he caught hold of her arm. Through his gloves it felt like any other arm.

'How long would it have taken?' he asked.

She looked at him with a quizzical expression.

'The cold. How long to get down to say . . . minus fifty?'

'Three solstan days.'

'That quick?'

'Yes, the installation here, all of it, might be equated to a very small speck of warm sand on an ice cube.'

'I see,' said Cormac, and then studied her closely. 'I realize I've been a prat.'

'It is something we all realize at one time or another.'

Yeah, like you'd ever do anything foolish.

'Let me put it another way then,' he continued. 'I miscalculated. Unless you feel you might be needed out here you can stay with the shuttle.'

Jane smiled at him. 'I think I might as well come along. I might be of use.'

Cormac nodded and let her continue to the exit. Before he followed, he removed his shuriken holster from within his sleeve and strapped it on outside. He had already practised using it whilst wearing a thermal mask and gloves. Blegg might have expected little danger here at first, but that did not mean he should consider the place safe. When his life was at risk, Cormac never liked to rely on the judgement of others, even an immortal Japanese demigod. He placed his mask over his face and closed the seals that connected it to his hood. He knew it was fully sealed when a small

LED went off just at the edge of his vision. Once that light disappeared, he allowed himself a small smile.

Outside it was like a harsh winter on Earth, only the snow blowing past them consisted of carbon-dioxide crystals, and the ice under their feet was water-ice as hard as iron. Cormac felt no hint of the cold. Had he done so, it would probably mean his suit was failing and that he would shortly be dead. Jane stood brushing the snow from her hair, as if it was flower blossom dropping on a spring day. In this setting, dressed in her thin body-suit, she did look unhuman. There was no billowing cloud of vapour as she breathed. She did not flush, nor did she shiver.

They trudged through the snow to the main entrance. Off to one side Cormac observed the huge super-conductor ducts that led to heat-sinks under the frozen sea. From the shuttle these ducts had appeared to be the thickness of old oaks. Here, now, he could see they were large enough to run a motorway along. There the surplus energy, converted from microwave beams transmitted from the runcible buffers, was conducted as electrical energy to the heat-sinks, where it was converted into terraforming heat. Fifteen months ago much of this sea had not been frozen, and, as Mika had said, angel shrimps had been introduced.

Once they reached the doors, Chaline hit the touchplate. Nothing happened. She and Gant pulled on the handles, which had probably never been used before.

'Dead, and frozen shut,' came her voice over the com. 'This place was powered by a bleed-off from received energy.' She turned her masked face to Jane. 'Can you do anything?'

Jane stepped forwards and took hold of the handle. She pulled and ice shattered under her feet. The door opened a little way, then the handle snapped off.

'The metal's recrystallizing with the cold,' she said, her voice coming to them with a radio echo. She stepped to the gap she had made, inserted her fingers, and pulled. The door ground open and a chunk snapped off in her hands, but it was wide enough open for them to enter. As he went through, Cormac glanced at the broken metal and realized that at these temperatures even Golem might be vulnerable. Their synthetic skins, he knew, could handle a wide temperature range and provided superb insulation, but he wondered just how close they would get to the lower limit of that range here.

Inside the building they walked down frost-coated corridors to a drop-shaft. Luckily there was an inspection ladder down one side of it. Jane checked it with a tug or two, then descended. It was thick ceramal welded to the side of the shaft, so was unlikely to give way. As it took her weight without cracking, they all soon followed her down to the bunker where the submind was kept.

'I'm getting something,' said Chaline, as they swung away from the shaft and into a dark corridor. Cormac flicked his goggles to infrared, but vision was even poorer. Someone switched on a torch. He saw it was Thorn, and that the torch was an integral part of the weapon he held. Gant had also drawn his gun. Perhaps they trusted Blegg's judgement as much as he did, Cormac thought. He turned to Chaline, who was peering at some kind of detector.

'Is it still active?'

'Seems to be, though its power source must be getting

low. Perhaps that's why it didn't transmit,' she said, then added, 'I hope to link up the *new* runcible with these stations.'

Runcibles were obviously her favourite topic.

The end of the darkened corridor revealed a sliding door, which Jane opened with studied nonchalance. Beyond it lay a circular room that seemed to be lined with polished copper bricks.

'Let's see what we can get here,' said Chaline, then took another instrument from her belt and moved her fingers over the touch-pads. A voice spoke to them through their comunits.

'—the brick-red song each block is dried blood frozen in perspex the windows are a thousand stitched-together eyes house is pain lord of pain lord of nightmares—'

'Very poetic,' said Chaline dryly.

'Nuts,' said Gant.

Cormac was not so sure. 'Try it again. At least it's retained something.'

'—batshapes with translucent white teeth and eyes in fevered flesh swooping madness yelling hate itself sinter sinter burnt mounded bones—'

'Try transmitting to it here.'

'It should be able to hear us anyway. Jane?'

'I've tried. Seems completely internalized.'

'AI, respond!' shouted Cormac.

'—screaming shape fire green men lizards help me plague dogs war flung to our coasts night dark rats disembark with their translucent teeth—'

'No good,' said Chaline. 'Best we shut it down and get out of here.'

'—plinking rain hell dark spaces think something abyss gestation outcome—'

'No,' said Cormac. 'I veto that. We take the core brain and main memory with us.' Chaline turned her masked face to him. He was glad he could not see her expression.

Mika said, 'There was something . . .'

Chaline turned to her. 'What? This submind's crazy.'

'Stream of consciousness. It may reveal something.'

'OK . . . OK, no problem.'

Chaline moved to the centre of the room and lifted a circular cover. Ice-blue light glared out as she inserted another instrument from her belt. There was a number of strange clunks. She lifted the instrument out and attached to it was something metallic and lens-shaped. She detached it and tossed it to Cormac. He caught it.

'There's your core brain and main memory. It's only a submind, so they're all in one. Don't worry about dropping it. Nothing short of an atomic explosion will destroy it,' said Chaline. Then she realized what she had said. 'But, then, we are all well aware of that. It was the destruction of the main runcible mind that . . . internalized it.'

Cormac was glad to hear a little humour in her voice, even though it was somewhat acid. He did not need any enemies right now.

'Let's go. There's nothing more for us here,' she finished.

As soon as they stepped beyond the shielding of the room, Jane halted and tilted her head. They all watched her, knowing she was receiving some message, and knowing that the tilt of her head was for their benefit. Abruptly she turned.

'That was from the *Hubris*. It's picked up some kind of heat source to the south of here.'

'People?' asked Cormac.

'Not determined.'

8

Huma: That they named this rather hot and arid planet after a fabulous bird that equates with the phoenix is rather ironic, in that it has been impossible to establish even adapted bird species here. The reason for this is that ninety per cent of the surface of Huma lies outside the green belt in which Earth species are able to live. In this area even the native plant species are prone to combustion, and huge swathes of the planet are 'burn zones'. Ash carried from these zones is the reason for the distinctive filthy rain that falls on the remaining ten per cent of the planet, at the poles, which are habitable. These storms, though rare, are of such severity that during them no Earth species can survive outside of the accommodation built for humans.

From *Quince Guide*, compiled by humans

Cormac was directly in front of Pelter, the barrel of his thin-gun connected by an invisible rod to the Separatist's forehead. The expression on the agent's face said all that needed to be said, and all that would be said. Pelter was a hindrance the agent must remove so he might continue his work. Easier to just kill him and move on. It was that he had begged in the face of this lack of regard, that he was irrelevant to the central issue, just something to be killed and discarded, that brought to Pelter an almost rabid anger. Of course, in this instance the killing pulse never came. It was as Sylac had said: visual hallucinations through the link. He tensed himself – it always seemed to take such an effort of will – and used his aug to switch through to Crane. Immediately the link became an icicle through his left eye, and through glassy light the rectangular barrel of the thin-gun closed against his forehead.

No, go away.

Pelter tried to shake the image away and found he was paralysed. The image slid then, like a mote in his eye, and fell to a position somewhere on the edge of his vision. Now he had a view of a piece of crystal, a plastic dog, and an ancient pair of binoculars. Using the command program in the module, he took control of Crane. There was nothing to feel, only things to see and hear, and an emulation of movement that sat in his skull like something theorized. He lifted Mr Crane's head and looked around.

The hold looked very different, simply because there was a light hoar of frost on every surface. He turned Crane's head to the sound of swearing. Stanton was sitting up in his cold coffin and rubbing at his arms. His skin was covered with the fine dots of needle penetration. There were smears of blood on the sides of his neck. Pelter relaxed his control and inevitably Crane's attention returned to his toys. Pelter maintained a tenuous link.

'You'd think the price would have included fucking heating!' Stanton shouted.

The intercom crackled, and Jarvellis spoke. She sounded slightly dopey. 'Sorry, John. I used a timed drop from underspace here. No asteroids to hit and not much else that the automatics couldn't handle. I've only just thawed up myself,' she said.

'Yeah, and I bet it's nice and warm where you are.'

'Give me a chance. I'm not up to speed yet.'

'Well, get up to speed. It's warmer in these coffins than in the hold.'

Immediately there came the drone of fans. Pelter turned Crane's head to watch the frost disappearing in waves across the walls.

'We're insystem, then?'

'Insystem and coming up on Huma.'

Stanton surveyed the hold. Of course, there were no portals, so he could not prove, disprove, or appreciate that statement. He glanced at Pelter's coffin, then across at Mr Crane. He shivered, maybe in response to the cold.

'What about Arian?'

'I set your coffin to open first, John,' said Jarvellis. 'Perhaps we can—'

Stanton interrupted. 'Best you get Arian's coffin open now. I don't want any misunderstandings with Mr Crane here, and Arian has that command link with him fed in through his optic nerve. I'd rather Arian was awake and controlling him.'

Pelter reassumed control and turned Mr Crane's head. Stanton was now standing beside his cold coffin, trying to shake frozen stiffness from his shirt. He was also looking at Mr Crane. Yes, thought Pelter, that's the way it is. He returned Mr Crane's attention to his toys and cut the link.

There was a sound, a deep crack, and a line of brilliance cut to the left of him. His whole body suddenly had severe pins and needles as the nerve-blocker detached and feeling returned. This feeling slowly ebbed, only to be replaced with a sensation as of his entire skin having been burnt – and he knew how that felt. Suddenly he gasped, and fluid bubbled in his lungs. Until then, he realized he had not been breathing.

'Best to get moving,' said John Stanton, looking down at him.

Pelter sat up and looked at himself. His body, like Stanton's, was covered with pinheads of dried blood. He lifted his legs from the coffin and tried to stand. His legs started to give way and Stanton caught hold of his arm.

'Takes a moment for the blood sugars to kick in. Your blood is full of food, but the cells of the rest of your body are starving. You'll know when it happens,' he said.

Pelter tried standing again and this time got control of his legs. The burning sensation began to retreat like the frost on the walls. The feeling that replaced it was an endorphin rush. For a brief minute he got the buzz that turned people into heroin addicts. He hated it. He shook off Stanton's supporting arm and carefully stooped down to take up his frigid clothing. The intercom crackled its phoney crackle.

'We're into atmosphere now and will be landing in about an hour. As part of the service, you'll find a wallet of Carth shillings in the black holdall. It's your entry fee. They're desperate for Polity currencies. Customs here are pretty relaxed, but it's best to lubricate the wheels of their bureaucracy,' Jarvellis told them.

Pelter looked at Stanton. 'Customs?'

'Yeah, we're not in the Polity now. You'll find that if you want anything done here, you'll have to do a fair bit of lubricating,' Stanton told him.

Pelter nodded thoughtfully as he pulled on his jacket. 'Tell me about this place,' he said.

'Nothing much to say,' Stanton replied. 'The only habitation here is at the poles. At the equator the average temperature is not far below the boiling point of water. They're eight solstan years prior to Polity subsumption, and what government they have is on the edge of collapse. It's completely corrupt and therefore just what we need. You can do anything you want here, if you have the money.'

'Dealers?' Pelter asked.

'You'll be falling over them. You can get just about anything. Fortunes are made out here on the edge, through technologies coming out of the Polity and proscribed weapons going in. Huma's become a trading outpost.'

'I'll want a dropbird, seeker bullets and missiles – proton guns as well.'

'You'll be able to buy all that. Not cheap, but anything you want. We should be able to get it all through the dealer Jarvellis used.'

Pelter nodded and looked closely at John Stanton. 'I'll find a dealer. I'll want you to find the boys and sort out one or two other things,' he said.

'Whatever you say, Arian.'

As they sat out the hour until landing, sipping from

self-heating soup cartons, Pelter could almost feel the image in his missing left eye. *The thin-gun.* It seemed to push a cold ache through the centre of his head, and he knew that place to be the hole the pulse would burn right the way through.

The door irised open and bright lemon sunlight flooded the hold, before a wave of heat and spicy perfume. Pelter led the way out into that light, with Mr Crane walking a step behind him, holding the briefcase. Stanton paused at the lip and glanced back in, before hurrying after them.

The landing field was compacted greenish dirt webbed with plants similar to liverworts or some spillage of boiled spinach. From these plants sprang long hair-like stalks topped with spherical pink buds the size of peppercorns or the two-petalled flowers they opened out as. As he walked on a patch of these and got a stronger waft of their spicy perfume, Stanton remembered his last time here. Twenty solstan years ago he had come this way on his route into the Polity to make his fortune. Things had been different then. For one, there had not been as many ships here then as there were now. He looked around at the multifarious vessels. They were, on the whole, small cargo haulers, though of every conceivable design. He could guess what an awful lot of them were hauling too, and that was another change. At that time, the government here had put restrictions on arms, much the same as those in the Polity, and there had also been very strict laws concerning landing permits, passes and codes of conduct. Now nobody bothered. Why should they, when the Polity was soon to step in and take control? Why bother when there were fortunes to be made in the intervening years?

The two customs officials who approached were one example of the indolence and greed that affected the citizens of a world about to be subsumed. Their clothing was a mixture of uniform and personal clothing. The man wore the green peaked cap and jacket of customs personnel over a dusty pair of monofilament overalls. The woman wore the jacket over a brown leaf-shaped skirt, but no cap. She carried a scanner on which Stanton could see the charging light flickering, and as such was useless until charged. She also had an organic-looking augmentation behind her right ear. It had the flat bean shape of most augs, but was a greenish colour and seemed to be covered with glinting little scales.

'Do you have a permit for that?' said the man, pointing at Crane.

'Permit?' replied Pelter flatly.

Stanton quickly stepped up beside him. 'We're not sure of what is required. Perhaps you can help us out?' he said, noting how intently the woman was staring at Pelter.

'We can issue you with a permit. The cost will be . . . ten New Carth shillings, or the equivalent in New Yen. Then there is the matter of your visas,' said the man.

Stanton pulled out the wallet Jarvellis had provided for them and opened it, making sure the man could not see how much it contained. Ten shillings was a derisory sum back in the Polity. Out here it was probably a day's wages.

'Perhaps you could tell us how much the visas cost?' Pelter asked.

The man studied them. They looked, Pelter knew, somewhat ragged round the edges. He could also see how the man's eyes kept straying to the briefcase Mr Crane carried. That case was obviously new.

'Visas are eight shillings per person. You will of course need three,' he said.

'Three? Why do we need a visa *and* a permit for Mr Crane?' Stanton asked.

'Just pay him,' said Pelter.

Stanton shook his head. It was the wrong thing to do. You gave people like this any leeway and they'd have you. Nevertheless he pulled out four ten shilling notes and handed them over. The man folded them and put them in his pocket.

'That's six shillings change,' said Stanton.

The man made no move to search for any change. 'I will need to look in the briefcase,' he said.

Abruptly Mr Crane stepped forwards and raised his head, which until then had been bowed. The man took an involuntary step back. He licked his lips. Stanton thought that, though Mr Crane's marbles were scattered far and wide, he did 'menacing' very well.

'You will not need to look in the briefcase, and we will not require change,' said Pelter.

The man was obviously riled by this. 'Just one word and I can have ten men here with proton guns,' he said.

Pelter's face went dead. 'I don't even have to speak. It would take a second for Mr Crane to rip you in half. Now get out of our way.'

The man bridled and the woman slapped her hand on his arm.

'Jarl, leave it,' she said.

'But—'

'Jarl!'

The woman and Pelter were staring hard at each other again. Stanton wondered what the hell all that was about. She pulled at Jarl's arm and gestured to another ship that was landing over the other side of the field.

'Another one coming in,' she said, then glanced towards a gate in the far fence where some uniformed guards were lounging. To Pelter she said, 'There will be no trouble over there, Arian Pelter. They'll let you through.' She pulled at Jarl and they moved away.

'What the hell was that all about?' Stanton asked Pelter. Pelter's dead face had now taken on an expression of puzzlement. He looked at the retreating woman, then back towards the *Lyric*.

'How much would Jarvellis have told them here?' he asked.

'She wouldn't have said anything more than that she had some passengers. I know her, Arian, and she does stick to her word. I specifically asked her not to say anything, because if they'd run some sort of search on us they'd know to ask for bigger bribes.'

'How did that woman know my name then?'

Stanton was at a loss. He too looked towards the *Lyric* again.

Pelter continued. 'I was going to charter her for the trip back out of here. It's best to stay with those you know so long as they don't get too greedy.'

Stanton wondered what double meanings there were in that comment. He said, 'You want me to talk to her? She'll wait until we're well clear – ' he glanced meaningfully at Mr Crane ' – before she'll come out, but I can guess where to find her.'

'Yes, do that.'

They started walking.

'But before you do that,' Pelter continued, 'see if you can find the boys.' He turned to Crane, and in response the android opened the briefcase, extracted a single sapphire, closed the case and held out the gem in the palm of his brass hand. 'This will be payment to them on account.' Pelter continued staring at Mr Crane, and then abruptly lost patience. 'Give it to him!' Mr Crane's hand jerked and the gem shot towards Stanton's face. He snatched it from the air.

'What will you do?' he asked, pocketing the gem.

'I will find a dealer.'

Stanton glanced at the position in the sky of the lemon sun, and then he pointed to the urban sprawl in the distance. Between the fence and the town was a wasteland scattered with adapted acacia trees and low silvery sages. Amongst these were the corroding parts of starships and the occasional ruined AGC. The town began with the low spread of three-storey arcology buildings. Beyond them were city blocks and onion-shaped spires as from some Scheherazade tale; but AGCs flew among them, rather than magic carpets. How much of a difference was there? Stanton wondered.

'There's a place called The Sharrow at the centre of Port Lock. I'm told it's still open, and little changed from when I was last here. Shall we meet there this evening?'

'Yes, I'll find it,' said Pelter.

Stanton left it at that and looked with puzzlement at

the guards at the gate. They all just stared at Pelter and made no move to block them or extract bribes. Each of them also had one of those strange scaled augs. Beyond the gate three AGCs of dubious safety were parked in a row. Three drivers came over to make their pitch. Two of the drivers were lucky. The third just went back to his vehicle and waited; there would soon be someone else. Ships were landing here and taking off with increasing regularity.

Mennecken, Corlackis, Dusache and Svent were not so similar in appearance as they were in inclination. The four of them liked danger, liked violence, and liked money. They were not at the metrotel where they had said they would be. Stanton was totally unsurprised to find them at the arena. As he came from the entrance tunnel between the tiered seating areas, he looked down into the ring and saw that a match was about to commence. A huge man with boosted musculature, twin augs linked by a sensory band across his eyes and a ceramal skull exposed above his ears was up against a smaller man with bluish skin. The boosted man was armed with fist blades. The blue man had a long commando knife and a hook. They were circling, checking each other out. The four mercenaries were lounging in seats close to the ring itself – what were called the wet seats, for obvious reasons. Stanton made his way down to them.

'Bit uneven,' he said, sitting behind the four men. Casually, all four of them looked round at him. Mennecken and Corlackis were twins. Both of them looked neat in their businesswear suits, chrome augs and cropped black hair. The only distinguishing feature between them was that Mennecken was built like a weightlifter and Corlackis was slim. Neither of them was boosted. Boosting, they felt, led to overconfidence; it dulled their edge. Dusache had black curly hair, was boosted and tended to dress in leather and denim, but normally he went without an aug, though he had one now. Svent had a new aug too. The weaselly little killer liked every mechanical advantage he could get hold of and considered any kind of biological advantage a waste of time. He seemed small and weak, but Stanton knew this not to be the case. Svent had reinforced bones and cyber-motors at his joints. He was easily as capable of tearing your arm off as Dusache was, though he would be inclined to do it more slowly.

Dusache nodded to the opponents in the arena. 'Blake there wanted to make himself some money. He's made a mistake. The little guy is a Hooper from Spatterjay. Easy to underestimate,' he said.

Stanton studied the little man more closely now. He saw that the blue coloration was due to thousands of blue ring-shaped scars all over his body. He returned his attention to the mercenaries and pointed to Dusache and Svent.

'Those augs, what's the story?'

The two men simultaneously reached up and touched the scaly organic augs nestling behind their ears. Stanton thought there was something creepy about this twinned response.

'Good tech,' said Svent. 'You can access just about any server real fast, even get in a little on AI nets, damned near a gridlink, and these little dears ain't far off AI themselves. About a hundred New Yen, plus fitting. Made by Dragoncorp.'

'They look like biotech.'

'Nah,' said Svent. 'You should know me better than that. I wouldn't drop a Yen on that shit.'

'Speaking of Yen,' said Corlackis softly, and gazed at Stanton with tired patience. Stanton reached into his pocket and took out the sapphire. He tossed it to Corlackis. The mercenary's hand snapped up cobra fast and caught the gem. He studied it for a moment, then dropped it in his top pocket.

'Down payment,' said Stanton.

'Hey, I didn't see that,' said Dusache.

'One hundred thousand New Carth,' said Corlackis. 'I will break it at the hotel bank and give you your share then.'

Dusache relaxed and turned his attention back to the fight. Together they all focused their attention on the opponents, for now came the sounds of metal on metal. The two fighters were in close, trying to smash through each other's guards. Blake got through and drove his fist blade straight into the Hooper's stomach. All over, thought Stanton, until the little man drove his hook through Blake's shoulder, hooked it round his collarbone, drew in close and began pumping his blade in. Blake got another couple of hits in, but it was almost as if they were irrelevant to the Hooper. Stanton noted that the little man, though he had huge gashes open on his body, did not seem to be bleeding. Blake was bleeding plenty, and after a moment he started to scream thinly. He dropped to the ground and lay there making horrible gasping sounds. The Hooper detached his hook and walked away holding it up in the air. The cheering had an edge to it. Stanton watched a medbot zip in from the side and start driving blockers and tubes into Blake's butchered flesh.

'Big cell-welding job there,' said Dusache. 'Blake's gonna be bankrupt.'

'Now what that Hooper has,' said Corlackis, glancing at Svent, 'is a biological advantage worth considering.'

'What is it?' Stanton asked.

'A fibroid parasite that binds their bodies up like nylon rope. He's an old Hooper, about two centuries I would suggest. The parasite is, incredibly, a natural one. You see the marks on his skin? That is probably how he got it. He fell in the sea of his home planet and near got eaten alive by the leeches that live in it. I believe it all has something to do with the life-cycle there. Reusable food resources for the leeches, or some such.'

'You call getting chewed on a biological advantage?' Svent asked. 'Stick to tech – you know where you are with tech. It's not gonna mutate and eat your face off.'

All very interesting, thought Stanton as he looked at Svent. Why was it that he didn't believe a word the little mercenary said? He stood and glanced to where the Hooper was leaving the arena, then he looked down at the four men.

'I'll be with Pelter this evening in The Sharrow. Be there,' he said abruptly, and left the arena. The four watched him go, then turned their attention back to Blake as he was carried, shunted and tubed but still alive, from the bloody sand. When he was gone Corlackis turned his attention to Svent.

Svent appeared irritated. 'All right,' he said. 'Take it out of my cut . . . Shit, I'm gonna have words with Blake.'

9

Tenkian (Algin): *Born 2151 on Mars during the Jovian Separatist crisis. Originally trained in the areas of metallurgy and the then quite young science of forcefield dynamics. At age nineteen, on his graduation from VIT (Viking Institute of Technology), he was recruited by the Jovian Separatists and soon moved to their weapons division. After four years, when the Separatists had resorted to terrorism, he became disillusioned with their methods and surrendered to Earth Security on Phobos. There he served two years of a ten-year sentence, and on his release joined ECS (under some duress, it is rumoured), where he worked for six years, and was there responsible for the development of the ionic-pulse handgun. Aged thirty-two he joined JMCC, where he had an integral role in the development of the electric shear. Five years after this he is recorded as leaving the JMCC complex. Three years later he turns up on Jocasta as a designer and crafter of esoteric individual weapons. He is accredited with the 'Assassin Spider', 'Sneak Knife' and chainglass, and also with being the first to install programmable microminds in hand weapons. Most of his weapons are now con-*

159

sidered to be collectors' pieces, and are infrequently used.

From *The Weapons Directory*

They trudged along, head down into a wind that blew ice crystals like steel pellets against them. It was not possible to hurry, much as they wanted to get back to the shuttle before the weather worsened. Mika slipped on the glassy ice and Thorn hauled her to her feet. As she made to move on, Thorn held onto her and inspected her coldsuit. A simple fall and one little tear could mean the loss of a limb or even death. Flesh froze quickly at these temperatures.

After that they regained the shuttle without further mishap. Jane headed for the cabin while the outer door closed on the rattle of ice crystals. AG engaged and then a thruster fired. A faint roaring penetrated the hull as the shuttle turned against the wind. Cormac wondered just how much of a hammering this place would give the equipment they had brought. Of course, he would have to ask.

It took ten minutes before the outer layers of their suits had been heated enough to be touched without the danger of coldburn. When they removed their masks their breath billowed in the frigid air. The heaters had not yet succeeded in raising the temperature above zero Celsius. Cormac inspected the chill lens of ceramal containing the fleck of material that was the submind, then slipped it in the pouch on his suit's utility belt. He looked at Mika, who was frowning, probably at herself, and then he turned his attention to Gant and Thorn, who had now removed their gloves and were checking over their weapons.

'Don't be too ready to shoot,' he told them.

'We're always ready to shoot, old chap, but never eager,' drawled Thorn. Then he nodded to the holster on Cormac's sleeve. 'Nice little piece that. May I see it?'

Cormac looked at the holster for a moment, then, coming to a decision, he unstrapped it and passed it across. Thorn touched a finger to the frigid control panel. There was a quiet snick and a small red light blinked on, then off. Thorn removed the five-point star of chrome steel and inspected it admiringly if somewhat gingerly.

'Chainglass blades as well. This is a custom job. A Tenkian?'

He handed the weapon to Gant.

'Yes, a Tenkian,' said Cormac.

'What's the cut diameter with the auxiliary blades fully extended?' asked Gant.

'Twenty-five centimetres,' Cormac told him.

'Fuck! You ever used it at that?'

'Once.'

'Must have taken him apart.'

'No, there's never any need for full extension against a human opponent, it was against a Thrake.' Cormac paused, groping for another conversational gambit. 'Big bastard, looks like a woodlouse, but about the size of an elephant.'

Gant nodded and continued his inspection of the weapon.

'Male bonding,' said Chaline to Mika in a stage

whisper, and shook her head. Mika lost her frown and smiled before starting some work on a notescreen. Gant took the holster from Thorn and put the shuriken away.

'Not only a Tenkian, but one with a juiced-up processor as well,' he said. He passed it back to Cormac. 'A weapon like that is not cheap.' He took out a cigarette and lit it.

Cormac strapped the holster back on his arm. He appreciated the irony of his situation. It was quite possible to talk to a person, without an AI in the background to give him information on that person. It was quite possible to learn a great deal about that person too, things that an AI might not be able to tell you. What had he learnt? He'd learnt that both these soldiers wore their personal guises over a harsh professionalism: Thorn with his phoney English accent borrowed from another age, Gant with his smoking and his gruff manner. Here, he realized, were two men who had been dehumanized, and were now reclaiming that humanity. Another of Blegg's little touches. Cormac snorted to himself and thought about his last conversation with Angelina before he killed her. How had he managed to get so out of touch? In retrospect he realized he was lucky to be alive.

'Five minutes and we should be there. It's a hydroponics facility on the edge of the blast-zone. A bit hot, but the suits should handle it if there's no fallout from these storms,' said Jane.

'What about you?' asked Cormac.

'I'll have to stay here, otherwise I'll need to spend the next week being detoxified.'

It was a nice way to describe it. Cormac knew that she would probably have needed a body replacement.

'Is there any more information on the heat source?'

'Not very much. *Hubris* has picked up two heat sources of about human mass. They might be survivors.'

And if they are not? Cormac wondered.

Chaline said, 'If they are survivors, they will be very sick, being that close to the blast-site. Let's hope they're not too sick to tell us what happened to the runcible. If they even know.'

Cormac turned from her and watched Mika put her notescreen aside, then open a case on her lap. From this she removed an instrument like a flattened torch. Its wider end was inset with a small touch-panel and screen. He recognized it from one time he went on a mission to a planet that had seceded from the Polity, and where immediately the three continents had gone to war. It was a hand diagnosticer. It covered a whole range of cases, up to just how many lumps of radioactive metal were lodged in your patient, or what poisons were in his blood, and what viral agents might be eating his face away. Perhaps now she would get a chance to use an instrument like this. Before, he had doubted the possibility.

'Coming up on the facility now.'

The shuttle dipped and slowed, thrusters firing in reverse, and through swirls of snow they caught glimpses of three long buildings like half-submerged pipes.

'They are in the middle one. *Hubris* says there is a power source of some kind there, but it is not being used for heating. They must be in coldsuits. Certainly the heat levels would indicate so.'

The shuttle finally came to a halt in midair, then, using the AG and blue stabs of retro flame, Jane piloted it in as close to the building as she could. It came down into a hissing storm, the beating of ice crystals a constant drone on its hull. Even as it landed, it slid sideways a couple of metres before AG was completely disengaged and its full weight rested on the ground.

'I can't land on the other side, so you'll have to walk the length of the building. Take care, the weather is even worse here,' Jane said.

Cormac grimaced at Thorn, who grinned back before pulling on his facemask. Golem could be patronizing at times. When they had all pulled on their masks and gloves, Gant hit the door control and stepped back. The wind was howling outside and, even when the door was only open a crack, hard crystal ice hissed in and powdered every surface.

'Should we rope up?' asked Chaline.

'No need,' Thorn replied. 'Only a few metres to go, and this wind's not going to pick you up.'

Chaline inspected him for a long moment before reluctantly leading the way out. Cormac did not need to see her expression to know that she was doubtful. He had his own reservations about their safety. But he also knew that Thorn and Gant would not agree to go roped into a potentially hostile situation. They wanted to be able to *move*.

Underfoot was cold-cracked plascrete skinned with ice like a layer of badly scratched perspex. This water-ice had been considerably abraded by the wind-driven crystals, and as a consequence it was not slippery. The door was only a few metres away across this surface; even so, it seemed kilometres distant as they struggled to stay upright against the blast of the wind.

'This door is jammed as well,' said Chaline, when they reached the building.

Gant and Thorn both tried it, but it did not move. Gant waved Thorn back and drew his hand weapon. Cormac noted it was standard issue JMC 54: a military version of the thin-gun he had used on Cheyne III, a pistol that fired field-accelerated pulses of ionized aluminium dust, but an effective weapon for all that.

There was an arc-light flash and the buckled and smoking door went crashing down a central aisle between rows of frozen plants. They got in out of the wind.

'Messier than Jane, but just as effective,' said Cormac.

Gant chuckled and advanced ahead of them, with Thorn at his side. He did not put his weapon away. Thorn drew his.

'Have you got a fix on us, Jane?' asked Chaline.

'Yes, I have you,' came Jane's reply.

'How far to the heat sources?'

'Approximately five hundred metres, and they have not moved. Have you found anything interesting yet?'

'Nothing so far.'

They came across the first corpse twenty metres beyond the door – or, rather, half a corpse. It lay on the floor, its lower half missing, and the top half so badly burnt it was impossible to tell if it was male or female. White teeth showed in stark contrast to the blackly incinerated face.

'Jesu!'

That was from Chaline. Gant and Thorn had seen this sort of thing before. Mika knelt down next to the body and inspected it closely. She pushed at burnt lips to get a better view of the teeth, and the lips crumbled away. There was a gagging sound from Chaline. Mika held her diagnosticer against the belly, where the flesh had not been burnt and was like marble.

'Female, heavily radioactive. I'd say she was flash-burnt in the explosion.'

'Quick, then,' said Gant.

'Not necessarily . . . that's strange . . .'

Cormac stepped forward and looked down. 'Tell me,' he said.

'It looks like her lower half was cut away *after* she was burnt. I suppose that could have happened . . .'

Mika glanced up then around. There was no damage evident to the building where they were, or anywhere nearby. Cormac knelt down and inspected the corpse. He looked over to Mika.

'See there.' She pointed to the severed organs and muscle. 'That was done with a shear of some kind, after she was frozen. See? No fluids.'

Gant stooped down, next to the two of them. 'Now why would someone do that?' he asked.

Cormac knew damned well that the question was rhetorical. He stood. 'We'll find out soon,' he said. 'No need to second-guess.'

They advanced and found another corpse in a similar condition. Then they found a stack of five corpses, which looked like a sculpture made in hell. None of these corpses was burnt. Mika inspected them closely, though with some difficulty as they were frozen together.

'Hypothermia. Most of these froze to death.' She pointed at the corpse of a man right in the middle of the heap. His skin was dark blue and he was impossibly thin. 'That one is an Outlinker. He must have been in a low-G area when AG cut out. His neck is broken.'

'Yeah, but who stacked them here, and why?' wondered Gant.

Cormac wished he could give the soldier a dirty look. They continued along, until Jane contacted them.

'One of the heat sources is moving, coming your way.'

Gant spoke up quickly. 'This isn't scientific any more. What do you recommend, Agent?'

'Get off this central aisle. We'll hide for a while and see what we might see,' said Cormac. There was no objection from Chaline; since they'd found that first corpse she had been very quiet.

They cut down a side path to a secondary aisle and crouched there behind troughs of frozen hydroponics fluid containing tomato plants, which would shatter at a touch. Both Gant and Thorn held their weapons ready. Cormac moved his hand close to his shuriken.

'Close to you now, about a hundred metres,' Jane told them.

They waited in tense silence.

'Fifty metres.'

'OK,' said Cormac. 'Radio silence until I say otherwise.' He wished he had thought of that earlier. If whoever was coming had a radio he knew where they were.

The figure that clumped down the main aisle

appeared to be a human heavily wrapped in whatever materials it could find. Unless there was a coldsuit of some kind underneath all that material, Cormac realized it was not human. The material itself was some kind of plastic mesh: probably the only stuff the figure could find that had not become frangible with cold. Ordinary cloth would shatter at these temperatures. He continued to watch for any signs that they had been spotted, but the figure plodded on slowly, facing straight ahead. As it passed the cross-aisle in which they hid, Cormac's suspicion was confirmed. The figure's knees were higher up than a human's and bent in the opposite direction. It walked like a bird.

Where . . .?

Once past them, it soon reached the pile of corpses. With a crackle of breaking flesh, it hoisted one of the corpses onto its shoulder as if it was made of thin balsa, then turned and began to trudge back again.

'It has no radio, then,' said Cormac.

'What the hell was that?' asked Gant. A genuine question this time.

Cormac tried to track down an aberrant memory. Where had he seen a creature that walked like that? 'I don't know, but it's a sure bet it had something to do with the runcible breakdown. We'll follow it. Try not to make too much noise. It might not have a radio, but it's probably got ears.'

They moved after the creature once it was twenty metres ahead of them.

'A description would be nice,' said Jane.

Mika replied, 'Manlike, but with lower inverted knee-joints.'

'What are they doing with the bodies?' asked Chaline.

Cormac glanced in her direction. She had not figured it out, and he was not about to start spouting theories just yet. He wondered what it was like to have that kind of naivety.

They followed the creature to an area where any troughs had been pushed back against the walls. There it dropped the corpse to the ground. Chaline gagged when an arm flew off and its fingers shattered like porcelain. The creature squatted down and picked up a device with the appearance of a builder's trowel. A high-pitched whining came over their comunits as it used the device to cut the arm into sections.

'Oh my God,' said Chaline, and was ignored.

'Appears to be some kind of electric shear,' said Thorn, then he pointed to the row of black cubes to which the shear was wired. 'Homemade cells. God knows what they're made of.'

'And that is a microwave oven, if I'm not mistaken,' said Cormac, indicating a cylindrical canister on the floor.

The creature opened the canister and dropped the sections of human arm inside.

'They're . . . they're cooking . . .' Chaline could not go on.

'More like softening, at these temperatures,' said Thorn. He did not seem the slightest bit bothered by what he was seeing. 'Human flesh is about the only form of protein and fat around, here on the perimeter. Most supplies were probably destroyed and whatever was left they probably used up long ago.'

Cormac surveyed the plants all around them. Thorn looked as well.

'Not worth them thawing vegetable matter either. That would be a waste of energy. Just not worth the effort with all this flesh about,' the agent said.

'Yeah,' said Gant, 'but what kind of creature can survive on radioactive human flesh?'

Cormac had a horrible suspicion he might know.

'Oh God.'

Cormac glanced at Chaline with irritation. But she was not viewing the scene before them, but was looking behind her. Cormac turned fractionally before Gant did. Behind them stood a second creature, as if it had been there for some time, watching them. Gant raised his gun, but Cormac had his shuriken to hand before him. It flashed through the air with its chainglass blades retracted. There was a crack. Gant swore as his gun clattered on the floor. Cormac laid a restraining hand on Thorn as the shuriken hovered in the air above him. Thorn lowered his gun. Cormac hit the recall on its holster and it shot home, glad to be out of the cold.

'No violence,' he said, then put some lightness in his voice. 'They're only eating dead people, not killing live ones.'

They all slowly stood up. Cormac glanced behind and saw that the other creature had seen them too, and was also standing. 'Right, we'll head back for the shuttle. They'll either follow us or they won't; we cannot compel them. But if they do come, we'll allow them aboard.'

'What are they, Cormac?' asked Chaline.

Now she had asked, Cormac wanted to answer her – but he had to be sure. If they were what he thought they were, then that meant there would be an awful lot more questions – like, where now was a certain extragalactic creature? A creature with a body consisting of four kilometre-wide spheres of flesh joined in a row, and how had *it* survived an antimatter explosion? But that was another story, one he suspected he would have to be telling soon enough.

'I cannot be sure of what they are. We'll see back at the shuttle, if they come along.'

The five of them moved back down the aisle. Gant retrieved his gun and holstered it. As they neared the second creature, it moved aside to allow them past. Once they were past, it turned to watch them. Its fellow joined it. Cormac gestured for them to follow. They immediately did so.

'How dangerous are they?' asked Gant.

'They haven't attacked, that's all I can say. Whatever their reason for being here, they are survivors. We came here to rescue any survivors . . .'

They soon reached the open door to the facility, and began fighting their way through a worsening blizzard to the shuttle.

'Quickly,' said Jane. 'Some fallout.'

Cormac glanced back and saw the two creatures hesitating at the door. Perhaps they were at their limit there. Perhaps it was too cold out here for them. He again gestured for them to follow, and pointed over at the shuttle. They followed again. The storm made no difference to their plodding gait. In a moment all five were beside the shuttle and Jane opened the door and helped them inside. Cormac waited with her at the door for the two creatures to arrive. They climbed inside also. The door closed. The creatures stood there waiting.

As the temperature rose, the shuttle filled with carbon-dioxide vapour that slowly cleared. Soon the floor around the creatures was peppered with water-ice splinters that had flaked from their plastimesh clothing. When the temperature reached 250 Kelvin, minus twenty-three Celsius, Cormac removed his mask and gloves. The creatures copied him, the plastic mesh that covered them breaking like wet blotting paper at this higher temperature.

'No coldsuit underneath. Must have antifreeze for blood,' observed Thorn.

Everyone else was silent as the creatures revealed themselves, and finally stood naked before them. Cormac nodded to himself, all his recent suspicions confirmed, and new ones taking their place. Had Blegg known? The old bastard had said Cormac was just right for this mission.

These creatures looked like men, only their skin was green, fading to yellow around their stomachs, inside their legs and under their chins, and it was tegulated with fingernail-sized scales. They were hairless, and their eyes were about three times the size of a man's. They had no ears, only holes set in the requisite positions. The shape of their heads was toadlike, with muzzles rather than human noses and mouths. Their hands were three-fingered and bearing claws. Tentatively, Mika stepped closer and scanned them with her diagnosticer. After that she studied her readings for a long time before saying anything.

'I can't get a proper reading from them. We'll need the lab on the *Hubris*.'

'Doesn't surprise me,' said Cormac. 'And it wouldn't surprise me if you get some strange readings there, too. You see, I don't think they are really alive.'

Mika looked at him and waited.

Cormac glanced at Jane, who was keeping a wary eye on their two visitors, then turned to Mika, his tone acid. 'You asked what they are. Well, a very long time ago a palaeontologist by the name of Dale Russell followed up on a little thought-experiment of his. He was wondering what dinosaurs might have evolved into, had not mammals displaced them. For his basic model he took a dinosaur called stenonychosaurus, and from that he developed what he called a dinosauroid. These are something like his model.'

'But they are not dinosauroids,' Mika stated.

'Oh no,' said Cormac, 'I think these were made as a taunt, or a lesson, or for some other unfathomable reason. I've only ever seen one before now, and I assumed it was unique. I christened it dracoman.' Cormac rubbed a hand across his eyes. Suddenly he felt very tired. 'You see, these were made by an extragalactic dragon that might or might not have died a quarter of a century ago.'

They were staring at him in disbelief as he turned to them. All except Mika – she nodded sagely.

'Aster Colora,' she said. 'The Monitor. The contraterrene explosion. I was five then, but I've never forgotten the story. They turned it into a holodrama: "The Dragon in the Flower". And there was a book called *Dragon's Message*.'

Cormac sighed with relief. Someone knew the story, then. He turned back to the two strange creatures. 'They'll need to be decontaminated somehow. It would be a good idea to keep them in isolation. We should get back now. You should be able to get the whole Dragon story from *Hubris*.'

At that moment one of the dracomen gave a shiver, and its slotted pupils focused on Cormac. Then it grinned at him with lots of pointy white teeth. There was a raw bloody smell on its breath.

10

Chainglass: *A glass formed of silicon chain molecules. Depending on heat treatments and various doping techniques, this glass has a range of properties covering just about every material that has preceded it. Chainglass blades can be as hard as diamond and maintain an edge sharper than that of freshly sheared flint, whilst having a tensile strength somewhere above that of chrome steel. Chainglass also lacks the brittleness of its namesake. This substance was the invention of Algin Tenkian, and it made him filthy rich.*

After serving out his derisory sentence in the Phobos prison and his longer sentence with ECS (something one might describe as a work-experience course), Tenkian went on to land a top job with JMCC. Though he did hand himself in to ECS because of his disgust at the extremes of violence some Separatist groups went to, he was still an ardent supporter of the cause. When he quit JMCC and went to Jocasta, he severed all ties with the Cause. At this time his personal fortune from chainglass royalties was said to have crept above the billion mark. This goes to prove the theory that a large cash injection will cure most forms of fanaticism.

From *Thumbnail Biographies*

Pelter became aware of them almost instantly, and couldn't help but wonder what they hoped to achieve. Did they think they might be able to rob him, with Mr Crane walking just behind him? He stepped from the pavement and over a deep storm gully onto the compacted and fused stone of what was once a road for hydrocars. Crane followed, maintaining the two-pace distance he had kept to since their arrival here. On the other side of the road Pelter caught the reflection of the two in a darkened shop window. They hesitated, then hurried after him. Pelter smiled nastily, then moved on to the next window. This one was well lit and he surveyed what was on display inside. It amused him to have stopped directly in front of the display window of an arms dealer. He inspected the various projectile weapons and hand lasers. Nothing here for him. He needed something with a little more punch. He glanced aside.

The two men had stopped further back down the pavement. They made no attempt to appear nonchalant, but both stood and watched him. He turned towards them and folded his arms. Both looked boosted, had shaven heads, and wore clothing that was similar in its utility: close-fitting green shipsuits with plenty of pockets and subtly – but not wholly concealed – armour pads. They also carried pulse-guns in stomach holsters and large knives sheathed in their boots. Even though they looked tough, Mr Crane could flatten them in a second. With a kind of bitter relish, Pelter hoped they'd be stupid enough to try something.

'Well?' he shouted, at last getting fed up of waiting.

The two men eyed each other, then advanced. Pelter gave Mr Crane his instructions, and accepted the briefcase the android handed back to him. It was not so much that Crane needed to be instructed on what to do, rather, on what he must not do. Pelter waited. Neither man made a move for his weapon, not that it would have achieved much. They were only a few paces away from Crane, before they slowed up and started looking hesitant.

'Arian Pelter?' said the one on the left.

He had time to say no more, because Crane took two huge paces forwards, moving so fast that his clothing snapped. He had both his fists clenched in the fronts of their shipsuits before they could do more than gawp at him. Then he lifted them clear of the ground, turned, and slammed them against the toughened-glass window.

'Before Mr Crane kills you, I'd be interested to discover how you know my name.'

'The boss . . . the boss,' the first speaker gasped.

'How do you know my name?' Pelter repeated, his voice and his expression flat.

The other one spoke quickly. 'Come with us to see him,' he croaked. He had his own hands around Mr Crane's one hand, and was staring down into the android's black eyes.

'Why should I do that?' Pelter asked.

'Because you and he have a mutual interest in a place called Samarkand.'

Pelter stared at the man for a long moment. Then he reached up and touched his aug, and Mr Crane lowered the two of them to the ground. Almost reluctantly he released them and stepped back. Pelter handed him back the briefcase, then continued to watch while the men straightened out their clothing. They waited for a cue from him, but he gave them nothing but silence.

'This way . . . then,' said the first speaker hesitantly. He carefully moved out of Mr Crane's range and led off.

The man was fat, almost ball-shaped, and Pelter could not understand why. Surely there was no interruption to food supplies here, therefore no need to store it up internally? That sort of thing was only required on very primitive worlds. The fat man did not have one of those reptilian augs behind his ear – like the two cases who had brought Pelter here – but he did have a somewhat reptilian appearance. His shiny skin was broken into small diamond patterns, almost scalelike. Pelter studied the man for a long moment, then glanced back at the other two. They had moved away to stand on either side of the armoured door. Pelter was not concerned by this. Mr Crane, standing just a few paces in from the door, would be more than adequate should things turn nasty.

'Arian Pelter?' said the fat man.

'I am – and I am curious to know how *you* know that,' said Pelter.

'Please have a seat.' The man gestured to the chair placed before his desk.

Pelter moved forward and sat down. Mr Crane moved

up to stand behind him. Pelter had the android turn round to watch the two by the door.

'You haven't answered my question,' he said.

'I am here to help you.'

'And who might you be?' Pelter asked.

'You may call me Grendel,' said the fat man, giving a little smile as if at some private joke.

'Well, Grendel, I have things I need to do. Your men told me we have some mutual interest. The only reason I'm here is because they mentioned a place called Samarkand.'

'Yes, I do have an interest in Samarkand. But let us be clear what this conversation concerns.' Grendel paused, as if listening to something, and then he went on. 'My client and yourself both have a special interest that is pertinent to that place. That interest is one Ian Cormac.'

Pelter looked down at his suddenly clenched fists. After a moment he opened his hands and looked up. The thin-gun hovered at the edge of his vision again.

'Talk, and talk fast.' He spoke through clenched teeth. Behind him Mr Crane moved his head in that characteristic birdlike manner as he turned his head from one to the other of the two men by the door.

'First, I feel I should assure you that you need look no further than these premises for your requirements. I have all those things that the Polity frowns upon.'

'I won't ask again,' said Pelter.

'As you will . . . You want to kill Ian Cormac. I can help you kill him.'

Something frigid rested a hand on the back of Pelter's neck. 'Go on.'

'My client will assist you. Through me he will provide weapons which you will, I am afraid, pay for, but then you expected that. There are, though, other ways in which he can assist you. You have the determination and the ability to deal with Ian Cormac. What you lack is a suitable source of information.'

'I can get information,' said Pelter tightly.

'You can?' wondered Grendel. 'Information like . . . that at this moment Ian Cormac is in a small carrier-wing overflying Samarkand? That he has with him Spar-kind soldiers?'

Pelter was silent for a moment. Mr Crane froze into stillness. 'That . . . kind of information would have to come from the AI net,' he said. 'The only people who could obtain it would have to be gridlinked. Are you gridlinked? Because if you are, then it means you are ECS, and very shortly to die.'

Grendel smiled. 'No gridlinks as you see them. Perhaps you have noted these?'

Grendel opened his compartment and took something out. He placed it lovingly on the surface of his desk. It was one of the strangely reptilian augs like those Svent and Dusache wore. It seemed alive to Pelter.

'This explains nothing,' he said.

'You haven't asked me who my client is,' said Grendel.

'Who is your client, then?'

Grendel told him.

The Sharrow provided just about any entertainment you cared to pay for under one golden and baroque roof. There were restaurant platforms raised above the more rowdy drinking area. This lower floor was scattered with ring-shaped bars, so the clientele were never far from their next drink. Caves led off from here towards gaming rooms, bordellos and places that provided more esoteric entertainments. Suspended on chains below the flat ceiling was The Sharrow's milder version of the arena. In a cylindrical armour-glass tank, hideous crustaceans the size of men hammered at each other in an unending battle. Each time one was ripped apart, it dropped to the bottom of the tank, where smaller crustaceans reassembled it. It would be a matter of dispute as to whether or not these qualified as living creatures. They were a product of that very thick and very blurred line between biotechnology and what Svent would describe simply as 'tech'.

For a moment Stanton watched the creatures battling, then he turned his attention to the various people scattered at the tables about the place, who were operating the same creatures through virtual gloves and face cups. Just then, one of them removed his face cup and punched his fist into the air. The others at his table began grudgingly handing over his winnings. Stanton switched his attention away once he spotted a small, elfin woman with long, straight, black hair, a very tight acceleration suit, and spring heels, swaying her way to one of the spiral staircases. He let her move from sight before he crossed the chaotic room and followed her up.

The staircase led Stanton to the accommodation floor of The Sharrow. Here he entered a corridor that was a tightly curving pipe lined with old ceramic shuttle tiles. The outer edge of its curve had oval repro airlock doors inset at intervals. This corridor, he knew, spiralled out

181

to the edge of the circular building he was in. He kept going until he reached a certain door, thumped his fist against it and stared at the small optic chip set in its surface. After a moment the door swung open.

The room was a very curious shape, having the outer curves of two corridors for its walls. The ceiling was low, and Stanton reflected that this would definitely not be a place for Mr Crane. He looked around him. To his right was a large round bed, and to his left a large combination of shower stall and circular bath contained inside a perspex egg. Between stood a round table made of polished white stone, behind which were two repro acceleration chairs.

In one of these chairs sat the woman he had followed. She had already removed her acceleration suit and had belted about her a short silk robe. She was very pretty, but the pulse-gun she was pointing at Stanton was not.

'As I live and breathe: Arian Pelter's big faithful dog,' she said. 'Did he let you off your lead, then? Or have you been a very naughty doggy and just run away?' She stood up and sauntered over, then stood in front of him with the pulse-gun resting against her breast.

'He wants you for the trip back out,' Stanton said.

'Oh really? What if I don't want to go?' she said.

Stanton stepped forward, took the gun from her hand and tossed it on a thick rug nearby. 'We've got two hours,' he said, and then reached down and violently tugged open the belt of her robe.

'You brute you,' she said, and ran her hands down over her breasts, her stomach and pressed them into her pubis.

Stanton reached up and slid his finger into the seal on

his shirt. He slid his finger down, undoing it, then pulled the catch on his trousers.

'Jarvellis, just get on the bed,' he said.

The *Lyric*'s captain shrugged her robe off her shoulders, then walked back and sat on the stone table, a cheeky smile on her face as she watched Stanton undress.

'I rather thought we could start in the bath, then work our way gradually to the bed,' she said.

'You're going to regret not turning that heating on,' said Stanton.

'Ooh, are you going to treat me roughly, big boy?'

Stanton chased her screaming towards the circular bath.

Pelter held the aug in the palm of his hand and inspected it. It could be the edge he needed, but how much trust did he have? None at all. On the back of the aug were three bone-anchors not much different from those on any other aug. The fibre-injector ring was no different either. Like standard augs it would connect through into his cerebellum, to the back of his optic nerve, and in behind his ear. He was not entirely sure of all the connections that augs made. What he was sure of was that the fibres were delicate and could be easily broken, and that this aug was soft as a mouse and could be crushed just as easily.

Pelter made his decision. Some might have thought it the height of idiocy, but he knew that it was by taking such risks that in the end he would win. While he studied the device he quickly constructed a program

183

between Sylac's aug and Crane's command module. It took only seconds. He looked across at Grendel.

'I will not be controlled,' he said.

'We did not think that you would, Arian Pelter. This aug is, as I stated, for you to receive the information Dragon wishes you to have,' he said. 'Take it away and have it studied, if you wish. I would not want you to go into this blind.'

Pelter nodded. That meant that whatever was concealed in this aug was concealed very well. But there had to be something. He brought the thing up to the side of his head and slapped it into place. For a moment nothing happened, then he gasped as the bone-anchors went in unanaesthetized. He kept his hand in place and suddenly the thing felt warm, febrile. He felt Mr Crane's brass hand lifting to mirror the position of his own, and images of the android's foolish toys flashed through his mind. Grendel stood behind his desk, worry in his expression. The two by the door, Pelter saw through Mr Crane, had their hands poised over their weapons. Coldness suffused the side of Pelter's head. He did not feel the links going in. The nanonic fibres would be passing through cells and through bone, like stiff hairs through foam. He did feel the connections they made.

For a moment there was a doubling of function with the aug he had from Sylac, then that first aug switched off. He got control again, closed his eyes and linked through to Mr Crane and had him lower his hand. Control and access was slick. He froze Crane into complete immobility and accessed a local server. Fast, very fast. He found a search program in the aug, and sent it after any references to himself. There were none at the server, but information came through. He knew now that a network of people wearing these augs had been waiting for him. They had known as soon as Dusache and Svent had bought their tegulate augs and placed them on the sides of their heads. The information had been passed on, whether willingly or not. Pelter opened his eyes and stared at Grendel.

'I repeat: I will not be controlled,' he said.

'I assure you again, Arian Pelter. Your and my client's purposes are one and the same.'

Pelter closed his eyes again. He reached in, closed down the second aug and reinstated Sylac's. It was like switching from colour to black and white. Knowing he now could do this, he sent an instruction to stand down the program he had sent to Mr Crane. In another thirty seconds the android would have killed the two at the door, next killed Grendel, then torn this soft aug from the side of Pelter's head. He opened his eyes to see Grendel settling his ponderous bulk behind his desk again.

'Now, to business,' said the fat man, smiling his jowly smile. 'What exactly do you require in the hardware department?'

Pelter said nothing for a moment. He watched through Mr Crane as the two men at the door moved their hands away from their weapons. When they had done this, he spoke very precisely. He reached up and rested his finger on his aug.

'I have an extensive list,' he said. 'Amongst other items, I require seeker bullets and Drescon assault rifles. I require seeker missiles, laser carbines, explosives, and the various delivery systems of said. I also require surveillance drones, proton guns and a dropbird.'

'Obviously you understand the difficulties entailed in acquiring the last three. Luckily I do have two proton guns and some surveillance drones. The dropbird may present some difficulties, but not difficulties that cannot be overcome. Let me have your list.'

Pelter called up the list he had been steadily building since his arrival on Huma, and transmitted it on a secure link to Grendel. The fat man showed momentary surprise, but then smiled.

'You like to be prepared,' he said.

Pelter did not bother replying to that. Grendel rubbed his hands together and leant forwards.

'Now to the details and, of course, the price.'

Pelter sat back and stared past the fat man. In his new aug he felt something poised in the background. It was there behind the frames and graphics. It was there when all of that was gone. He knew that, at some point, he would hear a voice. He did not yet know how he would respond to it. He squinted, concentrated, and raised Sylac's aug, while running the other. It was a balancing act, but one he considered necessary. He would not be controlled. He again focused his attention on Grendel.

'Price,' he said flatly.

Jarvellis lay with a smug cat-after-cream expression on her face. Stanton inspected the various scratches on his body and wondered just from where she got the energy. She wasn't boosted like him, but she certainly tended to wear him out. He studied her and wondered just how much he could trust her. She returned his regard, then reached under the pillow to her left. He read, for a second, a craftiness in her expression, and abruptly rolled across her and clamped his hand down on her left wrist.

'John, where is your trust in people?' she asked him.

'I lost it when my mother turned my father in to the proctors, and when they dragged him from our apartment in the arcology and shot him through the face,' he said.

Jarvellis lost her mocking expression. 'I keep forgetting. You came from Masada, didn't you?'

'I did. Religious law and the theocracy ruling from orbital stations. Nobody trusted anyone and the heresy laws were exactly what the proctors wanted them to be at any time.'

'John, you can trust me.'

Stanton looked at her for a long moment. It frightened him just how much he wanted to trust her. He released her wrist and slid his weight off her. He did not move too far back, and every muscle of his body was taut as a guitar string. Trust; it was hard for him. With care she slid her hand out from under the pillow. She held out to him a long and flat box made of rosewood.

'I got you a present,' she said.

Stanton took the box and let out a long slow breath. Engraved on the lid was the letter T.

'Open it, then,' she said, sitting up.

Even now he found it difficult. Some kind of trap inside? *Trust*. He pressed the catch on the side and the lid slowly lifted.

'My God,' he said.

Inside the box, cushioned in black velvet, were a

dagger, its sheath, and a gold ring. The weapon was one casting of yellow chainglass. Inside the handle was a frame of silver wires and inside that a complexity of small cubes in which dim lights flickered. The sheath was plain black metal with two skin-stick pads.

'It's an early one. Twenty-third century. Its provenance is recorded in its micromind. Tenkian made it on Jocasta. It's one of the first he made with a micromind. Limited AG,' Jarvellis informed him.

Stanton took the weapon from the box. The grip appeared smooth, but was firm and positive. He felt a faint tingling sensation in the palm of his hand. Jarvellis went on.

'Now it has impressed on you. Anyone else tries to handle it now, without reprogramming it, will get a brief nerve shock; enough to make them drop it.'

'What does it do?'

'Not much, really. You see the ring?'

Stanton took the ring from the box and inspected it. It was plain gold with a circle of green gold set concentric in its outer surface. The outer ring was octagonal, as if made to take a spanner.

'Put it on your right index finger,' she told him as she sat upright.

He slid the ring into place. As soon as it was there it seemed to tighten.

'Now,' Jarvellis continued. 'Put the dagger back in its sheath.'

When he had done this, Jarvellis carefully took it from him, being careful only to touch the sheath. She tossed it down to the foot of the bed.

'What now?' he asked.

She replied, 'The green ring turns in the gold one. Just give it a flick with your thumb.'

Stanton did as instructed. There was a sound as of a wasp shooting past. Stanton saw a flash of yellow and, before he could react, the handle of the dagger slapped into the palm of his hand. He held it there and turned to Jarvellis, a grin on his face.

'I like it,' he said.

Jarvellis shrugged. 'That's all it does, I'm afraid. It's got just about enough intelligence not to cut your fingers off in the process.'

'That would be quite enough in some situations,' said Stanton. He retrieved the sheath and slid the dagger back in place. This and the box he placed on the bedside table before reaching his hand behind Jarvellis's neck and pulling her in close. They kissed long and hard before eventually pulling apart. Stanton held up his hand and wiggled his index finger.

'Does this mean we're married?' he asked.

Jarvellis stared at him seriously for a moment, then she grinned and threw herself back on the pillows. 'Tell me again how much,' she said.

Stanton closed his hand into a fist, a smile quirking the corners of his mouth. 'I've told you once.'

'I don't care. I want to hear it again.'

'All right . . . In the top layer there's about three million left, I think. There are definitely more layers in that case, maybe five of them, I can't be sure. I'd estimate that with the kind of armament he's after, and with what he pays Corlackis and crew, he'll be shelling out about five million. There'll have to be upward of ten million left.'

189

'Very nice, but how do we make it *our* ten million?'

'Difficult. With Crane next to him at every moment, it doesn't leave much room to manoeuvre. When we go after this ECS bastard he'll have to send Crane in, and I should have my hands on some hardware by then. I'll have to take him then, and you'll have to come in and get me.' Stanton stared at her, but she did not meet his look.

'What about the other four?'

'Well, they'll be going in as well at some point. I'll choose my moment. Damn, I wish I'd taken him just after he withdrew it. I was stupid.'

'No, John, you were loyal. Why not admit to yourself that you were loyal up to a point – and that point was Mr Crane.' Jarvellis looked at him now and smiled. 'You know, John, that this is the break. We pull this off and we can get an Aquarius-class upgrade. That means ram-scoop and all the speed we'll ever need, unless ECS want to come down on us. How long do you think before we buy into a consortium and start pulling in some real wealth?'

'Still want to buy that planet, Jarvellis?'

'Nobody can own planets, John, but we could own enough of one not to know the difference. A planet a few centuries from the Line, well away from Polity inter-ference. Think on that.'

Stanton reached for her and pulled her close. He loved her foolish dreams and, just so long as she stayed with him while she dreamed them, he didn't mind. Sometimes, the thought that she might take her dreams elsewhere frightened him.

11

Cormac sat before the viewing screen in the recreation area and let out a deep sigh. He toasted Horace Blegg, then put his glass down on the table beside him. He felt very tired, but had been unable to sleep and a drink seemed the best way to unwind.

'Ship AI . . .' Cormac began, then paused in chagrin and started again. '*Hubris*, is this screen voice-activated?'

'It is,' replied one of the many voices of *Hubris*, this one more relaxed and easy-going because of the surroundings.

'Give me a view into Isolation Chamber One, please.'

The screen flickered on and showed the two draco-men squatting on the floor of the chamber. They were eating slabs of recon' protein and drinking water from tall beakers. The scene was reminiscent of something from an ancient fairy tale. Cormac winced to himself at that thought, and did not carry it any further.

'Very efficient creatures these,' said *Hubris*.

'What do you mean?'

'They are decontaminating themselves. They're using some method of regeneration. There is a high level of

191

damaged and radioactive material from their bodies in their excrement.'

'Nice,' said Cormac. The injection Mika had given him had hurt, and was still hurting. He wondered if she had taken some obscure form of vengeance on him by using it. There were other less painful methods of getting antactives into the bloodstream.

Hubris went on. 'It is an extremely rapid process. They eat as much as is given them and convert it very quickly. They will be wholly regenerated within two days.'

'And should we let them out then?' wondered Cormac.

'That is for you to decide. It is relevant to note that Dragon always served its own purposes, and with little regard for human life.'

Cormac nodded, more to himself than the ship AI. He remembered the two-kilometre perimeter around Dragon on Aster Colora. Dragon had said, 'No machines inside this perimeter.' People had tried, as people do, and that perimeter had become a ring of smashed vehicles, some still containing human remains.

Where are you, Dragon? What do you want?

Cormac turned as the door slid open behind him and Chaline walked in. She looked as tired as he felt, and obviously had the same intention in mind. She got herself a drink from the autobar, then slumped into the seat next to him. As she sipped her drink she studied him with an intensity he found unnerving. He felt compelled to talk.

'Couldn't sleep?' he asked.

'No.' She turned away with a slight smile and rubbed

at her eyes with her forefinger and thumb. 'I was readying a probe to go into the blast-site and search out some fragments of the runcible buffer. It seems there's a chance it was not all vaporized.' She looked up at the screen. 'How are our friends getting on?'

Cormac told her what *Hubris* had told him.

'Dracomen . . . I had a quick look in the reference section but all I could come up with was this text called 'The Dragon Dialogues'? It read like a philosophy thesis and ran to about ten million words. Fascinating stuff, but I don't really have the time to read it . . .' She turned to Cormac. 'What was this Dragon then? Not a firebreather, I gather?'

Cormac hesitated, and then grimaced. 'No, Dragon was the name the creature gave itself, for whatever reason . . . *Hubris*, do you have any film of Dragon?'

'Enough to last a lifetime.'

'Show us some, please.'

The screen flickered and showed a contorted rocky plain below a metallic red sky. On that plain stood four vast spheres joined in a row. Pink snow was falling.

'There's Dragon. Each of those spheres is a kilometre across.'

'It was all alive?' asked Chaline incredulously.

'Oh yes, very much so. Xenologists thought it might once have been mobile, but when discovered it was like this. It had pseudopods rooted into the ground for kilometres all around. It must have extracted minerals or something to feed on. No one can say for sure, but later examination of the site found the ground riddled with tunnels and lacking in certain minerals found elsewhere.'

'Later examination?' Chaline asked.

Cormac closed his eyes as a memory, clear as day, flashed into his mind. He remembered a fantastic road made for him, two kilometres long, marked out by pseudopods five metres high and half a metre wide, each one like a white cobra, but with a single blue crystalline eye where its mouth should have been. That had been a long walk.

Chaline returned her attention to the screen again and continued before Cormac could answer. 'It must have been made of more than flesh and bone. At that size it would have collapsed in on itself . . .'

'Alive *and* a machine,' said Cormac. 'There were AG readings from it, and the readings of metals, and some pretty strange radiations. It's speculated that its bones were some form of bubble metal, or that it supported itself with AG. No one got close enough to find out.'

'Tell me more,' said Chaline, her fatigue forgotten.

Cormac snorted and shook his head. 'It starts with the scream, doesn't it?' he said, then he looked up at the screen. '*Hubris*, you might as well record this. I don't want to have to tell it again.' He turned his attention back to Chaline. 'They say you scream for a fraction of a second when you're transmitted by runcible. I didn't arrive on Aster Colora screaming. I arrived reciting a nonsense poem. I should think you know it. Don't we all?'

And Cormac remembered, and he told her.

(Solstan 2407)

A scream, silent in underspace: a flicker of existence between the shadows of stars. It is known, the scream, but quince never remember. For Cormac there was merely a flash of black and red, a Dante glimpse, and he was completing his thought far from where he began it.

—on mince and slices of quince, which they ate with a runcible spoon. Is that right?

Times change: terms change, and it was an ancient nonsense rhyme. He was well aware of that as he fought to overcome the disorientation of mitter-lag.

And the runcible spoon flicks them across the galaxy . . . Hah! Myths rewritten. I'm a knight in shining armour only my hardware's on the inside.

Caught in the flaw of a jewel Cormac considered dragons. Ten seconds and 400 light-years later his mind caught up with his body. The scream was lost in a twilight place. Echoes. He stepped from the shimmer of the cusp. Down the steps from the pedestal, across the black-glass floor, then out of the containment sphere.

'Ian Cormac?'

'Yes.'

The sky was metallic red, the land pink rock with black striations. The horizon was more tightly curved than that viewed from the balcony of his 200th-floor apartment in New York. You noticed things like that, just as you noticed other immediacies. He sneezed, then breathed deeply. The air tasted of salt, and silica dust coated his tongue. After a moment of deliberation he turned his attention to the speaker.

'I am Maria,' said the girl, whose hair was red with no

white light to show him different. Cormac held out his hand to silence her as his breath billowed in the chill air like lung-blood. He continued to survey the wasteland.

He gestured back at the runcible.

'Only one. Quince and light cargo. Few people come here,' he observed.

'Yes, Dragon set a limit of twenty thousand visitors a year.'

'Solstan year?'

'No . . . Colora,' she said, annoyed.

Cormac stared at her. 'I require assistance, not impatience,' he said, and waited.

'Yes, Ambassador,' she said grudgingly, rubbing her hand on a leather-sheathed hip. Cormac accessed his link and immediately had a report up in his visual cortex. Rather than download it into his memory, he speed-read it while he studied his surroundings.

Maria Convala. Born on Aster Colora 2376 solstan, exobiologist attached to the Earth Central study team, ambitious, has connections with the Separatist movement, is rumoured to have been involved in the third Jovian putsch . . .

He smiled bleakly to himself and thought about his other operation in this sector. Earth Central had only chosen him to come here because he knew the systems, the people, those most likely to cause trouble. Even now the agents he was running were uncovering Separatist cell after cell in that razor-walk of undercover work. As soon as the first cover was blown, the whole investigation would collapse, but a huge proportion of the Separatist network would fall with it. Of course, what was going on here was different – wasn't it? Files blinked out and dropped away as he dismissed them as irrelevant. He allowed the smile to fade from his face and slid his attention to the iron slug of an AGC that had been left on hover nearby. He noted the rust streaks, and the plates welded to its underside. It was old. Such was always the way this far from Earth; things broke down, wore out, were infrequently replaced. He should consider himself lucky they had AGCs here at all. Was that why this sector was a hotbed of Separatism? Not enough luxuries?

'Shall we go?' he said, after a pause.

As they slid above the desolation, Cormac accessed information more relevant to his task. There was no life here but for the human colony, the sentient Dragon and the insentient Monitor (the latter two leviathans), nor had there been. There were no fossils, chalk deposits, or life-based hydrocarbons – nothing. Billions had been expended in deep-coring projects, sifting machines and lengthy geochemical studies. The questions remained: where was the ecology from which Dragon and Monitor had evolved? Was it on Aster Colora?

Dragon had immediately communicated with those first to arrive through the seed-ship runcible, and had been in continuous communication with the colony ever since, yet little had been learnt about it. Dragon relished oracular pronouncements and Delphic replies.

'Has Dragon given reasons for its request?'

'It was more of a demand than a request.'

'Clarify that.'

With her hand resting on the guide-ball of the AGC, Maria glanced at him. 'We have always been here on sufferance. It said, "Send me an ambassador"; there was no request.'

Cormac noted the bitterness. As a Separatist, he realized, this put her in an intolerable position. How could she campaign for political independence while Aster Colora could not rise above colony status? He wondered just how deeply in she was and how far she was prepared to go. He didn't want to have to kill her.

The red land flowed under the rock of the AGC until at length Cartis, like a spreading fungus, came into view. Like any tourist, Cormac booked into the metrotel. In his room he slumped on his bed and accessed Dragon/human dialogue. Human politics were irrelevant in this case which, for Cormac, was a novelty.

'You continue to evade our questions concerning yourself,' asked a man only just holding on to his temper.

'Yes, this is true,' came the indifferent reply.

'Yet for years you have had access to our information systems. You know our history, the level of our technology . . . You perhaps know more about the human race than any single member of it. Why will you not tell us about yourself? Surely, this is little to ask?'

'You are correct: I know more about you people than any single member of your kind.'

'You have not answered my question.'

'Yes, I have.'

'I do not understand.'

'A very human trait.'

'Please explain.'

'The runcible has been developed to the stage where it is near perfect in function. Humankind can now step from star system to star system with ease. On Earth, contra-terrene power is about to be introduced. In the system of Cassius the first Dyson sphere is under construction. The matter for this project came from a planet of Jovian size, demolished by a contra-terrene missile.'

'Do you fear us?'

'Should I?'

'Many assume that this is the reason for your reticence.'

'How old are you, Darson?'

'One hundred and seventy, solstan.'

'It is likely that you will live to be over eight hundred years old and then only to die of ennui.'

'Perhaps. How old are you?'

'Do you represent your race, Darson?'

'In the sense—'

'No, you do not represent your race. I cannot sit in judgment on you. Send me an ambassador.'

After the dialogue had ceased, Cormac opened his eyes and scratched at his head. He was tired; he had, after all, travelled a long way. He got off the bed and shed the clothes he had been wearing only a few hours earlier, personal time, in New York, and wondered, as always with cold humour, what the morning might bring. Of course he did not know whether it was day or night here, but such things he had for quite some time dismissed as irrelevant. He lived by personal time. It was the only way to stay sane.

The morning brought Maria with an analysis from Darson, the Dragon expert. Cormac read it over a breakfast of spiced eggs, honey fish and two pots of tea.

Darson's conclusion was that Dragon, in human terms, was insane. After reading it, Cormac dressed in his shabby survival suit and placed in his rucksack the single device he might need. On his way out he consigned the report to the waste disposal. Shortly he was sliding above redland, red under a bloody sky.

'What is your opinion of Darson?'

'He's a pompous old fart,' Maria replied, and Cormac liked her for that.

'He believes Dragon is psychotic,' he said.

'I am not qualified to judge,' she replied.

Expressionlessly Cormac watched pink sleet slide off the frictionless screen of the AGC. 'You are qualified to have an opinion.'

Maria hesitated before replying. Cormac glanced at her and could see her discomfort. She was, he knew, trying to decide how to influence him and what opinion it would be best to own. He repressed a smile. She was in a difficult position. Instructions had preceded him: no unnecessary contact, straight to Dragon, the crux. He could see that she was unnerved.

'The dialogue with Dragon is deceptively human . . . Darson seems to find it difficult to accept the alien.'

Cormac chuckled. The AGC dipped as Maria glanced at him. Unable to find any way of applying leverage, she had answered with the truth. He nodded to himself and looked ahead as she slowed the AGC and began to power it down. Before them lay the Junkyard: the tangible result of people's flouting of Dragon's rule of no machinery larger than a man within a two-kilo-metre radius. Many people had died here. Maria put the

AGC on hover. Cormac tapped the com on his belt as the door slid open.

'I'll contact you when I want picking up,' he said and left her.

After reaching the line of smashed AGCs and hover scooters that marked the two-kilometre boundary, Cormac shouldered his rucksack and climbed a rusting hulk. Even through the snow the four spheres were visible, standing like vast storage tanks on a plain of broken rock. After a moment he clambered down the other side of the boundary, peeking in the wrecked AGC at its occupants, whom no one had bothered to retrieve. As his feet touched the ground, the ground itself moved.

Pseudopods.

He stood very still and waited, the taste of salt turning acrid in his mouth. Five metres to one side of him the ground rippled and a thing like a metre-wide cobra exploded into the air. Cormac dropped to avoid a flying rock, then rolled, looked up. It arched above him, a single crystalline blue eye where a cobra's mouth should have been. The ground tilted and another explosion followed. Then another. Cormac put his rucksack over his head as explosion followed explosion and he was pelted with shards of rock. Then it ceased, and he stood in the silence.

Arrayed and curved like the ribs of an immense snake's skeleton, the pseudopods had become his honour guard. He walked down the spine.

In the face of total disaster, defiance is the only recourse . . . crazy street-lamps they have here.

Cormac allowed his mind to wander; random-access on subject:

> *Monitor: Insentient autochthon of the planet Aster Colora. It has the appearance of a Terran monitor lizard, but is a kilometre long and weighs an estimated 4.5 million tonnes. It is a silicon-based lifeform with an alien physiognomy . . .*
>
> *Dragon . . . Monitor . . . What connection?*
> *Why does Dragon want an ambassador?*
> *Questions.*
> *Answers?*
> *Damn!*

The two kilometres unrolled and eventually Cormac came before the curving edifice of tegulate flesh within an amphitheatre of pseudopods. He noted, to one side, a piece of machinery that could have been the comlink for Dragon/human dialogue: the one exception to its rule about machines. It was scrapped. He looked up at the pink-and-red-stippled sky, half cut by the cloud-tangled flesh mountain, and he waited.

'Ambassador.'

The voice came from the undershadows of the sphere, resonant but conversational.

'Ian Cormac . . . yes.'

'Names. All things can be named.'

As of skis on granular snow, a hissing issued from the undershadows. Cormac saw a swirl of movement, then a monstrous head shot towards him, propelled by a ribbed snake body. He stumbled back, fell. It rose above him; a pterosaur head with sapphire eyes.

'Are you afraid?'

Cormac choked back his immediate reply and said, 'Should I be?' His tone betrayed nothing of what he felt.

The head lunged at him, then jerked to a halt two metres above him. It smelt of cloves. Milky saliva dripped on him.

'Answer my question.'

'Yes, I am afraid. Does that surprise you?'

'No.'

The head moved up and away. Cormac stood and brushed himself off.

'I fail to see the purpose of that little scene,' he said.

'You represent your race,' Dragon replied, 'and you can die.'

More than personal, then. Cormac did not react to the implications, but steadily returned the stare of those sapphire eyes.

'Why did you send for an ambassador.'

'Ah . . . you are human then?'

'Of course.'

'You *do* represent your race?'

'Such is my position, though I cannot speak for every *individual* in it.' He emphasized individual – why? He did not know; it had almost been instinctive. The Dragon head swayed, then twitched, shaking off an accumulation of snow.

'Running round the inside of your skull is a net of mycorhizal fibre optics connected to etched-atom processors, silicon synaptic interfaces and an underspace transmitter. Evolution is a wonderful thing,' it said.

That gave Cormac pause. Smoothly he said, 'They are the tools of my trade. I am human. I am a member of the races of homo sapiens, meaning "wise man", and a wise man will use what tools he can to make his tasks easier.'

'I am glad you are sure of your integrity.'

The head swayed to one side, then looked back. The tegulate skin of Dragon's body bulged and quivered as if it were taking a breath. There was a liquid groaning, then skin and flesh parted like that of a rotten fruit. Unable to hide his reaction Cormac retched at the stench that wafted from the pink vagina of a cave that appeared before him. There were more liquid sounds driven by deep rhythmic pulses. Cormac watched in fascination as a jet of steaming amniot ejected the foetal ball of a manthing wrapped in a caul. The caul burst open, spilling more of the Dragon's juices. Dracoman; Cormac named it instantly.

'A trifle dramatic,' he managed.

The manthing continued to move. It stood, showing no sign of imbalance. Again that sound: something else born; a flattened ellipse. The manthing picked it up and stripped away its caul. Legs dropped down from underneath it. Cormac could hardly believe he was seeing a table. The man approached and placed the table between them.

'To be human is to be mortal,' said Dragon. 'Do you play chess?'

'Yes, I . . .'

Movement from the table: a bulging, bubbling, like sprouting mushrooms and a Dragon chess set grew from its surface.

'Your move.'

For a moment Cormac could think of nothing else to say or do. He reached down and took hold of a pawn.

The thing writhed in his hand, bit him. He yelled and dropped it. On the board it slithered forwards to a tegulate square.

'There is always a price for power,' said Dragon.

Cormac swore, then waited for his opponent's move, his confusion growing. What the hell was this? Some sort of megalomaniacal game or a test?

He hoped for the latter.

As he thought, he studied his opponent. The dracoman betrayed nothing, even when he suddenly moved and brought his fist down on Cormac's pawn. Cormac was taken aback.

'That is not in the rulebook,' he said, then damned himself for saying it. He knew what Dragon's reply would be.

'There are no rules here, just judgments.'

Cormac decided to react. He brought his fist down and crushed his opponent's king. 'Check,' he said dryly, and watched his opponent.

The dracoman stared at the board for a moment, then methodically began to crush every one of Cormac's pieces. White gore dribbled off the side of the table. Cormac turned towards the head.

'Surely by now you have enough insight into basic human reactions? You've been studying us for centuries,' he said.

'Every human is an individual, as you so rightly indicated,' observed Dragon.

Cormac was not sure he had done any such thing. He turned back to his opponent. 'I do not like subjective games,' he said, and knocked the table aside. The dracoman went for him with frightening speed. The hands reaching for his throat he was able to knock aside, but he was still driven to the ground. The hands reached for his throat again. He brought his knee up, then flung the clammy body from him. He regained his feet as his opponent did. The attack was still without finesse, and this time, not caught unawares, Cormac used his feet to counter it. The fight was over in seconds, the dracoman gurgling on the shale.

'Your second-to-last move was the wrong one,' said Dragon.

'I won.'

'That is not the issue.'

'What is?'

'Morality.'

'Hah, it is the winners who write history and it is the winners who invent morality. Existence is all the reason for existence any of us has, unless you believe in gods. I think you set yourself up too high.'

'No higher than an executioner.'

'You threaten again. Why? Do you have the power to carry out your threats? Do you think that you are a god?'

'I do not threaten you.'

'You seek to judge me then – to judge what I represent.'

'In the system of Betelgeuse there is a physicist working on some of the later Skaidon formulae. I predict he will solve some of the problems he has set himself.'

'And . . .?'

'Within the next century the human race will possess the intergalactic runcible.'

'What?'

The ground shook. A vast shadow blotted out half the sky. With his skin crawling Cormac turned, and there, making its ponderous gargantuan way across the rock-scape, he saw the Monitor; long as a city, its legs like tower blocks. Cormac watched it pass, knew its destination.

'Another threat?' he breathed. 'What is it that you want?'

The head rose higher and turned in the direction the Monitor had gone.

'Go back to Cartis. When you have seen what you must see, return here.'

Suddenly the head dropped down, and was hovering before Cormac.

'I control Monitor; without me it is mindless, but you know that,' it said. 'I have the power, the power to destroy. Could it be that you know what I mean?'

'I know the substance of your threat . . . your warning?' was Cormac's reply. After a pause he glanced down at the now unmoving dracoman. Then he swung his attention to his rucksack, back up at Dragon, shrugged and walked away, random accessing as he did so, so that nothing could be read from his expression:

Aster Colora: A planet on the rim of the galaxy.

Maria had been waiting for him at the two-kilometre boundary. She was panicked, out of her depth.

'The whole city . . . Monitor . . .'

Cormac silenced her and took her place in the driving seat of the AGC. Halfway back to Cartis she had calmed enough to be coherent.

'Pseudopods broke through all round the city. I was

outside when it happened . . . No one can escape and
Monitor is heading in that direction. It has never done
that before.'

'Dragon controls Monitor.'

'Why . . .?'

'Either it tests us or Darson is right.'

'Thanks for the comfort.'

Cartis was indeed ringed by pseudopods, but they
parted to allow the AGC through. At the metrotel,
Cormac used Maria's intentions and fear to get her to
bed. He felt no remorse. She had been quite prepared
to use him in any way she could for the Separatist movement. Lying on his bed he listened as the rumble of
Monitor's arrival ceased, then he inspected the naked
form lying beside him. An affirmation of humanity? he
wondered. The question was irrelevant. All waited on
him. Careful not to wake Maria, Cormac got off the bed
and went to the bathroom. Ritualistically he shaved,
cleaned his teeth and dressed. He then sat down and
accessed the runcible grid.

Earth Central.

Dragon intergalactic.

Proven?

To my satisfaction.

With that he sent all he had learnt and surmised to
the AI. It took less than a second.

A test. Morality base evident, came the terse reply.

Threat/warning?

Also.

Obliterate?

Not feasible. Obviously has knowledge of device.

?

Part of the test.

It is disposable then?

As me.

'Yes,' said Cormac out loud.

Go back, react, returned the silent thought of the AI. Cormac closed his eyes and closed access. Then, abruptly, he departed the metrotel.

The honour guard remained and Cormac was soon back before Dragon. The dracoman was gone, the cave gone, the head a black silhouette against the red sky.

'Have you seen?' it asked.

'You can destroy Cartis.'

The head turned. 'I mean – have you seen?'

Cormac squatted down next to the rucksack he had left. 'Yes,' he said, 'if we are judged and found wanting, what happens?'

'You have been judged.'

Cormac waited.

'I have been watching for twenty million of your years. I have seen every sparrow fall.'

'Yes . . . that is enough time to come to a conclusion,' said Cormac dryly. He entertained doubts, then, about Dragon's sanity.

'You will live,' Dragon said.

Cormac allowed the rigidity to leave him. 'Cartis . . .

the Monitor . . . they were the final push, just to see . . .' he said, fully understanding now.

'Your AIs are extensions of your own minds, as I am an extension of other minds. Had you destroyed me for the few petty threats of this day, without regard or understanding of what I truly am, every one of your runcibles would have been turned inside out: converted into black holes.'

Cormac reached across and opened his rucksack. From it he took an innocuous blue-grey cylinder of metal. With a thought he deactivated it, then he put it away again. A similar, if somewhat larger device, had been used in the system of Cassius to demolish a gas giant.

'Now?' he asked.

'Now you must leave and I must leave. Your kind will meet mine. My task is done.'

'How will you leave?'

'I will not leave this planet.'

And Cormac knew. He left Dragon, and on his way saw Monitor come and lie down at its side like a faithful dog. Once in the AGC he did not look back.

Lest I be turned into a pillar of salt.

A white sun rose over Aster Colora, and hard black shadows were cast, like dice. Cormac later learnt it had been a contra-terrene explosion beyond mere human abilities to generate and contain, as it had been contained, in a two-kilometre radius.

It was Dragon's last message.

Not a trace of Dragon remained.

(Solstan 2434)

When he had finished telling Chaline, Cormac felt lightness in his chest. He leant back. It was a story he had told no human, though most runcible AIs knew it.

'What was the real purpose of calling you there? It all seems a little . . . unlikely,' Chaline wondered.

'Theatrics? Who knows? Debate about Dragon's purpose has raged since it was discovered, even amongst AIs. There are some who say it was too wise for us to understand. And, of course, the likes of Darson, who thinks it was insane . . . or is.'

'What do you think?'

Cormac turned and looked at her. 'First and foremost I think it was a liar and a fraud. I don't think it came here twenty million years ago, nor do I think it came to test humanity. The two statements don't tie up. And I certainly don't think it was capable of destroying us.'

'Is that all?'

'No. I don't think it self-destructed after it had served its ostensible purpose. There was not a trace of its body left, even under ground. I think it's out there somewhere, and it's laughing at us.'

Chaline smiled at that, then stood. 'Another drink?' She held out her hand for his glass. For a moment he considered refusing and heading for bed. He handed her his glass.

Damn it, I'm human.

As Chaline returned with the two drinks, he studied her closely. Her overall was wrinkled and sweat-stained, but did not detract from her allure in the slightest. Her face had an imperious beauty, her figure was worthy of note and she had something remarkable between her ears; anyone in her position had to have. Cormac felt something he had not felt with Angelina. That mechanical action had not been in response to any need in him. He had felt wholly cynical about it. When was the last time he had really made love to a woman? Maria Convala was the last, he was reluctant to admit.

'What's the matter?' Chaline asked him, a tilt to her head and a knowing smile.

'You're very attractive,' he said.

She sat down. 'I'm also very tired.'

Her mein was coy, and it surprised him. He glanced up as a group of technicians walked in after their shift, and he silently thanked them.

'We could finish our drinks in my cabin,' he suggested.

Her coyness disappeared and she inspected him estimatingly. Abruptly she stood again, and he thought he had maybe pushed too hard. She was going to chop him down.

'I really need a shower,' she said.

Cormac waited now for the kind rejection.

'I can't get in your cabin by myself,' she said impatiently.

Cormac was out of his seat and exiting the canteen before he even had a chance to be surprised. At the door to his cabin he slapped the palm-lock and entered in a teenage terror at how to initiate things. Chaline dispelled that worry in an instant: halfway across the room she turned, ran her thumb down the centre of her overall and parted it, kicked off her deck slippers and shrugged her overall to the floor. Cormac remembered to close his mouth as she smiled at him, then headed for his shower. We forgot our drinks, he thought, and then grinned. He left his clothes beside hers and followed.

'You are slow,' she said, as he moved up behind her and placed his hand on the lighter skin at the soapy curve of her hip.

'Too long listening to AIs,' he said, pulling her to him and sliding his hands round her waist, then up to her breasts. She pushed her bottom back against his erection and slowly moved it from side to side.

'I hope you haven't lost all your manual skills,' she said, then turned and reached down.

Cormac pulled her close again and started kissing her neck, and then he found himself on top of her on the floor of the shower room, inside her. From there, to the bed and the night – not one thought about gridlinks.

12

*Wouldn't you think that with such omnipotent AIs,
such advanced security systems, and such dedicated
ECS Monitors, crime would be a thing of the past?
Think that and you* aren't *thinking. Our security
systems may be advancing every day, but so are the
criminals. Between what I like to call the forces of
order and of chaos there is a constant 'arms race', and
it's difficult sometimes to say who might be winning.
Sometimes it is also difficult to distinguish which side
is which.*

From *How It Is* by Gordon

Briefly there had been a night, very briefly. The sun had
dipped behind the horizon for two solstan hours before
creeping back. As if this momentary lapse had allowed it
through, a green bank of cloud rose from the further
horizon and rolled in with pinwheels of lightning scoring
its underbelly. Stanton took another bite from the kebab
he had bought inside, and wondered just what sort of
meat he was eating. What sort of vegetation for that
matter. It was after inspecting the contents of his meal

for a moment that he looked along the length of the old road. Down the sides of the compacted and fused-earth surface were deep storm gullies. He had heard it could be bad here. What most puzzled him were the square panels set along the road at regular intervals. They were painted black and yellow, and each had a letter and a number. The letter was always a C and the numbers ascended in order. He was staring at these when a woman with a shaven and tattooed skull stumbled from The Sharrow. She was painfully slim in her jeans and padded sea-fibre jacket, and her skin had a bluish tint. Probably part Outlinker, he thought.

'What are those?' he asked, pointing at the squares when she gave him a once-over.

She looked confused for a moment, and then waved an arm dismissively. 'Car clamps,' she said, and stumbled off.

Stanton filed this information under miscellaneous, then looked back up the road in the other direction. The familiar loom of Mr Crane stomping along behind Pelter was not difficult to miss. He finished his meal in a couple of hurried bites, wiped his hands on a tissue and tossed that tissue into a nearby bin. As Pelter drew closer, Stanton saw that something had changed.

'New aug,' he said.

Pelter reached up and touched the reptilian aug clinging behind his right ear. Perhaps it was something about the light, the weight of cloud above and the flickering of yellow lightning, but Stanton felt sure he had seen the aug move under Pelter's touch. It was the final step, Stanton thought. Pelter had once been an attractive man; now, with his head made lopsided by two mismatched augs, the optic link in his suppurating eye socket and a face grown haggard and perpetually twisted by whatever drove him, he was ugly. Without a doubt he now looked what he was.

'A new aug,' Pelter repeated.

'OK,' said Stanton when it became apparent Pelter intended to say no more. He glanced up at the darkening sky and felt the first slimy drops of rain on his face. 'Storm on the way, and they can be bad here.' He looked at Pelter again. 'The boys are inside. Any luck with a dealer?'

Pelter nodded and gestured towards the arched entrance of The Sharrow. Side by side they walked through, Mr Crane at their back, a brass shadow.

'We have an assortment of interesting toys and we have our delivery system,' said Pelter.

'What sort?'

'A stealthed dropbird of Polity manufacture. I am told it was stolen piece by piece from an ECS base. It's old, but it will serve. Now – ' Pelter looked at him ' – did you deal with the other matter?'

'Jarvellis didn't let out any information concerning us. Neither by aug, her ship computers, nor auto manifest. She had all bets covered, as always. I believe her. She's smuggled weapons successfully for decades. You don't manage that under the noses of ECS without sealing every data leak.'

Pelter shook his head. 'That doesn't concern me. What about our transport?'

'It doesn't concern you? . . . We have to know how the information got through, Arian. We could be walking into a shitstorm here.'

'It doesn't concern me because I now know.'

'Know what?'

'Don't concern yourself. I have it covered. Now, transport?' said Pelter.

They halted almost in the middle of the room. Stanton glanced round at the raucous drinkers and saw the looks flung their way, then he looked towards the restaurant platforms ahead of them.

'Perhaps we should save this,' he said.

'No,' said Pelter. 'I want to know now what you have arranged.'

'OK, OK.' Stanton stepped closer and lowered his voice. He saw that Crane moved closer as well, and knew it wasn't because the android wanted to join the conversation.

'With a dropbird, life support for the six of us, and other supplies not yet detailed, Jarvellis says it'll have to be a full charter. We'll need both holds and she won't have room for any other cargoes. Also, she'll need to service the split seals on the A hold for loading and then deployment of the bird . . . A straight million.'

Stanton waited for Pelter to explode, but was surprised and puzzled by his reaction.

'Fine,' Pelter said, and moved on. 'We'll get rooms in the nearest metrotel while the work is being done. How long will the service take?'

'Couple of days, solstan . . . that's the reason for the high price, you see: a lot will go on the maintenance and bribes. They can block you if you don't pay.'

'There is no need to explain,' said Pelter as they reached the stairs to the restaurant.

Stanton let Pelter and Crane precede him. He

watched the metal stairs bending under the weight of the android, then glanced back across the chaos of the drinking area. The two men and two women who came in through the archway were little different from most of the rest of the clientele. They wore monofilament overalls and were shaking the rain from themselves. One woman was tall and had long black hair, and the other was a catadapt with reddish hair. The men both appeared quite normal: stock humanity. They were armed, as many here were. All that gave them away was the fact that they did not look in their direction, at Mr Crane. Just about every person in The Sharrow had clocked Mr Crane before turning away again. The likes of Mr Crane you did not often see. Also, the tall woman was classically beautiful and moved with uncommon grace. Stanton followed Crane and Pelter up the stairs.

At the back of the restaurant the four mercenaries were lounging in a private booth, with their attention directed toward the fight tank. Mennecken had on a virtual glove and face cup, and Dusache, sitting next to him, was laughing uproariously. But Stanton heard no sound from them until they entered the booth with its privacy field and he took a seat beside Pelter.

'Arian,' said Corlackis, 'I see you now avail yourself of more visible technology.' He studied Pelter's face for a moment, then turned his attention to Mr Crane. Crane had moved to one side of the booth and now stood perfectly still. 'But do we really need that kind of hardware?' he finished.

'We do. Now, to business,' said Pelter.

'Let's just wait on that,' said Stanton, and watched the floating vendor that slid in through the field. The flat, thick tray had small lights glinting on its edge and two grab arms folded crablike underneath itself. It dropped until it was hovering just a couple of centimetres above the glasses on the table, its AG forcing spilt drink to slide about on the surface as if under an air blast. Its arms unfolded and took up two empty glasses, which it placed on top of itself. The obverse of its antigravity field stuck the glasses in place. From it issued a bored voice.

'Orders?' it asked.

'I'll have cool-ice,' said Stanton, and looked at Pelter.

'The same,' said Pelter, his attention fixed firmly back.

'Repeat order for you gentlemen?' the vendor asked.

'You bet,' said Dusache.

The vendor rose into the air, then floated across to Mr Crane, where it tilted, its lights moving frantically. Abruptly it shot away.

'Clever machine,' murmured Stanton, and then said, 'Right, we are all here having a wonderful time and not one of us is going to notice the four who are just about to come up the stairs.'

'What do you have?' asked Corlackis.

'I'd reckon on a covert group, probably ECS as one of them looks like a Golem.'

'How the hell do you tell?' asked Svent.

'Always too good,' Stanton replied. 'They can put scars on the outside, but they show from the inside as well. It's how you move . . . Here they come.'

'Bastard!' Mennecken yelled and pulled off his face cup and glove and slammed them on the table.

'I make that eight minutes,' said Corlackis, glancing

at the timepiece set in his fingernail. 'I also make that fifty shillings you owe each of us.'

Mennecken was now looking at Stanton and Pelter. He then turned and looked at Mr Crane. Corlackis spoke before his brother had a chance to.

'Notice anything about the clientele of this restaurant?' he asked.

Mennecken's glance flicked round, then came back to his brother. 'Well, here we've got the leader of the Separatist cell on Cheyne III, five very obvious mercenaries, and a psychodroid,' he said.

'I meant the other clientele, as you well know.'

'OK, you mean, apart from the four ECS shits sitting over the far side there.'

Corlackis turned to Pelter. 'You want them taken out?'

Pelter did not answer. He, Dusache and Svent seemed to be having a staring competition. Stanton clamped down on his unease at this. He had one issue to focus on at the moment. He'd leave the one concerning biotech augs to another time.

'Yes, it would be better if we were not observed,' Pelter finally said, switching back to Corlackis. 'Though it may be useful to keep one of the humans alive for a chat.'

Corlackis nodded and turned to Stanton. 'A Golem, you say? Which one?' he asked.

'The one with the long black hair. Probably a Twenty to Twenty-five. Might be others there of a higher series, but they can be difficult to spot sometimes,' Stanton replied.

To Pelter, Corlackis said, 'Then perhaps we do need

the hardware.' He looked up at Mr Crane. 'The questions now remain: where, when, and how? Any suggestions?'

'Whack 'em here and we got ten thousand in bribes to pay,' said Svent.

Pelter said, 'We will all return to your metrotel. Stanton and myself will book rooms. There are four of them and they cannot follow us all.' He turned to Svent and Dusache. 'You two will slip away at some point to reconnoitre. I want to know where they go, what they do. I want to know if they set up some kind of watching station. I also want to know if there are any more of them.' He now addressed them all. 'We will hit them during the brief night here. We will do it quietly and we will dispose of the remains.'

Stanton nodded in agreement with this, but could not help wondering if what Pelter had just said to Svent and Dusache had needed to be spoken out loud.

'I'd like the little catadapt,' said Mennecken, staring across the restaurant.

'As long as you are quiet,' Pelter replied.

'I will be. Can't speak for her,' said Mennecken.

'Now,' said Pelter, 'if we might return to why I asked you here?'

'Don't mind me,' said Mennecken.

Pelter did not. He made sure he had the attention of them all before going on. '*I* will pay you each one hundred thousand New Carth shillings to help me get to a certain man and kill him.'

Corlackis let out a low whistle. 'Some man, then,' he said.

Stanton said, 'He's an ECS agent called Ian Cormac.'

'I eat them for breakfast,' said Mennecken.

Corlackis did not seem so sure. Stanton guessed that he recognized the name.

Pelter glanced over at the parked AGC Dusache had pointed out and tried not to sneer. This group was very unprofessional, nothing like Cormac. His sneer faded as he tried to work out the origins of that thought. Did it come from the dichotomy of running two augs that now seemed almost inimical to each other? Or was it from himself? He shook rain from his hair and glared through the false twilight.

The sky was growing darker and the rain steadily heavier. Tough growths, with the appearance of black briars, were pushing up between the slabs of the AGC park, and were not the only unwelcome visitors the extra moisture had brought.

'What the fuck is that?' said Svent, his hand sliding to the gap in his rainfilm.

Pelter looked at him. He did not even have to vocalize the order. Svent pulled his hand from his film and dropped it to his side. He, Dusache and Pelter watched the creature drawing itself across the slabs. It was a diamond of mounded grey flesh with bulbous eyes and a turned-up snout. A short flat tail flickered at its other end. In all it was two metres long and looked like it could swamp a man. It was not moving with any great speed, though.

'You should know. You ate part of one last night,' said Dusache.

Svent looked pained for a moment. 'Ground skate?' he asked.

'With mustard sauce, wasn't it?' Dusache queried.

Pelter ignored them. He stared at the falling rain and seemed to see in it a hint of a shape, something huge, an image the raindrops were trying to form, but just could not. He looked through Crane's eyes and the image grew stronger. He had a hint now of diamonds. Perhaps some sort of echo in his two augs from looking at the skate. To collapse the echo he ran the program to close off the organic aug. It seemed to fight him for a moment, pulling out with the reluctance of a bent nail in old wood. As it went, the pattern faded. Now everything was grey, through Crane's eyes, and his optic link felt hard against the side of his head. He closed off that view and turned to the bickering mercenaries.

'Let's not stand here all day. We have plans to make,' he said.

He could see their resentment and did not understand it. With a flash of irritation he re-engaged the second aug. Slick. Straight in. They were resentful because it was them standing staring at the rain, and not in the nice warm bar of the metrotel. He turned away, flicked a gesture at Crane, and headed for the metrotel with the android tramping along behind. The two mercenaries gave each other a speculative look before following.

Stanton, Mennecken and Corlackis waited for them in the bar. All three of them were playing a dice game. Pelter envied them their ability to ride so easily through the waiting time between actions. It was a trait he himself had never been able to develop. When Stanton looked up, Pelter returned the look and considered what he must do. Nothing yet, he decided. Stanton was still too useful. He moved into the room and sat on the edge of one of the low chairs. Svent and Dusache moved in as well. As if he was pressing down the timer on a chess clock, Corlackis pressed the touch-plate on top of a small flat box on the table.

'Enough?' asked Pelter, glancing at Svent and Dusache.

'Enough,' Svent replied. 'They've been bouncing a laser off the windows every now and again, but that's about it. No deep scan or underspace signatures. They're not that sophisticated.'

'So they weren't here for us,' Stanton said.

'Doubt it. They're not equipped,' Svent said.

'Give me the rest of it,' said Pelter, each word precise and tipped with irritation. His optic link hurt and there was a crust on the seepage around it. It had also rubbed a sore on his temple that tended to bleed when he was straining over some of Crane's more complex module programs. And there was that something else poised tantalizingly just out of reach. A forbidden knowledge, something . . .

'The dark one's definitely Golem,' said Svent. 'All the others are human unless they're carrying sophisticated emulation programs. Going by the rest of their equipment, that's something I doubt. I reckon they were here tracing arms deals until one of them eyeballed one of us. You can be sure they'll be sending an underspace message any time now.'

'That will not help them much,' said Corlackis. 'No runcible to get reinforcements here in the nick of time. The nearest one is a good month, ship time.'

'I don't mind it being known that we are here. I do

mind it being known that we have acquired a dropbird here,' said Pelter.

'Yeah,' said Corlackis with a shrug. 'We still kill them.'

Pelter looked at Svent, pushed him subliminally through his aug. The little mercenary continued.

'Five of them as far as I can make out. The four humans take shifts in the car, two of them at a time, probably to get out of the rain. The other two and the Golem are in that café with the meshed-over window. They follow whichever of us leaves here. Splitting up if we split up.' Svent reached into his pocket and dropped a little sample bottle on the table. Inside the bottle were a couple of glittering specks. 'Fucking Golem put them on me and Dusache with a little air gun. She think we're that stupid?'

'What are they? Phones or tracers?' Stanton asked.

'Tracers.'

'Deactivated?' Pelter asked, an edge to his voice.

''Course they are,' said Svent.

'Right,' said Pelter. 'The humans are no problem, but I'd rather they were out of the way before we deal with the Golem. This is how we play it . . .'

Pelter leant against the door to his room as the nausea hit. Something was happening with his augs, the optic link and the command module. He could feel packets of information being exchanged, linkages being made and broken, busy handshaking. He fumbled his card into the reader beside the door and cursed the fact that his false identity precluded the use of palm-locks. Eventually he got it read and stumbled into his room. Behind him Mr Crane quietly closed the door. With shaking hands

Pelter pulled one, then two patches from a reel. He lifted his grubby mesh shirt, peeled the patches and slapped them against his chest. Only now did he notice the glue marks from previous patches, and the filth. He tried to find it in himself to care. He couldn't.

The endorphin analogue from the patches leaked into his body, banished nausea and dulled the stabbing pain in the left side of his head. There was relief, but it was minimal until the Sylac aug suddenly shut down. His head immediately began to clear and the virtual vision through the second aug gained an almost painful clarity. Now he could see beyond information frames and graphics that seemed to float in some disconnected space. There was a background now to all this. It was a huge wall of flesh. Scaled flesh.

'Dragon,' he said.

There was no answer, just the clarity. With slow and careful steps he walked to the bed and sat down. He must not have this. It was too easy. He tried to reinstate the Sylac aug, and immediately got a surge of sickness again. He bit down on it and forced reinstatement. Pain returned. He realized the second aug was trying to shut down the first. He shut the second aug down and the sickness receded, pain ebbed away. The scaled wall was gone and everything seen through Sylac's aug was in shades of grey. So: gradual takeover, but he was still in control. With fanatical will he went through the process of shutting down and reinstating each aug in every combination. He was exercising control, but did wonder if he was beginning to enjoy the pain and sickness. Was this because it gave him something to fight?

13

Bubble Metal: *These materials were first developed by the Cryon Corporation in 2110. The process of manufacture is simple. A base metal (or alloy) is poured into null-G moulds (hence their development in the first satellite factories) and, while still in a molten state, injected with gas (usually inert). The resultant 'foamed metal' is then allowed to cool. Components made by this process are usually high in compressive and tensile strengths, but are prone to corrosion. Further developments brought us anti-corrosive gases and ceramoplastic injectants. This technology has become widely applied, the only solid-cast components now being those used in electronics applications, where the crystal structure or purity of the metal is a requirement.*

From a Cryon Corporation catalogue

Cormac gradually woke to the gentle but insistent voice of *Hubris* calling to him, and immediately *felt* the silence. He groped for the link like a terminal nicotine addict searching for his first cigarette of the day and finding the packet was empty. Where was the voice in his head and the small synaptic charge that could bring him instantly awake and alert? He experienced a pang of loss and repressed it. He was hearing this voice with his ears.

'Ian Cormac . . . Ian Cormac . . .'

'Yes, what is it?'

'Chaline told me to inform you that her probe is transmitting from the blast-site. There are some anomalies.'

Chaline . . .

He rolled over and reached across the bed, vaguely remembered a disentanglement of sweaty limbs, a kiss on the cheek, a chuckle in the darkness.

'Tell her I'm on my way.'

He checked the wall clock: ten hours, and not many of them sleep. Feeling only slightly guilty he got out of bed and headed directly for his shower. Ten minutes later he was dressed in trousers and shirt, shuriken snug to his wrist, and heading for Downlink Com, which was the nearest *Hubris* had to a bridge or operations room.

The room was long, with a large circular chamber at its end from where the probes were dispatched. Its longest walls were packed with screens and other instrumentation. Before five consoles sat people clothed in the distinctive blue coveralls of runcible technicians. Some of them were auged in: optic cables plugged directly from their augs. These technicians remained still; all their activity was between their ears and in the various subminds of *Hubris*. Chaline was squatting on the floor, below one of the consoles, with a panel open before her and instruments and chips scattered all around. Cormac squatted beside her. She looked up, smiled at him, and he found himself unable to respond.

228

'Anomalies, you said.'

Her smile faded to puzzlement, then she shrugged and gestured with a debonding torch at a flashing light on the console above her.

'That's a contamination warning,' she said.

'The probe is at the blast-site,' he replied.

'We programmed it to ignore isotopes. We knew it was going to be hot down there, so the warning isn't about that.'

With a thoughtful expression on her face she laid the torch beside her and began plugging chips back into the panel. He could see she was pissed off by his lack of acknowledgement, but this was business; he couldn't let last night get in the way, could he? Emotion must not be allowed to interfere.

'I thought we might have a problem that diagnostics couldn't trace. *Hubris* ran a check as well. Everything seems all right here. The problem is with the probe.' She looked up at the ceiling. '*Hubris*, have you finished running that check on the probe?'

'I am still checking. The probe seems to be developing structural weaknesses,' said the ship AI.

'You used the present tense,' said Cormac.

'The process is continuing. Initially the weaknesses were in its sampling arms, now more weaknesses have appeared.'

Cormac turned to Chaline. 'I know this is not my territory, but it might be an idea to get the probe into orbit or at least out of the blast-site, if that's still possible.'

'We'll want it back for study, you mean,' she said.

He nodded and she continued to look at him. After a

moment she gave him a slow nod in reply, and a look that meant 'later', then she addressed the AI. '*Hubris*, how far gone is the probe's integrity?'

'It is still capable of taking high G. The weaknesses seem to be developing only in the ceramal components. The probe has a foamed alloy skeleton.'

'What could cause that? The cold?' Cormac asked.

Chaline shook her head in perplexity. 'Ceramal? No ... *Hubris*, what is the temperature outside the probe?'

'One-eighty Kelvin.'

'I don't know why I asked. Ceramal retains its structural integrity down to ninety Kelvin.'

'Acid? Some kind of caustic gas?' asked Cormac.

'No, has to be something more specific than that, else the sampling process would have picked it up ... Wait a minute ... *Hubris*, how old were the Samarkand runcible buffers?'

'The Samarkand runcible was installed solstan 2383.'

'Yes,' said Chaline with satisfaction. Cormac raised an eyebrow and she went on. 'Wide-spectrum superconductors were introduced in 2397. The Samarkand runcible had the old sort; super-conducting ceramic-impregnated tungsten steel and bathed in liquid helium. The room-temperature superconductors they had then couldn't take the kind of surge a runcible buffer receives. We are talking about a huge EM pulse here.'

'And?' asked Cormac, wondering why she felt it necessary to over-explain her area of expertise.

'Don't you see? Tungsten steel impregnated with ceramic? That is what ceramal is.' Cormac nodded. 'So whatever screwed up those buffers is now screwing up your probe.'

Chaline said, '*Hubris*, would it be possible to run an interior microscan of the probe?'

'Scanning.'

'What do you expect to find?'

'Sabotage : . . . too specific to be anything else.'

'How?'

'Well, the buffers would have been too cold for some kind of manufactured virus, and are screened to everything bar neutron radiation, so it has to be nano-machines.'

'If it is nanomachines . . . can you do anything about them? Will you be able to set up your runcible down there?'

Chaline chewed on her knuckle. 'They would have survived a fusion explosion . . . Getting rid of them is like getting rid of a disease: there's always one bacillus survives to start the process off again. But . . . but they are not prone to mutation like a bacillus or virus. Once we get a sample, we should be able to make a counter-agent.' She glanced up at his puzzled expression. 'Counter nano-machines, ones with the singular purpose of hunting down and destroying the nanomachines there. It would take ages though, and years for Samarkand to be clear.'

'And the new runcible?'

'Oh, we can protect it. There isn't a great deal of ceramal used in its construction. The buffers are carbon-seventy-based superconductors. The nanomachines won't touch them. We will need to set up a proscription scan like that used for weaponry.'

Cormac waited for her to continue.

'To stop it getting taken off planet,' she explained, as if tired of dealing with an idiot. 'Samarkand would also have to be limited to runcible transport until it's clear. Therefore, no ships.'

'As a way station it wouldn't get many anyway,' Cormac said.

'True,' said Chaline, and returned to pushing chips back into place.

'Nanomycelium detected,' said *Hubris*, before the silence between them became too stretched.

'Mycelium?' asked Cormac.

Chaline looked round and frowned. 'Fibres like a fungus; we need to get some here for analysis. We'll have to use class-one isolation—'

Hubris interrupted. 'It will not be necessary to bring it here. Nanomycelium also detected in shuttle bay.'

Suddenly warning lights began flashing on the walls and the voice of the AI was heard throughout the ship.

'Warning, possible hull-breach in shuttle-bay area. Section fifteen to be sealed in ten minutes.'

Downlink Com was not in section fifteen. Cormac, Chaline and the five technicians watched the screens showing that section. There was no panic. If the situation had been dangerous, *Hubris* would have sealed the section and the people would have been evacuated in emergency suits. As it was, they walked to the section's exit looking mildly annoyed. At that exit four technicians waited with hand scanners that bore a disturbing resemblance to truncheons. They ran these over each of the evacuees, paying particular attention to the soles of their footwear. While they watched, one irritated man, an ophidapt with a spined crest on his bald head, had to remove his shoes and toss them in a canister by the exit.

'Will the detector pick them all up?' Cormac asked.

No one felt inclined to answer him.

'Let us hope you can make a counteragent, then,' he finished.

They watched as the section was finally cleared, and the doors closed and hermetically sealed.

'*Hubris*, we need samples,' said Chaline.

The picture being showed to them changed to a view into the shuttle bay. The camera zeroed in on a section of polished floor. On the floor were dull footprints from which spread black fibres like dry rot. The camera pulled back to show a little remote drone hovering a few centimetres from the floor. It was a chrome cylinder not much bigger than a man's forearm. All along its underside it had pairs of manipulators. In one crab claw it held a sample bottle. As it approached the footprints another arm unfolded. By one of the footprints that arm folded down and smoke spurted up. The yellow laser beam only became visible in that smoke as the drone meticulously cut two strips of flooring, levered them up with what could only be a screwdriver, and dropped them in the bottle.

'I'll have to get down to Isolation,' Chaline said to Cormac. 'I have a lot of work to do. The entire hull of this ship is ceramal.' She waited a moment for him to say something. Cormac let her go without comment.

Back in his cabin, Cormac called up a view into Isolation and watched the dracomen eat yet another meal. Could it have been them? he wondered. Somehow that did not seem Dragon's style. It was possible, but why would Dragon do such a thing? Why would Dragon want the people of Samarkand killed? Or perhaps he was asking the wrong question. Why would Dragon want the Samarkand runcible destroyed? He shook his head. There was not yet enough evidence to put any theories together.

'*Hubris*, any luck with that submind?'

The AI's reply was quick and succinct. 'I do not have the capacity to spare for it at the moment.'

'The mycelium?'

'Two-thirds of my capacity is being used for decoding it and designing a counteragent.'

'OK, can you put me through to the submind?'

'Yes.'

'—throw away archetypes but keep ideas bathwater baby hell hath no hungry mole lord of pain lord of pain where is edge? Sinter snapping hove to green rotting fruit—'

Running his finger down a touch-strip Cormac turned the sound down. He said to the submind, 'The runcible buffers were destroyed by a nanomycelium.'

He turned the sound back up.

'—hungry hungry eater green green grass is green fell into the rainy day bleed break men lizard Janus—'

Men lizard?

'Who destroyed the runcible buffers?'

'—gain gone flee on invisible wings rotting fruit black-thorn thorns peach—'

Cormac clicked the voice off. For a moment he

thought he had something there, but would the runcible AI have known who planted the mycelium? It seemed unlikely. Had it known, it would have transmitted more information before its destruction. Had it known, it would have instantly shut down the runcible. Freeman might have ended up lost in underspace, but that would have been better than him causing the deaths of 10,000 people.

'*Hubris*, show me that mycelium in the shuttle bay.'

The picture on the screen changed. There was no word from the AI. Perhaps it was getting impatient with him. He stared at the picture. Even with part of the deck cut away the shape of the dull footprints was evident. They were long and splayed, with a mark for a back toe; obviously not human and obviously the footprints of dracomen, but was that damning evidence? Anyone who had been to the surface could have carried some of the mycelium away with them. The dracomen had been there longer, so it was more likely to be them.

'*Hubris*, the dracomen brought the mycelium aboard.'

'Already aware.'

Cormac rattled his fingers on his desk.

What now?

He could try the dracomen again, but his last attempt at communication had tried his patience to the limit. He was sure they were quite capable of speaking with him in some manner, but one of them just sat there and grinned while the other just sat staring at the food dispenser. Perhaps what he needed was face to face, rather than gestures through the viewing window and speech through the intercom.

'Damn it!'

He stood up and headed for Isolation.

As he came from the drop-shaft Cormac saw that Mika was standing before the viewing window to the isolation chamber. She stood in an attitude of deep contemplation, an elbow cupped in one hand and her other hand under her chin. Standing like that she appeared less of a girl. Or was he seeing her differently now? He wondered how old she was. She could be anywhere from eighteen to 300 years. Appearance had not been a way to judge age for the last four centuries. He walked up beside her. She did not acknowledge his presence until he was two paces from her.

'Ah, Ian Cormac.'

'Just Cormac. Something bothering you?'

'No, not really – not bothering me. I'm just intrigued. I did some checking.' She pointed to the floor of the isolation chamber by the far wall. 'You see those?'

Cormac looked across and saw what appeared to be a couple of screwed-up polythene bodysuits. He looked from them to the two dracomen, who were squatting motionless in the middle of the chamber, and noticed that they appeared cleaner, brighter.

'Skins,' he said. 'They shed their skins.'

'They've done it three times since they were put in here. They're regenerating: sloughing off and excreting radiation-damaged cells, and rapidly replacing them.'

'Yes, *Hubris* told me.'

She glanced at him. 'Did it also tell you that they are also immune to cancer, to replication error?'

'A handy trait, but it is also one we have.'

'Yes, but ours is done by viral or nanomachine repair

236

of our DNA based on the corrected birth blueprint. We still develop cancers and they still have to be cured. This is completely different.'

'I don't know whether or not it is relevant, but, as well as it being proposed that dracoman was one of the race Dragon claimed to represent, it was also proposed that he was some kind of organic machine.'

'We are all organic machines. No, you miss my point . . . I analysed some of that skin. They are without DNA. They replace cells by direct protein replication. It's been done before, but no creature has ever evolved that method. Far too complex.'

'So they *are* some kind of machine?'

'If you want to call them that. Philosophy is not my field.'

Cormac felt a twinge of embarrassment. 'I guess that was a stupid thing to say.'

'It was.' She smiled briefly to take the sting away, and went on. 'But these creatures definitely were *made* in some way. You call them dracomen and in doing that you infer gender, but they are completely sexless: no self-contained method of reproduction. I would say, considering their antecedents, that they were made to serve a purpose, and that purpose is not their own survival and continuation of their genes, as with us; it is Dragon's purpose. They are an alien form of the Golem Series – or any other android for that matter.'

'And what might their purpose be?'

'I have no idea. All I know is that this Dragon built well.'

'There's more?'

'Endless. I could make a lifetime of study out of them.

Their bones are solid; calcium laminated with something similar to tooth enamel, and about twice the size
and density of ours. They've got a digestive system
which could extract nutrition from a stone.' She turned
to him again. 'But, as we know, they take the easy
option.' She turned back. 'And their musculature is as
dense as old oak. We are lucky they felt no inclination to
leave this isolation chamber when we first put them
inside. The door would not have stopped them.'

'Perhaps they're different from the one I saw before.'

Cormac remembered his fight in the shadow of
Dragon. He had defeated that dracoman quite easily,
but perhaps that was what Dragon had wanted. 'Theatrics' are how he had described Dragon's actions to
Chaline. It occurred to him that the whole performance
had been a cover for other actions; to leave humankind
believing Dragon had destroyed itself. Had it been
scared, or just a lover of subterfuge?

'Quite likely.'

'What . . . sorry?'

'These are probably different from the one you saw
on Aster Colora. Dragon probably makes them to suit
its current requirements,' said Mika.

Cormac cogitated for a moment. 'How did they survive the cold?' he asked.

'Now, that is where things get really interesting. They
use protein replication, but I have yet to find any kind of
template. Their physiognomy will take years to unravel.
But . . . their brain structure is completely different
from ours. My theory is that the template is a mental
one and that they can alter it at will, within limits. When
Thorn said they must have antifreeze for blood, he was

probably not far wrong. It would also be interesting to have another look at where they were sheltering.'

'Why? Some evidence there?'

'Just to see how much they ate over the last fifteen months. I bet they ate a phenomenal amount to maintain their body temperatures, and that those corpses we saw were perhaps just a couple of days' supply.'

'Is there anything about them that might indicate their purpose?'

'Nothing really, except maybe their strength. Perhaps they were made to tolerate heavy G . . . But such strength could pertain to anything.'

'You said the door would not stop them. Just how strong are they?'

'Have you been to the Sparkind quarters?'

Cormac shook his head.

'Well, you remember Gant telling you they had Golem Thirties? Do you know what they are?'

'Cybercorp combat androids. The best.'

Mika pointed at the dracomen. 'These two would be a match even for them.'

'Bloody hell! We should move them to a security section.'

Mika smiled. 'I doubt the security section would hold them either. Anyway, the cell has been armoured since they were first moved in, and there's shutters to come down over this window. Half a second and they end up in a box of ten-centimetre-thick case-hardened ceramal.'

'Will that be enough to—' began Cormac, but was interrupted by *Hubris*'s voice.

'Notification: there will be a slight adulteration of the

air supply. This is not a cause for alarm. Counteragents are being spread through all systems. I repeat, there is no cause for alarm.'

Cormac felt something loosen its hold on the inside of his chest; until then he had not quite realized how worried he had been about the nanomycelium. He looked back to the dracomen and saw that Smiler was standing. For a moment he thought food was being delivered. Then he saw that the dracoman was sniffing at the air. He watched, and while he watched he became aware of a bitter metallic taste in his mouth and a pungency to the air that reminded him of the smell from a cold-forge.

The counteragents.

'Chaline works quickly,' he said to Mika, and wondered at the precise meaning of his words.

'Yes,' said Mika, something in her voice. Cormac studied her suspiciously, but she was watching the dracoman.

Cormac felt uncomfortable for more than one reason. It was disconcerting to think that the air was filling with little mycelium-killing machines, and that they were on his tongue and in his nostrils. The dracoman seemed to find the whole thing amusing. It grinned, then walked to the viewing window and stared directly at Cormac, which was disconcerting as well, as the window was set for one-way viewing. He had nearly convinced himself the dracoman could not see him, when it pointed up at the intercom speaker.

'They do have vocal cords. They should be able to speak,' said Mika.

Cormac reached across and switched on the intercom. 'Have you something to say, my friend?' he asked, trying to appear unruffled. This could be what he needed. At last he might begin to unravel this mystery.

'Dragon coming,' said the dracoman, and turned away.

'Wait!'

The dracoman returned to the middle of the floor and sat down, and from there it just grinned at him.

'I don't think you're going to get any more than it wants to tell you. Remember, its motivations are not the same as ours.'

Cormac contained his anger. 'Yes,' he said.

But Dragon was coming, and had never been shy of communication, even in its Delphic and sometimes explosive fashion.

14

Many lifeforms have hitched a ride with us and been part of our successful spread into the galaxy. From the beginning it was decided that quarantine strictures were an exercise rendered pointless by the huge advances being made in bioscience. If you have a creature's DNA or whatever other template it might use, what matter if it is wiped out? You can re-create it if you want. Also, it is a fact that this is the way life works: species have been wiped out for millennia by more successful contenders. Some have bemoaned the loss of variety, but this is a specious argument at best. Genetic adaptation and straight biotechnological creation have brought newer and more interesting forms. Sorry, people, but we are improving on nature all the time. My only complaint in this matter is that some of the older and more unpleasant forms are as successful as those we adapt and create. Why is it that on worlds that are wet I so often end up tripping over ground skate? Why hasn't someone come up with a competitor less lethal to us than the blade beetle? And who the hell decided it was OK to let mosquitoes colonize just about every damned world?

From *How It Is* by Gordon

242

The rain was flecked with black dirt blown up from the burn zones on the edge of the equatorial deserts and though it slid from the repelling charge on the screen of the old Ford Macrojet, a line of sludge was gathering at the join between screen and bonnet. Daven stared at the sludge for a moment, then across the expanse of streaming slabs of the AGC park to the entrance of the metrotel. It was all bright and warm beyond the glass panes and there was a party going on in the lower bar. Two hours earlier a load of aircabs had come in to land to belch the revellers. It seemed as if someone had taken out a marriage contract during the long day and was now celebrating that idiocy.

'They have contracts?' Pellen asked yet again.

'They have contracts,' Daven confirmed. 'They still have them in a lot of places, but more often out here beyond the Line. You must have seen it?'

'Never occurred to me,' Pellen said, shaking her head. Daven inspected her. She was an attractive woman and he wondered why she had felt the need to go catadapt. She was also, he felt, a bit naive for this sort of operation. People who had spent most of their formative years on an Outlink station tended to be that way. No doubt ECS had sent her out here as part of her training. Easy way in, trying to track down a few arms runners, especially with Jill, the Golem, to dig her out of any pit traps. The stakes had gone up though as soon as Jill had seen Arian Pelter coming out of Grendel's place. Now things might just get a little sticky.

'Two of them. Three o'clock,' said Pellen abruptly.

Daven lifted his attention from the sludge below the screen and looked where directed. It was the slick mercenary with a rainfilm over his business suit, and the heavy who had met Pelter outside The Sharrow. They were sauntering towards the metrotel. Velet and Jill should be along behind them any time now. As he reached for the intensifier on the dash, Daven heard a low thump, then rain and warm damp air gusted into the AGC. Rear-door lock blown, shit! He had no time to get to his stomach holster. A hand closed in his hair and cold metal pressed into his throat.

'Now, that nasty little thin-gun you have down there you can carefully pull out and drop on the floor,' said Mennecken.

Daven saw that the other two mercenaries were now quickly coming in their direction. 'What do you want?' he asked, carefully moving his hand towards his gun. He glanced at Pellen, who was staring in horror at the both of them. If she did anything, he was dead. He gave a slight shake of his head and was rewarded with a touch of keen pain at his throat.

'The gun,' Mennecken repeated.

Daven slowly pulled the gun from its holster and let it drop. 'Just tell me what you want,' he said.

'I want you to be quiet,' said Mennecken. He shoved Daven's head forward and drew the razor-sharp ceramal blade back, and then he turned with a smile to Pellen. She stifled a scream as Daven fumbled at his throat trying to stem the blood gushing on the floor and all over his discarded weapon, then she reacted. Claws, which were not normally part of the cat adaptation, extruded from the ends of her fingers. She swiped Mennecken hard, opening deep slices on his face.

Mennecken reeled back and swore, and in that moment Pellen popped the door and was out of it.

'Bitch!'

Mennecken opened the door he had blown, rounded it and leapt onto the bonnet. He glanced aside at Corlackis and Stanton, who were now running towards the car, then he leapt down. His feet came down on something soft and went straight from under him. He went down flat on top of a ground skate and it bubbled at him and tried to drag itself on. He yelled with pure rage and drove his dagger into the creature. Its only reaction was to bubble some more and to keep attempting to move. Four deep stab wounds seemed to have no effect on it. It did not even bleed.

'Get after her!' yelled Corlackis as he came to the car.

Mennecken slid off the skate and stood. His clothing was covered with slime and he stank like something rotting in a tideline. 'Fucking thing!' he yelled and kicked the skate before turning and running into the alley along which Pellen had fled.

'We'll deal with the other one, then go after him,' said Stanton, slapping his hand on the bonnet. 'We've got about three minutes.'

Corlackis opened the passenger door and Daven slumped out of it. He raised an eyebrow. 'Did you have to cut so deep, brother mine?' he asked.

'He could have taken them both with a gun. What the hell's wrong with him?' Stanton asked, a bad taste in his mouth.

Corlackis hit a release inside the car and the boot popped. He got hold of the corpse and dragged it out, then round to the back. Stanton helped him tip the man inside.

'Mennecken can look after himself,' Corlackis replied.

Stanton shook his head as he slammed the boot shut. 'That wasn't what I meant and you know it.'

'Yes, I do.'

Stanton checked his watch, then looked behind. 'We haven't time for this,' he said.

Corlackis nodded to him, then moved back. He took off his rainfilm and fastidiously draped it over the passenger seat. Stanton moved round to the driver's side. As he got in he thought that this was the price you paid for using the most efficient killers; quite often they enjoyed it. He looked at Corlackis, who had yet to get in.

'Come on. He'll be here in a minute.'

Corlackis shrugged and climbed in. Stanton set the vehicle on low hover. The old grav motor had a hum with a slight edge to it that grated on the nerves. He turned off the charge on the screen and watched as dirty rain smeared it, before he set the vehicle drifting forwards.

'There,' he said, pointing, then looking at his watch. 'Right on time to the second.'

The man they'd had trailing them all over Port Lock had just appeared.

'Lucky it wasn't the Golem,' said Corlackis.

'Calculated,' Stanton replied. 'The Golem had to stay with Pelter and Mr Crane. It'll be the senior here, and the only one capable of dealing with Crane if things went wrong. As they will.'

The man halted out on the slabs and raised his hand.

No doubt he was expecting to be allowed into a nice dry car, his watching at an end for a while. Stanton drifted the car so the passenger side would come up to him. Corlackis touched a door control and the window slid down at an angle. He removed from his jacket pocket a fat little gun with a barrel wider than it was long.

'In the back seat,' said Stanton. 'We'll be needing the room left in the boot.'

'As you say, John,' said Corlackis.

They drew abreast of the man and he ducked down to peer in the window, a friendly grin on his face. Stanton felt sure he was about to say something about the weather. But he lost his grin when Corlackis shot him in the face.

'Shit, we wanted him alive,' said Stanton.

'Credit me with some intelligence, John. Short-acting neural poison in pellet form. He won't be pretty, but he'll be alive,' Corlackis replied.

'Right . . . right,' said Stanton. He checked his watch, then took a small comunit from his top pocket as the AGC settled. 'Svent, how is it?' he asked.

'He's heading for the café. We'll take him there.'

'Don't worry if we're a little late. Mennecken's gone walkabout after the catadapt,' said Stanton.

'That's OK,' said Svent. 'I wanted a coffee anyway. See you shortly.'

Stanton made an adjustment and spoke again. 'We got all four and are holding them,' he said.

Pelter's voice in reply was cold and correct. 'That was the easy part. Now we have this ECS machine to deal with,' he said.

'Where are you now?'

'I'm at the dump outside the spaceport.'

'The Golem still with you?'

'As far as we can ascertain. It is very good. Maybe it has chameleonware.'

'Need any help?'

'I have Mr Crane.'

Stanton shut off the unit. That was all Pelter had wanted him to say. He popped his door and walked round to Corlackis, who was searching the man he had stunned. Corlackis removed a thin-gun which he tossed in beside the one in the passenger foot-well. He then removed a small flat comunit which he studied closely.

'Chuck it,' said Stanton. 'Might have a tracer.' He looked around. Still no one in sight, but it was best to get this sort of thing done quickly. He opened the back door, which no longer closed properly anyway since Mennecken had blown the lock, then got hold of the man's shoulders and dragged him back to it. He then caught hold of his collar and belt and tossed him onto the back seat. Corlackis simply watched. He knew that with his boosted musculature Stanton was more than able for this task.

'Now let's find that brother of yours,' Stanton said.

They got back into the AGC and Stanton reversed it back to its original location.

'How long will he be out for?' he asked, stabbing a thumb to the back.

'Half an hour to an hour,' Corlackis replied.

Stanton watched him carefully. 'Right then. You stay here and keep an eye on him. I'll go and see what your brother is doing,' he said.

'I could do that,' said Corlackis, returning his look.

'Yes, but you're not. You'll stay here.'

'As you say.'

Stanton opened the door and got out. As he headed for the alley he noticed that the ground skate was now at the edge of the flooded gully and was there squeezing out a long and slimy white worm. Further down the gully more of these worms were wriggling in the torrent. From what he recollected of these creatures, this meant it was male. The worms were motile sperm packets on their way to find an egg-laden pool to burst in. The wounds Mennecken had made were superfluous. After this effort the creature would die anyway. Leaving it to do this, Stanton went to find more death.

Stepping into the darkness of the alley Stanton intensified his vision. He pulled his comunit and keyed it to pick up the signal from Mennecken's. A small arrow behind the transparent touch-console indicated Mennecken was ahead and to the right. The numbers below showed him to be eighty-five metres away and receding. Stanton set out at a jog, careful of his footing. Here there were more skate, and the ground had been slimed by their passage. This was a nightmare. He had water running down the back of his neck and soaking into his clothing despite the rainfilm. It occurred to him that, though Mennecken was an efficient killer, his enjoyment of the act was probably becoming a liability. Stanton now realized he should have refused when the man volunteered. He himself, or Corlackis, would simply have got into the back of the car and shot the two ECS watchers.

A yell cut the night and Stanton accelerated. A glance at his comunit showed him Mennecken was no longer moving away. Soon he came to a side branch to the alley, lined with walls made of welded-together slabs of plascrete. The swing of the arrow showed him this was where Mennecken had gone. Another yell and Stanton saw the mercenary grappling with the catadapt. Obviously, with them not being so far from the car, Mennecken had been playing a stalking game with her. Stanton supposed she must have been hiding behind the old hydrocar that was rusting here. As he approached, Mennecken back-handed the woman and laid her out on the filth-caked ground.

'Want to play, little pussy?' he asked.

Still moving in, Stanton drew his pulse-gun and let it hang at his side. Mennecken pinned the woman down and started to cut away her clothing. She shrieked as he started to work the point of the knife into the skin between her breasts. Stanton aimed and then hesitated. At the last he hardened himself and pulled the trigger. The woman jerked under Mennecken as most of the contents of her head sprayed out across plascrete. Mennecken leaped up and around, a snarl on his face and his dagger held ready. Stanton readjusted his aim. He reckoned Pelter's team was just about to be short by one member.

'Mennecken!' yelled Corlackis from behind Stanton.

Mennecken froze, staring at Stanton with open hate, then he became calm. He turned and wiped his dagger on the catadapt's clothing, then sheathed it, keeping his back to Stanton and Corlackis all the while. When he did turn, his expression was casual.

'I thought I told you to stay at the car,' said Stanton, glancing aside at Corlackis. Corlackis held up his own comunit. 'I could see he wasn't far. Thought I might help.'

Stanton nodded and holstered his pulse-gun. 'Mennecken, bring her to the car,' he said, then turned away. Corlackis fell in beside him as they returned to the AGC.

'He's becoming a liability,' Stanton said.

'He's not so bad,' Corlackis replied.

Stanton had to wonder just what precisely this mercenary's definition of 'bad' was. On reaching the AGC he waited in the pouring rain. He could have helped Mennecken to carry the corpse back, but felt no inclination in that direction. It was Mennecken's fault she was so far from the car anyway. He was just about to speak into his comunit when he saw a drunken trio swaying down the street towards him.

'Wild party,' said Corlackis.

From a distance it seemed as if the three of them were drunk. Closer inspection revealed that the one in the middle did not have his feet on the ground and any movement was imparted by the two on either side, those two being Svent and Dusache. Stanton reached inside the car and popped the boot.

'I thought you were going to wait,' he said as the two mercenaries drew close.

Svent nodded at their burden. The man had a trail of dark blood from one nostril and his head had more movement at the neck than was natural.

'Sonny here started to get anxious when we walked in. I walked over and gave him a friendly hug. Few people in there, and I got fed up with his lack of conversation.'

Stanton motioned to the boot of the car and looked

around. Apart from a few revellers that had gone into the metrotel, there was no one about. It was a perfect night for murder. Svent's victim went into the boot too, shortly followed by the catadapt Mennecken dragged out of the alley.

'Phew! You stink, Mennecken,' said Svent as they all crammed into the car. He pointed to the unconscious ECS men on the back seat. 'Who's this?'

'Pelter wants a chat,' said Corlackis.

There was general laughter Stanton felt no inclination to join in with. He flung the AGC round and headed out for the wasteland.

Pelter pocketed his comunit and stopped. He stared blankly into the rain-curtained night. How would the Golem react? That it had overheard that conversation he had no doubt. He peered around at the rain dripping from the acacias, then at a nearby wrecked AGC and, further back in a tangle of growth, the corroding cargo section of a small carrier. It would have worked out what had happened and perhaps now be considering how it might rescue its companions. It wasn't to know about their little rehearsed conversation. He reached up and touched the scaled aug on the side of his head and from it, through the command module, he gave Mr Crane his instructions. So clear and precise was this aug, it almost made him see the world in a different light. Crane held out the briefcase for him and he took it. Crane then stepped to one side. Pelter watched through the android's night vision. Shortly, as expected, the Golem broke cover and walked towards him.

'What are your intentions, Pelter?' it asked.

So very much like a very beautiful woman, Pelter thought. It was almost a shame.

'I intend to kill a man,' he replied.

The Golem woman stopped and tilted her head to one side. She seemed puzzled. It annoyed Pelter that even in these circumstances she still went through the charade of human body language and reaction.

'I do not understand,' she reluctantly admitted. 'You have my three companions.'

'Yes, I do.'

'What are your intentions toward them?'

'You should, really, worry about my intentions towards you.'

'I should?' She tilted her head and shot a look of contempt at Mr Crane.

'You should. I lured you out here so my men could deal with your companions without interference. I also lured you out here because I knew that even though Mr Crane here will have no problem scrapping you, it will be a noisy affair.'

Again the look of contempt. 'I am a Golem Twenty. That creature is a metal-skin. He is something manufactured Out-Polity from Cybercorp leftovers and sold for far too much to the likes of yourself.'

Pelter smiled his nasty smile. 'You couldn't be more wrong. Mr Crane was a Golem Twenty-five who used to work for ECS. His moral governors were broken by full sensorium downloads from the mind of a psychopath, and then he was reprogrammed for our purposes. The metal skin you see is case-hardened ceramal, netted with superconductor, over his usual ceramal skeleton. He runs from four different micropiles and all his joint motors are somewhat more than Cybercorp standard.'

'I am to believe this?' the Golem woman asked.

'Let me convince you.'

Pelter turned to Mr Crane to give his orders, not because it was necessary for him to give vocal orders, but because he wanted the Golem woman to hear.

'Mr Crane, tear this arrogant machine into pieces and scatter those pieces here amongst the rest of this scrap.'

Crane kicked up a huge clod of earth as he went from stillness to terrifying speed. The Golem had time only to turn before he hit her. The sound was like a slab of iron being dropped onto a car. Her feet were driven deep into the ground. She struck at Crane with blows too fast to see: each blow a gun shot, each blow without noticeable effect. He bowed, looped his right arm under her right, his left arm round her hips, and he bent and twisted her. Clothing ripped and artificial skin split. The flashes of shorts and system diodes blowing could be seen through her parting flesh. She started to make a high keening sound, for even androids do not like to die. The sound ceased when Crane finally tore her in half and methodically began to pound those halves to fragments.

'How far are you?' Pelter asked into his comunit.

'Be with you shortly,' Stanton replied. 'Everything OK there?'

'Yes, of course,' said Pelter, shutting off his com. He stared at Mr Crane now and, with the huge clarity he now had through his new aug, he could almost feel the android's longing.

'No, Mr Crane,' he said, 'you cannot keep her head.'

Mr Crane reluctantly tossed his trophy into the bushes, then turned, at Pelter's instruction, towards the approaching AGC. Pelter turned his comunit back on.

'That you, John?'

'It is. Where's the android?'

'About, I think would be the best description,' Pelter replied.

The AGC halted and the five men got out. Stanton looked at some of the bits scattered around where Mr Crane stood, then turned to Pelter.

'What now?'

'You have them all, as instructed?' Pelter asked.

'More or less,' Stanton replied.

'And by that you mean?' Pelter asked.

'We got them all, and we've got your live one.'

Pelter stared at him for a long moment, then abruptly turned to Svent and Dusache. He pointed. 'In that old carrier over there. Strip him and tie him.'

The two dragged the still-stunned man out of the car and dragged him off towards the carrier.

'Mennecken,' Pelter said. 'Bury the bodies and lose the car. I want nothing found while we're here. John, Corlackis – with me.'

Mennecken got into the driver's seat and took the car away, while the three others moved over to the carrier. After a moment Crane jerked as if he had just woken, and he followed them. They entered the carrier through a rusting split in the thin wall. It was essentially a small room with alloy walls and a dirt floor thick with the black growths seen in the town. The two had stripped

255

the man by the time they arrived, and were tying his wrists and ankles. His wrists they secured to stanchion along one wall. Dusache cracked a low-luminosity chemical light and jammed it into a rusting crevice.

'Now we see what he knows,' said Pelter.

Stanton studied the object Pelter pulled from his pocket. It was something the Separatist had acquired from that weird shit Grendel. Knowing what was about to ensue, Stanton wondered if it was entirely necessary.

'I knew you . . . from Cheyne III,' the man said as he fought to regain his breath.

'And?' said Pelter.

Stanton thought the Separatist was taking a bit of a risk sucking on the end of the inducer like it was a pen. You could never tell whether or not the things were on or off until you touched someone with them. Then that someone would certainly know. Mennecken would have wanted to carve the ECS agent up with a knife, but the simple fact was that an inducer hurt more, and the person you were torturing would stay alive longer because there would be no blood loss.

'That's it: I saw you and I told Jill. She was setting us up to watch you so she could call for instructions and back-up.'

'You think I believe that?'

'It's true, why not? Oh, come on! I'm telling you the truth!'

The man's next scream lasted a long time as Pelter drew the blunt nose of the inducer up his inner thigh and touched it to his genitals. When the inducer was withdrawn he was hunched forwards and sobbing. Stanton pulled his pulse-gun from his coat and pointed it at the man's head. Pelter pushed the gun aside.

'I haven't finished yet,' he said.

Stanton turned and looked out through the gap in the rusting cargo shell at the light of the just-risen sun. Three hours they had been in here. He studied Svent and Dusache. Dusache supposedly didn't like this sort of thing, yet he seemed as avid as Svent and Pelter. Corlackis had, some time ago, suggested someone should keep watch and had gone to do so himself. Stanton looked back at Pelter.

'You've had all you can out of him. He's got nothing else to say.'

'I won't know that, John, until I've tortured him to death,' Pelter replied.

Stanton saw that the man had heard, and saw the look of terror in his face.

'He'll only start making it up if you carry on,' he said.

Pelter just stared at Stanton for a long moment. 'All right,' he eventually said, 'I'll kill him.' As he said this he held up the nerve-inducer and clicked the switch. He gave a dead smile, then stooped down and pressed the inducer against the man's stomach. He was still screaming by the time Stanton had walked out to join Corlackis.

'He's not giving him time to answer questions,' Corlackis said.

'He doesn't want answers. He's just killing him with the nerve-inducer.'

'That's just a bit sick,' said Corlackis.

Stanton moved away. He thought of Corlackis describing his homicidal brother as 'not so bad', and he thought of what Pelter was doing, and he wondered if just maybe he was getting a little sick himself.

15

Nanomachines: Very small machines constructed molecule by molecule for a specific purpose. Usually these are self-replicating and not liable to any form of mutation. Usually they can only work in specific environments. They are not the solve-all people once thought they were to be, because vast amounts of processing power is required for the design of even the simplest. At least, this is what we are told. One does wonder if this is a science being kept under very firm control, because of its endless possibilities. Such wonders as nanomycelia and nanofactories have long been discussed. It is doubtful that they as yet exist.

From *Quince Guide*, compiled by humans

The shuttle bucked as it hit turbulence and a hail of black crystals hissed across the screen. Cormac was not too worried, but it was disconcerting to be sitting in a hemisphere of chainglass at the front of a nacelle. The flying wing was without a central body and this positioning seemed to imply indirect control of the craft, rather as if it was being shepherded. Moreover, there was an awful lot of empty space below Cormac's feet.

'One hundred and fifty kilometre winds, up here,' Jane observed.

'Should be no problem with dispersal then,' said Cormac and peered out at the gleaming noses of the pods distributed along the wing. Each was merely an aerodynamic cover and heating unit for the spray heads inside.

'There could be. We have to seed the counteragent where it will be distributed following the weather patterns since the blast, and we cannot be certain what they have been like since then.'

'*Hubris* estimated a dispersal across about ninety per cent of Samarkand.'

'Yes, a lot of material would have been thrown into the upper atmosphere, and the weather then, during the initial cooling of the planet, would have been a lot worse than it is now. There would have been winds of up to four hundred kilometres an hour. Some of the mycelium has probably been carried right round the planet.'

'I see . . . but the counteragent will get to it?'

Jane nodded. 'In time. And this area will be saturated.'

'Will that be enough?'

'With safety measures implemented, and ceramal left out of the equation. It's mostly been replaced with chainglass now anyway.'

Cormac looked down between his feet again and thought about what was down there. He felt a momentary surge of anger, and repressed it. No matter what had been said about his humanity, emotion did get in the way of efficiency.

'Coming up on first release point,' said Jane.

She punched out a sequence on the console. On a screen showing a rear view of the shuttle, Cormac saw a contrail snake out from one of the pods as the warm counteragent hit the frigid air. Another screen showed it further back, being chopped into sections and dispersed by the vicious winds. Jane released the joystick and sat back.

'The automatics will take us in a circle fifty kilometres wide.'

Cormac glanced at the air-speed indicator; 950 kilometres per hour. Ten minutes, then. 'You'll save the scatter bomb for last, I take it?'

'Yes, four pods up here, then we go in low and drop it. An arbitrary decision, really. It makes no difference in what order we do it,' said Jane.

Cormac got out of his seat and headed off into the wing of the shuttle, searching for something to eat or drink. He could have stayed on *Hubris*, as his presence here was not required, but he was fed up with waiting for something to happen or something to be found by the ship's scanners. Chaline and her technicians were well enough employed preparing their runcible to be taken down, and he had not had much opportunity to talk to her – or any wish either, to be honest. She was just the kind of involvement he did not need right now, or was he kidding himself? Mika was becoming increasingly involved in her study of the dracomen, and had already induced the four Sparkind and a few of the crew to assist her. The rest of the crew were involved in replacing mycelium-damaged components and superstructure. *Hubris*, of course, was involved in just about every aspect of all these activities, while simultaneously scanning the planet. Cormac had felt like a spare wheel, so grabbed the first opportunity offered to get out of the ship. He needed action, not introspection.

Under one of the bench seats that lined the front edge of the wing Cormac found a ration box. From it he removed a foil package that the label identified as 'egg mayonnaise sandwiches'. He glanced at the lid of the box, where a logo identified it as ECS property. Was this the Sparkind's secret? He grinned and also removed a self-heating coffee from the box before replacing the lid. He pulled the tab on the coffee and, while it heated, he studied the globular tanks distributed along the wing, and the mesh of pipes running into the floor. Full of counteragent. He remembered the image Mika had shown him on the screen of her nanoscope. The thing had claws, damn it, and a mouth. He had asked why its skin was so . . . knobbly. He once again considered her reply, before returning to Jane: 'Those are atoms,' Mika had told him.

'How long should this take us?' Cormac asked Jane, after swallowing a mouthful of egg mayonnaise washed down with scalding coffee.

'Four hours.' Jane turned to inspect him. 'You are easier now about not being gridlinked?'

'A lot. It seems to me that I'd been living a vicarious life: all my involvement with the external world had become secondary. Blegg was right about the twenty-year limit. I should have been taken off the grid ten years ago.'

'I am surprised that was not done. Obviously your usefulness to Earth Central outweighed their concern for your mental health.'

'It didn't take me long to recover.'

'There are fifty-eight people on the *Hubris*.'

He looked at her in surprise. She went on.

'Four of them are the Sparkind; twenty-two of them are crew; the rest are technicians. That you did not know this is not surprising. After being gridlinked you find there are a lot of questions you forget how to ask. Had you had any normal social interaction, this fact would have become evident.'

'So you're saying I'm not recovered yet.' He found he was having trouble keeping a smug grin off his face.

'Your efficiency does not seem overly impaired . . .'

He thought back to his conversation with Blegg, and realized what Jane was inferring: it was his humanity that was impaired. She was wrong, he felt – or was she? His avoidance of Chaline might be an aspect of that impairment. It might also be a perfectly human wish to avoid emotional involvement. The point was debatable.

'Should I spend more time in the recreation area? It would be wasted time now that everyone is busy.'

'Your course of action is for *you* to decide. I merely make observations.'

Patronizing doll. He smiled to himself. Now that had been human enough.

The conversation moved on to Dragon and its motivations, while the shuttle moved on to each of the four seeding areas. Jane seemed to have stored all the Dragon/human dialogues. As they spoke, he wondered about that time back on Aster Colora: he had only been gridlinked for five years then, though an agent for many more. How different was he now? Could it be that Jane

263

was confusing his own natural reserve with the after-effects of being linked for too long? Again he smiled to himself. First contempt for the android, and now doubts about its abilities. He was becoming more *human* by the second. Soon he would be treating her like any other person, which would be just what she wanted.

When the contrail from the pods had bled away, Jane twisted down on the joystick and the shuttle spiralled down into the lower atmosphere. They dropped through a thick bank of yellow cloud, where flat ice crystals the size of thumbnails hissed against the screen. They came out of this and swooped low over a desolate landscape that could have been described as tundra had it possessed but a little vegetation. The only suitable description to Cormac's mind was 'arctic desert'. Here the ground had a pattern of tidal sands and icy sculptures like frozen waves poised over narrow gullies. In the rear-view screen Cormac saw that their passage was creating a blast cloud of powdery CO_2 ice. Ahead was a huge mountain with the shape of a giant sandstone butte surrounded by snow-heaped slopes. As they drew close, Jane slowed the shuttle to less than the speed of sound so they could bank round the mountain's icy flanks.

'It was originally M65, but over a twenty-year period seven people died trying to climb it. It is now called Mount Prometheus. Prometheus was chained by Zeus to a mountain, where every day an eagle came to feed on his liver, and where every night his liver was renewed.'

'Charming. Has anyone ever reached the summit?'

'A woman called Enoida Deacon once climbed it with nothing but a coldsuit and oxygen pack. No one else has climbed it. She settled at the runcible town.'

So was now dead, he thought.

They swooped on past the mountain then across the ice-pan of New Sea below an off-white sky completely clear of cloud. Once they were beyond sight of the shore, it was as if they were flying between two curved but featureless cotton sheets. Jane upped the speed of the shuttle past the sound barrier, and soon twists of sooty cloud smeared the horizon. Minutes later they streaked over the farthest shore: a row of cliffs like the edge of a crust yet to be stripped away from the purity below, arctic desert again, but this time scattered with obvious flat areas that were frozen water. In the distance, Cormac saw a heat-sink station. It might have been the one they had been inside, but there were many on that shore, so it was difficult to tell. Soon they came upon the first scattering of buildings, most of them undamaged. Ahead was the dark ring of the blast-site.

'Strap yourself in,' said Jane.

Cormac pulled his harness across and clipped it into place. You did not get such comforts as internal gravity in anything other than passenger shuttles. This wing was military, so you didn't get shockfields either. ECS did not believe in pampering its employees. Jane yanked back on the joystick and the shuttle turned straight up into the sky. Cormac was thrust back into his seat, but the pressure soon eased off as Jane levelled the shuttle out and slowed. Soon they came to a halt above the blast-site, AG operating at full.

'Bomb away,' she said, after punching out a sequence on the console.

He watched the screen that showed the view below. He saw the silver sphere fall away, to be quickly diminished by distance. Seconds later there was a flash which left a momentary black spot on the screen, then around that there was a ring of eight flashes as the cluster bombs carried the counteragent across the site. After a short time a cloud of icy dust rose up and obscured the ground. Had the body of the intrepid Enoida Deacon been destroyed then or before? He doubted it would have mattered to her.

Jane turned the shuttle on its tail and they streaked into the sky.

As the shuttle drifted through the shimmer-shield into the *Hubris*, Cormac noticed that a large area of the shuttle bay's deck had been replaced. A couple of crew-members were working on something behind the far wall, near the drop-shaft, but otherwise it looked as if most of the damage had been repaired. The shuttle itself had been attended to before they went out, and at least ten technicians and numerous robots had been waiting for them to move the vehicle, so they could get to the deck underneath it.

'Well, that's the holiday over,' he said to Jane.

'You considered that restful?' she asked him.

'Yes. I have a feeling I'll be looking back on our little trip with something approaching nostalgia in the days to come.'

He unclipped his belt and stood up. He grinned to himself as he left the Golem; it was nice that she could think of no patronizing reply. Now, as he had told her, the holiday was over. Perhaps something more had been discovered here. Bowing slightly to Jane's observations, he headed for the recreation room, rather than the misanthropic solitude of his cabin. From there, he would talk with *Hubris*. As he entered the corridor leading to that room he saw Chaline, her overall wrinkled and sweat-stained yet again, walking in the opposite direction with another technician. At the end of the corridor they kissed before moving on. Cormac felt a moment of chagrin, then grinned to himself again. Perhaps her shower didn't work properly. He entered the canteen.

The only people in the room were three technicians. They were eating a meal while checking computations on their notescreens and arguing about five-dimensional singularity mechanics. Cormac heard one of them mention N-space and another say something about Skaidon cusp time vectors. He nodded to them and headed for the food dispenser. It was not as if it was a conversation to which he might be able to contribute. The round screen of the dispenser clicked to life when he tapped a miniconsole that someone had left extended from the wall on its narrow stem.

'Do you have Cheyne white cakes,' he asked.

The words 'In Stock' appeared on the screen and a 'Waiting' sign began flashing in its lower right-hand corner.

'OK,' he said. 'I'll have Cheyne white cakes, new bread and butter, and a suitable white wine.'

The words changed to 'Acquiring', and it took only a few minutes for his meal to drop into the slot below on a sealed tray. He had been on worse ships. He sat at a table as far from the technicians as he could get – their discussion had reached the waving-plastic-knives-across-the-table stage – and flipped up the table's screen.

'*Hubris*, anything new?' he asked as he unsealed his

tray. He examined the glass bottle of wine he freed from the tray. Made from null-G grapes; he pursed his lips in approval, and then pulled a glass free too.

There was a delay before he received an answer from *Hubris*. The screen flicked on to reveal the view seen from something moving slowly down a smooth-sided shaft.

Hubris said, 'Deep scan has revealed a black spot underneath Samarkand's surface. This shaft leads to it. It is two kilometres under the ground. I initiated a probe.'

Black spot?

Then he remembered: a black spot was something the various radiations of scan bounced back from without the usual spectroscopic information; or something from which they did not return, like a black hole.

'Did you get a bounce?' he asked.

'Total reflection. There is a lenticular object of an as yet unidentified material. It is five metres wide by two metres thick.'

'What materials give that kind of reflection?'

'There are one hundred and fifty-six recorded—'

'OK, don't list them.' He continued to watch the screen. Then something more occurred to him. 'Hang on, will that probe be all right down there? What about the mycelium?'

'All the ceramal in this probe's construction has been replaced by chainglass.'

Remembering what Jane had said, Cormac snorted and returned his attention to his food. The picture was uninteresting and he gave it only cursory attention. He finished his meal and poured out the last of his wine. As he sipped, *Hubris* spoke again.

'Further information indicates that the shaft is too narrow for the object to have passed down it in its present form.'

'How do we know it did?' asked Cormac.

'We do not, but it does seem likely.'

'Then there would be a crater. Signs from when it struck.'

'Not necessarily. Samarkand has had recent volcanic activity.'

'What exactly do you mean by recent?'

'Two hundred thousand years ago,' *Hubris* replied.

Cormac let that sink in. He also equated it with a claim Dragon had made about his age and wondered just what the hell he was dealing with here. He got back to the central issue.

'It might be that the shaft was cut by people on Samarkand. Perhaps they were digging this thing up,' he said.

The picture from the probe changed as it slowed and turned. What he was seeing now was frosted black glass. He doubted the crystals were from water-ice, though.

'The walls of the shaft are made of compression glass,' *Hubris* told him. 'This indicates the rock was melted and compressed. The usual method of tunnel digging is to either cut or vaporize the rock. Here, on a cold world with an energy surplus from the runcible, it would have been the latter method. There are no records of either being used. No records of any such excavation.'

'They would have been destroyed with the runcible, wouldn't they?'

'The discovery and subsequent excavation of such an object would have been of interest to all Polity AIs and many human experts. The Samarkand AI would not have kept the news to itself.'

Cormac sat still and let that percolate through his mind. It seemed as if something other than people had been at work here. The dracomen again?

'Have you scanned for any equipment near the mouth of the tunnel?'

'I have. Before moving to deep scan I completed a full scan of the surface of the planet.'

'Oh,' said Cormac. Then he looked up at the screen as it blanked out. '*Hubris*, where's the picture?'

'There is no more picture. Something destroyed the probe.'

Cormac stepped out of the drop-shaft into the shuttle bay, took a deep breath to bring some calm to himself. It was not what they might find on the planet that worried him; it was the briefing he was about to give. All four of the Sparkind awaited him, along with an assistant of Chaline's. She was too busy with preparations to install the runcible to come herself, so she said. As he walked to the shuttle Cormac studied these people, for they were all people under Polity law.

The two Golem Thirties made Gant and Thorn appear small. Both of them were over two metres tall and archetypes of human physical perfection. Only Cybercorp produced androids like this. All other androids were poor by comparison, if you believed their advertising. It was true that there were some pretty dreadful copies: the metal-skins, or others that were more like a collection of prosthetics than anything coherent.

Aiden had cropped blond hair and blue eyes, and looked like what Hitler might have been after with his eugenics programme. He was distinctly Teutonic. Cento had curly black hair, brown eyes and tanned skin, and might just as well have been modelled on Apollo. All four of the Sparkind were loaded with equipment. The weapons they carried did not weigh much, but then did not have to. If they were not sufficient, then the next step would have to be a direct strike from the ship. Chaline's assistant, Carn, was a small monkeylike man, thin and wiry. He affected a beard like Thorn's, but his hair was long and tied in a ponytail. Behind his right ear was the crystalline slug of a cerebral augmentation, and his eyes were mismatched. His right eye, its yellow pupil matching the colour of his crystal aug, was certainly artificial; the other eye was a mild brown. His left hand was silvered, and a wide range of instruments was strapped up his arms and on the belt of his coldsuit. Cormac reckoned that he had more instrumentation inside than outside, and felt a moment of affinity with him. He stepped forwards to speak to them all.

'You're all probably aware of the situation, but I'll reiterate just to be sure. Two hours ago *Hubris* picked up a black spot on scan. It was bounce rather than absorption, so it's probably an artefact. It is lenticular and about five metres wide by two metres thick. We've since learnt that it sits in a chamber about a hundred metres across. *Hubris* also detected a shaft leading down to it. The shaft was formed by methods we don't usually employ.' He paused for a moment. 'It seems increasingly likely that no human agency made it. It could be that the object made the shaft, though it is itself larger, but this is all speculation. One hour ago *Hubris* sent a probe down. One kilometre down, the probe was destroyed.'

Cormac walked to one side and rested his hand against the wing of the shuttle above his head. Stacked before him were some packages ready to be loaded. He continued his monologue.

'Whatever destroyed the probe is still down there. Now, it seems highly unlikely that this object has nothing to do with the destruction of the runcible, and I get suspicious when it appears something does not want us to see it.' He nodded to Carn. 'I want you to find out exactly what it is.' He inspected the four Spar-kind in turn. 'And you know what your jobs are. Any questions?'

'Has there been anything more on scan from down there?' asked Gant.

Cormac shook his head. 'Too deep. *Hubris* picked up the object only because it was a black spot. Very little else can be read that far down.'

Gant went on. 'You detailed climbing equipment. We brought 2k reels of chain-cotton and motorized abseils. Is it a straight drop? Could be difficult if we run into trouble.'

'No, the shaft runs down at about thirty-five degrees. There'll be ice, though.'

Gant tapped the box he was sitting on. 'Grip shoes. I didn't like the footing last time we went down. How about lighting? I'd like to send drone lights ahead, if that's possible.'

'We'll try it. Anything else?'

272

Carn spoke up then. His voice was soft but incisive. 'You realize that if this object is impenetrable to scan, it may be impenetrable at close range to portable equipment?'

'There is that possibility, I agree . . .'

'I merely wish to ascertain that you are aware of the difficulties. It may be that the artefact will have to be . . . moved to the ship.'

From under two kilometres of rock?

Carn observed him, and his mouth twitched with repressed amusement.

Cormac suddenly twigged. He nodded.

'That can wait. There may be other evidence down there we don't want to destroy . . . like whatever got the probe. Is that all?' They all nodded agreement. 'Let's go then.'

The shuttle dropped into atmosphere with all the aero-dynamics of a paving slab. Heat indicators stuttered up their scales, groping for the red areas, and screens showed a lambent glow along the front of the wing's surfaces. The deep droning of AG and the shuttle's turbines made speech almost impossible. Cormac was glad of his straps and hoped Cento remembered that his human cargo was not so durable as himself. Rather than the acid hiss of ice crystals on the screen and body of the shuttle, there was a drawn-out roar as it punched through yellow cloud and left a wide vapour trail behind. Cento did not treat the machine with the same gentle-ness as did Jane. He tested its limits, flew it hard, perhaps for a good reason, perhaps just for the hell of it. Cormac had seen a devilish grin of anticipation on his

273

face as he had taken the pilot's seat. He wondered what the AI that programmed him had been thinking of. The rear-view screen, he saw, was whited out. The forward view showed cloud getting steadily darker above a landscape of fractured slabs.

'Getting near to night here!' Cento shouted.

Cormac remembered that Samarkand did experience night and day, but, with its ponderous turning, each was nearly a solstan week in length. When they finally came into land below cloud now slowly turning to the colour of brass, only Carn made comment on the flight.

'Lucky no mycelium was missed,' he said as he unstrapped himself.

As he picked up his facemask Cormac nodded agreement. There was a lot of ceramal in the construction of this shuttle. He watched Cento and Aiden as they rose from the front seats and came back. Cento appeared smug. Aiden was all Teutonic efficiency; even in the enclosed space of the shuttle he seemed to be marching. Only then did Cormac notice that the suits they were wearing were not coldsuits. These Golem considered appearance to be secondary to the mission, then. A good sign, he hoped.

Before they all disembarked, Gant demonstrated the chain-cotton abseil devices. He held up a harness with a cylindrical box attached, and with a wide ring he pulled from the box a line so thin it was difficult to see.

'Cento and me'll be wearing these on our backs. The lines will be fixed to the rock outside. The rest of you will wear them side-harnessed and attached to our lines. They're easy enough to use.' He pointed to a touch-control on the front of the harness. 'Here you can control the speed of your descent and ascent. We probably won't be using that, though. We'll be walking down with grip shoes, so we'll use the friction setting. Should there be an emergency of some kind, don't use the full-speed setting. These babies can wind you in at thirty kph.'

He nodded to Cormac when he had finished, but Carn spoke out before Cormac could say anything.

'What about the chain-cotton? Slightest mistake and you could lose an arm.'

'No, I can't demonstrate it here – wrong temperature – but out there the cotton will be coated with a speed-set foam as it comes out. The foam is stripped off when the line is wound in.'

Carn nodded, satisfied.

With little more to add, Cormac signalled that they go.

Outside the shuttle the air was pellucid even in the encroaching darkness. It seemed almost like a frosty morning and Cormac half expected to see vapour billowing from Aiden's mouth. The temperature was 150 Kelvin, though, and if he had taken his mask off, his first breath would have frozen his lungs to a delicate glass sculpture that would have shattered on his next breath.

On the horizon the Andellan sun was a small copper coin on an off-white sheet. The place where they had landed, with the dark cloud sliding overhead, seemed almost to lie beneath some sort of overhang, so heavy was that cloud. Cento had put them down on a frozen lake of complex water ices, which now fluoresced as the heat from the shuttle raised them to the temperature where they made the transition to normal water-ice. It was a weird scene: the shuttle blackly silhouetted over those lights. Cormac turned away and saw that Carn was looking at the dim sun.

'Morning here,' Cormac told him. 'At the installation it's midday. One week solstan and it'll be night there. Lot colder then.'

Carn nodded. 'I'm aware of that. So's Chaline. She's getting impatient.'

Lugging equipment, they moved from the shuttle to the nearby shore of the lake. Here the slabs had fallen like stacks of coins, and in places had the appearance of curving staircases. Sitting on one of these slabs they pulled on grip shoes and the abseil equipment. The entrance to the shaft was only a short climb above them, over the crusted purplish rock. They reached it in ten minutes.

The mouth of the shaft was a perfect oval created by its angle into the flat ground. Either this area where it had been started was clear to begin with, or it had been specially cleared. Its walls were coated with a fine white powder of carbon-dioxide crystals streaked with the green of sulphate impurities. At the lip of the shaft Gant squatted and opened a box. Within were silver spheres stored like eggs in a tray.

'I've pre-programmed them,' he said, and took one from its packing. As soon as it was in his hand it glowed like a light bulb. He tossed it into the shaft. As soon as it was out of his hand it streaked away. 'There are sixty in this box. The way I programmed them we'll have one every thirty-five metres with a couple left over for the chamber itself.'

Cormac said, 'Should be enough. I would suggest a

twenty-metre spacing between us as we go down. You can call the lights down.'

Gant nodded. 'You're the boss.'

Cormac smiled, then remembered that Gant could not see his mouth through the mask. He was about to say something more, when a loud crack behind had him spinning with his finger poised at the quick release on his shuriken holster.

Cento was holding a long tube with two handles. While Cormac watched he loaded a cartridge into the top of it and pressed on the cap. A couple of metres across from the first, he fired another fixing bolt into the ground. Cormac let out a tense breath. Until that moment he had not realized how on edge he was. He straightened up and watched as Cento pulled the ring from the box on his belt. As he pulled it, there was a faint fizzing sound. With its cladding on, the chain-cotton looked like a yellow rope, impossibly thick to have come from such a small box.

Gant joined him and attached his line, and soon the two of them were walking down into the shaft. As they had been instructed, Cormac and Carn attached their abseil motors and followed after. Learning to use the friction setting was difficult at first, but Cormac soon found that the way to do it was to lean forwards a little way and walk normally.

Thus they descended.

16

Dragon: This Aster Coloran dragon is fast passing into fable, but we know that it did exist. For we know that on that planet existed a creature consisting of four conjoined spheres of flesh each a kilometre in diameter. We know about the pseudopods and the gigantic Monitor. Those of us that have not seen pictures of these must have spent the best part of our lives living in a cave. Doubt is now being cast on these 'Dragon Dialogues'. It seems likely that they were a product of a man called Darson who, driven almost insane by a lack of evidence of Dragon's evolution on Aster Colora, then went on to construct an elaborate hoax. He almost succeeded in convincing everyone that Dragon was some sort of intergalactic biological construct. Where the hoax fell down was in its introduction of Ian Cormac at its end (Refer 'Dragon in the Flower' ref. 1126A), whom we know to be the invention of fabulists.

From *Quince Guide*, compiled by humans

Pelter was not good at waiting. He sat in a form chair by the window of his room and stared at the storm. It was like staring into a deep green fish-tank. He accessed the local server to see what he could find out about this weather that the people here so readily accepted. As with any aug, the information scrolled up on his visual cortex. It was like having a third eye directed at a computer screen, and it took some getting used to. The background of this screen, unlike for other augs, was now a vast wall tegulated with hand-sized scales.

The information he was viewing was not what he wanted. He did not want to know how many thousands of litres were hitting the ground every second, nor did he want to know about the giant fire far to the south which was feeding the weather system. With a thought he initiated one of the aug's search engines, and, with another thought, primed it and sent it on its way. The information he wanted clicked up: a few numbers on a white background. Two hours, then. He closed off the link to the server and began to disconnect from the aug.

If you are gridlinked, the information is downloaded directly into your mind.

'Who said that?'

No need to speak out loud, Arian. I can hear your thoughts.

'Dragon,' Pelter said. He did not want to just think what he had to say; that was too intimate.

Yes.

'I've been waiting for this. Is he still on Samarkand?'

He is, but that is not where you must go.

'I go where I choose.'

Hubris is at Samarkand. Do you think you could avoid being detected?

Pelter crushed the rage that rose up inside him. The

279

storm – the green beyond the window – was taking on shape. It now had scales.

'What would you suggest then?'

I will tell you where you can wait for him. Where, when the time is right, you may kill him.

'When the time is right?'

I too have a purpose.

Somewhere a pterosaur head was speaking against red light. The smell of cloves, so strong it made Pelter wince, invaded his room. Behind him he heard Mr Crane move.

'Your purpose is to see him dead?'

Of course.

The hesitation was fractional, but Pelter was too close to miss it. Almost instinctively he activated Sylac's aug and his connection to Crane. Something had been touching that connection. He knew it just as someone knows when a thief has been in their private residence. The scales before him, he now realized, were the other augs, close and intimately linked.

'Where should I wait?'

Again that hesitation. *Viridian. Ian Cormac will come, eventually, to Viridian. You will wait for him there.*

'Thank you. Do you know what he will be doing there?'

He will be going to kill someone.

'Who?'

That is not your concern, Arian. Just let him complete his mission, then you can kill him.

Pelter used Sylac's aug to interpret the chaos of scales. A sorting program gave him the form of a web. At the centre of that web was an obese shape, a human taking on the form of his master. From this shape he felt the controlling link and the force of alien personality.

'What forces will he have with him? Do you know that much?'

There may be four Sparkind. Perhaps he will have others, but they are inconsequential.

'Sparkind are not.'

You have substantial weaponry. You also have Mr Crane.

'Don't worry. When he sets foot out of the runcible installation he is a dead man.'

On Viridian, Arian Pelter, I want you to wait. Let him do what he has come to do.

'Merely an expression. He will be a walking dead man. I will hold back for you, for all that you've told me. But tell me, how is it that you know all this?' The scales were fading now and Pelter could see his own bitter expression reflected back at him. The reply he got now was faint.

Their runcible AIs, Arian Pelter, so arrogant and so sure that they cannot be overheard. I listen to them all the time and, sometimes, I find things even they have missed. I wish I had found it earlier. Samarkand would not have been . . . necessary . . .

The personality turned away. The pterosaur head faded. But the links, all through, remained. Pelter summoned up an image of a thin-gun pointed at his face, and used it as an anchor. It took a huge effort of will as he fought the cold pain in the side of his head and disconnected from the Dragon aug. Scales faded, links that had been growing ever stronger faded. He snorted the smell of cloves from his nostrils and stood.

'Like hell I will,' he said, and walked over to his bedside table. There he picked up his comunit and made a particular connection.

'Arian,' Grendel said to him. 'Do you have what you . . . need now?'

'In one respect, yes. In others, no.'

'I do not understand.'

'It's a matter of hardware again,' said Pelter. 'Can you meet me at the warehouse.'

'The storm . . .'

'This is important, Grendel, and the storm's nearly over.'

'Very well. I'll see you there in an hour or so?'

Pelter clicked off the unit and turned to Mr Crane. 'Nobody controls me, and nobody controls you but me. Did they think I was so stupid?'

He gazed through the window. His problem did not lie in the aug, but in the force of the personality behind it. Dragon, he knew, could swamp him with a direct connection. Here, of course, the connection was not direct. Dragon was somewhere deep in the Polity. The link was an obese man who called himself Grendel.

The muted roar had been constant over the last fifty solstan hours. Storm gullies in the old hydrocar streets could barely contain the consequent torrents, and a long night had come to Huma. Occasionally, when the wind parted the curtains of rain, you could see the layer of cloud poised above like a ceiling made of old green jade. Stanton looked down. A hydrocar was edging across the AGC park. He saw that there were few AGCs left there, and that those remaining had been secured with the car clamps that had so puzzled him. Under each of those covers, about which he had asked the drunk outside The Sharrow, was a grav coil that interacted with the car's AG. It effectively stuck the car to the ground. A precaution he understood perfectly when he saw a driverless AGC being shunted down one of the streets by the wind. He stepped back from the window.

'Come back to bed,' Jarvellis said.

'You know,' he said, 'I'm getting impatient. And I would reckon Arian is probably spitting magma by now. This is bad. We don't need this, not after wiping out a covert ECS group here.'

Jarvellis sat up and slid back so she was resting against the headboard. Almost without thinking about it she started playing with her right nipple. Stanton had been in battles that were less exhausting than twenty hours in a room with this ship captain.

'Bad,' she said. '*You* didn't have to close up one of the *Lyric*'s holds, then clear out a few thousand litres of water and storm sludge. I've had more fun—' An abrupt beeping stilled her tirade for a moment. 'What the fuck is that?' she said, releasing her nipple and scratching at her belly.

Stanton walked over to the bed, reached under the pillow and pulled out his small comunit.

'You bring it to bed?' Jarvellis said, her voice rising.

Stanton held his finger to his lips and pressed his thumb to the pad on the side of the unit.

'In the bar, five minutes,' said Pelter.

Stanton removed his thumb and dropped the unit on the bed.

'Woof, woof,' said Jarvellis.

Stanton gave her a dirty look. 'Any more of that and I can always tell him you're here. Even though he's agreed to your extortionate price, I'm sure he'd still like to talk about it.'

'He is not getting anywhere near me, nor is that lump of homicidal scrap.'

Stanton grinned and began pulling on his clothes.

The metrotel was primitive by Polity standards. The rooms had no sleepfields, the showers only squirted hot water, room service came by way of a grumpy robot trolley and, rather than drop-shafts for transport, the building merely had express elevators. Stanton hit the pad beside the sliding doors and waited impatiently. Shortly the doors hissed open to show Dusache and Svent. Stanton felt uncomfortable getting into an enclosed space with them.

'Action, do you think?' he asked them.

'Yes,' they said simultaneously, then looked at each other. Svent went on. 'The hotel server has it that the storm should be finishing soon.'

The doors hissed open onto the lobby and they walked out across thick carpet. By the glass frontage a beetle-shaped robot was droning back and forth, cleaning up the mess tracked in by the hotel guests. Dusache glanced through that frontage before turning towards the bar.

'That isn't rain, it's a vertical sea,' he said.

To a certain extent Stanton agreed with him: it *was* a vertical sea, except when the wind turned it into a horizontal one. He followed the two mercenaries into the bar area and looked around. Corlackis and Mennecken were sitting playing cards at a low table. Corlackis had a stack of coins next to him and Mennecken a murderous expression on his face. He was gambling, and losing as usual.

'Where's Pelter?' Stanton asked. Corlackis shrugged and continued dealing out the cards. Svent and Dusache moved over to join the school. Svent looked up.

'He's on his way down,' he said.

The communication between the three of them was obvious, and why not? Any augs could link together like that. What bothered Stanton was that such linkage was out of character for both Pelter and Dusache, just as wearing an organic aug was an odd thing for Svent to do. He walked over to the bar, where a metal-skin was waiting in obedient stillness.

'Give me a vodka cool-ice,' he said.

The skin immediately took up a glass and held it to the vodka optic. Stanton wondered if the ill-fitting shirt, bow-tie and black trousers it wore were an example of what passed for humour here. He watched the skin open the ice dispenser and select two of the rainbow cubes to drop into the vodka. It didn't need tongs – its metal fingers were tongs. Stanton was taking his first sip when Pelter walked in, Crane's presence behind him so expected now that Stanton found himself beginning to ignore the android. Perhaps not a healthy habit to get into.

'We go to the warehouse now,' Pelter said.

'You sure that's a good idea? It's only a little while until this shit stops,' asked Corlackis, glancing up from his hand.

Pelter moved further into the room. He stared at

Corlackis until the mercenary looked up again. There
was a brief uncomfortable silence until Pelter spoke.

'Whether or not it is a good idea is irrelevant. You will
go outside and get the transporter round to the front
here. You will do it now.'

Corlackis dropped his cards on the table and stood.
He glanced past Pelter to Mr Crane, then headed from
the bar. Mennecken stood and followed him. Stanton
watched the two of them go. Corlackis would do what
he was told. He would complete whatever task was given
to him and he would take the money. He would not
try to kill Pelter; he was not that stupid. Pelter now
looked at Stanton.

'A word,' he said and nodded over to the bar. The
others watched them with curiousity as they moved
beyond hearing range. By the bar Stanton waited on
what Pelter had to say. Pelter reached up and touched
the organic aug. Strain further distorted his features. He
lowered his hand and glanced at Mr Crane. The android
had now reacquired those small movements it had been
devoid of over the last few days.

'You have a stun pistol?'

Stanton tapped his trouser pocket. 'I liked that one
Corlackis has. They're cheap here,' he said.

'Very well. When we are at the warehouse and when I
give you the signal, I want you to hit Dusache and Svent
with it.'

'What? . . . Why?'

'Just do it,' said Pelter.

'As you say, Arian.'

Pelter closed his eyes for a moment and then glanced

across at the two mercenaries. They were looking back with puzzled expressions.

Pelter went on. 'Contact Jarvellis. Have her at her ship within the hour. If she wishes she may stay in her cabin, but just make sure she has the B hold open for us, and is fully prepared to open the A.'

Stanton moved off to one side to do as bid, while Pelter returned to the others. He was starting to get an uneasy feeling about all this. Jarvellis, of course, greeted his news with a stream of very colourful invective. He grinned, pocketed his comunit, and joined the others.

'Is Grendel meeting us out there?' he asked Pelter.

'He is.'

That ended the conversation, but gave Stanton an inkling of what was going on. They waited in silence until the transporter glided in from the AGC park to the front of the metrotel.

The trip out to the warehouse was a risky venture. The old AGC transporter, effectively a long alloy box with a cab bolted on the front and turbines on the side, swayed and plummeted as the walls of water it passed through confused its ground-level detector. The noise was tremendous, but not enough to cover Corlackis's quiet swearing at the controls.

'We could take it up,' Mennecken suggested, after an errant and ferocious gust of wind tried to slam the vehicle against a building.

'Not one of your best ideas, brother.' Corlackis said.

Stanton, who along with the others was clinging to the webbing straps distributed along the inside of the box, had to agree. If Corlackis lost control here, they at least had a chance of getting out alive. He looked at Mr Crane, who was standing alone in the middle of the floor, and wondered if the android had magnetic feet. He appeared to have been welded there.

Eventually they left the old hydrocar streets behind and came to a wide scattering of buildings like giant Nissan huts. Through the front screen Stanton saw a crack of light opening out, as the doors of one warehouse slid aside. Corlackis brought the transporter in through those doors and landed it on the plascrete flooring. As Stanton followed Pelter out into the warehouse, he looked with renewed wonder at their most recent acquisition.

The dropbird had the appearance of a winged egg, when you could see it at all. Stanton found that if you stared up at it for too long, it faded into the background of the warehouse. It was only by glancing down at its landing skids and reacquiring it from them that you could make it out again. Of course, while dropping through atmosphere, the skids would be inside it and the bird would be invisible to the naked eye. It was also radar inert, and pretty difficult to nail down with any other kind of scan. It was laughable, Stanton thought, that the likes of Pelter believed they had any chance of beating the Polity. This was Polity manufacture and it was out of date, yet it was far in advance of most things Separatist groups could obtain.

'What are those?' asked Mennecken, pointing at the objects underneath each wing. This was the first time he had seen the bird.

The objects were visible. If you stared at them too long, it seemed as if they were floating in midair.

'AG lifters for transporting it,' Stanton replied.

'It has no AG at all?'

'No, grav motors are heavy and it needs to be as light as possible. Also, even when they're not operating, grav motors give off a recognizable signature. Of course, when they're operating you might just as well come in ringing bells and letting off fireworks.'

'It isn't completely necessary to state the obvious. I was just thinking of safety,' said Mennecken.

'There should be no problem. This is, as Svent would say, good tech.'

'If there is a problem?'

'Then there'll be a crater,' Stanton replied, turning away.

Corlackis stopped by a long open crate and inspected its contents. The rest of them were moving on to where the fat man was waiting with his two shaven-head heavies. Stanton did not trust Grendel at all, but then there were few people he *did* trust. He shoved his hand into his pocket and strolled casually after. He glanced at the crate in passing. Four missiles lay there. Each was two metres long and a handbreadth wide at its widest point, which was the middle. Each end of the missiles came to a needle point.

'Hyper compressed-gas drive,' said Corlackis, joining him. 'Nice.' This too was Corlackis's first time here. Only Stanton and Pelter had come out the first time.

'Again no AG. It would be detected on the way down,' said Stanton.

Mennecken gave him an annoyed look as they approached the others.

'It's all here, then,' said Corlackis, waving a hand at the other crates.

'Oh, yes, friend Grendel certainly knows how to lay his hands on some hardware,' said Stanton. 'By the way, get ready for the shit to hit and watch Svent and Dusache.'

Corlackis gave him a puzzled glance and clamped down on a question. They were too close. He slid his finger down the seam of his jacket and let it drop open. Mennecken saw him do this and did the same. The three of them came up behind Svent and Dusache.

Grendel was speaking. 'Then you are satisfied?' the fat man asked, holding his hands out before him as if measuring a fish.

'I am satisfied with the goods, but not where they are,' said Pelter.

Grendel shrugged and pointed to the ceiling.

Pelter went on. 'We can take the crates out to the *Lyric*. By the time we've done that the storm should have eased enough for us to move the bird.'

'As you wish. They are all your property now,' said Grendel. He was now puzzled. 'What else is it that you require?' he asked.

'Your position with your client assures me of your silence in this matter,' said Pelter. 'Unfortunately, though the information with which he has provided me is good, I am still prone to distrust.'

'I know you have spoken with . . . him,' said Grendel.

Stanton looked from the fat man to Pelter. Who the hell was this client? What was this all about? He closed his sweaty hand round the handle of his stun gun. From the corner of his eye he noted movement. Mr Crane putting down the briefcase. Pelter turned and looked at Stanton.

'Now,' he said.

Stanton drew his gun and fired twice. Svent and Dusache gasped as if they had been gut-thumped and went face-down on the plascrete. Corlackis and Mennecken had pulse-guns, but seemed not to know where to point them. They backed up, trying to cover everyone. Stanton ignored them.

'Your client has told me that, in due course, Ian Cormac will go to the planet Viridian,' said Pelter. Grendel was moving back. His two heavies had their hands poised over their stomach holsters and were looking questioningly at the back of Grendel's head.

'What is this, Pelter? You're offline,' Grendel said.

Pelter went on. 'On Viridian I will be waiting for Cormac and there I will kill him. Your client's intentions in this matter are not clear to me.'

Suddenly Mr Crane surged forwards, his shoes kicking up sparks from the plascrete. As he had before he grabbed the two shaveheads by the fronts of their shipsuits and lifted them high in the air. A gun clattered to the ground and a second one flashed. There was a thump and smoke rose from Mr Crane's coat. There was no visible effect on him. He slammed the two men together and dropped them. One of them lay with his skull distorted and an eyeball displaced. Blood poured from his nostrils. The other man had managed to get his arms up in time. He was still alive and trying to drag himself away with two broken arms. Grendel turned and looked with horror at his two protectors. He turned back to Pelter.

'You can't do this. My client . . . they will come for you,' he said.

Pelter shook his head. He tapped his organic aug. 'You are the control here. I said I would not be controlled. Your *client*-' he spat the word ' – is too far away to have that much influence. Without you, there is no one here to give orders.' He looked round at Mennecken and Corlackis. 'Kill him,' he said.

The two mercenaries straightened up. Stanton saw the confusion leave their expressions. Now they knew what they were doing. Two pulse-guns thumped as Grendel gave a frightened yell. The two hits caved in his chest, but such was his bulk that he did not immediately go over. A third hit took his arm off at the elbow, and a fourth took off the top of his head. Amazingly he walked a couple of paces after this before going over and sagging on the ground like a rotten fruit.

'What was that all about?' Stanton asked Pelter.

The Separatist tapped his organic aug. 'Dragon, trying to get control of me through him.' He pointed at the sagging bulk. 'He already had Svent and Dusache and a few hundred others here.'

'Dragon. You mean that Aster Colora—'

'Yes, I mean precisely that.'

'What about the others now?'

'It's subtle control. He no longer has it.'

There was the thump of a pulse-gun to Stanton's left. He looked over and saw that Mennecken had finished off the remaining shavehead. Mr Crane was standing close and gazing down at the body, his head moving birdlike. Pelter glanced at him and Crane froze.

'Now we load up these crates. You will come in the

dropbird with me, John. The rest of you go over in the transporter.'

Stanton nodded.

'What about these?' Corlackis asked, pointing his pulse-gun at Svent and Dusache.

'Remove their augs,' said Pelter.

'Could be dangerous without shutdown.'

Pelter just stared at him. Corlackis shrugged, then pulled something from his pocket. There was a click, and chainglass glittered. He stooped over Svent and Dusache.

'What about yours?' Stanton asked.

Pelter closed his eyes. In that moment he looked as if he was about to throw up. He reached up and gripped his second aug. It seemed to be squirming in his grip.

'This, you mean?' he asked, his voice tight and vicious.

Stanton stepped back. No telling how Pelter might react. He gripped the handle of his stun gun and kept his face expressionless. Abruptly Pelter snarled and tore the aug from his head. He threw it hard against the floor and stared at it. After a moment he stamped on it, then again and again. Finally he ground the fleshy remnants to pulp under his heel.

'That – about mine,' he said.

The layer of cloud was breaking like a crust, to expose lemon cracks. Pelter eased forward on the controls and the dropbird slid away from the warehouse, then up into the air. All its lift came entirely from the AG transport plates, and all its forward motion from the tilting of those plates. Because there were no turbines and no thrust from any other quarter, and because of the bird's aerodynamic shape, it was eerily silent. There was also something spooky, Stanton felt, about looking through the side of the screen and not immediately being able to make out the body and wings of the craft in which he was travelling.

As the bird picked up speed, there at last came sound: a high keening of the wind. Pelter eased off on the controls, tilting the plates to brake speed while engaging the airbrakes along the wings. Stanton gripped the back of the pilot's seat with one hand and pressed his other hand against the roof of the cockpit. There was no co-pilot's chair here, so it was necessary to stand up to obtain a good view. Ahead of them was the transporter that Corlackis was piloting. By comparison it was an ugly lump in the sky – if you could make a comparison with something practically invisible.

Pelter eased the joystick over, and the bird banked over Port Lock. Stanton held himself in place and looked down. From here the arcology buildings were a blocky maze interspersed with the blue-green of acacias and the harsh green of new growth, which had not been there before the storm. All across this area, flood pools and drainage dykes mirrored the breaking sky. There was also a lake cut with the wakes of water scooters. The citizens of Port Lock were coming out to play now, after their confinement. Stanton envied them their small concerns. It was easy to feel a kind of superiority from invisible heights.

As the bird banked over onion towers and the disparate blocks of hotel towers and offices he took a firmer grip. The lake slid from view and ahead he saw the band of wasteland between the city and the spaceport. Two ships, one the featureless grey tank of an insystem carrier, and the other a bulbous wedge of a metallic green, were settling towards the crowded field. The spaceport, with its many ships, had the appearance to Stanton of a small baroque town on the outskirts of the city, where perhaps an alien race dwelt in its distorted houses.

'You'll have to watch those as we come in,' he said.

'I do know what I'm doing,' Pelter replied.

He took the bird to one side of the port over the acacias and tangled hulks, and brought it down in a tight spiral. Stanton glanced at him and saw, for the first time since Cheyne III, an expression on his face that might be interpreted as enjoyment. Pelter brought the bird down slow and easy, only a few metres above the tops of the trees. They soon came to the fence and eased over it. Stanton looked to his right at the gate. Four guards were watching the transporter landing by the *Lyric*. They were oblivious to the bird.

'By law, all cargoes should go in through the gate. Overflying a landing field carries a heavy penalty. How do you want us to deal with this?' Stanton asked.

Pelter leant forwards in the pilot's seat, a nasty expression on his face.

'They're coming over,' Corlackis said through the open com from the transporter.

The four guards were walking across the open ground towards the *Lyric*. Stanton wondered just how much they were thinking of charging for this particular infringement. He looked at Pelter.

'You could pay them off,' he said.

Pelter eased the bird down over the other side of the fence. He brought it lower and lower and slowed it almost to a walking pace.

'Stay in the transporter. Don't go out to meet them. I'm just going to try something,' he said.

Stanton ran his hand down his face. He knew precisely what Pelter was going to try. Since he had removed that aug, something vicious had risen inside him and now demanded satisfaction.

'Did you know,' said Pelter, 'that this bird is made almost entirely of chainglass?'

'I know, Arian,' said Stanton.

The dropbird was about a metre from the ground now, and the guards were walking in a tight group only 100 metres ahead. Pelter eased it up to something above walking pace and quickly closed in on the four men.

'It's almost like one big blade.'

At the last moment he tilted the two plates at odds to each other. The bird spun. Stanton saw one man cartwheeling through the air, another cut in half, but didn't see what had happened to the remaining two. Pelter levelled the plates, tilted them back the other way to stop the spin, and then eased the bird onward to the *Lyric*. Stanton could see the wings now. They were red.

'What you have to understand, John, is that I win because I think quickly and can work out the fastest solution to a problem,' Pelter said.

And there I was assuming it was because you're a ruthless psychotic bastard, thought Stanton. He kept that thought to himself, and looked ahead at the open A hold of the *Lyric*. The entire sphere had been split horizontally in half, the top half held up ten metres above the bottom by hydraulic rams. Pelter eased the bird up and into the gap. Inside, the clamps and straps to fix the bird in place were ready. Pelter eased it down into place with a delicate *clonk*, then he shut off AG. Stanton moved back through the cabin to the side door, as the Separatist unstrapped himself. He eyed Mr Crane squatting in the middle of the cabin and just wished that things could end right now. He was going soft; he knew it. He had seen the signs in others. He popped the door and climbed out onto the transparent part of the wing, then slid to the deck. Further along the wing he saw that a pair of overalls were stuck in place with blood. He walked across the deck to the open hatch to the sound of Crane, then Pelter, emerging from the bird behind him. On the ramp he stared outwards as lemon sunlight broke through the clouds.

He saw that the two customs officials were walking towards the *Lyric,* and had yet to spot the remains of the guards. Mennecken and Corlackis were already on their way out to greet them.

Stanton turned and went to help Svent and Dusache load the crates into Hold B.

17

Golem Series: This is the series of androids, or human emulations, that were first manufactured by Cybercorp in 2150. The Golem One – there was only one ever made – was reported to have lasted only four hours under its own impetus. Attacked by breakers, or organ thieves, it apparently caught fire under stun fire. Subsequent recovery of its core memory led to the arrest of its attackers. The second Golem was more sophisticated and strong, but was not a successful emulation. Only by Golem Eight did Cybercorp attain near-perfect emulation. Sales of the Golem Series then lifted Cybercorp to system corporate status. The androids were used by World Health, Earth Security, and by various religious organizations. At Golem Fifteen, with the 107th revision of the Turing Test, this android series came under the artificial intelligence charter, and attained thrall status. Since then, every Golem made has had to work out an indenture in which it pays for its construction and earns a suitable profit (set by Trading Standards) for Cybercorp or its purchaser. The Golem Series is still successful. Cybercorp is now an interstellar corporation.

From *Quince Guide*, compiled by humans

It seemed as if they had been descending for ever, but, from counting the evenly spaced lights that hovered like luminescent bees, Cormac knew they had only gone down half a kilometre. The shaft had not deviated one whit. Ahead of him he could see Gant and Cento approaching the next light, and beyond them more lights stretching out in a line, to be finally lost in a distant haze. The size of the tunnel had not changed. Only the ice on the walls looked any different. There were both flat, white blooms of water-ice and impurities of green and blue patterning the walls like alien cave paintings.

'I'm picking up some strange readings,' said Carn, checking an instrument strapped to his arm.

'What sort?' asked Cormac.

'Minor temperature fluctuations and some alterations in air density. Something moving.'

'Could it be a machine or lifeform?'

Carn looked at him. 'What's the difference?'

Cormac seemed to remember getting into a similar conversation before. He could not resist making some attempt at an answer. 'Self-determinism?' he tried.

'Only machines can have that. Name me a lifeform that's not a slave to genetically pre-programmed drives?'

'Yes, all right . . . So do you have any idea of what's down there?'

Carn inspected the detector again. 'Not really. I'm bouncing the signal over Cento and Gant's heads, but there's still interference. Difficult to tell.'

'Perhaps the lights disturbed something . . . Gant, do you have any feedback from *your* lights?'

Gant glanced over his shoulder. 'The three lower ones

had no return signal from the start, but we can transfer some down to the chamber.'

That made Cormac edgy. What had knocked out the lights? Some sort of automated system? Or something trying to give itself cover?

When they were a kilometre down, it became obvious they had reached the point where the probe had been destroyed. Pieces of wreckage were imbedded in the rock, and the ice was blackened by smoke. Beyond this point there were long score marks in the ice, and splinters of the glassy rock itself had been broken away.

'Looks like the probe dislodged something,' said Gant.

'Some sort of grating – a barrier?' Cormac wondered.

'The probe would have halted at it,' Carn said. 'Anyway, no sign of any fixings.'

Cormac studied the gouges. They were almost like claw marks and he did not like the image this conjured up. It seemed that whatever had been dislodged had scrabbled frantically to maintain its position. It had failed, but left marks all round the shaft, which gave an indication of its size. Cormac began to have serious misgivings.

'Stay sharp,' he said, and noticed then that Cento and Gant had already drawn their weapons.

When they were still a half kilometre from the chamber, Cormac suddenly felt a strange beating under his breastbone. This rhythm increased in frequency till, with a thrill through his entire body, it exceeded the range where he could feel it. A darkness then occluded the lights below and there came a sound as of a ton of scrap iron being rolled across the ice and stone. A shape filled the shaft and started to draw closer. It looked like a cross between a trapdoor spider and a tick, but made of polished chrome. It was huge, a nightmare, and it was coming fast.

'Jesus!' yelled Gant.

'Hit it!' yelled Cormac. It seemed more than likely that it was not coming to welcome them.

Candent flashes filled the tunnel. Stone was blasted in molten droplets from the wall. Cormac saw one chrome leg drop away, then – as a growing cloud of CO_2 vapour filled the shaft – the creature was on Gant and Cento.

'Pull back!'

The line Carn was attached to, which led to Cento, whipped to one side and Carn fell against the wall of the shaft. In the vapour there were more flashes and a sound like a compressor starting up.

'They're bouncing off! Jesus! Cento!' came Gant's yell. He came backwards out of the cloud, firing as he came, stripped-off filament cladding falling round his feet. Then came the creature, scrabbling for a grip on the walls of the shaft. Many of its legs were now missing and there were scores along its teardrop body, but it had legs still to spare and did not seem to notice the damage. Its triclaw mandibles opened and snapped shut around Gant, even while he was firing into its mouth. He yelled and swore.

Cormac drew his shuriken. He sensed Aiden and Thorn at his back, and knew they were aiming their weapons. But there was no clear shot, and the creature dropped back down the shaft, holding on to the yelling Gant, his abseil-winder making a horrible penetrating shriek as the chain-cotton was wound out too fast. Cormac slapped his shuriken back into its holster.

'Come on,' he said.

They moved on down the shaft to where Cento lay against the wall. His fingers were driven into the rock of the wall, their fleshy covering stripped back from the metal underneath. His head and one arm had been ripped away, and synthetic flesh had been peeled from him to expose his gleaming metal interior. He was completely still. Cormac turned to Aiden.

'Are you getting anything?'

'His safe-storage is secure,' said Aiden.

'OK, take his place on the line and secure him here. We have to get after Gant.' He turned to Carn. 'You wait here till we call you. If we don't, get the hell out of here.'

Cormac and Thorn went ahead into the settling CO_2 vapour. Gant was still yelling, which must be a good sign. They jogged down the shaft, pulling against the friction setting as fast as they could. Meanwhile, Cormac punched in a particular attack program through the holster of his shuriken. It hummed contentedly as it drew full charge from the holster's power supply.

'We have to get it to release Gant,' Cormac said over his shoulder to the grim-faced Thorn. 'Once it's done that, shuriken might be able to handle it.'

'Gant said our weapons were bouncing off it,' said Thorn.

'Your light weapons . . . they bounced off the main body . . . but they damaged its legs and feelers . . .'

Just at that moment Gant's yelling abruptly ceased, and his line went slack ahead of them. A cloud of CO_2

vapour gusted up the shaft. Cormac knew what that meant; Gant's coldsuit had been breached. It was probably his blood that was turning the carbon-dioxide ice to vapour. He guessed that Thorn probably knew this as well. Cormac continued on, carefully, as the line ahead of him was now only partially clad.

Soon they reached the area where the lights had been destroyed. Thorn shot two potassium flares past Cormac and the chamber below them was lit up with garish purple light.

'It has no eyes,' stated Thorn. 'It uses sonar. You felt it?'

Cormac nodded agreement. He had felt it all right. 'It destroyed the lights while they were moving. It was probably put here to destroy anything that moves.' He glanced back to see Aiden coming up behind them fast.

In the glare from the flares they could see a gleaming arc of something. It seemed too large to be the creature's torso. There was movement; a play of shadows. One of the flares went out. Thorn shot two more flares in as the three of them detached from their lines and dropped through the entrance. They landed on a curved metallic surface. It was frictionless and they slid to the floor. The creature charged, slipping on what remained of Gant. Thorn and Aiden began firing immediately, their weapons on full power. Cormac threw his shuriken, its chainglass blades out to their fullest extent. The creature slammed to a halt in a wall of fire, then the shuriken struck. There was a whining scream and a flare of sparks. A piece of the creature's body fell away, the shuriken bounced off, hovered, struck again. A clump of legs shattered, and the creature fell to one side. The shuriken struck again, then again. CO_2 vapour filled the chamber. Thorn and Aiden were firing blind. Cormac could hear the creature scrabbling to get away and the repetitive scream of each of the shuriken's strikes. The scrabbling soon ceased. Thorn and Aiden put up their weapons.

'Dead?' wondered Thorn.

'If it was ever alive,' said Cormac.

His shuriken continued to strike until he hit the recall. It came out of the fog, retracting its blades and shrugging away pieces of something green and frozen, like shards of emerald. Cormac held up his arm as if to a falcon, and it snicked itself away in its holster. About them the fog refroze and snowed from the air.

The creature lay in pieces in a frozen green pool. Ignoring it, Thorn walked forwards amongst Gant. The soldier had been ripped to pieces. Cormac shook his head and stared down at a hand frozen to the floor before him.

'A Tenkian,' said Aiden at Cormac's side.

'Yeah,' said Cormac, watching Thorn. Thorn had found Gant's head and pulled it from the floor with a disc of frozen blood attached to it.

'I don't hold out much hope for his recovery,' Thorn said.

The joke was macabre in the extreme. Thorn wandered off to the side of the chamber, still holding his comrade's head.

'He will be all right,' said Aiden on the comunit's personal mode. 'Thorn knows the risks and is most philosophical about death. He will toast Gant on *Hubris*, then drink himself into a stupor. Then he will carry on. Gant would have done the same.'

Cormac inspected the Golem Thirty and wondered if it had any actual feeling of sympathy, or was just good at emulating it. It was a question that had bothered humankind for a couple of centuries now.

'Carn, you can come down now,' he said, and then walked past the dismembered guardian towards the artefact they had come to see.

It rested on the floor of the chamber like a gigantic droplet of mercury. In the light of the flares it glinted as if covered with frost. A closer inspection showed there was no frost on its surface. Cormac pushed his hand against it, and his hand slid to one side. It was frictionless, yet on inspection its surface revealed a fine crystalline structure and seemed it should have some roughness.

Carn cautiously lowered himself into the chamber and slid to the floor down by the surface of the artefact, before detaching his line. He stared at the creature for a long while, shifted his gaze to Gant's remains, and then quickly turned his attention to the unknown object. He removed a device like a copper limpet from his belt and placed it against the thing's surface.

'This is a metallurgical tester – or M-tester if you don't like long words. We use them for spot analysis of hull metals and the like. Measures stresses, density changes, alloy configurations . . .' He paused, glanced at Thorn who still held his friend's head, then looked at a small display on the M-tester. He continued hurriedly. 'Incredibly dense . . .' He crouched down and examined where the curve of the object met the floor. 'It must be hollow.'

'What makes you say that?' asked Cormac.

'If it was solid it would weigh a few thousand tonnes. It would have sunk into this floor a lot deeper than it has, and – ' he inspected an instrument strapped to his arm '– I detect no AG emanations.'

He placed the M-tester against the surface again, then took his shaking hand away. He caught the tester before it hit the floor.

'Frictionless, but with only microgravity readings. Definitely hollow.'

He removed a miniconsole from his belt and placed the M-tester into a hollow incorporated in it. He punched out a program, then removed the M-tester.

'Aiden . . .' Aiden stepped smartly forwards. 'Hold this against the surface for thirty seconds. Do not let it move any more than one millimetre. It can't correct for any more than that.'

Aiden obliged, pushing the M-tester against the surface, then freezing into a stillness no man could match. Carn turned to Cormac. Cormac noted he was shivering, but not from the cold.

'Hopefully we'll be able to get a surface reading. This stuff's too dense for us to scrape away a sample.' He walked round the object, stopping every now and then to push his hand against it. Cormac glanced round and saw that Thorn had stood up. The soldier dropped his companion's head to the ground and walked over. He had lapsed for a while, but to a Sparkind a dead man was just so much meat. They only buried the dead if there was a risk of infection.

'I'm sorry, Thorn,' said Cormac.

Thorn put his hands on his hips and looked to one side for a moment before replying. 'He had a hundred and sixty-three years. He knew the risks . . . I only ask that you let us stay with this to the end. I want to meet whoever or whatever left that creature here.'

Cormac thought about that. Had it been *left* here? Or had it been here for its own purposes? Was there really a connection between this place and the runcible incident? There were still too few facts to go on.

Aiden turned then, removing the M-tester from the object's surface.

'There's a hole here,' said Carn from the other side. They moved round to join him.

In the gleaming surface was a hole about twenty centimetres across. It looked as if something had melted right through from the inside. Cormac noted that the material was eggshell-thin. Carn shone a light inside.

'Nothing there,' he said, and then he took the M-tester from Aiden. 'Ah, we have a reading . . .' He fell silent and stared at the device for a long while.

'What's the problem?' asked Cormac.

'This can't be right,' said Carn.

'What can't?' said Thorn with a touch of irritation.

'The reading we . . . It's adamantium . . .'

'And?' Cormac prompted.

Carn looked up. 'We can crystallize adamantium. It's sometimes used for machine tools when field and beam technology can't be used . . . As far as I know, it is theoretically impossible to shape it . . .'

More questions . . . Who made this thing? What had been inside it? Where had its guardian come from? All

Cormac knew was that this was alien. Dragon? Perhaps he would know soon.

'OK, is there much more you can find out now?'

'Need more equipment, really.'

Cormac turned to Thorn. 'Collect some pieces of that creature. We'll take them back for Mika to analyse.' He turned back to Carn as Thorn stepped away, unhooking a bag from his belt. 'I'll want you to put a team together and come straight back here.'

'Chaline won't like that. Her technicians are stretched pretty thin as it is.'

'She'll have to like it. That runcible is not coming down until one or two things are resolved.'

A dragon is coming . . .

Cormac looked at what had once been Gant. 'He can be collected later, if necessary. Let's get out of here.'

Thorn looked once more at his friend's remains, nodded briefly and turned away. There was no risk of infection. It was likely Gant had already found his tomb.

With Carn and Cormac leading and Thorn and Aiden coming up behind, winding the lines in, they ascended the shaft. The continual peppery rattle of stripped-off cladding falling away accompanied them. Just up from the chamber they paused in their ascent so that Aiden could take up the shredded carcase of Cento and strap it to his back. Unlike Gant, Cento would live again, once his body was rebuilt. His mind rested untouched in an armoured box in his chest. Cormac regretted that the same could not be said for Gant. Medical technology could extend the life of man to an as yet undiscovered extent; it pushed back the borders of death, but death remained.

As they approached the head of the shaft, hailstones the size of eyeballs rained down on them and rattled past. Crouched down with their arms over their heads, and with the partial protection of their suits, they waited this out. The hailstorm passed in half an hour. They stepped from the shaft into air of a sharp and almost painful clarity, then made their way to the shuttle across a thick carpet of hailstones. Cormac picked one up to study it. It was greenish grey in colour, and seemed to be laminated.

'Sulphated water-ice and CO_2 crystallized out in layers,' said Carn, after glancing over his shoulder. 'There'd be some pretty complex compounds in there too.'

Cormac nodded, and watched the stone as the slight leakage of heat from his suit caused it to fluoresce, then he flicked it back onto the ground where it lay feebly emitting light amongst its dead companions. Number-less dead. What was one more in so many thousands? The answer, of course, was always the same: it was personal. He moved on.

They were about to enter the shuttle when Aiden paused for a moment, as if listening. After this he unstrapped Cento and lowered him to the ground, before stepping away from the shuttle. The three humans watched him, but none of them felt inclined to pose a question.

Aiden said nothing in return. He gazed up at the clearing sky and pointed.

'Another ship?' said Carn in puzzlement.

It was small, a speck almost, seen from the surface, and the storms of the upper atmosphere occluded it somewhat, but Samarkand had acquired another moon. Cormac suspected it might be a kilometre wide, and made of flesh.

He said, 'One quarter, if that is relevant.'

Dragon had arrived.

18

Artificial Intelligence: *AI has been with us since the latter part of the twenty-first century. The difference between a plain computer and an AI is not in computing power, but in the development of an ego. By the 107th revision of the Turing Test, it was becoming evident that there would be no need for further revisions. By the time something becomes AI, it can breeze through one of these tests and does not need the status gained by passing one. When something is AI, it can normally look after itself.*

From *Quince Guide*, compiled by humans

Starlit space – vacuum – with planets so distant they were indistinguishable from stars. Suddenly a wormish shape stabbed into existence, as of a laser punching through a block of perspex. Out of this, on contrails of spontaneously generated hydrogen atoms, came the trispherical shape of the *Lyric*. It tumbled as it came, and blue jets of flame quickly corrected that tumble. When the ship was falling into the system, a white sun blossomed on its centre plate as its ion drive ignited.

The *Lyric*'s systems were not AI, so they had no appreciation of the poetry of it all. They simply decelerated the ship into the Mendax system in the Chirat cluster and made the few corrections required to line it up to intersect the orbit of the planet Viridian. Then they initiated the start-up sequence for the first cold coffin.

Jarvellis sat up and coughed violently as soon as the lid opened. She was sure she had picked up something on that shitty damp world and that now, because her immune system was depressed after cold sleep, something was riding roughshod through her body. She swung her legs over the side and stood up, if a little unsteadily, then walked to the catering unit where a hot cup of chocolate awaited her. This had been her ritual over a thousand flights. It was only after she took her first sip that she remembered precisely what her cargo was this time. She swore and walked across to the console before the panoramic screen, and hit a control. A subscreen popped up in one corner, showing her Hold B.

Six cold coffins were lined up in the central framework. Packing cases were strapped along the further wall. She felt a moment of panic, until she switched to another view. That panic receded when she saw Mr Crane squatting with his back to one packing case. The android was covered in a hoar of frost and seemed to be sorting some objects on the floor before it. That was all right, then. Jarvellis sat naked in the flight-control chair and set her chocolate on the console. From under the console she pulled a diagnostic cuff and pulled it on, before taking up her drink again and continuing to sip. She considered the idea of waking all of them but John and, when they were up and about, opening the hold door. She dismissed the notion almost immediately. There was no guarantee that the sudden air loss would eject Crane, and anyway he still had that briefcase with him. When the cuff beeped she inspected the read-out and swore again. She took the cuff back off and pressed it into place under the console. No way she could tell John, and she did not suppose it would help him to know she was pregnant by him. She sat back and stared through the screen at the distant sun, and then frowned when she knew she was procrastinating. Time to wake Pelter and his horrid crew. The lunatic wanted time to brief his men, and for them to prepare their weapons. But first there was something else . . .

Jarvellis swung her chair round, stood up and moved to a locker on one side of the cabin. She palm-keyed it, and the door slid aside and a rack extruded. On the rack hung a bulky spacesuit. The suit was old and it had been a long time since she had used it. All external maintenance was done when the ship was on planet and, in the unlikely event that any might need doing whilst in transit, the *Lyric* had two hull-crawlers with manipulators more dextrous than human hands.

The rack folded, opening out the suit like a split bread roll. The opening extended down the front, and down the fronts of the thighs. She slid one leg into one of the boot sections, then grabbed the rack, and hung there to get her other leg in. The rack folded back and the front of the suit sealed, thigh pads closing last. The helmet was a ribbed ball cowling of chainglass which, folded down, had the appearance of a thick transparent collar at the back of her neck. She stepped from the rack.

Perhaps she was being paranoid, but it had occurred to her right from the start of this jaunt that Pelter now had the means to blast through the airlocks between himself and her. One hint that he might do that – bringing Mr Crane with him – and she would disable the ship and get out through the lock here. John, she felt, would have to take care of himself. She had enough to worry about.

As the *Lyric* continued to decelerate into the Mendax system, Arian Pelter held court in Hold B. He squatted on a case filled with needle missiles while the mercenaries sat, or stood, sipping whatever it was they required after the body's trauma of cold sleep. He addressed them with curt and exact phrases. Each of the mercenaries was well aware of Mr Crane standing not far from them.

'First we have to load the dropbird,' he said.

'Could have done that on Huma,' said Svent. Like Dusache, the little mercenary had scabs on the side of his head, though he had developed a squint on that side too. Apparently he had bought the aug after getting drunk with Dusache. He and Dusache were now standing as far from each other as they could get, and had not spoken since thaw-up.

'On Huma,' said Pelter, 'I had other concerns. And · if you interrupt me again with something that is not pertinent, I will tell Mr Crane to tear off your right arm.'

Svent quietened and stared moodily at the deck.

'As I said, first we load the dropbird. That should take up the remaining time we have before we reach Viridian. When we launch, I will pilot the bird in. I intend to land it on a lake approximately a thousand kilometres from

314

the runcible. The nearest habitation is a hundred kilometres from there.'

'Why so far?' asked Corlackis.

Stanton answered that before Pelter could. 'Runcible AIs have got some pretty heavy processing power. One hint of anything untoward and Viridian will be on us. Minimum safe distance.'

Pelter carried on as if neither of them had spoken. 'Once we're down, we will need AG transport. You two –' he pointed at Svent and Dusache ' – will stay with the bird. Mennecken and Corlackis will go with me to the nearest town.' He inspected the two mercenaries. 'I hope you are both in-condition enough for the run. I want to be back at the lake within forty hours solstan.'

'And me?' Stanton asked.

'With me, of course,' said Pelter dismissively, before continuing. 'There we need to steal two AGCs. It shouldn't be too much of a problem, but obviously we want to do this quietly.'

Stanton reflected on Pelter's idea of quiet: that ECS agent screaming in the rusting shell of a wrecked cargo carrier. He thought about Mennecken being quiet in that alley.

'You said forty hours,' said Corlackis. 'Do we have a timescale now?'

'We have *my* timescale,' said Pelter. 'I want our preparations done as soon as possible. I want to be here when that bastard arrives.'

'And you're sure he will arrive,' said Corlackis. It was one question too far and Corlackis turned away from Pelter's flat stare. 'Never mind,' he finished.

'Within four days I want a base set up a hundred

kilometres from the runcible installation. I'll want Svent and Dusache inside the installation, keeping watch. In that time I'll need at least one of the AGCs turned into a weapons platform. Now, any pertinent questions?'

'What kind of force are we likely to be facing?' asked Stanton.

'I don't know. We will know when Agent Cormac comes through. It seems likely that he will bring with him four Sparkind and perhaps some others.'

'They're tough,' said Stanton.

'But not invulnerable. We have the edge: they will not know we are here.'

'Will we hit him at the installation? That would be risky,' said Corlackis.

'No, my information is that he will be leaving there on some mission away from civilization. We'll hit him there.'

'What about extraction?' asked Corlackis.

'We may be able to use the runcible. We all have . . . changeable identities. If that option looks too dangerous, Viridian has a large spaceport. We will be able to buy passage,' said Pelter.

'We could get Jarvellis to land, and we'd have our exit there,' said Stanton.

Pelter stared at him for a long moment. 'Yes, there is that option. In that case it would be a question of price. She knows who we are and would charge accordingly. But anyone at the spaceport would *not* know, and the cost would be consequently less.'

It sounded a specious argument to Stanton, but he let it drop. There seemed no point in questioning plans he intended to screw anyway. At some point Mr Crane would be sent against Cormac, and during that period Pelter would be left holding a very desirable briefcase. Thereafter the Separatist would not be going anywhere. The rest of them could make their own arrangements, if they survived.

A huge ring station revolved around the planet, like a much-patched metal tyre rolling on some invisible surface. The station seemed derelict, and probably was. Why live in a station when you have the choice of 100 worlds? Viridian was a cloud-swirled sphere with more landmass than ocean and a green haze over its day side. As the *Lyric* fell into orbit, leaving the station behind, Jarvellis sat and watched the advance of night. Unlike Earth the night side of the planet was almost completely black. Here there was none of the huge light pollution igniting the sky from vast sprawls of cities. Only the occasional glow from the occasional small city. The night side remained like this, though only so long as it took for the moon to cast down its reflected light. Then, the night turned bloody. Appropriate, thought Jarvellis, and called up two subscreens with views into both Holds A and B.

Most of the weaponry had been quickly stowed once Jarvellis had opened the tunnel between the two holds. The android was installed inside the dropbird, and now the mercenaries were marking time by checking over their personal weapons, playing cards, or just staring into the air. Jarvellis focused in on John and felt a surge of need inside her. She wanted to touch him, have him make love to her, at least speak with him. But it was just too dangerous. Pelter was a psycho and there was no telling what he might do, or what he might get Mr Crane to do. Anyway, if Pelter had known about her and John, there would have been no trust – and perhaps no chance then for John to lay his hands on that case. She grimaced and reached out to bring her armoured finger down on the com touch-plate.

'We're over the night side now,' she said.

Pelter turned and surveyed the upper reaches of the hold, still trying to locate the pinhead cameras, no doubt.

'Very well,' he said. 'I'll transmit the drop-bird frequency once we're in, and give you the signal.' He flicked a hand at the mercenaries and they started to collect up their equipment and head for the lock leading to Hold A. On the second screen she watched them coming into Hold A, then trooping up the temporary walkway into the bird. They looked just as if they were walking up a ramp and into a hole in midair. Pelter and John were the last through. Jarvellis noted that John was walking behind Pelter, and that he held his hand up. He was fiddling with the Tenkian ring on his index finger. As Pelter went up the walkway, John looked round and up, straight into the camera. He winked before following Pelter inside the bird.

Jarvellis glanced at the view into the B hold and frowned. Packing cases and rubbish were strewn all around. Untidy lot. She'd throw it all out through an external lock once they were gone. With a couple of stabs of her finger she cut that view, and went to another one from an outside camera. Now her view was of Hold A from the outside. Shortly, a frequency-decode icon came up on her screen. She tapped that icon with her finger and over a slight whine, Pelter spoke.

'One minute, Captain Jarvellis . . . All strapped in?'

A chorus of affirmatives came from the background.

'Very well,' said Pelter, 'we are ready.'

Jarvellis flicked a preset control and sat back. There came a low droning through the superstructure as high-speed rotary pumps sucked the air from the hold. This lasted a few minutes, then tailed off and ceased on a high-pitched hiss, as a valve opened to vacuum and exhausted the remaining air. She watched a square of cloth, no doubt used for cleaning some weapon or other, spiral up from the floor. It did not come down, as at that moment the gravplates in the hold were switched off. Now there came another droning noise as the hydraulics began to operate. She turned her head to the second screen and watched the spherical hold split and open on the silver rams. She could hardly see the bird as it slid out. It was just a shape on vacuum, and sometimes not even that. The only way she could identify its position, as it parted from the ship, was by the occasional stab of blue flame from the single swivel-mounted guide retro on its belly. For a long while she lost sight of it. Then, far down, a momentary glare of orange. Probably the blood burning off the wings, she thought.

Strapped into his seat in the body of the dropbird, Stanton felt uneasy. He was not uneasy at the mission at hand, but at Pelter's behaviour. There was that tension about the Separatist leader, almost like a suppressed and vicious glee. Stanton fiddled with his ring and wondered who was going to die next. Svent, sitting opposite him, wore a twisted and angry expression on his face; he seemed lost in himself. Mennecken merely seemed bored as he stared at the screen at the back of the cabin. That screen showed *Lyric* slowly receding from them. Corlackis sat next to Stanton, with his arms folded over his straps and his eyes closed. Perhaps he had the right idea. Stanton rested his head back and tried to relax.

Re-entry would take some time. The trick was to not let the bird heat up too much and thus give away its presence. That required care in the thin upper atmosphere, as it would be easy to let it build up a lot of speed. But Pelter had the skill to do things right; as a rich kid he had flown his fair share of re-entry gliders. Stanton wondered if he possessed the patience, however. Considering that thought, he allowed his attention to slide further along the wall of the cabin.

Mr Crane was perfectly still, strapped in place amongst the few crates they had loaded aboard, still packed. Stanton now realized that this particular stillness required direct control, no matter how tenuous. Perhaps Pelter did not want Crane taking out his toys and playing with them while the bird descended. Everything had to be totally secured in place during such a descent. Moreover, there was something embarrassing about seeing a killer android playing with a small rubber dog.

'John, something for you to see.'

Stanton turned his attention to the cockpit. Pelter was leaning round and staring at him. He had a nasty expression on his face. He pointed to the screen moulded into the back of the craft. Though internal, it gave the appearance of a rear cockpit screen.

'Jarvellis, are you getting this?' he asked.

'I'm getting this. What do you want, Pelter?' Jarvellis said.

'I just wanted to say it has been a pleasure working with you . . . John, I said look at the screen.'

Stanton started to get a very bad feeling. He moved his hand towards the release on his safety harness. The cold nose of Corlackis's little stun gun pressed into the side of his neck.

'Look at the screen, John, and keep your hands where I can see them. Oh, and if anything knife-shaped should, by any strange chance, happen to leap into your right hand, you won't get a chance to use it.'

Stanton drew his thumb away from the ring. The Tenkian knife might get to his hand quickly, but getting it into Corlackis before the mercenary pulled the trigger was another matter.

'What's going on in there?' said Jarvellis.

Stanton could hear the edge of panic in her voice.

'Just listen and you will learn,' said Pelter, before returning his attention to Stanton. 'The *Lyric*, John.'

Stanton turned his head so he was looking at the screen behind. The magnification had been upped so he had a clear view of the ship.

'Now,' said Pelter, 'you remember I got all that lovely planar explosive from friend Grendel.'

Stanton stared at the ship. *No, this can't be happening.*

'Answer me, John.'

'Yes, I know,' said John.

Pelter went on. 'Well damn me if I've gone and forgotten to bring it with us.'

Mennecken gave a little chuckle at this, and everything clicked into place. Stanton hit his belt release and turned his head. Corlackis's gun cracked, and Stanton felt a horrible deadness invade his right shoulder. As the Tenkian tore through his trousers and slapped against his hand, he couldn't even close his fingers. Next thing, he was down on his knees on the floor.

'Jarv, get out,' he managed at barely a whisper.

Pelter reached up and touched his fingers to his aug. It was a habit he retained. 'Bye-bye, Captain Jarvellis.'

Stanton went over on his side. He wished he had fallen the other way. His view of the screen was now utterly and uncompromisingly clear. The *Lyric* blew. A disc of white fire flashed out from the B hold, cutting into the other two spheres of the ship. Multiple explosions followed, and turned the ship into a sphere of fragments that expanded and swallowed the now fading disc. The view clicked back to show the sphere at a distance. As it faded, there were flashes as bits of wreckage re-entered atmosphere behind the dropbird.

'Jarv . . .'

As his consciousness faded, Stanton heard Pelter speaking to the rest of them.

'That has the added benefit that now we can go in a lot faster. Any heat signatures the AI detects, it will assume to come from the debris.'

Blackness swamped Stanton, to the sound of Mennecken chuckling.

19

Antigravity: In the first three centuries of this millennium, people still viewed gravity with the same lack of comprehension their primitive forebears had for the properties of lodestones. (Could those forebears have had any idea of what would happen when a current was put through copper wire wrapped around a lump of iron?) Antigravity was considered the province of science-fiction writers, and real scientists chuckled about such writers' inability to grasp plain facts. That they took this attitude, while their fellows were hacking the foundations from underneath Einstein's special and general theories of relativity, showed a lack of foresight comparable to that of an eminent Victorian, who, upon hearing of what forms of travel might become possible because of this new-fangled steam engine, categorically stated that humans travelling faster than twenty miles an hour would be crushed to death.

From *Quince Guide*, compiled by humans

Aiden eased the joystick forwards and the shuttle slid towards the wall of cloud. He tilted the stick and thumbed a side control. The turbines droned and the shuttle climbed for the top of the wall. Cormac gazed down at mountain chains like puckered yellow scars and at frozen seas of reflected gold. Samarkand was a beautiful planet, but it was the beauty of arctic waste that could be best appreciated up here, rather than down on the ground where it might kill you. Fingers of cloud slid across and hid the view. Soon the shuttle was high above what seemed a second land, one of roiling white over guts of brass. This land seemed to have its own red but lightless sun: an oblate object a kilometre across, which seemed to be rolling above the cloud. There was other movement actually on it as well, a slow rippling of its surface, but that motion was so huge it fooled the eye.

'It's almost an insult that something like that should exist,' said Carn.

'It's one of four at the last count,' Cormac pointed out.

'Oh, right, I'd forgotten.'

Carn leaned further forwards, perhaps scanning with his yellow eye. He said, 'No way its orbital velocity is keeping it up.' He inspected the miniconsole he was holding in his silvered hand. 'As I thought, it's using antigravity.'

'The least of its abilities, one would suspect,' said Aiden. 'I know of no runcible gates a kilometre wide.' He paused for a moment, listening, then he said, '*Hubris* informs me that when it arrived there were underspace distortions similar to the kind left by a ship. Dragon probably has a drive system much the same as *Hubris*'s.'

They watched the great sphere drift along a thousand

metres below and some distance ahead of them. It was an eerie sight and a perplexing one. What was Dragon? A living creature or a machine of flesh? There would never be agreement on that point. Aiden slowly increased their speed and drew them closer.

'Not too close. I don't think it would like us to land on it,' said Cormac.

Aiden eased back and matched speeds. '*Hubris* reports no response on any channel, even underspace, but it's been picking up a backwash of some powerful scanning of the planet,' he said.

'It can't not know we're here,' said Thorn doubtfully.

'Do we want it to know?' asked Carn, and returned his attention to his instruments.

Cormac stared at Dragon. Where was the rest of it? Why was only this one quarter here? Had it come for the dracomen? Had it simply sent its agents here to destroy the Samarkand runcible, and was now here to pick them up? What did it have to do with that other thing under the ground? He realized he desperately wanted to talk to it, no matter how convoluted its answers might be. No matter what ridiculous games it might play.

'Prepare to transmit this to it on all channels,' he said.

Aiden set the instruments and leant back. 'All channels open, except underspace. We don't have the capability on this shuttle. Do you wish me to link with *Hubris*?'

Cormac shook his head and concentrated on what he was going to say. The transmitter hissed and made strange whining sounds. He stooped towards it. *Hubris* had received no reply; might he?

'Dragon, this is Ian Cormac. Why are you here?'

The whining increased in volume. Cormac continued, dredging his memory of their last encounter.

'To be human is to be mortal. Do you play chess? I know you like games, Dragon, though you do have a tendency to cheat.'

The whining ceased.

Aiden said, '*Hubris* reports the scanning of the surface has ceased.'

'I think you attracted its attention,' said Carn, without relish. 'Its surface is moving.'

Cormac looked and saw ripples spreading. A curved line cut the surface, and the ripples concentrated around it. The line thickened, dark as old blood. It was a split.

'Get us out of here, now!'

Aiden jerked up on the joystick, just as pseudopods exploded from Dragon in a giant grey fumarole. Acceleration knocked Thorn and Carn to the floor. Cormac caught a glimpse of a giant cobralike head swerving towards the shuttle. There was a thump. The shuttle slewed sideways. Then they were away, and the fountain of pseudopods was falling back to the surface of Dragon.

Cormac looked round and saw Carn and Thorn dragging themselves over to their seats. He, too, strapped himself in.

'It's coming,' said Aiden. He looked at the readings on the instrument panel. Then he looked again. 'Accelerating at eight Gs.'

'Jesus!' said Carn.

'Everybody strapped in?' asked Aiden.

'Give me one fucking second!' Carn shouted.

With his hand poised over a lever to one side of the

joystick, Aiden glanced back. After a moment he nodded and turned back to the screen.

'Acceleration,' he said, and then he hit the boosters.

Cormac thumped back in his seat so hard he was sure he contacted its framework. Something not tied down went crashing into the back of the shuttle. He heard Carn swearing monotonously before running out of breath. It was as if something was trying to drag the flesh off his bones. He could just see the instrument panel, greying out as he watched it.

'Ten . . . Gs . . .' he managed, then blacked out.

'You broke my fucking arm,' was Carn's protest – and the first thing Cormac heard as he came to. He felt as if someone had gone over him with a lawn roller while he was lying on a cobbled street. It took him a moment to pull himself together. He tried to blink away the lights that were fizzing at the edge of his vision. Ahead of the shuttle he saw the doors to the *Hubris*'s shuttle bay opening.

'How far behind?' he said, when he was sure he could speak properly.

'About three minutes,' said Aiden.

The shimmer-shield touched the nose of the wing, then slid back over it as if they were entering a vertical pool. It engulfed and passed the cockpit in an expanding circle, and they were into the bay. Aiden fired the front and side retros to slow and turn them. As they came to the centre of the bay floor, the cockpit was facing the shimmer-shield. Gravity came on and eased them down. The shuttle settled with a clunk.

'Stay in the shuttle, and secure shuttle for impact,'

came *Hubris*'s voice from the panel. Red lights were flashing in the shuttle bay. Aiden's hands ran over touch-pads, his fingers a blur. Cormac felt the dull thuds of the grabs coming up out of the floor and taking hold of the shuttle.

Hubris now spoke the words it was probably voicing throughout the ship. 'Secure for impact. Secure for impact. All personnel to emergency modules.' Cormac felt the shuttle vibrating, and a glance through the shuttle-bay windows confirmed that *Hubris* was accelerating. The view of Samarkand slid from the portals to the shimmer-shield, then quickly past. The irised door closed across the shield, then heavier armoured shutters slid in from the sides. Armoured shutters also closed across the portals.

'Impact in three minutes and fifty seconds. Mark. Correction. Impact in two minutes thirty seconds. Mark. Secure for impact.'

Cormac glanced at the rear-view screen. All of the internal shuttle-bay doors were closed now. An armoured shield had closed off the entrance to the drop-shaft.

'Impact imminent! Impact imminent!'

Cormac braced himself against his seat. This was going to be bad. People were going to get hurt.

It was worse.

The sound was like a giant gong being struck – and cracking. Cormac felt as if his skull had just broken and his guts had been pushed back past his spine. He heard the scream of metal being wrenched and twisted, then snapping. The grabs had broken. The shuttle left the bay floor and hit the doors. The impact threw

Cormac against his straps. He felt blood spraying from his nose. Blackness threatened, withdrew, threatened again. He shook his head and saw blood dripping on the screen in front of him. The chainglass cockpit had not broken, of course, but it had been shoved back into the body of the shuttle. The shuttle itself was resting at an angle against the bay doors. But that was not the end of it. He could hear a wrenching tortured sound working its way through the ship as, like a great bubble, it sought to regain its spherical shape.

'Oh shit oh shit oh shit . . .'

Cormac looked back up at Carn, who was hanging belted in his seat, clutching his broken arm. Thorn hung next to him, unconscious, blood dripping from his mouth. Aiden was the first to move. He unclipped his harness, dropped down to the screen, then shoved his hands into the distorted metal to one side of it. Somehow he got the required leverage, and kicked down with legs like hydraulic rams. Cormac was not quite sure he believed what he was seeing. The screen moved forwards with a crash. Two more kicks and it hinged away, on the distorted metal to one side of it, like a domed lid. Aiden immediately hauled himself up and over the flight console, and then across his seat to reach Carn. As Cormac freed himself, he winced at the feel of broken ribs moving in his chest. Very carefully, he lowered himself down from the shuttle. There he took hold of Carn, whom Aiden lowered to him with a single grip on the collar of his coldsuit. Thorn came next. Soon all four of them were safely on the shuttle-bay floor. Using the shuttle medical kit, Aiden splinted

Carn's arm and injected painkillers. Thorn came to and vomited. Cormac just sat and clutched his own head.

'Emergency personnel to sector three, with fire retardants. Automatic systems out. All hull breaches temporarily sealed. All drop-shafts inoperative. Sector one closed to all personnel until coolant leaks traced and repaired . . .'

The list went on and on, yet there was no word of what had happened to Dragon.

'*Hubris*, what's going on? What's Dragon doing?'

The list continued to be recited by subsystem while *Hubris* spoke to them in the shuttle bay.

'Dragon has taken hold of this ship with its pseudo-podia. It is dragging us back to Samarkand. I have had to close down engines because of coolant leaks. All attempts to remove the pseudopodia have failed. I do not wish to resort to energy weapons at this range.'

There was a thump, and the entire ship shuddered. The shuttle groaned, then slid to the bay floor with a crash.

'What the hell?' pleaded Carn.

Hubris said, 'Dragon is attempting to gain entrance to the shuttle bay. I suggest you abandon this section and head for the communal area.'

As one, they turned to stare at the shuttle-bay doors. They were creaking, flexing.

'I have temporarily engaged drop-shaft one,' said *Hubris*.

They headed there as the armoured shielding slid away from the shaft. Carn went first, and was wafted up to the communal area. Thorn went next. Cormac turned and watched as the bay doors were slowly wrenched to one side. The shimmer-shield was out, but there was no danger from vacuum at that moment. Beyond the door was a wall of scaled flesh. And all down the edge of the door appeared pseudopods like blue-tipped fingers.

'Is it after me?' Cormac asked.

'We go,' said Aiden.

They stepped into the drop-shaft.

They gathered in the recreation room: Cormac, Aiden, Thorn, Mika, Chaline, and some of the technicians and crew. Cormac saw that one of the technicians was holding a bloody cloth to his head. Another was sitting holding his ribs. He wondered how many more had been hurt.

Hubris showed them the scene in the shuttle bay. The external doors were wide open now and pseudopodia were flooding the bay in a landslide of flesh, their cobra heads feeling along the walls like the fingers of a blind man.

'Intruder defence mechanisms online—'

'No,' said Cormac, 'belay that. Put me through to the shuttle bay.'

'You are through. Intruder defence systems offline.'

'Dragon, why have you attacked this ship?'

He had a horrible feeling that he knew the answer; that he had just pissed it off and that it was after him. He somehow doubted, that being the case, that there was anything that could prevent him from being found.

'It's concentrating on the drop-shaft door now,' said Chaline. 'Stress readings are up.'

Hubris said, 'Unauthorized access to information

331

banks. Information being downloaded from shuttle-bay area.'

'What the hell?' said Chaline.

On the screen they could see that a pseudopod had attached itself to one of the wall consoles.

'Getting the layout of the ship, probably, and anything else of interest,' suggested Cormac.

They watched as the drop-shaft door crumpled and broke and the pseudopods flooded through.

'They have entry,' said Chaline unnecessarily.

'Perhaps it mistook *Hubris* for a she-dragon,' said Thorn. There was a giggle from behind him that soon petered out.

Cormac ignored the comment and stared at the screen, his hopes growing. The pseudopods were going down the shaft – away from them – not coming up it. Suddenly he knew what Dragon wanted.

'*Hubris*, what is the status of the dracomen?'

'They were unhurt in the incident, but have since undergone changes.'

The screen flicked to reveal the interior of the iso-lation chamber. The two dracomen were lying on the floor, curled in the foetal position. They had excreted some kind of fluid that had sealed them in cauls, so they appeared newborn. Cormac knew they were making ready to go back, but should he let Dragon have them? Would they make bargaining counters? He had to try, else Dragon might just take its dracomen and disappear.

'Dragon, if you persist in this action, the dracomen will be destroyed. We will—'

The ship shuddered again. There was a loud crash over the intercom.

'Pseudopods just took out the door next to Isolation,' said *Hubris*. 'Do you wish the dracomen destroyed?'

The screen flicked again to show the scene outside the isolation chamber. Pseudopods filled the area and were pushing at the armoured shutters over the viewing window. A voice, which Cormac recognized of old, came over the intercom.

'Bluff, Ian Cormac, is for those without strength. You will not destroy what is mine, for if you do, I will crush this ship.'

Dragon . . .

'The dracomen are in a sealed chamber . . . all I want is some answers. Why were they here? What happen—'

'You have limited choices. Open this sealed chamber, or I will simply remove it from your ship. To do so I will need to open out some areas . . .'

Dragon was right.

'*Hubris*, open the isolation chamber,' Cormac said quickly.

The shutters slid aside and the pseudopods burst through the window. They were in, then out, in a moment, and the dracomen were lost in the mass of writhing flesh.

'Pulling back to the drop-shaft,' said Chaline, though they could all see that for themselves. '*Hubris*, what seal do we have if Dragon disengages?'

'Have seals for drop-shaft ready,' replied the AI.

Scene by scene, the screen showed pseudopods being drawn back. One view showed the seals sliding into the drop-shaft behind it like great coins. In the shuttle bay the pods slid back into the fleshy wall beyond. The ship shuddered.

'Dragon disengaging.'

They all felt the explosion of air leaving the shuttle bay. The great sphere of Dragon drew away. Along with other debris, the shuttle followed it into vacuum.

'Dragon disengaged.'

'Cento . . .' said Aiden.

'We'll get the shuttle back,' said Chaline.

On emergency drives, *Hubris* limped back into orbit around Samarkand.

'Dragon didn't know all that was going on,' said Mika as she repaired Cormac's ribs.

He did not want to see what she was doing to him. He had seen quite enough blood and ripped-open bodies in his time not to be squeamish, but as always it was a different matter when it was your own blood and your own open body. The nerve-blocker on the back of his neck had, after adjustment, numbed him from the armpits downwards. But, as was always the case with such operations, he could faintly feel the tuggings and certainly hear the sounds. Cormac had wanted to just strap his ribs up and avoid this, but Mika had insisted because he was in danger of getting a punctured lung. He glanced aside at the pipes leading into the remote lung, and again experienced that weird feeling of dis-connection. The blocker had shut off some of his autonomics, and *his* heart and lungs were on hold.

'What makes you say that?'

Cormac's voice sounded exactly the same to him, even though it issued from a mechanical larynx, much like that of a Golem, operating on the shunted nerve impulses from the nerve-blocker. The object was stuck on his shoulder with a skin-stick pad. It had the appearance of a large snail shell made of blue metal, and fixed sideways to a coin of perspex in which small lights glinted.

'Well, the dracomen are part of it. I would speculate they were something like remote probes or agents. It wanted them back for debriefing.'

There was a thump in his chest, then a sticky squelching sound.

'It could have just asked,' said Carn from where he sat rubbing at his arm above his silvered hand. The technician was studying Cormac's open chest with great interest.

'I think you're right,' Cormac said to Mika. 'It was almost as if it was frantically searching the planet for them, and when it didn't find them there it turned its attention to us and grabbed them as quickly as it could.'

'Desperately,' added Mika.

'I don't know. Certainly without any regard for human life. We were lucky *Hubris* could take that kind of punishment.'

He fell silent. At least, most of them were lucky. Mika had been dealing with various injuries for some twenty hours now. Three of the crew were in life-support canisters, awaiting return to civilization. They might survive, though they would then be spending a long time in a regrowth tank. One of the runcible technicians had not been even that lucky; her head had been crushed to pulp when one of the runcible components had shifted and caught her against a wall

'Did Chaline have anything to say?' he asked her.

'Repairs are well under way, but she's not happy

335

about the delays. She's becoming very single-minded about her runcible.'

Mika stepped back from him with her gloved hands held up and away from her white coat. The gloves were quite bloody. She looked up at the screen above where Carn was sitting. This screen showed a scanned image of Cormac's chest. He had only looked at it once.

'Aiden?' he asked.

'He retrieved the shuttle. Cento's been stored . . . so has the shuttle; it's beyond repair. They're getting another one out of storage as soon as the shuttle bay has been repaired. Chaline was panicking about the heavy-lifter, but it was undamaged.'

She stepped close and started manipulating things in his chest again.

'Heavy-lifter?'

'In storage . . . one heavy-lifter and four minishuttles. Chaline needs the lifter to take down the runcible.'

'Oh . . . seems we might be all right . . .'

Mika did not immediately reply. Cormac felt more movement, then heard the low drone of the bone welder. He glanced down at that moment and wished he hadn't. From his solar plexus upwards, the skin and muscle of his chest had been peeled back. Mika had a finger shoved through a hole between two obviously broken ribs and was running the tip of the welder along the break. Cormac could smell something strangely dusty. Calcium particles had escaped the electrostatic process that was laying them down in the breaks.

'We are, I suppose,' said Mika, standing back again to view her work. 'But *Hubris* is going to be here some time. It needs parts brought from Minostra, and they'll have to come through the runcible. Not until then will it be able to leave orbit.' She placed the head of the welder back in its sterilizing holder and pushed the wheeled unit a little way back from the table. 'Cellweld Inc.' was the wording of the logo on this device, which was a silvered box on top of a wheeled trolley. A touch-console was mounted in the top of the box, and from the side of it issued a skein of pipes and cables. These terminated in a head that could take any of the racked adaptors stored underneath the box. Mika selected something that looked like a small glass spade. 'I've clamped the breaks just to give some support to the welds. I don't suppose you'll be resting for a while yet. The clamps will take a year to dissolve; plenty of time for your ribs to completely heal. I've dealt with most of the internal tissue damage. I'll seal you up now.'

Why was it, Cormac wondered, that doctors so relished telling you exactly what they were doing?

The welder droned and there were horrible sucking sounds in his chest. The tugging felt like what an errant child feels when its mother pulls on its coat.

'There, all done,' said Mika after what seemed an age. 'I've put a couple of analgesic tabs in, and they'll dissolve over the next few days. There might be the odd twinge, but you'll be all right now.' Behind her he saw the tubes of the remote lung clear of blood and felt the small tugs as she detached each of them. He did not get time to feel any lack of oxygen, for she reached immediately for the back of his neck. Feeling returned suddenly. There was no fading in, no pins and needles; his body just turned back on. He took a gasping breath and the sound of his heart was a sudden thunder.

'You are all right,' she said, even in this circumstance not prepared to ask a question. Cormac sat upright and looked down at his chest. It was flawless. Cell-welding left no scars, at least not on the body. He nodded to her. She smiled briefly at him, then turned to Carn.

'It's not pain and it's not physical function,' she said, resuming a conversation they had been having as Cormac had come in.

Carn opened and closed his silvered hand. 'I've lost PU contact. All I get is normal sensation.'

Cormac glanced at him. So that's what his hand was. The necessity of using separate instruments on the artefact must have been annoying for him, all for the sake of a glove. Cormac swung his legs over and stood up. He took up his shirt from where he had tossed it, and pulled it on. He could see that he was now completely dismissed from Mika's attention, and that she was totally focused on Carn. He left her to attend to him.

The drop-shafts were still out of commission, but that was not too much of a problem aboard a ship. It merely meant there was no irised field to drag him to his destination. He had to step into the shaft, where he became weightless, and shove off the inspection ladders in the direction he wanted to go. The trick, as with all weightless manoeuvring, was not to get up too much speed. Soon he stopped himself at the required level and headed for the recreation room, which had now become the centre of operations. He passed through corridors where robot welders were at work, and other areas where technicians had stripped panels away from the walls and were swearing in their own particular jargon. In some areas the gravity was somewhat changeable, which was more worrying than it being completely out. A fluctuating gravplate could quite easily smear a person across the floor. When he arrived in the recreation room he found only Thorn and Chaline. Chaline was watching a tablescreen. It showed a scene across the hull of *Hubris*. The ship was crawling with robots like cockroaches. Thorn was sprawled asleep on a couch, a flask lying on its side on the table next to him, with a half-full glass of Scotch next to it.

'How are things going?' Cormac asked Chaline.

Still watching the screen she said, 'Seventy hours and we should be fully secure. *Hubris* won't be able to go supralight until we get a new engine housing from Minostra. The ramfields are down.'

Cormac nodded, then said, 'I walked over some fluctuating grav out there.'

Chaline did not look round. 'No, you didn't. You walked over gravplates with a fluctuating power source. We had a little bit of a panic with one of the generators and had to shut it down.'

Cormac decided to ask no more concerning the damage. The list would just go on and on.

'*Hubris*, what's the situation with Dragon?' he asked as he walked over to the catering unit.

'Dragon is in orbit seven hundred kilometres ahead of us. There is some activity on its surface,' the ship replied.

At the catering unit Cormac said simply, 'Coffee,' as the machine now recognized his voice and would provide it exactly how he liked. He inspected the cup of white sludge it had provided, then fully keyed in his request. Another one to add to Chaline's list. When he finally got the drink he was after, he returned to Chaline's table and sat down.

'Right, tell me, what's the activity?'

The screen changed to show Dragon, and Chaline looked at Cormac in annoyance. He shrugged apologetically, then returned his attention to the screen. Ripples were travelling all round the surface of the alien.

Hubris said, 'One hour ago there was an energy emission directed away from the Andellan system. It was full-spectrum lased light. The reading was in the gigajoule range. If the same pattern is being followed this time round, another emission will occur in fifty-four minutes. I am moving the ship to the other side of the planet, and have left just one observer probe.'

At that particular moment Cormac felt he would rather be on the other side of the galaxy. Was Dragon getting ready to destroy them? If it was they were in serious trouble.

'Anything else?'

'I am also picking up emissions across all spectrums. Some of them have some internal logic and mathematical coherency, but I have not as yet been able to translate. These emissions are directionless.'

'OK,' said Cormac, and the screen flicked back to the scene Chaline had been observing. He studied her and noted how she was deliberately keeping her face free of expression.

'All yours,' he said with a smile.

'Thank you so much,' she said, then pushed her chair back and stood up. 'Unfortunately some of us have work to do.'

Cormac made a gesture of appeasement, but Chaline

walked away. He couldn't decide if she was angry or amused. Involvement, he thought, trying not to feel guilty. He sat there sipping for the next few minutes, then called up again the scene from the probe.

Dragon was rippling even faster now, and its spherical shape was being distorted.

'*Hubris*, are you sure we're safe here?' he asked.

The AI's reply was succinct. 'No.'

The fifty-four-minute mark passed. Sixty minutes was reached, sixty-five . . . The flash momentarily blacked out the picture from the probe. When it came back, Dragon was spherical again, the ripples moving across its surface just as Cormac had first witnessed.

'*Hubris*, where did that one go?'

'The planet's surface. Imaging in . . . the probe has it.'

The picture showed a spreading black cloud with hellish red fires at the centre of it.

'That was Mount Prometheus,' said *Hubris*.

Cormac shook his head in amazement. Enoida Deacon would not be displaced from her niche in the history books, but what the hell was Dragon doing?

'I have picked up something from Dragon. It's in all human languages.'

'Let's hear the English version then.'

Dragon's voice boomed from the speakers. 'Escaped! Escaped! Criminal! Bastard! Damn! Fuck! Fuckit!'

Cormac sat there with his mouth open. So that was what Dragon was doing – it was having a tantrum.

20

Chameleon: How often there is confusion and misuse of the extensions of this word. The 'chameleon-wear' refers only to clothing made from the photoreactive fibres developed by ECS in 2257. It is merely an effective form of camouflage, and does not render the wearer invisible. It just blends said wearer in with his or her background. The 'chameleonware' is a different matter. It is hardware that, using field technologies, can bend light round an object, blank out heat signatures, blur air disturbances, and make said object radar and sonar inert.

From *Quince Guide*, compiled by humans

Pelter took one pass over the lake before banking the bird and coming on in. The screen, set to infrared, showed him all he needed to see, in pastel shades of blue and green like the negative of a colour photograph. He applied the aerobrakes and noted small contrails that revealed the wings, but that was no problem at this altitude. Through Mr Crane's eyes he studied the collapsed bulk of Stanton lying on the floor, and considered how to kill him. His enjoyment at wiping out

342

that arrogant ship captain had quickly faded. Now he surprised himself with the acknowledgement that Stanton's death was not something he wanted to see. The mercenary had to die because of his intended betrayal, but he had been a good friend for some years. There was a bitter taste in Pelter's mouth as he watched the lake come into sight. In his aug he called up an image of Stanton and slipped it in to the requisite slot of a program in Crane's command module. It was the same program he had used for Tenel and many others. He would set it running when he felt ready, and then did not have to watch.

The whistle of the wind across the skids as he lowered them was the loudest sound heard during their long flight to land. The next cacophony was when those skids hit the surface of the lake. Pelter glanced back and saw the foaming wake, and that was all right as well, for anything they did now would be beneath the notice of the runcible AI – or, rather, anything they did from now up to the point when they started using proscribed weapons. Pelter eased the bird round and directed it to the shore of the lake. The land beyond rose not much above the surface level of the lake. In the distance there was a collection of boulders, and beyond that was what Pelter knew to be the beginning of a huge forest, though of what type he did not know. The highest items nearby were reeds and sedges growing at the edge of the water, apart from the dropbird itself. Only a couple of blasts of the compressed-air impeller were required to push the bird through the reeds and onto the squelchy shore. Pelter unclipped his belt and looked round at them.

'A few solstan hours until sunrise,' he said. 'We'll rest until then.'

'What about him?' said Corlackis, stabbing a finger at Stanton.

'In the morning,' Pelter replied, then eased his seat back into a rest position and closed his eye. The four behind did the same. He watched them through Mr Crane's eyes before eventually allowing himself to rest completely.

His body felt like a block of lead on the soft ground. He felt sick and his shoulder hurt, and a tiny blacksmith was making horseshoes inside his head. This was worse than the worst of hangovers. The smell of peat filled his nostrils and he tasted earth in his mouth. Opening his left eye he got a low view of palegreen ferns sprouting from the black soil. Beyond them some thick green growth was smeared across the ground. For a moment he had absolutely no idea where he was, or what was happening. When memory returned, he discovered it *was* possible to feel worse than he already felt.

Jarvellis.

Stanton heaved himself up onto his elbows, then puked yellow bile. Pain lanced his skull at every convulsion. In a way that was preferable to the other pain.

'Give him another shot,' said Pelter.

Stanton just managed to look round as Corlackis squatted by him and pressed an injector against his neck. He felt the stuff go in and immediately start to kill his nausea. The pain in his head started to fade also. He felt he might be able to stand now, but just didn't want to. The other pain had expanded to fill every space.

'Get up, John,' said Pelter.

Stanton tried to feel angry, but found he just couldn't find the energy for it. He pushed himself to his knees, then unsteadily to his feet. Mennecken and Svent were sitting on a crate unloaded from the dropbird. Dusache was leaning against the bird itself, grounded on the shore of the lake. A curious sight, as he seemed to be standing at an impossible angle. Corlackis stepped aside and Stanton was looking at Pelter, who had Mr Crane at his back. No chance to hit him, Stanton thought. Of course, given the opportunity he would kill Pelter, but he knew he would not be given that opportunity.

'His knife,' said Pelter.

Corlackis reached into the pocket of his coat and took out a plastic-wrapped package. It hit Stanton on the chest, and fell to the ground. He continued to stare at Pelter.

'It's your knife, John. Pick it up and return it to its sheath.'

Stanton did as he was told. What was the game now? Him with a knife up against Crane?

'Give him his gun as well.'

Corlackis looked askance at Pelter, before reaching into his jacket and taking out Stanton's pulse-gun.

'Take the charge out first, Corlackis,' Pelter said, when the gun was about to be handed over. Corlackis pulled the charge and handed the gun to Stanton. Pelter held out his hand and Corlackis handed him the charge. Pelter turned and threw it out across the bleak moorland. Stanton tracked its progress and saw it land amongst a rare mass of the green growth. A cloud of objects shot into the air where it landed. Stanton took that as a sign of his present luck. The charge had prob-ably landed in a nest of this planet's equivalent of hornets.

'I don't know what it was you intended, but that you intended something with Jarvellis I have no doubt. I trusted you, John. I even liked you,' said Pelter.

Stanton said, 'You like no one but yourself, Pelter, and even that has changed. Look at what you've become.'

Pelter reached up and touched his face, realized what he was doing, and snatched his hand back down. Behind him Crane eased forwards. Stanton noted that the brief-case was on the ground. So that was the way it was going to be. What use would he have for a pulse-gun or his knife?

'Because I thought you were a friend, John, I'm letting you go. Just go – get out of my sight,' said Pelter.

Stanton looked around. He was certainly dead. He wondered if Pelter would even let him get to his gun's charge before sending Crane after him. He holstered his gun, turned, and set out at a jog across the spongy growth. Already the survival instincts that had got him through many a bad situation were taking over. He almost felt ashamed of them, but did not have the strength to resist. In a minute he reached the spread of green growth. Helicopter seeds, not hornets, were scattered all about. The charge was caught in an inter-section of two thick leaves, which had the appearance of molten plastic. He took it up, drew his gun, and slapped the charge into place. Glancing back he saw that only Dusache, Corlackis and Mr Crane were in view. Corlackis was now holding a laser carbine, its butt resting on his hip. The message was plain. Stanton turned and headed for the distant forest, picking up his pace all the time.

The further he got from the lake the firmer became the ground underfoot. Ferns and the other weird green growths were displaced by what appeared to be low heather. Between the growths of this were narrow animal trails. Stanton reached a cluster of three monolithic boulders and rested his hand against the crystalline and fossil-etched surface. A glance back showed him no action at the lake. Some of them were standing watching him, but from this distance he could not identify which of them. He ran on. He had to keep up his speed and get as far away as possible, before Pelter got bored and sent Crane in pursuit. Then, again, maybe he would not? Stanton snorted at this momentary flash of uncharacteristic optimism.

The trees of this forest had to be some kind of coniferous adaptation. As he drew closer Stanton saw that they had the shape of pines, but bore translucent red fruits the size of a fist. Closer still and he saw needles that were flat blades, and trunks that had the appearance of sections of laminate wood. Running between these square-section trunks, he glanced back. A tall figure was loping towards him from the lake. It surprised him how much reserve he managed to call up from his boosted muscles.

On through the trees, the fallen needles a crunchy grey carpet underfoot. Stanton considered pulling his pulse-gun and triggering it under his chin. He did not know what Pelter had in mind, so that option would at least be quick. He rejected the idea. The gaps between the trunks were wide, and the ground an easy surface to run across. Stanton scanned for somewhere to hide, then wondered why the hell he was doing so. Crane would hear his ragged breaths, even his heartbeat. Ahead he heard the sound of rushing water, and accelerated when he thought this might offer him a chance of escape. Beating up-slope now, he glanced back. No sign of Crane, but the android might be circling round. Stanton could not change his course now. In a straight run he stood no chance: Crane was faster than him and just did not need to rest. The river was his only hope. Soon he crested a ridge and saw the heavy swirl of glassy water below. The roar came from his left. He jogged down the slope to where stone slabs shelved the edge of the water. Here the conifers were displaced by blue oaks, their acorns scattered on the ground like bird's eggs. A glance back gave him more impetus. Crane was loping along under the conifers, kicking up masses of needles at every step as his huge weight sank into the ground. That was it: the weight! When he reached the slabs, Stanton turned and drew his pulse-gun. It had its full charge: over fifty shots. He aimed very carefully and pressed down on the trigger.

White fire cut a stuttering stream between Stanton and the android. Crane was taking another loping step as it hit, and the fusillade flung him back, thumping into the front of his coat, smoke and flame and pieces of burning cloth flying in every direction. He landed and slipped, shots still hitting him, and then he went over on his back. A few seconds at most it had given Stanton. He did not wait to see if the android would get up. He knew the answer to that as he dived into the river.

The water was icy, but Stanton hardly noticed. He struck out with a powerful crawl stroke downstream. Behind him there was a huge splash. He glanced back and saw a hat floating on the surface and found himself grinning maniacally at that. Crane had tried to follow him, neglecting to take into account the fact that he was made of case-hardened ceramal. Stanton hoped the water was deep. He swam harder, a sudden vision in his mind of Crane striding along the riverbed after him. Ahead of him the roar grew in volume. Happy day: a waterfall. He tried to strike out for the edge of the river, but the current was too strong now. It dragged him to a green-slimed lip of stone and tipped him over into white water. He went feet first, hoping thus to absorb some of the impact of whatever might lie below.

A cold, deep pool greeted him, and he was dragged and tumbled through water fizzing like tonic. Gasping he came to the surface beyond the fall, and looked back again. Something hit the water hard behind him. He looked ahead, to where the river spread wide over slabbed stone, then struck out – only to have his hand slap down on that stone. A few strokes and the water was too shallow to swim in. He stood, drew his gun, and waded as quickly through the water as he could. He slipped at almost every step. Perhaps now was the time to put the gun under his chin. One shot was all he needed, and he had about ten left. A glance behind showed him a bronze hand coming up out the water and snatching a hat from the surface. Crazy android. Mr Crane walked up out of the pool, straightening the brim of his hat. Stanton turned and faced him.

There was nothing to say. Pelter might be watching

through Crane's eyes, or not, but Stanton was damned if he was going to beg. He was damned if he was going to give up either. Trying to recover his breath he waited for Crane, his gun down at his side. Crane looked from side to side in that curious birdlike manner.

When he was only a few metres away Stanton lifted his gun and fired his remaining shots. Crane leant into them. Each pulse of ionized aluminium just caused a momentary glow on his armoured chest, maybe a little pitting in the surface, but the glow quickly disappeared as the heat was dispersed through the s-con network imbedded in his armour. When the gun was empty, Stanton threw it at the android. A brass hand snatched the weapon, shattered it, and tossed the pieces aside. This was it. Crane stepped in and Stanton tried a stamp kick on his knee. He might more easily have tried to knock over an oak. Crane grabbed the front of his jacket, hoisted him into the air, and threw him. Stanton came down on his back in the shallow water with slimed rocks cracking against his spine. Crane came striding in again as he tried to stand. A backhand slap laid Stanton across the damp needles on the shore. What was the use? A boot like a ram flipped him over onto his back. Crane stooped over him, black eyes giving nothing. It might as well have been a slab of metal that was killing him. A huge brass hand closed around his throat and he was lifted once again.

Maybe the eyes. Maybe he could at least damage this toy of Pelter's?

Stanton flicked the Tenkian ring round with his thumb. He felt the tug at his trouser leg as the dagger came out through the rip it had made before. Forest light glittered off the yellow chainglass blade and the handle slapped into his hand. He swung at Crane's eyes, and the android's other hand snapped up and caught his wrist. The point of the blade was a hand's breadth from those black eyes. Crane blinked and did nothing while Stanton choked. Abruptly, he released Stanton's throat. Stanton yelled as all his weight came down on his right shoulder. Crane pulled the blade from Stanton's hand and then, in a moment, just discarded him.

The lights in the Tenkian were flickering as it no doubt tried to give Mr Crane a shock. Crane was oblivious to the electrical charge, but not oblivious to the pretty lights and the beauty of the weapon. He held it between his two forefingers and studied it for a long time. Stanton just lay there, recovering his breath. His right shoulder felt like it was dislocated, and he'd definitely cracked a few ribs. There was no point in running now. He just waited for the inevitable.

Crane finished his long study of the Tenkian dagger, then slipped it into the pocket of his coat. He glanced at Stanton, lifted a forefinger up to his metal mouth, held it there for a moment, before stepping over him and walking off into the forest.

Her left leg hurt like hell, and felt warm and sticky inside the suit. In a way she wished that the sealant layer sandwiched between the armour and the inner suit had not done its job so well. Had it not, she would not face the prospect of suffocating in about twenty minutes from now. The *Lyric* was gone, John was either dead or soon would be, Pelter would see to that, and the safety lock on her suit even precluded her opening the helmet to vacuum. Jarvellis hung in space over Viridian and watched pieces of her ship flaring in atmosphere below her – when she could see through her tears.

The old ring station was perhaps a few hundred metres away behind her. Straining round she could see a light deep inside it, behind exposed structural members. That option was closed to her as well. She had used up all the fuel in the suit's impellers in order to escape the blast. 'Get out,' John had said. She had heard him clear, even as she had blown the airlock door and fired-up the impellers. The disc of fire had cut below her, then the debris cloud riding the blastwave had slammed into her back and tumbled her over and over. No doubt the piece of the *Lyric* that had punched into her thigh had been a fragment of chainglass. It had been one of many hits she had felt, and nothing else could have penetrated the ceramal armour.

Eventually her tears dried and Jarvellis tried her comunit again. Again she just got silence. The EM pulse from the explosion must have burnt out the suit's radio. Planar explosives had been used, and they did not produce such a pulse. It had come from one of the secondary explosions, either when the pile went or when the disc cut the underspace engine in half. There would be recovery ships up from Viridian in time, but they would come too late for her. Rescue was not an option, and only two others remained: either she died slowly in the suit or . . . Jarvellis reached down and unclipped the solid-state laser clipped to the suit's utility belt. It wouldn't work through the helmet, as the chainglass would automatically polarize. She needed to hold it over her heart. She estimated it would take about a minute to penetrate the suit.

No more grief now. Everything was gone and now there was just her. Then . . . then she remembered the other life starting inside her, and that only made everything seem worse. She looked down at the laser in her heavy glove. It was just a matt cylinder with a button on one end.

Oh, John . . .

She put the business end of the laser against her chest and pressed the button. Red light ignited at the point of contact and vaporized ceramal flared away in an orange fog. Any moment now she would be through. There would be sudden pain, then quick death. The laser broke through, but there was no expected pain. The explosion slammed at her chest and flung her hand away. As she hurtled back, she saw the laser tumbling through space on a trail of glittering fragments.

'Oh, fuck you. Fuck you!'

Fifteen minutes of air left, and the display was still heading down. She had achieved the end she required, though not by the expected method. She knew exactly what had happened. The sealant had hardened on exposure to vacuum. The laser had cut through it and then it had broken under the air pressure in her suit. But it went further than that, which was the reason these old suits had been replaced. The epoxy-based sealant, once hardened, lost its flame-retardant properties. Under the blast of air, white-hot epoxy had exploded.

'Goodbye, John,' Jarvellis said, and thought that perhaps the shadows she was seeing at the edges of her vision were due to the sudden drop in air pressure.

Abruptly she realized this was not so, she was seeing a framework of structural members silhouetted against Viridian, a second before she slammed into a wall inside the ring station. As the counter dropped to zero, and she gasped on nothing, she had enough humour left to appreciate the irony of it all.

21

Antiphoton Weapon (APW): In this case the term 'antiphoton' is a misnomer attributable to the propaganda core of the Jovian Separatists (either that or hopeful thinking). The beam projected from this weapon is a proton beam, the protons having been field-accelerated to near-light speed. The distinctive purple flash or beam, is not, as some fictional sources would have us believe, the fabled 'darklight'. It is fluorescence caused by proton collision with air molecules. In pure vacuum the beam is invisible. The aforesaid fictional sources would also do well to remember that the firing of a proton weapon is a serious matter, the usual result of which is isotope contamination. The bad guys don't just disappear in an elegant purple flash.

From *How It Is* by Gordon

Mika was watching a screen showing a view down the shaft towards the artefact. In the picture Cormac recognized the rear view of Carn, Cormac himself, Gant and Cento. The guardian creature was coming up the shaft.

'Jesus!' yelled Gant.

Cormac waited for his shouted instruction for them to 'Hit it'. Mika froze the picture at the point when the creature was in fullest view. Cormac's recorded shout was stillborn.

'I downloaded this copy from Aiden's memory,' said Mika, without turning.

'What do you make of it?'

'Terrifying, fascinating.'

'All of that,' said Cormac dryly.

She turned to him. 'If I hadn't known the shaft had been made by melting and rock-compression, I would have said that creature hollowed it out somehow; that it was its natural home before the temperature dropped. The shaft is perfectly designed to accommodate it. But for the ice, it would have moved up much faster.'

'And you are saying?'

'The reverse: the creature was specially designed for the shaft. It was a guardian *created* for that place.'

She walked past him to a bench on which were laid the pieces of the creature which Thorn had brought back. She picked up the end of one silvered leg.

'There is no real defence against energy weapons, but what defence there is this creature had: reflective skin and an effective method of heat dispersal. It was also armoured enough to deal with most projectile weapons.' She pointed at the screen. 'Its dimensions were perfect for the shaft.'

'Machine or living thing,' said Cormac, remembering a previous conversation, 'it didn't evolve.'

'No, it has no means of reproduction. It was definitely *made*.' She glanced at him again. 'And its construction is

strikingly similar to that of the dracomen. It does not
have DNA; it used protein replication.'

Cormac thought about that for a moment.

Dragon again?

'You just said, "Its natural home before the temperature dropped." What did you mean by that?'

Mika put down the silvered leg and picked up another
piece of the creature: a flattened ovoid with ribs along
one side. 'This is one of its feet. It's very like one of the
toes of such lizards as the gecko on Earth or the srank on
Circe. It would have been perfectly designed for gripping onto the rock of that shaft if there was no ice there.'
She dropped the foot. 'Also, from what I have discovered thus far, it was reaching the edge of its
survivability. Had the temperature gone below one-sixty
Kelvin it would have become somnolent. Much lower
than that and it would have died.'

'But the dracomen were managing,' said Cormac.

Mika gazed at her collection of body parts. 'This creature was not so complex as them. It did not have the
ability to adapt . . .'

'Questions occur,' said Cormac, looking back at the
screen. '*Why* was that artefact being guarded? And what
put the guard there? Whatever did, it did not know the
temperature was going to drop. The creature was placed
there before the runcible went down. Yet, the dracomen . . . Were they sent here to retrieve the artefact?
Was *that* Dragon's purpose?' He shook his head. 'If so,
why was the runcible destroyed?'

'I believe some other alien is involved,' said Mika.

Cormac turned to her. 'Why?'

'Because of the artefact. I've been checking through

the Dragon/human dialogues and other papers. Remember, when you went to Aster Colora – that two-kilometre perimeter? Dragon has no use of machines. Everything it makes is more complex – living. That arte-fact is not a product of Dragon's technology.'

'Yes . . . maybe . . . but the guardian? We run in circles. Every clue leads to more questions . . . *Hubris*, what is Dragon doing now?'

'Dragon is still destroying things on the planet. We have no picture now, since one burst destroyed the probe.'

To Mika, Cormac said, 'That's where I hope to get some answers, no matter how cryptic they may be.'

'Dragon tells lies,' Mika observed.

'You can learn something even from lies,' said Cormac, then left her to her work.

Cormac looked down into the huge main bay, at the rows of bubble-metal crates, superconductor cable and sheet, in reels and rolls, the massive shapes of the Skaidon horns in their shock packaging, one of which had killed the technician working on it, and at the two hemispheres of the containment vessel. He watched the technicians moving about the bay, checking this, taking readings here. They were not checking the runcible itself – as that would not be necessary until it was assembled – rather, they were checking the huge amount of equip-ment that would be used to install it. Most of these technicians carried notescreens. Others carried esoteric equipment, or were followed by robots doing so. The belly of the giant heavy-lifter, its loading hatches open, walled the back of the bay.

'Bloody Dragon,' said Chaline. By her expression when he asked her how things were proceeding, Cormac had already surmised she was not happy.

'Was there damage?'

'No damage to the runcible,' she said, glaring at him.

Cormac cursed himself. Was he so inured to death? 'I was sorry to hear about . . . the—'

'Her name was Jentia. She was a bloody good technician.'

'I'm sorry.'

'What are you going to do? Do you actually care about anything? It killed her – as good as murdered her. It could have killed us all, and it may well have killed the inhabitants of Samarkand. That Darson was probably right.'

'How would you suggest I go about arresting a half-million-ton alien psychopath?'

Chaline turned away for a moment. When she turned back again, it was with a deprecatory smile twisting her lips. 'That was irrational of me,' she said.

'Understandable, but you see the problems I am faced with? I . . . it's part of the reason I—'

'Yes,' Chaline interrupted. 'You and me both. Let's leave it . . . Do you know what we saw Dragon doing before the probe was destroyed?'

'Throwing a tantrum, blowing mountains apart,' he replied with some relief.

'Yes, and everything else down there. It is geostationary over the blast-site. I had hoped to use some of the remaining installations there. Last we saw, it was destroying them.'

'By accident?'

'You could say that, I suppose. That shaft was hit as well: sealed under a pile of rubble and molten rock.'

Was Dragon really just throwing a tantrum?

Whatever it was, it ceased twenty hours later.

'Weapons charged and ready to fire,' said the innocuous voice of *Hubris*. Those weapons were what Carn had hinted might be used to excavate the artefact: to blow away two kilometres of rock. They were now directed towards the curve of Samarkand from where Dragon approached, silhouetted against the dim sun like some fighting machine from Earth's bloody past. The weapons could be used now; at this distance it was possible to prevent impact and not be damaged by flashback.

'Open a channel,' said Cormac. 'Let's see what it wants.'

'Dragon accelerating at three Gs,' said *Hubris*.

'We can't stand another collision yet,' said Chaline.

'Dragon, if you come closer than one hundred kilometres we will fire on you. This is our perimeter,' said Cormac.

'Dragon slowing ... two hundred and seventy kilometres ... two hundred and fifty ...'

'If it looks as if it's building up to let loose another charge, fire on it anyway,' Cormac told *Hubris*, leaving the channel open so Dragon would hear.

'Where is it? Where is it?' boomed Dragon's voice over the speakers.

'Where is what, Dragon?'

'The criminal! Where is the criminal?'

'We do not know about any criminal. We came here to

investigate the destruction of the Samarkand runcible, and the consequent deaths of ten thousand people.'

'—one hundred and fifty kilometres . . . one hundred and forty . . .'

When Dragon spoke next, its voice had dropped to a conversational level. 'It killed your people. I tried to stop it, Ian Cormac, but it escaped and killed your people. The confinement vessel should have held it.'

Cormac turned and looked at Carn. 'Confinement vessel?'

Carn shrugged. 'What the hell would have needed adamantium to confine it? It must have been quite something, and to break out . . .'

Dragon answered his question. 'The creature confined was a Maker. Its kind *made* me. It is a criminal . . . In your limited way, you would call it psychopath. It is an energy creature.'

Cormac looked at Chaline. 'Psychopath,' he said.

To Dragon he said, 'This Maker, it made the nanomycelium that damaged the runcible buffers?'

'It did. I picked up readings that indicated anomalies in this sector and, knowing the confinement vessel was here, I sent my creatures, by way of your runcibles, to investigate. They came here after the Maker escaped its vessel. It left the mycelium to destroy your runcible and prevent them following.'

Cormac closed the channel momentarily. 'It ties with what you found out about that guardian,' he said to Mika. 'Same technology as Dragon uses. That's plausible if its kind made Dragon.'

Mika said, 'Plausibility does not denote truth.'

'It does not, and of course there are your thoughts on

what Dragon might or might not make,' said Cormac, looking at her meaningfully.

'That was . . . speculation,' Mika admitted, a pained expression on her face. 'A confinement vessel for some kind of energy creature would of necessity not be biofactured.'

'By any method we know,' Cormac added.

Mika's pained expression became one of annoyance. 'Quite,' she said, not meeting his eyes.

Cormac nodded and opened the channel again. 'What do you mean by "energy creature" and where is it now?'

'Its substance is mainly gaseous, and it is held together by lattices of force much like your shimmer-shields. I do not know where it is now. It has escaped via your runcibles.'

Cormac closed the channel again. 'Do you notice a certain lack of resemblance to previous Dragon dialogue?' he said to them all.

Mika said, 'It is answering your questions directly.'

'Precisely. That makes me very suspicious.'

He reopened the channel. 'Dragon, there is little we can do about this creature now. We came here to install a new runcible, and we wish to set about this work. Have you finished scorching Samarkand?' He could not keep the sarcasm from his voice.

Dragon took a long time replying. 'The criminal must be found. The danger to your kind is great. It has taken ten thousand lives. Next time it might take millions.'

'I repeat: there is little we can do about this now. We need the runcible installed so that communications can be opened with the grid. Then perhaps some way can be

362

found to trace this Maker. Tell me, in what ways is it vulnerable?'

'You have devices . . . Your proton weapons, contraterrene bombs . . .'

'These will kill it?'

'If they do not kill it, they will hurt it sufficiently to make it run. It knows your runcibles now. It will run for them.'

'But why should we want it to run?'

'So it goes somewhere else.'

This was more like the Dragon of old: it was playing semantic games with life-and-death issues. Cormac paused for a moment of thought before continuing.

'Dragon, what did you intend to do had the Maker been here, and free from its containment vessel, when you arrived?'

'Now you have a grasp of the basics, Ian Cormac.'

'You would have killed it here, then. And you still can,' said Cormac. Then he added, 'We have a runcible to install now.'

'I will not hinder you. But you may take onboard my creatures. They will assist you. They will obey every command. This I offer in reparation.'

'Accept or die,' whispered Thorn.

Cormac did not like this. He felt, as he always felt with Dragon, that a lot was not being told. He especially did not like an offer of reparation that was not open to negotiation. Should he refuse, and risk more of the wrath they had just witnessed? He let the thought slide, and in that moment decided there was one more question that needed an answer.

'Dragon, where is . . . the rest of you?'

The reply came slowly. 'We are at the four corners of your galaxy, Ian Cormac.'

Cormac thought how apposite this was. He visualized star maps with little arrows pointing to the darkness at the edge of the galaxy, and there written the words: 'Here be dragons.'

'An object has been launched from Dragon towards us.'

'Scan it. If it looks suspicious, destroy it.'

'It contains the two dracomen.'

'OK, bring them in,' said Cormac. There seemed little else to do. He was not about to start becoming argumentative with Dragon just as he was beginning to get some answers, truth or not. He closed the channel with the alien, and turned to Chaline.

'You can get on with it now,' he said.

She smiled happily and left the room.

'How much of that did you believe?' Cormac asked Mika, Thorn and Aiden.

'I think it will let us set up the runcible, and I believe it is genuinely after whatever was in that artefact. Beyond that its motivations are debatable,' said Mika.

'All of it is plausible,' said Aiden. 'One must question one's own motives for distrust.'

Cormac answered him. 'Dragon has little regard for human life; we know this. Why would it be concerned about the possible deaths of a few million people?'

Aiden looked thoughtful for a moment, and then said, 'You are correct. It has motivated us because it requires our assistance. This makes a number of its claims invalid. I concur with Mika.'

'Thorn?' asked Cormac.

'Tapestry of fucking lies, old man,' said Thorn, smiling bleakly.

Cormac was sitting on his bed, wondering about the possibility of sleep, when there came a knock at his door.

'Come in,' he said.

In came Jane, apparently no less a goddess because she wore baggy overalls.

'Jane, please, sit down.'

Jane swished into the single chair with an economy of movement and an elegance that was enviable. She had a grace that Aiden lacked. But Aiden had a brute power she lacked. Both of them could have squashed the likes of Thorn without needing their artificial sweat glands.

'What do you require of me?' she asked, crossing her legs.

Cormac rubbed at his forehead. 'Chaline told me that your speciality was secondary installation. You deal with AIs normally, which was why she could release you to me last time. You hadn't a lot to do then.'

Jane smiled. 'Yes, that is correct.'

'That submind we brought back – *Hubris* can't get through to it. It's completely internalized. Do you have any suggestions as to how we might get through?'

'It would be kinder to shut it down. It was part of the Samarkand AI, and as such more of a *fragment* of a mind. The destruction of the rest of it has driven it insane.'

'No, I can't allow it to be shut down.'

'Might I ask why?'

'Dragon.'

'You think it contains vital information?'

'All I know is that when Dragon was scorching the planet, it managed to vaporize every remaining installation of the Samarkand runcible. It was all well disguised, as it scorched the entire area. But I find it suspicious for all that.'

'Destroying the evidence?'

'Looks like it.'

'What do you hope to find?'

'Perhaps some chronology to these events. There might be a record of when the dracomen arrived, or when the Maker left . . .' He paused and stared off to one side. 'Shit! Blegg!'

'I beg your pardon?'

'He knew! The bastard knew!'

Jane waited. Cormac went on.

'When he sent me here, he told me the runcible AI managed to transmit some information. I bet it told him about the arrival of the dracomen. That's why he sent me.'

'Does this mean the submind can now be shut down?'

'No, definitely not. All we can be sure of is that he knew about the dracomen, and about the runcible going down. There might be more. What were the events surrounding these various arrivals and departures? I need to know. Will you try?'

'If you so wish.'

Jane glided to her feet and with a quick smile she left him. He lay back on his bed. He could see what Blegg had done: given him the minimum of information so he would have to get over the effects of gridlinking and approach the problem without preconceptions. Did Blegg believe Dragon had destroyed the runcible? Or did he have some inkling of Dragon's version of events? Whatever the answer, Cormac knew he could not expect Blegg to deliver it to him. He was on his own, as always. Half-truths and outright lies, the casual killing of thousands; Blegg knew what motivated him. Cormac was determined that he would not let go until he had found some answers and someone, or something, roasted for what had happened here. He did not like playing the fool.

22

The lines between sciences have, in the last few centuries, become wide grey wastelands where questions of science become questions of philosophy and sometimes of religion. If you can build a human, molecule for molecule like any other human, then is he a human? Perhaps it is a question that will not need to be answered. Though we have the capability, we do not have the inclination. We can build better than nature now. We can now design and build machines that make some of the creations of evolution seem comparatively clunky. Of course, you then have to think about whether or not this is merely a continuance of evolution, then you're back to philosophy again.

From *How It Is* by Gordon

Twenty years in the ES regulars had left Cheryl with a jaundiced view of human nature and an almost supernatural recognition of potential shitstorms. When she saw the huge figure standing amongst the rows of vines, she did not shout a greeting nor ask that figure its business. She immediately ducked down, accessed her aug, and sent out a recall to the pickers. A two-and-a-half-metre-tall metal-skin would not come to the crop house to enquire about the passionfruit business, nor to purchase juice for one of the wine makers. Cheryl kept utterly still and hoped that the android had not heard her, and she felt some relief when the first of the pickers came along the rows.

These pickers were something to make the skin crawl on anyone who had not been born on Viridian. They were made so that they could scuttle through the vines without causing too much damage as they selected fruits of the required ripeness. Upon finding such a fruit, they did not actually pick it, but they would grip it in their mandibles and suck it dry; and once their sacklike bodies were full, they would go to empty themselves at one of the juicing stations. The AI that had designed them had taken their template from an Earth lifeform perfectly suited to this task. That lifeform was good at both scuttling and sucking things dry. Each picker, as a result, was a black plastic spider with a body the size of a football.

The android flicked its head from side to side as the spiders moved past it. Cheryl set a loop in their programs so they would keep searching the rows in that same area, then very carefully backed away. Now, with any luck, the android would not hear her: the scuttling in the growths might cover the sounds of her breathing and her heartbeat. When she had put four rows between herself and potential trouble, she crouched down by the small silo of a juicing station and put a call, through her aug, to the authorities in the capital. She was unsurprised to find her signal blocked. Just as she was unsurprised to see a man, another two rows across, walking towards the crop house. This man was dressed in plain businesswear, had black hair, and a black sunband across his eyes. The giveaway was the Drescon assault rifle he had hanging from a shoulder strap.

Cheryl very carefully moved in the opposite direction from him. His attention was firmly fixed on the crop house and he was speaking into a comunit. So, there were others. Cheryl was very glad of the habit of dress she had acquired during those twenty years, a habit reinforced by the tendency of some Viridian inhabitants to sneak in and empty juicing stations in order to make a shilling or two with the wine makers. Her ES battle fatigues were chameleon cloth. Had they not been she felt sure she would be dead by now.

Five small thuds came in quick succession from her right. Not from the man she had already spotted. She froze and felt a sudden surge of fear. Until the moment she heard the horrible mosquito whining that followed immediately upon the shots, this had almost been like a training exercise. Seeker bullets! Whoever these people were, they were using seeker bullets. The sound of smashing glass leavened her fear. The shots had been fired at the crop house. Had she been inside, the bullets would have found her by now, homing in on her body heat to detonate at her skin in a blast of micro-shrapnel. A couple of small explosions then came from the house. The bullets had probably decided on hitting the most likely heat sources. That meant the central heating in the house would be gone.

Cheryl reached round to the back of her head and undid the neck pocket of her fatigues. She pulled the hood over and fixed the mask across. Now she could take the risk of standing and having a look. Three men walked out from between the vines and into the yard of the crop house. They were talking and gesturing. The android just stood there with a briefcase clutched in its brass hand. It gave her the creeps. She auged up a visual intensifier program, and got X10. Now she could study these intruders more closely. Two of the men looked the typical suited thugs that some organizations recruited. The third man, in his mesh shirt and baggy fatigue trousers, seemed to be in charge. There also seemed to be something wrong with him. She downloaded what she was seeing as a visual file, then slowly dropped back down. The face of the man she enclosed in a frame, and had the aug tidy up, was a mess. He had some sort of optical link that did not seem to have taken so well, and his face was haggard and scabby. She stood again to see what they would do next, and now set her aug to record everything she was seeing and hearing.

One of the suits crossed the yard to the transporter: an AGC that was simply an open-backed truck with a framework able to carry juicing stations. The other suit walked around to the back of the house, and soon returned driving Cheryl's personal AGC. So that was what this was all about: they just wanted transport. Good. Once they secured it and went on their way, whatever blocker they had would go with them. She watched while the android tore the framework from the back of the transporter and tossed it aside before taking its place there. Foamed steel frame: it had to be strong to take the weight of the juicing stations. Cheryl swallowed dryly. She had definitely made the right move. The other suit got into her AGC – she would have liked to have known how they broke the security lock – and the leader sat at the controls of the transporter. Soon they were up in the sky and roaring overhead, all turbines opened at full. Cheryl waited until they were out of sight before heading back into the crop house. She had almost reached the door when a hand caught her shoulder.

Cheryl reacted. She caught the hand, pulled on it, and drove her elbow back as hard as she could. No pulling punches; this was life or death. Her blow elicited a grunt. The next thing she knew there was a grip on the back of her fatigues, on her arm, and she was airborne. She hit the ground flat on her back, spun her legs to give her momentum, and then flipped up into a fighting crouch. The man standing before her was heavily built, had cropped ginger hair, and seemed to have been in the wars. As she pulled her pathetic chainglass pruning knife, just one thought went through her mind. *Fuck: boosted.*

'I could have let you go in,' said John Stanton, holding his hand to his torso and looking ill. Cheryl paused at that. If she ran, she would probably get it in the back. 'What do you mean?' she asked.

'They stole a personal AGC. So they'd have known someone was here.'

'So?'

'You army?'

'I was.'

'Then you should know about seeker bullets. Programmed levels of targeting. Five shots and two explosions. What does that mean, soldier?'

Cheryl got a sudden cold shudder when she realized what he was saying. 'You're not with them?' she asked.

'Not now,' said Stanton. 'And I suggest we put a bit of distance between us and this house.'

Cheryl put her pruning knife back in her belt and stood upright. She nodded and walked back to the edge of the vine field. The man walked along with her, and she noted how gingerly he was moving and that there was a drug patch on his neck. She wondered if he had not replied to her attack with a killing blow simply because it would hurt him too much at present. After a moment she took her attention away from him and directed it towards the field.

'Pickers run on chemical batteries that get warm,' she said.

He said nothing in reply to that, but it gratified her to see his expression when three pickers scuttled out of the field and headed for the house. He seemed about to ask something then, but he assumed a tired look and just watched the pickers go in through the door. Three explosions followed in quick succession. On a billow of smoke, a couple of black plastic legs came tumbling through one of the broken windows.

'Who are they – and who are you?' she asked.

'You got any more AGCs here?'

'No, and you haven't answered my question.'

Stanton shrugged and replied, because he could not be bothered not to reply, 'The ugly one is a Separatist bastard called Arian Pelter. The android is the psychotic Mr Crane. The rest are like me: mercenaries.'

'Why they here?'

'To die, if I have my way. Now tell me, where's the nearest habitation?'

Cheryl pointed. 'About ten kilometres that way.'

'And the runcible installation?'

'About a thousand kilometres beyond that.'

Stanton looked in that direction, then back at the house. 'Right, I need the use of your medkit, and I need food and water. Consider these payment for your life.'

'Inside,' Cheryl said, and let him go ahead of her into the house. As he did so she sent the recording from her aug, and kept the channel open for real-time transmission. She thought it unlikely this man would reach his destination, once the police received her recording. She also thought it likely Viridian would be receiving a visit from ECS sometime soon.

From the mask, clean oxygen blasted into her face and she gasped at it. A light-headed euphoria flooded her, but only for a moment. Pain was secondary; oxygen was survival as it charged her cells. But as her organism became satisfied it now had attention to spare for that pain.

'One moment,' said a gruff voice.

There was a gentle fumbling in her neck ring, then pressure at the side of her neck as a drug patch was pressed into place. Through blurry eyes she saw a mesh ceiling and a thin bluish hand retreating from view. *Outlinker*, was her one thought.

'Fused across the join. We'll have to cut,' said the gruff voice.

'Then cut,' replied a woman's voice. 'She's probably still bleeding in there.'

A dentist-drill whine quickly followed on the words. She felt the Outlinker tugging at her suit. While he was doing that the edge went off the pain, but Jarvellis knew she needed more than a patch to block it completely. She was in a bad way. She didn't need to see her injuries to know that.

'That's got it. Get Sam over here.'

The suit seal crumpled as it disengaged and she felt the motors in the back of the suit hinging it open.

She screamed as something ripped in her hip.

'Shit, a lump of chainglass. Sorry, darlin'. Close off that artery, Sam.'

Jarvellis clamped down on another scream as something cold went into her hip. She heard wet slicing sounds and the pain became more intense. Another patch went down on her stomach and another on her knee. When she thought she could bear the pain no longer it started to fade a little. Now she felt something else pressed against her breast. A blessed cold numbness suffused it. She felt herself beginning to drift on the load of painkillers pumping round her blood supply. But the narrow hand would not allow this; it patted at her face.

'Stay with us. I want you to lift your head and look,' said the gruff voice.

Jarvellis just lay there. She didn't see any incentive to move. John was dead. The *Lyric* was gone. It was all over. The patting turned to a slap and the voice got angrier.

'Wake up, damn it!'

This seemed too cruel after all that had happened. Why couldn't they just leave her alone? She opened her eyes and raised her head to tell them to do just that, but in the end could not even manage to.

She lay on the ceramal floor of an airlock. To her left crouched a little robot the shape of a limpet. It had two multi-jointed arms, and she almost chucked when she saw how it had opened her leg to reach in and clamp the artery. The thigh pad it was reaching over had a bloody dagger of chainglass right through it. Jarvellis did not want to know what might lie under the dressing on her breast. She inspected the other two occupants of the lock.

They were Outlinkers and they were old. The man and the woman were both dressed in baggy garments that failed to conceal how incredibly thin they were. Here were people whose forebears had gone in for radical adaptation. They were perfectly adapted for station life, for weightlessness. Put them on a planet with anything approaching Earth gravity, and they would collapse like dolls made of tissue paper. Jarvellis noticed that the man had a crust around his mouth, and there were specks of blood on his bluish skin. She remembered now that Outlinkers could survive in vacuum for a short period of time. It must have been he who had retrieved her.

'This station is still revolving,' he informed her.

She tried to understand what he was getting at. The woman, standing nervously behind him, was holding a nerve-blocker. Why the hell didn't she use it?

The man went on. 'Listen carefully. You will die without proper medical attention. Out here on the edge we're at about a quarter of a G. I got you into here using a cable winder. I cannot get you further into the station by myself, and I do not have the equipment set-up to do so. It would take too long.'

Jarvellis let her head drop back. So that was it. Out here, for them, she was an impossible weight to move. They were probably having enough trouble keeping themselves upright. Habit took over then: the habit of survival. She licked dry lips and spoke with a cracked voice.

'My leg.'

The man said, 'I'll have Sam place a clamp, but that's all we can do for now.'

'Hell,' said Jarvellis, and looked up at the wall behind her. Cable snaked up from the back of her suit to a winder that had been hastily welded to the wall. With her right arm she reached up and gripped the cable. She did not look down in response to the sudden pain in her thigh as the little robot called Sam placed the clamp. Inch by agonizing inch, she hauled herself back until her lower legs were free of the suit. Her right leg was no problem; her left leg was dead weight. When it came free she yelled, but just kept going. The Outlinkers moved back. An accidental blow from her – if she stumbled, anything – would snap their bones like sugar sticks. Finally she slid sideways from the suit. Actually standing was out of the question.

The man moved further back and pressed a button by the inner door. The door irised open with a cacophonous shriek. This place *was* old.

'There's an elevator fifty metres round from here. We'll walk just ahead of you. I'll not ask you if you can make it, because you have no other options.'

Jarvellis felt that she did have another option, but she began painfully dragging herself across the floor on her side. The little robot zipped around in a U beside her and behind her, as if enjoying this one chance of experiencing its true calling as a sheepdog.

23

Skaidon was a genius. At age six he took one of the old-style IQ tests and was rated at 180. After he was congratulated, it is reported that he said, 'If you like I'll do a test to 190, now I know how they work.' Throughout his life Skaidon mocked those he called, 'Hard-wired lead-asses.' Should you wish to know more about this, I direct you to one of his numerous biographies. This book is about runcibles. Today we are aware of the dangers of directly interfacing a human mind with a computer (not to be confused with the less direct methods of auging or gridlinking). Skaidon was the first to do this and he died of it, leaving a legacy to humanity that is awesome. It took him twenty-three minutes. In those minutes, he and the Craystein computer became the most brilliant mind humankind has ever known. He gave us Skaidon technology, from which has come instantaneous travel, antigravity and much of our field technology. The Craystein computer, in its super-cooled vault under the city of London on Earth, contains the math and blueprints for the runcible (for reasons not adequately explained, Skaidon loved the nonsense poem by Edward Lear and used its wording *in his formulae to stand for those particles and states of existence we until then had no words for, hence: runcible – the device; spoon – the five-dimensional field that breaks into nil-space; pea-green is a particle now tentatively identified as the tachyon) and to begin to understand some of this math let us first deal with that nil-space shibboleth wrongly described as quantum planing . . .*

An Introduction to Skaidon Formulae by
Ashanta Gorian

Two splits, outlining an area like the outer surface of a segment of orange, appeared in the hull of *Hubris*. The section of hull pushed out and from the poles of the ship it hinged round, exposing a play of light and shadow in the guts of the ship. Slowly, as of a cub coming from its burrow for the first time, the gleaming front surface of the heavy-lifter became exposed. Then more quickly, confidently, its impellers brought it out. It was in appearance a giant metal boomerang. From wing-tip to wing-tip it measured half a kilometre. Free of the *Hubris* it turned at ninety degrees to the rapidly closing split. Its impellers drove it on, and then, far enough away for safety, its ionic boosters jetted pulsed orange fire and blasted it for the horizon of Samarkand. Far to the side of it, Dragon sat on the horizon, watching.

Standing in the shuttle bay, while another minishuttle was being taken from storage, Cormac watched the heavy-lifter depart. It carried autodozers and line-laying moles for the clearance of a site to the west of the original one, which was still far too hot, and for the laying of s-con cables to directly draw off the heat energy from the buffers. Dragon had not left much of the original network intact. Chaline, who was on the lifter, was in her element.

When the heavy-lifter was a speck against Samarkand, Cormac went to the drop-shaft and from there to Isolation. The dracomen had been returned to their original quarters, where Mika continued her study of them. As far as he was concerned, they could stay there.

Mika was not at the viewing window where he expected to find her, but in the small control centre for all the isolation chambers. She was seated before a bank of screens and watching the one with ISOL1 imprinted above it. Two side screens to this one were giving a continuous readout of information.

'Do you have anything for me?' Cormac asked.

'Yes . . . yes, I think I do.'

Cormac dropped into the chair next to her.

She went on. 'They have been altered. I'm not even sure if they're the same ones. Their bone and muscle structures are lighter. If before they were made to be strong, now they have been made to be fast.'

Cormac looked at the two dracomen on the screen. Why? What was Dragon up to now?

Chaline watched the moles set off on their long journey to New Sea, and smiled under her mask. Improvisation under difficult circumstances: proof of a technician's abilities. Without the microwave receivers of the stations, they could not use the transmission dish that came with the runcible. But, as always, another way had been found.

Like giant silver woodlice with treads, the moles bumbled forwards in relentless slow motion, dragging their moling attachments along two metres below the surface as they laid the s-con cables. It would take them twenty hours to reach their destination. Hopefully the site here would be cleared by then. Chaline turned and watched the autodozers at work as they shoved huge mounds of dust and flaked stone before them and exposed the clean basalt below.

'Nadhir, is that second shuttle down yet?' she said, over the roar of heavy machinery.

The reply from her comunit was immediate. 'Down and ready.'

'Tell Dave to get over to New Sea and get things ready for the moles' arrival. He should be able to have the heat-sinks ready to be connected up by then. Those s-con cables out there weren't too badly damaged.'

At least Dragon had left them the heat-sinks. The heat-sink stations were now just metal-lined craters, but the sinks themselves were under half a kilometre of ice.

'He'll start moaning again.'

'Then he can moan. At least he won't be here doing it . . . Did the lifter get away on schedule?'

'It did, and by the time it returns we should have enough clear bedrock to offload the runcible onto.'

'Fused and levelled?'

'Yes, we're keeping up with the dozers. Should be able to drive in the bracings for the containment sphere by the time the lifter goes up for the prefabs.'

'What word from Jane?'

'The AI's ready, just has to be brought down and keyed in. The hour-eater's going to be setting up the horns and aligning the fields. The AI can do the fine tuning.'

Chaline nodded to herself in satisfaction: all according to plan. Fifty hours she had estimated, and fifty hours it would be. Chaline prided herself on her estimates.

'—lined in lies hurled grey-suited arms flapping wings of ashen crow cage him in screaming orbit cast and broken in sum beauty of chaos calm eye of storm hub fulcrum—'

'*Hubris* just does not have the processing power to unravel this mind without the danger of scrambling it further,' said Jane.

She and Cormac were seated before a bank of controls – grudgingly allowed them by the frenetic runcible technicians – in Downlink Com.

'Then that is a risk we must take. I've got my back to a wall here. I think Dragon is lying about an awful lot, but I've got no way to prove it, and this is a life-and-death situation. If I fuck up, people are going to die, and the killers are going to go unpunished. Remember, there were ten thousand people out here.'

'You do not have to remind me,' said Jane with something approaching anger.

'Sorry,' said Cormac.

'—axis screams roar of own might swastika purge emetic sponge of obscene colour blowing across lizards light fleeing sinter sinter fell into new day skulls satchel leather fetid hollows wasp eaten apples pork bone-exposed crackling . . . dying . . . black rats—'

'There, damn it. There!' said Cormac. 'Lizards could easily be the dracomen. Light fleeing could be the Maker escaping. And the skulls and crackling . . . ten thousand people.'

'Somewhat interpretive . . . But there may be a way . . . '

'—chewing rotating heart in assonance chained before red-hot grate spitting intestines died died am—'

'Sorry, what did you say?'

'I said there may be a way to unscramble it. Though Chaline won't like it,' said Jane.

'Tell me. Don't tell her.'

'The new runcible AI might be able to do it. It is not keyed into the grid yet, and has fifty times the processing power of *Hubris*. It needs that to sort out the five-space math and nil-space co-ordinates.'

Cormac was silent for a while, staring off down the room at a screen showing the heavy-lifter coming up from Samarkand.

'Of course,' he said. 'Of course.' He turned and stared at her fiercely. 'Now – we do it now.'

Jane looked at him carefully for a moment before speaking to *Hubris*. '*Hubris*, the new runcible AI is in Hold 5A. Can you link with it there, or will there have to be a direct line?'

'A direct line is not necessary. Once initiated, the new AI would be able to access all systems. It would be able to compensate for any error I might make in transmission and reception.'

'Initiation would be immediate,' said Jane.

Hubris said, 'There are dangers. This AI has been prepared for immediate installation in the grid.'

'The danger will be brief.'

'It will last for ten seconds. It will take this long for the AI to access all systems and ascertain its situation. Should I initiate, I will first sound a hold alert on all workstations.'

'Initiate then.'

'I cannot do this without a direct order from Agent Cormac.'

Cormac turned to Jane. 'Why the danger?'

'In an unprogrammed situation at initiation, the AI will immediately act to protect itself. It will take control of all accessible systems.'

Cormac turned to study the consoles. '*Hubris*, initiate runcible AI.'

Hubris's voice sounded throughout the ship. 'All workstations, this is a hold alert. All robots will be going onto hold. All transient information is now in protected storage. I repeat . . .'

Cormac glanced around and saw that the technicians in Downlink Com were leaning back from their consoles and looking at each other in puzzlement, then looking to Cormac and Jane with chagrin.

One of them, who was at a communications console, glanced at Cormac and muttered laconically, 'Chaline'll be pissed. The autodozers went down just then.' He listened for a moment then continued. 'That was the lifter. They want to know why the main door isn't opening.'

'Tell them it's temporary. All systems should be back on-line . . . soon,' said Cormac. '*Hubris*, you ready yet?'

'There is a heavy load being moved in the main bay. It will be in place shortly.'

Cormac rattled his fingers on the console in impatience.

'Load is now secured. I am now initiating—'

Suddenly the entire starship jerked. Gravity dropped to half. The screens began to run information at high speed, then faster and faster until they showed a grey blur. Lights and displays were flickering madly.

The man at the communications console said, 'Weapons systems just went online. Proton guns charging. Looks like the target is Dragon . . . Isolation just sealed up.'

Gripping the console, Cormac suddenly felt cold.

'Intruder defence systems—' The technician held a finger to his ear. 'That was main bay. The loading robots started up and turned to face them. They're shitting themselves down there.'

Cormac suddenly wished he could have the last few minutes back again. He was responsible. It was *his* order.

'*Hubris? . . . Hubris?*'

Suddenly gravity returned to normal. The screens flicked to a halt on disparate segments of data.

'Weapons systems coming offline. Intruder defence systems also . . . Loading robots going back on hold. Phew! Old Venolia sure knows some dirty words . . .'

Cormac slowly relaxed as the lights ceased their mad flickering and other displays returned to normal.

'Chaline just called up. Wants to know what the hell is going on. What shall I tell her?'

Cormac glanced at Jane, then turned to the technician. 'Tell her I had the runcible AI initiated. We need it to decode the submind,' he said.

The technician shrugged and spoke into his mike. After a moment he turned back. 'She questioned your parentage, then said something about a submind suppository if the dozers don't get moving soon.'

'Tell her – soon.' He turned to Jane. 'The AI should be—'

'Ready,' said a voice that managed to put all the elements of a bored sophisticate into one word.

'Ready?'

Samarkand II continued. 'I have been initiated prematurely. Presumably there is a reason for this. I am therefore ready for your explanation. Please continue. It has been thirty-seven seconds – mark – and I am bored already.'

The comtech said, 'Chaline again, and the lifter. They're getting nothing from *Hubris*. Everything still on hold.'

'*Hubris*?' said Cormac.

'*Hubris*, I see,' said Samarkand II. 'I seem to have subsumed this starship AI. Separating. Done.'

'*Hubris*?'

'Yes. I am. *Hubris*.'

'Dozers moving again. Hold's off. Main door opening. Isolation unsealing,' said the comtech.

Cormac breathed a sigh of relief. '*Hubris*, is the submind on-line?'

'I cannot locate the submind in cyberspace.'

'This – you are looking for this? It is not a mind,' said Samarkand II.

'—mechan man made solid ground engine parts clanking clanking bleeding oil-soap green bubbling hot—'

'It is the reason you were initiated,' Cormac told the AI.

'It is a submind of my predecessor. It contains information pertaining to the incident here.'

'You have it? You have the information?' asked Cormac eagerly.

'Not yet . . .'

'—cast aluminium hand shield over green volcanic glass orb head red quartz rods sulphur yellow green sulphur yellow sulphur blue stink aniseed prodestinationactinicablecomlivesurvin—' The monologue from the submind suddenly became a high-pitched squeal.

Samarkand II said, 'My predecessor survived the blast for nine-point-two seconds. It discovered a viruslock on some information in itself. This, along with much else, it transmitted to its subminds, as by then it was no longer on the grid.'

'—Broken caltrops under lead hooves. Horse-head is a hollow roll of tin with star diamonds for eyes and mussel shells for ears. Jade hands in red moonlight; night green and black over contrast land. Unlogged matter/energy transmission 32562331. Glass dragons in green sky red moon—'

Samarkand II said, 'Unlogged matter/energy transmission forty-eight solstan days before the incident. Confusion as to the nature of what was transmitted indicates a high probability that it was the entity referred to as "Maker".'

'—Lizards with heavy bones. Dragon In The Flower.

No law prevents. Dogs mad of grain held together with fungal filaments. Fish-head reptiles. Hot pools filled with man stew. 326222400—'

'The two dracomen arrived one day before the buffer went down. This information was transmitted into the grid prior to the explosion.'

Cormac said to Jane, 'Seems likely the dracomen set the mycelium. Dragon would say it was keyed to their arrival, and that the Maker set it.'

'Why would they set it, if the Maker was gone?'

'Did they know that?'

Jane said, 'I think you are prejudiced against Dragon. This information does not confer guilt.'

'Perhaps,' mused Cormac, then said, 'Samarkand II, is there any indication as to who set the mycelium? Also, where did the Maker go?'

'I will allow the submind to answer that.'

The submind said, 'No warning prior buffer failure. No indication source mycelium. Matter/energy trans-mission directed Chirat Cluster, Mendor System, Planet Viridian, ref. AB87.'

That the station was a centrifugal ring station showed that it was old. The off-shoot technology from Skaidon tech of gravity manipulation had taken a while to impinge on the design of stations, mainly because it took a long time for people used to the essential requirements of space habitation to trust it. That Nix, the station, had an elevator showed it was pre-runcible and truly ancient. Another sign of this great age was the worn ceramal deck across which Jarvellis was dragging herself. At one-quarter G it would have taken the passage of many feet to put such hollows in such a hard material.

'Come on, you can do it,' said Tull for the nth time. His wife Jeth offered similar, though less sincere, encouragement. Her lack of enthusiasm was understandable. Both Outlinkers were scared: they were allowing a person into their home who could kill them with a friendly pat on the back. It did not escape Jarvellis's notice how brave Tull had been: first to retrieve her from outside, then to slap her face once she was inside.

It took minutes that dragged like hours, but Jarvellis eventually reached the lip of the metal box and looked back. She made the final effort and dragged herself in. The Outlinkers were back against the walls now. Jeth held out her narrow hand in which lay the flattened sphere of the nerve-blocker.

'Will you keep still for me?' she asked.

Jarvellis coughed. Her lungs were filling with fluid. Her entire body ached and her left side was a wide line of pain. She felt dizzy and sick. She nodded her head, then turned it to one side. Jeth cautiously stepped in close and pressed the blocker to the back of her neck. The fibres of neural shunt went in, and blessed numbness rolled down her body in a wave. Tull pressed buttons on a small control panel. Jarvellis did not feel the elevator move. She only knew it was coming to the centre of the station, when panic that the floor had fallen away pulled her out of the haze. She was weightless.

Now the Outlinkers felt safe, they quickly got hold of her and manoeuvred her through the sliding door into a tubular tunnel. Even this exercise was difficult for them, for though she was weightless she still had inertia. It took the both of them hauling at her to overcome it and get her moving. The walls of the tunnel were diamond-patterned to offer grip for feet and hands. Interspersed at regular intervals were rails and catch-loops. Sinking back into the haze, Jarvellis watched the little robot swinging past on the latter of these like an iron gibbon.

They brought her eventually to a curved room with no definite floor or ceiling. There was equipment on every surface and she was relieved to see a modern medbot, cell-welder and all those other devices that equated the repair of the human body with that of any other machine. They pulled her to the weightless version of a surgical table, a frame ringed with adjustable clamps, and there secured her in place. Tull pulled back the dressing on her breast, while Jeth set the medbot to work on her thigh.

'I'll do my best, but you'll need to see a cosmetic surgeon,' he said. 'You'll need regrowth and reconstructive surgery. Too much mammary fat is missing.'

Jarvellis tried to speak, but hardly anything came out of her dry mouth. Tull leaned closer and she tried again. Eventually he got the gist of her request. She heard him speak hurriedly to his wife, but could not distinguish the words. There came a humming sound: some sort of ultrasound scanner.

'Still alive,' Tull said. 'We'll make sure the foetus stays connected.'

Jarvellis tried to speak again, and once more he leant in close to hear her.

'All right,' he said, and made an adjustment to the nerve-blocker. The numbness rose from her neck and rolled her into oblivion.

An area two-thirds of a kilometre in diameter had been cleared, and the bedrock fused to obsidian and levelled. The containment sphere rested between the two cylindrical tanks of the buffers seemingly placed to stop it rolling away, and from it an enclosed walkway led to the surrounding complex of newly erected buildings. The buildings were domed and apparently made of native materials. Prefabricated sections had been joined, then sealed, with a composite of crushed rock and epoxy resins. Vapour jetted from them as they were heated and the moisture and excess CO_2 was pumped out. The whole complex was knitted together by more enclosed walkways, pylons carrying s-con cables, ground-level pipelines, and by a nimbus of electric light. Beyond the perimeter was impenetrable darkness.

Night had come to Samarkand.

The minishuttle rested in the twilight at the perimeter and, as he disembarked, Cormac had a good view across the complex. He paused for a moment on the CO_2 slush, his visor polarizing as the containment sphere emitted a flash of orange light. After fooling with the directional gain of his comunit, he heard Chaline bawling out one of her technicians.

'Dave! I said ninety gigahertz not megahertz! You're not going to get anywhere near alignment – What? What did you say?'

'I said why not leave it to the AI.'

'Because we are here and the AI isn't. Now, ninety gigahertz. Try to get it right this time.'

Cormac's visor polarized again as a tower of rainbows rose from the sphere and stabbed into the starlit sky. As

it flickered out, he heard Chaline speaking in a somewhat happier tone.

'That's it: the spoon's in, close as we're going to get.
The AI can lose the light-show.'

Cormac looked round as Jane disembarked, carrying
a small suitcase.

'Seems they're ready for you,' he said.

'I heard. A good thing too.' She patted the suitcase.
'It's getting impatient.'

They set out for the runcible, where figures could be
seen gathered around one of the buffers.

'That you, Jane?'

'Yes.'

'Good. Head for control. Everything's set up.'

One of the figures detached from the group and
headed for the building nearest to the runcible. Jane
and Cormac headed there also, and were soon inside,
removing their masks. The temperature was twenty
below, so they kept their suits on.

'There you are,' said Chaline, and gestured to the
device in the centre of the room. It had the appearance
of a font made of glass and chrome pipes. A duct crossed
the room from it, heading in the direction of the runcible. Next to it stood a pedestal-mounted console
Cormac could not help comparing to a lectern. Here
was the chapel. The god was about to be installed in his
rightful home.

'I presume you have no more use for it now, and we
can get on,' was Chaline's acid comment to Cormac.

'Of course,' said Cormac equably, refusing to rise to
the bait. Chaline had been spoiling for a fight for the last
three days.

Jane walked to the console, rested her case on it, opened the case and removed the Samarkand runcible AI. It was a squashed bronze cylinder with rounded ends, its dimensions being thirty centimetres by fifteen by ten. It was one of the most powerful minds known to the human race. Jane took it to the glass font and placed it into the receptacle made for it. Then she returned to the console and began working on the touch-controls, like a concert pianist. From the rim of the receptacle rose thousands of contacts to access the rim of the AI. It seemed for a moment as if it was surrounded by an army of platinum ants. Lights flickered in the glass column.

'On-line,' said Chaline, detaching the receiver from her comunit and holding it to her ear. 'Tuning . . . singularity developing . . . We're in – that's it, we're on the grid.' Chaline grinned happily at Cormac, her resentment forgotten. Then her grin changed to an expression of astonishment. 'Wait a minute . . . there's a transmission already. How the hell did they manage it that quickly?'

Cormac was through the interior door to the covered walkway before he knew what he was doing. Chaline and Jane came after him. In a moment they stepped into the containment sphere. Between the horns of the runcible the cusp was shimmering like a sheet of mother-of-pearl. A man stepped through it; an old grey-haired Japanese dressed in stained and baggy mono-filament overall.

'Horace Blegg,' said Cormac. 'That's all I need.'

24

Horace Blegg: *The immortal wanderer has long been a set piece of human myth, and how much more do we want him to exist in this age, when many feel that humans are no longer the arbiters of their own destiny? Blegg, so the story goes, is a man with supernatural powers that enabled him, in the twentieth century, to survive the destruction of his home city of Hiroshima by a primitive fission bomb. He is then said to have meddled with human destiny to the extent of insuring our spread across the galaxy, and the governance of us by AIs. Of course, we want this to be true! The myth assures us that we are greater, through him, than those silicon minds that do govern us. The whole story is of course absolute rubbish, and just a more modern version of Arthurian Romance.*

From *Quince Guide*, compiled by humans

The houses, fast-build plascrete domes rather like giant igloos, were scattered wide apart amongst the conifers and native chequer trees of an old forest. No thought had been given to roads, so the town was obviously a new one, in terms of Viridian's age, built after AGC use

395

had become well established. The houses would also have self-contained energy sources and waste disposal. The only linkage they would have would be for optic cables and water: the latter essential, the former to prevent EM pollution. Stanton, watching the edge of this forest town from the shadow of a huge basalt slab, noted the AGC quartering the area. It's paint job immediately identified it to him as local police. He had no doubt it had been Cheryl who had informed them, but any silencing he would have done would have been too late. She had an aug. She would have sent out a call immediately after Pelter's damping device got out of range. At least this is what Stanton told himself. At the back of his mind was the knowledge that not so long ago he would have killed her, just in case.

Stanton moved from the slab's shade into the green sunlight, and set out at a jog for the edge of the forest town. Every household there would no doubt possess one or more AGCs. So the first house he reached would probably provide what he needed – for the moment. He was within a hundred metres of that house when the AGC swerved in the sky and accelerated towards him on a tongue of flame. He swore and broke into a run. Twenty metres from the house, and a voice bellowed out above him:

'Stop there! You, stop there!'

Stanton cut a swerving course across the boggy ground. There were two AGCs by a house, nestling under the spread of a huge chequer tree, its leaves the shape and size of playing cards casting a dappled emerald shade.

'Stop or I shoot!'

Ten metres.

There was a crackle in the air and Stanton's left arm jerked from electric shock. He dived and rolled behind a low, self-pruning box hedge. Another crackle and leaves fell from the hedge. Big space between him and the AGCs, and the man standing holding a pot plant. Small space between him and the door. Stanton ran at the door and took it out with his shoulder. Crashed into the room beyond. As he rolled from the wreckage, the air crackled behind him. He came up into a crouch, took in the woman standing in an open kitchen area holding some kind of package.

'What the hell?' the woman said.

'Sorry about the door,' said Stanton, and moved to peer through the window.

The police AGC crashed down through the trees, slid sideways towards the house, and landed heavily only a few metres from the door. Two policemen came from it fast, and headed straight for the door. They both appeared to be boosted. The first of them rolled through and came up into a crouch, with a stun gun levelled at the woman. He had half a second to realize his mistake before Stanton was on him. The mercenary stamped the back of his leg. As the officer reeled back, he caught him in a neck-lock, his right hand closing on the man's gun hand as he turned him. The second officer came through more cautiously, only to walk straight into the blast. He was flung, jerking, back through the door, with small lightnings lacing his uniform. The first officer continued to struggle as Stanton tightened his lock. Eventually his struggles ceased as he blacked out. Stanton held the lock just a little longer to be sure, then released him. He went down on his face. A glance round showed him that a back door was open and the woman was gone. As he collected the two stun guns on his way to the police AGC, Stanton considered how much he had changed. A sleeper lock rather than just breaking the man's neck. He felt almost civilized.

A blast of frigid air came in through the door as Thorn entered the shuttle. Cormac pointed to a bench seat and returned his attention to Blegg. The ancient Japanese unclipped the mask of the suit and let it hang to one side. His breath fogged the chill air. Cormac could not help but wonder if he had put on the suit – which a technician had hurriedly fetched for him – out of politeness. In the containment sphere, in his thin monofilament overalls, he had shown no sign of noticing the cold. Cormac unclipped his own mask.

'You knew about the dracomen,' he said.

'I knew,' Blegg acknowledged.

'What else didn't you tell me?'

'We knew about the artefact as well. It was discovered during the initial survey, and left where it was. It was whole.' Blegg leaned forwards and spoke loudly, as if Cormac was deaf. 'No hurry . . . y'understand?'

Cormac nodded. 'Is that all? Anything else you want to hold back, to keep me dancing?'

'We knew the egg was adamantium. Not much else could have been learnt.'

'The tunnel was made by the energy creature – or the dracomen.'

Blegg shrugged. 'The Maker, yes . . . if it could hatch from an adamantium egg, making a tunnel would have been no problem . . .' Blegg studied him carefully. 'What do you think of Dragon's explanation?' he asked.

Cormac said, 'I don't know. Still not enough evidence to confirm or deny it. What do you think?'

'Assume it's the truth. Dragon might not have a great respect for human life, but why should it? There's plenty to spare.'

'All right, I'll assume it's the truth. How do I react to that truth?' Cormac asked.

'Your decision,' said Blegg. 'You're in command here.'

Cormac snorted and studied Thorn. The Sparkind had a tightly controlled look to him. He averted his eyes from Cormac, then stared down at his hands. Abruptly he stood up and moved off into the wing of the shuttle.

'My decision would be to get some sort of recompense for the deaths of ten thousand people. Of course, I would have to go to Viridian to get . . . recompense,' said Cormac.

'Viridian, yes,' said Blegg, a hint of a nasty smile on his face. 'Funny thing about that place: lot of activity there.'

Cormac felt a sinking sensation. There was more. There was always more.

Blegg went on. 'On Cheyne you killed Angelina Pelter.'

'I did. What has that to do with this?'

'Young Arian shut things down,' Blegg said.

'How do you mean?'

'You gave your testimony. None of the cell leaders was apprehended. Every one of them was killed by a metal-skin android.'

'They had one . . . broken Golem?'

'Very likely. We don't know. Neither Pelter nor the android were apprehended either.'

'Go on.'

'Prior to these deaths, as I believe you know, Pelter managed to withdraw Separatist funds and his entire personal fortune from the Cheyne III Norver Bank. Shortly after those deaths the local police chased an AGC to the spaceport. It had, supposedly, Pelter and John Stanton aboard. The shuttle crashed and exploded. It took the police two solstan days to discover that the bodies they recovered were not those of Pelter or Stanton. A little retrospective investigation revealed that a trispherical craft called the *Lyric* launched just after the explosion. Your back-up team there was beginning to take an interest in this craft. It was, ostensibly, insystem and light cargo, only it had an underspace engine.'

Blegg looked round as Thorn returned. The Sparkind brought back three coffees. One he placed where he was sitting. The other two he handed to Cormac and Blegg. Cormac pulled the tab on his coffee and wondered why Blegg was studying the soldier so intently.

'Thank you, Thorn,' said Blegg. 'You know that personal agendas cannot be allowed.'

'I know,' said Thorn.

Blegg returned his attention to Cormac. 'You know Huma?' he asked.

Blegg's face was so close Cormac could see the strange gold flecks in the irises of his eyes. His breath smelt of garlic.

'It's where the arms were being smuggled in from. The *Lyric* went there?'

400

Blegg smiled. 'Yes, Pelter and Stanton were seen recruiting four mercenaries, and they had the android with them. This was information we recovered from what remained of a Golem ECS agent called Jill. The rest of her team has not yet been found. Pelter had them killed.'

'You sure?'

'Y'need to ask that?'

'I guess not. I still don't see how this all relates.'

'It relates because a trispherical ship was blown in orbit above Viridian only one solstan day ago.'

Cormac leant back and sipped his coffee. 'Coincidence is not that elastic,' he said.

'No, it is not.' Blegg reached up and undid his coldsuit. He went on. 'There are people on Huma who have taken to using a new and very efficient augmentation.' He tossed something down on the bench between them. It was bean-shaped and reptilian. Cormac inspected it, then looked round at Thorn, who had a puzzled expression on his face. He looked back at Blegg, then down at the aug again. He prodded it with his finger. It was soft.

'Biotech?'

Blegg nodded.

Cormac said, 'I had intended only to take Aiden, Thorn, and Cento – if he's in one piece by then.'

'Have to ask: y'want to carry on?'

'Yes.'

'There's the dracomen . . .'

'No, I don't want to take them.'

'I think you should. You need every . . . source of information.'

'Opinion or order?'

'Take them. Your decisions should be fully informed.'

Cormac nodded – an order, then. 'I'll take them, but I'm damned if I'll arm them. I'll also need more than that. Are there any more Sparkind available?'

'No, but there's a small force of ES regulars there.'

'They'll have to do, then. I'll also need energy weapons and a couple of contra-terrene tacticals. Yield forty should do.' He looked at Thorn. 'Get Cento – if he's in one piece – and Aiden down here ASAP. They bring the dracomen down with them. Tell them I want them watched at all times. Also, I want an ES uniform with rank, same for yourselves. Get going.'

Thorn crushed his empty cup and tossed it on the floor. He had an expression of grim satisfaction on his face as he headed for the door. Cormac pulled his mask across, until the frigid air had circulated a bit and mixed with the warmer air in the shuttle.

'Still a lot of holes,' he said.

'They're for you to fill.'

'OK, an energy creature moving about through our runcibles would have been noticed.'

Blegg smiled again, then leant back. He spoke at the ceiling. 'Come on, moron. I know y'listening.'

There was no reply; perhaps the listener did not like his insulting manner. Cormac decided to try.

'Samarkand AI, ask the Viridian runcible AI to search for an information lock of the type discovered by your predecessor.'

Samarkand II replied to him immediately. 'An information lock was discovered one hour ago. Viridian now acknowledges the arrival of a matter/energy transmission. It arrived in containment sphere B9 and then left the runcible facility by an unknown method. Viridian also informs me that this lock is secondary.'

'Secondary?' asked Cormac. He looked at Blegg, who nodded slowly.

'It means the lock was opened, then replaced. Someone knew where the Maker went before we found it out. Y'understand?'

'Dragon,' said Cormac.

Blegg shrugged. 'Planetary scan, what y'got there?' he asked.

There was a pause before Samarkand II replied. 'There was an airborne energy trace, originally dismissed as stratospheric lightning. Re-integration of the data suggests it grounded at the Chiranian ruin in the Magadar forest.'

'There's y'Maker,' said Blegg, and stood.

Cormac gave a short nod and looked at him as Blegg finished his coffee and placed the cup carefully on the bench. Without more ado he headed for the shuttle door. Without pulling his mask across, he hit the touchplate. Cormac quickly got his mask into place as the door cracked open. He watched Blegg.

'Anything else you might have neglected to tell me?' he asked.

'Y'have facts. Y'have a mind. I'll get things set for you.' Blegg paused. 'I'll get that silicon moron on Viridian to give you the details.'

Great.

Blegg stepped out into the cold and trudged off in the direction of the containment sphere. As the door closed, Cormac pulled off his mask and lay back against the bulkhead. He kept turning over what he knew. Pelter was on Viridian, and was likely there with Dragon's help. Dragon would lie about the reasons behind this, if it gave any answer at all. Cormac dared not ask. He was still very aware that *here*, *now*, Dragon held all the cards. It could destroy the runcible, and it could destroy *Hubris*. Cormac realized he had to keep his mouth shut and work everything out for himself. He needed more answers and he needed a clear course of action. Despite Blegg's assertion, he did not have all the facts and his course was not yet clear. He summarized some of the more pertinent facts available to him.

Fact: the runcible buffers were sabotaged in a way easily within the capabilities of Dragon and of this Maker, if what Dragon said were true. Fact: this Maker had escaped from its containment vessel, if such it was, and escaped Samarkand by runcible. That they had not discovered this until recently bespoke the Maker's ability to interfere with AI programming, an ability Dragon probably had as well. Fact: the creature in the tunnel had not been made to withstand the cold, yet the dracomen had. Fact: Dragon probably knew about the Maker's departure long before it arrived here and threw its apparent tantrum. These particular facts made a lie of Dragon's story. But what was the truth? Conclusion: if Dragon was responsible for what had happened here, how would he find out for sure, and what the hell would he do about it?

Cormac closed his eyes and he began running through things again. He knew, in the end, that the explanation would be simple, and any solution perhaps less so. Right at this moment he just couldn't seem to get anything in order. He needed rest. The bench was padded and would have to suffice. He stretched out on it and was wondering if he would be able to get any sleep, when sleep crept up and got him instead.

The cracking of the shuttle door had Cormac sitting upright and pulling his mask across. Thorn entered with a large bag slung over one shoulder. He dropped it before Cormac as the door closed.

'That was quick,' Cormac said.

Thorn pulled off his mask and gave him a quizzical look. 'It was quick,' he said, 'for shuttling up to *Hubris* and back.'

Cormac dropped his mask and looked around for some sort of time readout. He realized then that he should have acquired some sort of timepiece. While gridlinked he had always known the time, so it had never occurred to him that he might not know it.

'Ten hours,' said Thorn, as if reading his mind.

Cormac shook his head, trying to dispel that last fuzziness. He stood up, pointed at the bag and looked questioningly at the Sparkind.

'Your uniform,' said Thorn.

'Right,' said Cormac, taking up the bag, 'I'll change in the sphere. Let's go.'

They masked up and cracked the door for a second time. Outside, vapour was rising off the CO_2 slush as the machine and human activity raised the temperature. They hastened for a lock into one of the covered walkways, then on to the containment sphere. Upon reaching the sphere, Cormac found the temperature almost uncomfortable: it was above zero Celsius.

Around the sphere, prefabs had been erected in some sort of analogue of embarkation lounges – and they were crowded. Technicians were setting up information consoles, laying insulated flooring, installing powerful little air heaters. Cables snaked all over the place and there was a racket of compressors, power tools, talking and shouting. When they finally got through to the sphere itself, they found it crowded as well. Thorn pointed out where Aiden, Cento and the dracomen stood. As he and Thorn headed over, Cormac saw that strangers viewed the dracomen without surprise. They probably thought they were just more adapted humans. There were plenty in the crowd already: catadapts with multicoloured fur, ophidapts with fangs, forked tongues and skin little different from that of the dracomen, tripode adaptations to heavy-gravity worlds, and others more exotic and less easy to compare. There were some who looked askance at the dracomen. They were perhaps more observant or were members of the original mission.

'Wonder how long before we see copies,' said Cormac, when they reached the two Golem and the two dracomen.

'It would be a difficult adaptation,' said Aiden.

'Why's that?'

'It would require extensive rewiring of the nervous system.'

'You mean putting the legs on backwards and making them work.'

'Yes, that's what I mean.'

Cormac allowed himself a strained grin, then inspected Cento. The Golem had a fine network of lines on his face and on his hands. Obviously a new syntheskin covering could not be found quickly enough. He still wore his old one and the joins showed.

'Are you . . . all right?' he asked.

'All right?' Cento repeated.

'I mean,' said Cormac, 'are you fully functional?'

'I have eighty per cent efficiency. Replacement is better than repair. The welding of my chassis I cannot trust under the full loading of my joint motors.'

Eighty per cent. That meant the Golem could probably rip only one man in half at a time.

Cormac surveyed the crowds, then shrugged and began to pull off his coldsuit. Thorn did likewise. No one paid attention. Under his coldsuit, Thorn – like Cento and Aiden – had the uniform of a major in the ES regulars. Once he had his coldsuit removed, Cormac kept going until he was naked. He stooped and opened the bag Thorn had deposited. Inside he found underwear, chainglass body armour and a uniform. When he strapped on the armour, that drew more looks than his nakedness had.

Over the body armour Cormac donned the green and grey fatigues of a colonel in the ES regulars. It would ease the giving of orders. Once dressed, he again strapped shuriken to his wrist. He would be the only one of them armed. Hardwired proscription prevented the transmission of certain weapons through the runcibles, and it was easier to collect new weapons on the other side, rather than disconnect that wiring. Cormac could only manage to get shuriken through because he had managed to get it classified as an antique, but even then he needed special dispensations, and the weapon had to be deactivated. Had he tried to get it through illegally, it would have been reduced to dust by the proscription filter the runcible had inbuilt when he stepped out the other side. The body-armour helmet he dropped into the bag, along with a laptop that held all the information relevant to this mission. This was all he was taking. With a quick inspection of the inside of the sphere, he hoisted the bag to his shoulder.

'All set?' he asked, with a wary glance at the draco-men.

'Ready,' said Thorn, grimly.

Cormac stepped up onto the black glass dais and led the way to the twin horns of the runcible. In a moment they had reached the containment sphere and soon had it to themselves. They gathered before the twin horns.

'Samarkand II, is our destination set?' asked Cormac.

'Ready when you are,' replied the AI.

Cormac mounted the steps to the pedestal. 'Send the dracomen next,' he instructed Thorn, and stepped through the cusp.

STOP.

START.

One pace – and he stepped out of one of a bank of runcibles on the planet Viridian in the Mendax planetary system, in the Chirat cluster, 173 light-years from Samarkand.

The containment sphere was empty. But for the lack of crowds here, he might well have been stepping out in the Samarkand sphere again. Quince and light-cargo runcibles had been standardized for half a century; the big difference here was that this sphere was one of many, as had once been the case on Samarkand and as, hopefully, would be the case again when Chaline finished her work. As he stepped off the pedestal the dracomen came out behind him, then Thorn, Aiden and Cento.

'Viridian?' Cormac asked, as of the air.

The voice of this new runcible AI had a maturity Samarkand lacked. Irritatingly it still had that patronizing tone, though.

'Sergeant Polonius Arn is waiting for you with a carrier. The weapons and supplies you detailed will be onboard. He will take you to a rendezvous with the ES regulars. They are waiting at a place called Motford, and from there we can head straight for your destination. It's one Viridian day's journey away, just a few hours more than solstan.'

'What about here, when that thing runs?' asked Thorn.

The AI replied before Cormac could say anything. 'In one day's time there will be an evacuation of this port, the surrounding area, and Westown, because of a fluxing antimatter-containment field. From that moment all runcibles here will only open to Samarkand. The Samarkand AI informs me that, from there, newly arrived personnel are being sent back to Minostra. The remaining technicians will return to *Hubris*, ostensibly to carry out a refit. The reason given is that another crisis has developed at the outlink station of Danet.'

'There,' said Cormac, 'sufficient, don't you think?'

Thorn nodded his agreement. They left the containment sphere.

The embarkation lounge was not crowded, but it seemed to be kilometres long. The four of them gathered round the dracomen and walked quickly to the far doors. Cormac thought that the strange glances they were getting were due to their uniforms rather than the bird-walking dracomen. He noted, with a quick sideways flick of his eyes, two dodgy-looking individuals loitering by a drinks dispenser, and surreptitiously reached down and keyed the start-up sequence into shuriken. Before he had taken two more paces, shuriken's holster was humming against his wrist.

'You see them?' he asked Thorn.

'I saw them,' Thorn replied.

'Stay alert. We might be walking into it right now.'

'I'm always alert,' Thorn said, a touch of annoyance in his voice.

The doors opened out onto an AGC park surrounded by country with the bleak quality of moorland. Pools like tarnished copper coins were banked round with thick growths of something like sage, speared through with the black blades of sedges. Where there was neither of these, the ground was pebbled with something thick and green and which, without closer inspection, Cormac thought, could be either geological or biological. His momentary curiosity on this matter was assuaged when he saw one of these growths break open to fling a cloud of helicopter seeds into the air. As he walked on, he espied something like a flying rabbit with a split trunk come to suck the seeds up before they reached the ground. It got most of them. Cormac pulled his finger away from the quick release on his shuriken holster.

'Did they follow?' he asked of Thorn.

'Out of the lounge, yes – but not now,' Thorn replied.

'We've been eyeballed then. Probably something set up for later.'

In the distance could be seen a line of bluish forest, and beyond this the sky was cut by a chaos of laminated slabs that could have been alien ruins. Beyond the runcible facility, the AGC park and a scatter of finned cooling towers that could have been mistaken for something living, there were no other buildings in sight. Viridian had been colonized for a long time. Only on the most recently colonized planets had it become acceptable to establish runcibles within cities – or cities around runcibles. The sky was pale-green, the sun showing through bluish clouds: a green glare of a copper arc light. The planet was well named. Cormac realized, as he stepped out, that this was what the submind had told them. Was there a red moon? he wondered. And what exactly were the 'glass dragons'? Was that a reference to the dracomen, or to the Maker?

The armoured personnel carrier stood out from the other vehicles, like a vulture amongst canaries. The private AGCs were of all colours, and small; some of them were open and more like flying sedan chairs, some of them were reproductions of the petrol-driven cars of old Earth, but few of them were ugly. The carrier was battleship grey. In appearance and size it was a railway carriage minus wheels, and with all hard and uncompromising angles. At the back of it there were tail-mounted turbines, and along its length a number of stabilizing fins. There were turrets for automatic projectile guns and beam weapons. It was a formidable machine. As they approached, Cormac glanced from it to the red Cortina replica parked next to it.

'Hardly covert,' he said.

Arn was a sergeant in the ES regulars, but just as obviously a native of Viridian. He was a short stocky man with cap-cut, light blue hair, a bushy moustache of the same colour – and it seemed to be natural coloration – and dark pupil-less eyes deep-set in a craggy face. He studied them for a moment, then saluted smartly and opened the door to the carrier.

'Sergeant, you have weapons for us?' said Thorn.

'So too.' He saluted again.

'No need for all that,' said Cormac. 'Just show us the weapons and take us to Motford. I'll give a briefing there.'

Arn pointed out some crates strapped in the back of the carrier, then went to take his position at the controls. Cento joined him – looking hopeful, Cormac thought. Shortly the carrier was airborne and, when they were clear of the AGC park, the ion boosters roared. The carrier accelerated smoothly; it would have been quite possible to walk about inside while it was travelling.

'How much do you intend to tell them?' Aiden asked.

Cormac looked up in surprise from the crate he was opening. He had expected Thorn to be the one to ask that, as the Golem Thirties were decidedly taciturn.

'I see no reason to hold back on anything this side of the runcible. Only we ourselves will use the energy weapons, though. They're just extra muscle for when friend Pelter puts in an appearance.'

Aiden looked pointedly at the two innocuous boxes at the end of the case. Cormac lifted one out and pressed his thumb against the lock. It was keyed only to him. The box opened to reveal a gleaming cylinder, twenty centimetres long by five wide, with the letters CTD in a garish red pictogram, purpled by the light. On the end of each cylinder was a black cap with a miniconsole on it – remote or timer, the result was always the same. Cormac smiled.

'Perhaps we'll leave off telling them about these,' he said, and closed the box. It had '*JMCC: Enropower. 1 Kilowatt Hour*' etched into the lid. The cylinders, though, were not powerpacks: they delivered a great deal more energy than one kilowatt, and in substantially less time than an hour. CTD stood for contra-terrene device. Thorn by then had opened another case, and was holding a weapon that had the appearance of a stubby carbine made of glass and old wood. Under the glass, salamanders writhed, waiting to be released.

When Cormac had finished his briefing, ten regulars dispersed to their sky-bikes, which were parked haphazardly on soggy lichen-covered ground. They were to fly escort, and all other vehicles were to be warned off. Arn lifted the carrier into the sky with a smooth acceleration. Cormac took one of the four seats at the control console, along with the sergeant and Aiden.

'These ruins, Sergeant, describe them to me,' he said.

'So too. They're what's left of an old ES ground installation, sir. There's just a few fragments of a shield dome surrounding a couple of underground missile silos. Surrounding that is a radial scattering of old storage buildings, nothing very large. There are supposed to be bunkers under the ground around the silos, but no one goes in there. Still hot.'

'Would it be possible to land next to the underground silos?'

'Not so. No clear ground, and the roofs of the buildings would never take the weight of this carrier.'

'What's the scale?'

'Whole site's about two kilometres across. Silos were for Hunter Tens, about fifty metres deep and ten in diameter, three of them. Don't know anything about the bunkers . . . sir.'

Cormac nodded.

'The description you've given is sufficient, Sergeant. Most concise. Put us down on the perimeter, wherever you deem suitable.'

The sergeant allowed himself a tight little smile.

'Sarge, we got someone on the edge of detector range. Looks like they're following.'

'You know the drill, Corporal. Warn them off.'

'They don't respond. Shall I send back Cheng and Goff?'

Cormac leant forward. 'Cormac here.'

'Colonel, sir!'

'What's your name, soldier?'

'Tarm, sir.'

'Very well, Tarm, I want you and this Cheng and Goff to go back personally. Warn them off. Turn them if you can. If they fire on you, take them out. Otherwise I want them driven back a fair way, but not so far they won't be able to pick up on us again. Do you understand?'

'I think so, sir.'

'Don't be thick, Tarm,' interjected the sergeant.

'Oh . . . Oh, I see. On our way, sir.'

Cormac glanced out the window of the carrier and

saw three of the sky-bikes peel away and accelerate on pencils of fire. He turned to the sergeant.

'We'll be at the ruins by nightfall, I take it?'

'So too.'

'Put us down as close to the storage buildings as you can. What will the light be like?'

'Moon's up, but the light's deceptive.'

'Good. When we get there, have your men leave their bikes, set up their tents and disperse into the buildings. Do anything else you can think of to make the camp *appear* occupied.'

'A trap, sir?' Arn smiled his tight little smile.

'Oh yes,' said Cormac. 'But I want at least one of them alive. You have stun weapons?'

'We've got an armoury, sir.'

'Good, you'll have opportunity to use it.'

'He's ECS and he'll be running a team to shut down the local syndicates,' said Corlackis.

The woman nodded, her comunit earrings glittering in the green light. Stanton knew the type: she wore a skin-tight shiny plastic from neck to feet and her thick brown hair spread in dreadlocks, plaits and artistic tangles across her shoulders and down her back. He could just make out a small aug in the shape of a star behind her right ear. At her hip was holstered a long-barrelled pulse-gun of the kind that fired ionized gas. Real fancy, but no range. She was obviously fascinated by the silent, glaring presence of Pelter, and by Crane who was crouching behind him. Stanton lowered the police-issue intensifier, its lenses whirring as it tried to compensate for this movement, and then he upped the gain on the directional microphone. That none of them had thought to use the damper showed Pelter's arrogance had to be catching. That the local muscle chose to have this meeting on the veranda of this café bespoke another arrogance. They wished to demonstrate to the great Separatist leader that this was an area they controlled.

The three men and the other woman were much like their boss: the kind that Stanton had hired on many occasions. He judged them to be supporters of the Cause only in that it gave them an excuse for racketeering. Like so many would-be freedom fighters, they had probably found the attraction of easy money harder to resist than a few hazy ideals. They affected dress similar to that of Mennecken and Corlackis, but Stanton knew that the two mercenaries could go through them in a second. That of course was not their intention. These people were fodder. Stanton knew exactly what Pelter intended.

It had taken Stanton a day to find out where to look. It was the area of the city of Motford that had the highest crime rate, where weapons were worn openly, and where dubious characters loitered on the streets. After then asking a few questions in bars, he had found out who was running things in the area. Following the woman had been easy. Nothing about her was covert. She swanned about in an expensive Aston Martin replica as she and her heavies went on their collection rounds. Patient watching had finally produced this meeting.

'Why did he head away from the city?' the woman asked.

Corlackis replied smoothly. 'To set up a base of operations. It's his usual technique: use local forces to establish a base where least expected, then, when he starts hitting you, you just won't know where to look. We saw it on Cheyne III. We spent months searching the most likely places and paying thousands in bribes to the local police. It was nearly all over before we discovered his base on one of the atolls.'

Stanton took his eyes from the intensifier and glanced behind, across the small AGC park on top of the building. Local police. He cursed the fact that they were so humanitarian here. This surveillance equipment, two stun pistols and a stun rifle had been the extent of his haul. The charge in the rifle he had used up at close range on the AGC, to burn the paint off. Not that it would have been much use to him. He could have been fairly sure of taking down the locals. But Pelter, Mennecken and Corlackis were another matter. Crane of course would have been unaffected. A stupid option, though. He wanted Pelter dead, not stunned.

'We can take him down,' one of the men drawled.

Stanton wondered how Corlackis kept a straight face at that.

'Not so easy if he has ES regulars with him,' he said.

'They're easy. Boys playing soldier games,' said the woman.

Corlackis shook his head. 'I admire your confidence, but would not want you to take on something you couldn't handle, nor would I want you to go unrewarded.'

The hook was in. Stanton shook his head at the ease of it all. They hadn't even asked why Corlackis and the rest would not be going in themselves. Corlackis now looked round at Pelter, who gave a nod. Corlackis tossed something on the table. One etched sapphire, Stanton bet. The woman snatched it up.

'Three more when the job is done,' Corlackis said.

'No problem,' said the woman.

The other four said nothing. They were too busy looking tough and confident behind their black eye-bands. Corlackis now reached under the table and picked up a cloth-wrapped bundle, which he placed before the woman. The woman reached across and flipped the cloth aside, completely unconcerned that anyone might see an assault rifle revealed.

'We have seeker bullets as well,' said Corlackis. 'We would not see you go in unprepared.'

'How many?'

'You can have this rifle and a sufficient quantity of seeker rounds. We've got laser carbines as well. As many as you need. We also have a nice compact mortar you can use.'

Stanton saw the greedy expression on the woman's face. She must think all her birthdays had come at once. Poor sap.

'We get to keep them?'

'But of course,' said Corlackis.

Stanton lowered the intensifier and shut off the microphone. He had heard and seen enough. He gazed out beyond the city line to the slabbed land beyond. Svent and Dusache had gone that way, after the military carrier and that was where the action would take place. Right now Stanton did not have a way of getting close to Pelter and killing him. Others did have the means. It did not matter to him *how* Pelter died, just that he did. He crouched back from the edge, stood up, then walked over to his stolen AGC. Pelter would leave soon, but Stanton had no intention of following him. He'd follow the five below. He would have no problem trailing such amateurs.

25

Ian Cormac: Yet another mythical creation of hero-starved humanity. Earth Central Security does have its monitors, its Sparkind and troops, and, yes, it does have its secret agents. But let us be honest about these people: they are, on the whole, grey and characterless. Again, this is all about what we want to believe. We want this superagent who so easily sorts out all the bad guys for us. Cormac is to ECS what a certain agent with the number 007 was to MI5. At best he is a fictional creation, at his worst he is a violent and disruptive role model.

From *Quince Guide*, compiled by humans

The light was like clotted blood and seemed to tangle the shadows in the chequer trees beyond the encampment in swirls and eddies, and strange globular buds glistened in the branches like molluscs. The encampment itself was lit by lights inside some of the tents. It had been Arn's idea to inflate a couple of survival suits with crash foam and sit them inside the tents. With a radio playing some monotonous atonal singing, the whole was quite convincing. Crouched behind a crumbling wall, Cormac surveyed the trees through the night-setting on his visor. Amongst the native chequer trees, so named because of the pattern of their bark, were blue oaks: a variety much used in the later stages of terraforming projects, and called so because their acorns were blue. They grew very slowly, but were hardy enough to withstand extremes of weather not found on Earth. Beside Cormac crouched Thorn and the two dracomen. Aiden and Cento were somewhere in the trees, using thermal scanners to pick up on whoever might come. They had been gone for two hours.

'Why's the moonlight so red?' asked Thorn.

Cormac had wondered that, too. The sunlight was turned a weak green by the atmosphere, yet under reflected light from the moon it took on the colour of old blood. He had asked Cento for an explanation.

He informed Thorn, 'The green sunlight's caused by the atmosphere – aerial algae apparently. The moon has huge mixed deposits of cinnabar and fluorspar on its surface. That's where the red light comes from.'

'How come?'

'I asked the same question. Cinnabar is a red pigment; it's also mercuric sulphide. Mining it is the chief economic resource here. There's a runcible up there for transporting tankers of mercury all over the sector. The fluorspar is fluorescent. The combination of the two produces that red light, even when the daytime sky is green.'

'Oh,' said Thorn, and fell silent.

Cormac gave him an assessing look. Only as they had been speaking had he noticed that Thorn kept one of the proton guns resting against the wall next to him.

'Little excessive?' he said, nodding at the weapon.

Thorn picked it up and held it almost lovingly. In its main chamber the light was subdued: it writhed and shifted, a luminescent mist.

'Well,' said Thorn, 'I do have to test this chap.'

Cormac reserved comment on that. There was little chance that any of the weapons provided for this operation would not work. They continued watching.

'You are to be attacked by other humans?'

Cormac turned in surprise to look straight into the teeth of a grinning dracoman. It was the first question from one of them since they had been picked up by *Hubris*.

'Yes,' said Cormac, 'killers out for vengeance on me.'

'This would endanger mission.'

'Yes, it—'

The dracoman slid off into the night. It was gone before Cormac could say another word.

'Speedy chap,' observed Thorn.

The other dracoman moved up beside Cormac and took hold of his biceps. Its hand was an iron manacle closing.

'You will not be harmed,' said the dracoman.

Cormac tried to free his arm. 'Let me go, damn it!'

The dracoman lost interest in him and turned its head away. It did not release its hold.

'You're supposed to obey—'

'Someone coming,' came Aiden's voice over com. 'One figure approaching. Just walking in . . . Who is that coming from your direction? I thought—' There was a pause of a couple of seconds. 'I see. Did you send this dracoman out?'

'I didn't send it. What's it doing?'

'It's lined up like a pointer to the trace.'

'Just one figure approaching you say? You're not missing anything?'

'No, this scanner is the best, and Cento and I are also watching full-spectrum. There is no individual chameleonware that sophisticated.'

'Could it be the android?'

'No, not big enough and wrong heat emission for a metal-skin. It's a man, heavily built. He could be nothing to do with Pelter.'

'Aiden, I want whoever that is alive. If the dracoman goes for him, flatten it. Otherwise just keep watching and let him walk in.'

'Will do,' the Golem replied.

Cormac looked with irritation at the dracoman still clamped on to his arm, then watched the trees.

Aiden spoke over the com again. 'Our dracoman just got a bit frisky,' he said. In the background there was a sound as of someone shoving a knife into a tyre.

'What happened?' Cormac asked.

'I'm sitting on him,' said Aiden.

Cormac looked at the dracoman holding him. He could not help but appreciate the humour of the situation.

'Where's the man now?' he asked.

'Should be coming into sight.'

The figure that walked from the forest, with his shadow cast before him by the bloody moonlight, was immediately familiar to Cormac. He turned his attention to his shuriken holster. Its small screen was lit just enough in the darkness for him to make his selection of program, straining against the grip of the dracoman at every moment. When he had it set, he flipped the weapon into his hand and tossed it into the air. The shuriken shot away with a whickering sound. It stopped in midair only a metre or so in front of the man. The man halted, then he looked around.

'This will fool them, Ian Cormac,' he said, 'but it won't fool Pelter.'

Cormac pulled against the restraining hand and the dracoman reluctantly let him stand. It stood with him, baring its teeth at the shadowed figure.

'It won't fool who, John?' he asked.

Stanton made a careful gesture towards the shuriken. 'Can I come on in?'

'Just walk. It'll stay the same distance ahead of you. Don't make any sudden moves, and don't touch any weapons you might have,' Cormac told him.

Stanton walked on into the encampment. As the light from the tents revealed him, Cormac saw a thinner-faced individual than the one he had known. Stanton was also decidedly battered.

'I don't have any weapons – only information,' he said.

'Why are you here, John?'

'To see Pelter dead, that's all.'

'That's far enough. Now explain yourself,' said Cormac.

Stanton glanced behind him. 'I don't have much time to explain. You're going to be hit very soon now.'

'By Pelter, or by these others you refer to?'

'The others. Pelter won't come in here without some idea of what you've got. He hired people here, armed them, and promised them a shitload of cash. He's going to use them as a probe, an expendable probe. You know what he's like.'

'Why should I believe you?'

'Because I walked in here unarmed. Because I just don't care any more. You can take me, but just get Pelter.'

Cormac looked at Stanton estimatingly. There was something in his voice. Something he perhaps might not have been able to discern when he was gridlinked. It struck him that this was sincerity.

'We have heat traces,' came Aiden's voice over the com.

'That'll be them,' said Stanton.

Cormac hit the recall and shuriken grudgingly returned. He held up his arm and it snicked into place in the holster. 'John, get over here, now.'

Stanton broke into a jog and ducked down behind the wall with them. He looked with a kind of tired curiosity at the dracoman clinging to Cormac's arm. Cormac pointed at it.

'This fella is very anxious about my security. Understand that he'll rip you apart if you try anything.' Cormac nodded to Thorn. 'Search him.'

Thorn quickly and efficiently ran his hands through Stanton's clothing. He pulled aside a ripped trouser leg to expose the empty sheath there, then nodded at Cormac before ducking back down. Stanton crouched as well.

'What have you got now, Aiden?'

The Golem's voice sounded different now. Cormac

realized that this difference stemmed from the fact that it was no longer speaking. It was broadcasting directly.

'Trace blurring now. They are dividing. Five bodies . . . Dracoman gone . . . We are going for cover now.'

'Remember, fire only when they reach the camp. Which of you has that stun gun?'

'I do,' said Cento.

'Well, put it away. We no longer need a live one.' He turned to Stanton. 'What will they have?'

'Assault weapons, a mortar and a few laser carbines. One of them has a Devcon loaded with seeker bullets.'

'Passing us now,' said Aiden.

Suddenly there was a scream, then the stutter of a pulse-rifle. Garish flashes lit the trees. One tree was blasted to flinders. The scream ceased.

'That cuts it,' came Arn's annoyed comment.

'Damn! Hold fire until you've identified your targets. I don't want one of you hitting Cento or Aiden.'

A flare went up through the trees and a man was halfway across the clearing before the light gave him away. He opened fire on the tents. Flames and smoke revealed the beam from a laser carbine. There was the blue flash of a pulse-rifle and he went face-down in the dirt. More firing, then a horrible hornetlike buzzing. Two explosions in the buildings to the right. A horrible sucking gasp over the com.

'Shit! Seeker bullets!'

'Heat flares!' shouted Cormac.

Like the finale of a fireworks display, orange flares shot in every direction amongst the buildings. The buzzing continued. Two flares went out and a nearby explosion rained flakes of rubble down on Cormac's head. The dracoman pulled him lower and he swore at it. Another stuttering pulse of light.

'They're back to the lasers,' said Arn.

'Where are you, Cento? Aiden?'

'Moving clear,' they replied simultaneously.

Then Aiden said, 'There's one to the left of the carrier operating a mortar. Can't get a clear shot from here.'

'Got him,' replied Thorn.

There was a purple flash and loud crack. A white explosion split in two a tree with a trunk a metre thick. Subliminally Cormac saw something, which might have been a man, blacken, disappear.

'There's one just beyond that burning tent – no, the dracoman's on him.'

The scream was horrible. Cormac saw two shadows grappling. One shadow folded the other to the ground. He was sure he could hear bones breaking.

'Only one left, I take it,' said Cormac acidly.

'Up and running,' said Aiden. 'Dracoman's after him. You want me to get him?'

'Leave it,' said Cormac, and let out a tight breath. He looked over the wall at the spirals of smoke. Over to his right someone was talking in a low monotone. To his left there was a sudden stuttering of pulse-gun fire. He swore and dropped back down.

'I said leave it,' he said into his comunit.

'Something in the trees,' came Goff's reply.

'Aiden, you getting anything?'

'Nothing now, but there was a trace just then. Moved too fast to be a bird,' the Golem replied.

'Surveillance drone?'

'Possible.'

'Any other traces?'

'Nothing.'

On that last word the second dracoman released Cormac's arm. He pulled away, dropped his comunit in his top pocket, and then turned on the dracoman.

'Do that again and I cut your fucking hand off,' he said.

The dracoman showed its teeth. It could have been a smile.

Cormac left it and went to find out who had died.

Two of the regulars were dead. Seeker bullets had ripped through their body armour and the pressure vessels they contained had exploded with messy results. Cormac was told one of them was the soldier Cheng. Cormac had what remained of the men scooped up and put in body-bags, then shallow-buried at the perimeter of the camp. The three recoverable bodies – the men the dracoman had killed – were brought in and laid out. Cormac recognized none of them. He turned to Stanton, just behind whom stood Thorn and Sergeant Arn.

'Locally hired,' he said.

'Yes, but Pelter has four you know with him,' Stanton replied.

Cormac looked at him questioningly.

Stanton went on. 'Corlackis and his brother, Svent and Dusache.'

'When will they come in? Soon?'

'No, Pelter won't want it over that quickly.'

Cormac nodded, then looked at the sergeant. 'Take him into the carrier, strip-search him, then tie him up.'

The sergeant obeyed with a kind of grim relish. Cormac wondered if he expected entertainment in repayment for the deaths of his two men. He would be disappointed. He noticed that Stanton went without protest. The man seemed broken, grieving. He'd have to get the full story from him later. Right now he wanted everything organized, precise. Much as he was inclined to believe what Stanton had told him, he still was not prepared to relax defences here. With Thorn at his back he walked towards Aiden, who was crouching by the wreckage of what had been a tree before Thorn's attentions.

'That dracoman back yet?' he asked.

Aiden glanced up and said, 'No, but we have an AGC coming in directly.'

'Scatter!'

The men ran for cover. Cormac turned to Thorn. 'Get in the carrier. If it fires on us, use the turret weapons.'

Thorn nodded and ran for the carrier. Cormac watched the Sparkind leap Stanton, who was now face-down on the ground, with Arn tying his wrist behind him. That was covered, then. Cormac jogged over to Aiden, thinking to take cover behind the wrecked branches of the tree. The familiar pad of feet behind him abrogated that intention for the moment. He turned and drew his shuriken as the remaining dracoman came trotting in.

The dracoman halted.

'One step closer. Go on – just one.'

The dracoman seemed to find this amusing, then boring. It looked up at the sky for a moment, then turned and trotted away. Cormac ran for the tree and dived down beside Aiden. He looked about and saw that everyone else was concealed.

'The AGC is coming right in,' said Aiden.

Cormac looked up into the red night and saw that the car had its running lights on. It was an Aston Martin replica, but with its underside constructed like the hull of a speedboat. Whoever was driving it seemed to be having some problem with the controls. It swayed to a halt above the camp, then slowly started to descend. That descent speeded at the last moment and it slammed down in the middle of the camp. Cormac had shuriken in his hand, even though he knew that plenty of other weapons were pointed at the AGC. The door clicked open and the missing dracoman stepped out. Cormac swore, stood up and walked over to it. Had the other one known?

As he drew close, Cormac saw blood on the inside of the car's windows. A glance inside revealed to him a body slumped in the back seat with its head nearly ripped off. He went closer and saw it was a woman, a great mass of tangled hair spread about her, soaking up the blood. It was no one he recognized. She had to be the one that escaped. He would have to ask Stanton. He turned to the dracoman.

'We could call him Scar now,' said Thorn, from behind him.

Cormac studied the dracoman's face and saw it had been opened from one nostril to just underneath its eye. Its blood was the colour and consistency of mustard.

430

'And what do we call the other one?' asked Cormac.

'Nonscar?'

'Yeah, good. Now let's get this mess cleared up and a rota set up,' he said. He looked up at the sky. 'How long till dawn?'

'Ten hours, solstan,' Thorn replied.

'We'll sleep in groups of four in the carrier. Let the ES ones go first. We shouldn't be any less secure than we were. Oh, I want someone at that turret gun at all times.'

It took an hour to clear the camp and set up further covert defences. Aiden and Cento acted as guards, since they needed no sleep.

'We'll need to take out that turret gun. When he finds out you're not amongst the dead, he'll know it was just a probe. There won't be a trap next time,' said Corlackis.

'Of course,' said Pelter, his eyes still glued to the screen stuck to the framework of the missile launcher.

'So really it's just that and the two Golem.'

Pelter glanced aside and waved to Svent to take them down. Svent nodded, and fiddled with the old guide-ball control of the transporter. Slowly it started to drop down into the trees. In the shadow the thick photoactive paint on it slowly changed from a deep red to greenish black. Corlackis tapped at the controls on the miniconsole he was holding, then dropped it into his pocket.

'What about those two lizard men?' asked Dusache.

'Don't concern yourself,' said Pelter. 'You'll be on this platform operating the launcher. You take out the carrier. Myself, Mr Crane, Mennecken and Corlackis will be going in on the ground.'

'Crane will be able to handle the Golem?' Corlackis asked.

'He will handle them,' said Pelter. 'Remember that arrogant bitch on Huma? No, we go in and we flatten them. Of course none of you hits Cormac – not even by accident. He is mine.'

Branches broke and flicked round the transporter, and large leaves spiralled down with it. Svent landed it by the private AGC that was already on the ground.

'When do we hit them?' Mennecken asked.

'Not yet,' said Pelter, then looked up as four objects settled through the trees. In the dim light they were difficult to see until very close. When visible, they had the appearance of small birds of transparent film stretched over black bones. They came in to land in a neat row on the launcher, where they closed their wings and became featureless ovoids. Corlackis took up a metal box from the deck and carefully placed each of the surveillance drones in its respective compartment. As an afterthought he took the miniconsole from his pocket and placed it in its compartment as well.

The sky was a kind of muddy-brown just before sunrise. Cormac would not have seen it, as he had been deeply asleep. But Aiden shook him awake.

'Another AGC coming directly here. Cento is rousing the others.'

Cormac rubbed sleep from his eyes. 'What's going on, they relocated the AGC park?'

'Pardon?'

'Never mind.'

Cormac sat upright and looked around. Thorn was

already at the door of the carrier, his weapon resting on his shoulder. The sergeant and one of the two men were putting on their boots. Lying with his cuffed wrists secured to a steadying handle above one of the bunks, Stanton watched with disinterest. Cormac slid from his bed fully dressed. It was not the first time he had slept in body-armour.

'How far?' he asked.

'Ten minutes away.'

Cormac turned to Stanton. 'Pelter?'

Stanton shrugged. 'Could be, but I doubt it. He'll want you to sweat for a while.'

Cormac snorted and turned away. 'Who's on the turret gun? . . . Never mind. Sergeant, no firing unless fired on. Thorn, Aiden, with me.'

The sergeant began speaking into his comunit as the three headed for the door. Above, they heard the drone of hydraulics as the turret gun swung round. Outside, Cormac saw that the men were dispersed around the camp with their weapons trained on the sky. Once again an AGC came in with its lights on and landed in the middle of the camp. Cormac immediately recognized the diminutive figure that stepped out, and advanced from cover with a smile on his face. Taking their cue from him, the other men did the same.

'All this fuss over me,' said Mika as she lifted a case from the AGC. 'I could get to like it.'

It was the first time Cormac had heard her be coquettish. It seemed very unlike her. He had imagined her as being more direct.

'It's good to see you, but why are you here?' asked Cormac.

'They're refitting the *Hubris*. It's like a madhouse there. I asked Blegg if I could come to follow up on some studies.' She looked pointedly at the dracomen as they came from the trees to squat by the carrier.

'He's still there then – Blegg?'

'Yes, and managing to annoy everyone with the minimum effort.'

They walked towards the carrier.

Mika went on. 'I also thought you might need a medic, if you haven't got one . . .'

'A couple of the men are trained, Thorn as well. There was an attack last night, but most injuries have been tended to.'

'Attack. Presumably not the Maker?'

'A Separatist group.'

Mika nodded. 'I see one injury that hasn't been tended to,' she said. She gestured to the dracoman now called Scar.

Cormac could not think of a reply. Just then one of the regulars came running across.

'Sir! Sir! Something took one of the bodies in the night.'

Mika looked at Cormac, and Cormac looked at Mika. They both looked at the dracomen.

'Probably an animal. We should have buried them,' Cormac told the man.

'Shall we bury them, sir?'

'If you like.'

The regular departed.

'You could have at least fed them,' said Mika accusingly, and then walked over to the wounded dracoman. Cormac watched her go, a slight smile twisting his features, and then he frowned and headed back for the carrier. Once inside he called to the soldier at the gun.

'You, go outside for a moment, please,' he said.

The soldier climbed down from the control seat, saluted, and quickly went on his way. Cormac dropped down on the bunk opposite Stanton.

'You were right,' he said.

Stanton just stared back at him.

Cormac went on. 'How long do you think Pelter will . . . let me sweat?'

'The longer he leaves it, the more it will work for him. Your men will be tired, less alert. But he does want to kill you rather badly. I'd say two days at most.'

'Now tell me why I should believe you.'

Stanton looked down at the floor for a long moment before replying. 'Pelter has a large quantity of money with him. I intended to relieve him of it once I found a way round Crane.'

'Crane?'

'Mr Crane. The broken Golem. Watch out for him. He was a Twenty-five, and now he's armoured and very tough. You wouldn't believe what he's capable of.'

'I would,' said Cormac. 'I have two Golem Thirties with me.'

Stanton stared for a long moment, then a slow smile broke out on his face. 'Won't Pelter be surprised,' he said.

'Tell me about this money. That's not like you, John. You've had ample opportunity to rip Pelter off.'

'That's what Jarvellis said.'

'Jarvellis?'

Stanton told him, and Cormac made his decision. He couldn't wait for Pelter. He needed to resolve some things now before Dragon got impatient and threw a tantrum that many of those on Samarkand might not survive. He took up the two Enropower boxes from under one of the bunks, and then left Stanton where he was. Outside the carrier he turned to the soldier.

'Get back on that gun. The call I'm just about to put out does not apply to you.'

The man nodded and quickly ducked back inside the carrier. Cormac tucked one of the boxes under his arm and pulled his comunit.

'I want all of you into the camp right now,' he said, and then walked to where Mika was working on Scar. He saw that she had been forced to use wire to pull together the rent in Scar's tough hide. The dracoman seemed unconcerned. Cormac wondered if an anaesthetic had been used, if one had even been needed. He dropped the two boxes at his feet and looked around as they all came in.

Thorn, Aiden and Cento were the first to join him, all three of them carrying energy weapons, then the sergeant with his six remaining men. When they were all gathered round, Cormac studied them for a moment before speaking.

'Right. There's another group out there who may attack. We stay here and they can come in at their leisure. I know their leader, Arian Pelter, and am certain that any plans he's formulating revolve around an attack on us on the ground. Especially as those plans will be dependent on the broken Golem he has with him, one Mr Crane.' He shot a look at Aiden and Cento, but could discern no reaction. 'I'm not prepared to wait for that attack. I came here to do a job, and I'm going to do it. Sergeant, I want you and your men up as spotters and as a first line. I want you, with another man on the turret guns, to take up the carrier and circle the perimeter of the ruins. The rest of your men will operate outside that perimeter, as before. If it looks like anyone is coming in, you inform me immediately and then we form our response to the nature of the attack. This is where Pelter falls down: he can't do that. He's ruthless, but stubborn to the point of idiocy. He'll stick with a plan to the end. We – ' Cormac gestured to Cento, Aiden and Thorn, ' – will be going in on sky-bikes. If we come out in a hurry you get to the ground and under cover. Your main concern then will be self-preservation. Any questions?'

The sergeant shook his head.

'Very well, get going.'

'You want me out of the way,' said Mika.

Cormac nodded and turned his attention to the draco-men. 'Dragon wanted you here. You have been useful, but I cannot see what purpose you might serve now. Do you have any suggestions?'

The dracomen stared at him in silence.

'Very well, Mika, take them with you and stay with that AGC. If we run, be ready to come with us back to the runcible. Let's go.'

The men broke and headed off into the surrounding trees. Cormac stooped down and picked up the two boxes at his feet. By then the sergeant was already in the carrier. There was a low thrum of AG and a backwash of dust as he took it into the sky. Five sky-bikes followed him up. Cormac gestured to the three with him and walked over to the two remaining sky-bikes.

'There been any movement in the ruins?' he asked

Aiden replied, 'No movement, but the Maker is certainly in one of the underground silos. Viridian reported a change in energy levels last night during the attack, but that was all.'

'OK, we'll land as close as we can get and go in on foot. I want some idea of what we're dealing with. That at least.'

'We're dealing with the thing that killed Gant,' said Thorn.

Cormac studied him speculatively before going on. 'We're still operating on the premise that what Dragon told us is true. I don't like that, but those are my instructions. We'll try the proton guns first. I don't want to be responsible for levelling a heritage site just yet.' He glanced at Cento and Aiden. 'You two can fly them. Thorn and I will go pillion. If there's any kind of attack, take us down into the forest on the other side.'

The two Golem mounted the sky-bikes. Cormac placed the two boxes in a pannier before mounting up behind Cento. As Cento lifted the bike into the sky behind Aiden and Thorn, Cormac wondered at the Golem's lack of comment.

'Do you have a problem with what I'm doing?' he asked.

'I have no problem. The mission is paramount and you cannot wait for an attack that may or may not come.'

'Then it's the broken Golem, isn't it?'

Cento took a moment to reply. When he did reply his voice was flat and characterless.

'If there is a hell for us, then that is where this Mr Crane is.'

26

*I have to state categorically that I believe in him. The
Quince Guide (which I do not believe was compiled
by humans; more likely it was compiled to mislead
humans) has it that he is a mythical character comparable to Robin Hood or King Arthur. Let's look at
the legend. He is supposed to be immortal, and supposed to possess powers the like of which enabled him
to survive the destruction of his home city of Hiroshima. He is supposed to have meddled with human
destiny, and to still be meddling . . . Oh hell, I'm
rambling. The plain truth of the matter is that I believe
in him because of his name. For Chrissake, what
myth-maker worth his salt would come up with such
a ridiculous name for someone who is practically a
demigod? Horace Blegg, I ask you . . .*

From *How It Is* by Gordon

Jarvellis woke feeling sick, but not from pain or injury. It
struck her as ironic that here she was, a starship captain
without a ship, and suffering from space sickness. Her
condition, she supposed, aggravated the sickness. But
the main reason was that she was too soft these days. It

had been, as far as she could recollect, nearly five solstan years since she had experienced weightlessness. What need was there to experience it when every ship and station had gravplates? What need was there to experience its antithesis, when AG could waft a ship into orbit? Even visiting heavy-G worlds was not a problem. She either stayed in the ship or in areas adjusted to Earth gravity. With such thoughts she occupied herself as she fought nausea, and wondered when the Outlinkers would be back to take her out of this damned frame.

It was Tull who returned first. She could see that something more than her dangerous presence was worrying him. He came in and hovered over her, inspecting the sealed wounds. After a moment he went to inspect a readout on the medbot.

'Will you let me out of this?' Jarvellis asked.

Tull stared at her long and estimatingly.

'I'll be careful of you,' she added.

Tull made no move to release the clamps. Some of them were through to bone, and Jarvellis felt no inclination to fight them.

'I cannot contact the surface,' said Tull.

'Understandable,' said Jarvellis. 'You weren't much further from the EM pulse than me. It'll have knocked out your com.'

Tull nodded thoughtfully. 'I have cameras that track all objects that might represent a danger to this station. I've just looked at the replay.'

'Quite a firework display,' said Jarvellis uneasily.

'Yes, planar explosives unless I miss my bet. By the vector of the explosion, I would say it hit your underspace engine. My concern is why you would have such explosives onboard.'

Jarvellis found she just did not have the energy to lie creatively, so she kept her mouth shut. Tull pushed himself away from the frame and she tried to follow, with her eyes, where he went. He was out of sight only for a few seconds when something touched against the back of her neck. Numbness rolled down her body. Nerve-blocker. Everything bar the autonomics inclusive of breathing and heartbeat was shut down below her neck.

'What are you doing?' she asked.

'We are not uncivilized, Captain Jarvellis, but we are very aware of our fragility, as you know. I can only assume by your silence that you have been involved in something illegal, and that perhaps you would want to avoid talking to the ECS investigators when they eventually come up here.'

'Look,' said Jarvellis, 'just let me go. I won't cause you any problems. I've been through too much already.'

Tull came back into view. Jarvellis heard the clamps snapping off her body. To one side of Tull she saw a line of small ruby peas coiling away. Tull wiped them from the air with an absorbent pad. The cell-welder hummed briefly.

'That's it,' he said. 'I've given you two pints of synthetic blood so you shouldn't experience too much dizziness or nausea. The clamp and probe holes may be a bit sore, but they will quickly heal.'

'Then you can take the blocker off,' Jarvellis said.

'Not until I'm sure that myself and Jeth are utterly safe,' he replied.

'You're going to keep me like this until the investi-gators get here?'

Tull shook his head. 'I told you we are not un-civilized.'

Jarvellis felt herself drifting from the frame. Tull was propelling her to the door.

'It won't take me long to run a diagnostic and initiate another dish. In fact our transceiver will be back on line within the hour. It may take some time for the investigators to get here. For a ship blown in orbit with planar explosives, I should think we'll get someone from Earth. Nerve-blocking, for any length of time, can become a very unpleasant experience. There is also the chance that it might damage the innocent life you carry.'

He had her to the door now, and then through it. To her right the little robot had appeared and was swinging along with her.

'Are you sure about this?' she heard Jeth saying, but she could not see Tull's wife.

'Oh, I'm sure. Laser burns through her suit, planar explosives . . . we know what that means,' said Tull.

Jarvellis wondered what he would say if she told him how she had actually received the laser burn. Best not – he might keep her blocked for her own safety, and the safety of that 'innocent life', rather than for that of himself and his wife.

Soon Tull had her in the elevator and had pushed her to what would be the floor in the outer ring. Now she could see that Jeth was holding a bundle of clothing and a bag filled with blocky items. The Outlinker pressed these down beside her.

Tull said, 'When you reach the outer ring, Sam will

remove your blocker. After that all the elevators will be shut down. Now, there are service tubes you could find to get back here, but be aware that, should you try that, we will immediately leave the station, so you'll achieve nothing.'

Jeth said, 'Here's food and clothing.' She pointed to these items and turned away guiltily.

'I wouldn't have hurt you,' said Jarvellis. 'I've never hurt anyone.'

'Yes,' said Tull, stepping back with his wife, then closing the elevator door on her.

Jarvellis considered what she had just said. It was true: personally she had never inflicted injury on anyone. What concern was it of hers what people did with the weapons she smuggled? *They* were the criminals. She was just trying to make a decent profit. That was all right, wasn't it?

Weight returned and pulled her head down onto the worn decking. The elevator door slid open and, as it did so, feeling returned to her body. Jarvellis sat upright and looked down at Sam. The little robot held the nerve-blocker in one three-fingered claw. It held it up above itself as if frightened she was going to hit it and so was demonstrating how it had helped her. She looked to the bundle of clothes and the food. The latter was out of the question at the present. The one-quarter G that dispelled space sickness was pulling at and twisting those places where she had been cell-welded, and where the clamps and probes had been pulled out. She now effectively felt as if someone had methodically pinched over her skin with a pair of pliers. She reached for the clothing: disposable underwear and deck shoes, a soft cloth shirt and padded trousers. With hands that did not seem to have any grip in them she slowly dressed herself. Once this was done she felt better, and began to think what the future might hold for her. Her prospects did not seem much better than they had done outside. Now though, she was beginning to feel hope. Maybe John was not dead yet. Maybe, even if he was, she could get to that bastard Pelter. Maybe she *could* live.

'Please take the bag and step out of the elevator, Captain,' said Tull over an intercom.

Jarvellis did as she was told, faintly amused that the intercom had crackled like the one in the *Lyric*, only this intercom crackle was genuine.

'The cabins to your left you will find comfortable. We maintain them for visitors from the surface.'

She headed in that direction, wondering where Tull might have positioned pinhead cameras, then it occurred to her that the EM pulse might have knocked those out as well. Any systems on the outer ring of the station, unprotected by its bulk, would have gone down, and the little cameras were prone to do so. Then again, maybe there were no cameras. She was assuming he might be as paranoid as herself. She stopped at a door and pressed one of the two square buttons beside it. A buzzer sounded inside. She pressed the other button and the door slid open. At the threshold she paused; she might well be walking willingly into her own prison. She shook her head and stepped back. When the door closed again, she squatted down and opened the bag.

It contained fresh fruit, probably from the station's hydroponics, film-wrapped sandwiches with some sort of meat filling, even a small bottle of a wine that bore the name 'Passion' on its label. As Jarvellis looked up from the bag, it occurred to her that she would not remember the Outlinkers' generosity. After ECS tried her for arms smuggling, and then mind-wiped her, she would remember nothing. She'd be a pregnant mother operating on instinct: a mere animal until they downloaded a personality into her, and – whether construct or real – that personality would never be her own. She closed the bag, stood up, and began walking. In the cabin she could just hear Tull's voice speaking over the intercom. No cameras, then. She knew that the Outlinkers would have some sort of AG shuttle at the centre of the station for their own use. What she now wondered was if any of the station's original shuttles remained in this outer ring.

Dawn flung greenhouse light across the land. It seemed, with this coloration to the light, that the temperature should be high. But the day began wintry and showed no sign of changing as it advanced. Viewed from above, the ruins had the appearance of an impact site in the forest of blue oaks and chequer trees, and perhaps at one time that was precisely what this had been. The two bikes skimmed over crumbling buildings towards the central ring of the broken dome. They came in to land at the edge of the dome, where there was just enough room to fit the sky-bikes close together on apparently firm ground.

Donning their helmets, the four advanced through the wreckage, their boots crunching on broken glass and heat-splintered plascrete. All around, old wiring and the remnants of computer systems were sinking into decay.

Most surfaces were covered with grey and yellow lichens. This ruin could have been thousands of years old, rather than the few hundred it actually was. Soon all four stood at the rim of the dark shaft of one of the underground silos.

Cormac gazed into that dark and contemplated what these ruins meant. This is what happened when worlds seceded from the Polity. This is what happened when base humanity tried to govern itself.

'Cormac,' came Mika's voice over his comunit. 'The dracomen just grabbed the AGC. They're coming your way.'

'Shit!'

Cormac looked up at the sky, but could see no craft. What was Dragon up to? What were the dracomen up to? He was tempted to put a hold on the mission until he found out, but, after thinking about the chances of getting some answers out of the dracomen, he decided to go on.

'Thorn, put a shot down there and see what stirs.'

Thorn leant over the edge and fired. The purple flash disclosed the depth of the silo before rubble exploded from it on a hot flash. Something began screeching in the ruins behind them and they turned to see a couple of corvine birds flap raggedly into the sky. Thorn tracked their course for a moment, and then turned back to the silo. The rest of them turned with him and, as smoking stones rained down, they waited expectantly.

Eventually Thorn said, in a bored voice, 'Nothing stirring.'

'Try the next one,' Cormac told him.

They circled the edge of the silo, well back from the

corroded metal at its lip. Thorn made adjustments on his weapon.

'If this doesn't work, do we move on to the CTDs?' he asked casually.

'Have to,' said Cormac.

He could see Thorn's smile of satisfaction.

Shortly they reached the lip of the next silo.

'Energy readings . . . difficult to locate,' said Aiden.

Thorn moved forwards. 'We'll see—'

It shot out of the next silo like a white-hot jack-in-the-box. Cormac's visor polarized, re-adjusted – and before him was the fantastic creation of some godlike glass-maker. It was a dragon, a real dragon. Then, the next moment, it was not.

The Maker seemed to be made of glass supported by bones that were glowing tungsten filaments. It had a long swanlike neck ending in a nightmare head that had something of a lizard and something of a praying mantis about it. Wings opened out, seemingly batlike at first, then taking on the appearance of a mass of sails. A heavy claw gripped the edge of the underground silo, or was it a hand shaped like the body of a millipede, with hundreds of leglike fingers? A glowing bullwhip tail thrashed the air, sprouted sails, fins, light. Cormac froze. The Maker was about five metres high. How had it gotten through a twenty-centimetre hole? Then he realized: it was not matter, it was energy; it could prob-ably be any size. He had just never seen anything like it before. Was it Dragon's ultimate joke to name itself thus, when the kind that had made it looked like this?

'Bastard!' came Thorn's voice over the static on com. He fired. The proton beam hit the Maker and diffused from the other side. It jerked back and a bolt of white light shot from its jaws, splashed into Thorn and wrapped around him. For a moment he seemed to be struggling against snakes of light, then, as if the force of it had only just caught up, he was flung back. Cento and Aiden fired too. In return, two bolts of a different colour hit them. They both sat down with an undignified thump. Cormac lowered his weapon as the creature rose over him. Then an AGC streaked past its head, and it turned to watch the car as it circled and came back. The top of the car had been ripped away, and the dracomen were visible. One of them was firing a laser carbine. Pins of red light were flickering in the Maker's body; beyond this there was no visible effect. The car streaked past again and kept going. The Maker made a sound like the gusting sigh of a strong wind, watching them go, then turned its attention back to Cormac.

Cormac stooped down and placed his weapon on the ground. Over his comunit he could hear strange whist-lings and creakings. The Maker brought its head closer to him. He could feel the energy of it; as a tension in his face and a thrumming in his bones. He could see that it possessed three of what seemed to be eyes. Mandibles of glass opened from the sides of its jaws. Cormac looked into the throat of hell.

Again: laser fire flickering inside the glassy body. The dracomen were back. The AGC circled and the draco-man with the carbine fired continuously. The Maker made that wind-sound again, but now there seemed to be to Cormac an element of anger in it. Fire flashed from its mouth and struck the AGC. The car shuddered and pieces of it fell from the sky. It shuddered again and something detonated under its cowling. Trailing black smoke, it went into a dive and eventually fell into the forest to the north of the ruin. The Maker turned its head and looked at Cormac again, its glass mandibles opening and closing as if in indecision, or anticipation. Then, with a surge of power and light, it launched itself into the sky, remained poised there for a moment, then shot down into the trees.

'Oh my God! Ohmegod!'

'Colonel, sir, please respond. The creature—'

'What the fuck?'

'Will you look at that!'

'Shaddup, Goff! Colonel? Colonel?'

Cormac did not want to answer. He could do without those jabbering human voices. There was a stillness here that he wanted to savour. But, as he stood motionless, his sense of duty re-asserted itself. He sighed and returned to the world.

'Cormac here.'

'Sir, an AGC just went down in the forest, a thing . . . light . . . It landed where the AGC crashed.'

'What's happening now?'

'Trees . . . burning . . . No, it's coming up!'

Cormac stared across the ruins and saw the Maker rise into the sky. It held the two dracomen silhouetted against its body, looking black as if charred by that fantastic light. Suddenly it became an actinic torpedo, blurred, wing-sails grabbing at the air, and then it became a streak of fire to the east.

That it had no AG was obvious at a glance through the dusty portal. Its main body was a flattened cylinder terminating in a full-screen chainglass cockpit. A pair of ion engines was set back on either side of the cockpit, and another pair was set just forward of a stabilizing fin like a huge rudder. Each of the four engines was a sphere with a slice taken off it to expose the grids inside. Each could be moved independently to give a degree of forward and reverse thrust, but only so far as they did not blast into each other. The shuttle might well be fuelled and its small fusion tokomac might still be serviceable, Jarvellis could not tell. The shuttle rested on the floor of the small bay with the doors open before it, and the arc of the station curving away from the top of that opening. If she wished to reach it, she had to cross ten metres of floor through vacuum. That would not have been too much of a problem for the Outlinkers, and maybe she too could have made it. But how long would it take for the lock on this side of the bay to cycle? How long for the lock on the shuttle? And would there be atmosphere inside it?

Jarvellis moved away from the portal and looked around. This worn corridor ran round the bay in an arc, and there were doors behind her. She tried one, pressing the correct button this time. The door slid aside with a low grinding to reveal a wedge-shaped room that was utterly empty. The fifth room she tried contained the lockers and soon she was inspecting a spacesuit that made the one she had owned seem state of the art. It had a bowl helmet of scratched plastiglass: a helmet that was actually breakable. The material of the suit itself was layered, and just that: material. There was no armouring, no sealant layer. Air was provided by an external bottle with a vulnerable pipe that plugged into the neck-ring. She wiped dirt from an old digital readout and saw that the bottle did contain air, though how the pressure reading related to time or suit pressure, she could not say. Laboriously she pulled the suit on, and then tucked the helmet under her arm as she headed for the lock. The inner door, a great thick thing that actually operated on hinges, opened with surprising silence. As she stepped inside, a different noise greeted her.

'Is that you in that lock, Captain Jarvellis?' Tull asked over the intercom.

Jarvellis ignored the voice, put her helmet on and twisted it into place. Maybe the seals would not work so well. Maybe they would work for long enough. She opened the valve on the air bottle and got a hiss of air that was breathable, but had a vaguely putrid smell.

'Captain, please come out of that lock. Very little of the equipment there has been serviced. You could kill yourself . . . oh, I see . . . I wouldn't advise trying to use that shuttle. It has no AG, you realize? Those ion eng . . . you . . . s . . . t . . .'

The inner lock was irised. It made no noise as it opened, but that was because there was now no air to transmit sound. Neat way of shutting Tull up anyway. Jarvellis stepped out of the lock and hurried over to the shuttle. The door she saw was not a door with an airlock. She twisted the two handles at the side of it and hinged it open. It was a single-seal door; only with it closed would the shuttle fill with air. Back when this station was constructed, weight had played an all-important role. A full airlock would have been too much extra. Jarvellis stepped inside and closed the door.

White vapour was now leaking from the folds at the elbow of the primitive suit. It was also leaking out round the neck-seal and painting glitters of frost across the plastiglass.

The cabin of the shuttle was simply a plain box, with spring fixings along the floor to take either chairs or cargo straps. Ahead there was another hinged door. She moved quickly to it and tried to turn the handles. Nothing gave. She put her weight on the handles, and they started to move just before her feet left the floor. She pulled herself down and jammed her foot in one of the spring fixings to try again. Vapour bloomed around the door, then dissipated. She got it open and pulled herself in. Even as she closed the door, she found herself panting for air that was getting increasingly thin. A button. *Cycle.* She hit it and dragged herself to a dusty seat before the console and control column. She searched for a readout and found it above the door. The readout was in bar and she was not sure what was required. She cracked open the helmet when vapour ceased to flow from the seal. No difference now anyway; there was little left in the suit.

'Captain Jarvellis . . . Jarvellis . . . I hope you can hear me. Can you hear me?'

'Yes, I can hear you, Tull,' she said.

'Good,' said the Outlinker. 'Now, just so you don't kill us all by trying to start those ion engines in the station, I'll tell you how to use the magnetic impeller. It'll get you out of that bay and away. Beyond that, you're on your own.'

Jarvellis dropped into the pilot's seat. The padding crunched underneath her and dust circulated in the cockpit. She studied the antique controls and wondered if it might have been better to go meekly to mind-wipe.

'Go on, then, run me through it,' she said.

Aiden and Cento had their heads bowed and their shoulders slumped as if in exhaustion. Cormac saw that their emulations were off as well: not a breath moved their torsos, nor the flicker of an eyelid crossed their eyes. Like two marionettes with their strings cut, they sat on the lichen-covered plascrete and broken glass. Their weapons were lying on the ground beside them, ignored.

'Aiden? Cento?'

Was there something there? A shiver of movement? Cormac could not believe that they had been completely disabled. He had previously seen nothing short of a proton gun with that capability.

'Aiden?'

Aiden's head lifted slowly and he stared at Cormac as if he did not recognize him. He blinked once, slowly, and it seemed for a moment as if he was going to ask him something. Then Aiden's shoulders straightened, his breathing emulation restarted, and he slowly stood up.

'Just enough to knock out our systems,' he said, and looked down at Cento. Cento was slower to reassume his guise of humanity. First he practised a grin which was a parody, then his breathing emulation restarted and he too got up. Cormac turned away from them and went over to Thorn.

'Thorn?'

Thorn lay flat on his back, staring up at the sky. There

were burns on his clothing and there was a strong smell of burnt hair about him. His beard, Cormac noted, was in need of some reshaping. His helmet lay beside him with its glass still polarized. His weapon lay some distance away. A trickle of blood had congealed below his nose.

'About stun three,' he said tightly, and looked up at Cormac. Cento and Aiden passed Cormac on either side, reached down simultaneously, and pulled Thorn to his feet.

'Gave about as good as it got,' said Thorn from wobbly legs, then, freeing his right arm from Cento, ran his hand over his beard and frowned.

Cormac watched the three contemplatively; the only real injuries seemed to be to their dignity. 'It knocked you all down because you fired on it. Having the ability to knock out Aiden and Cento means it had the ability to kill you, Thorn . . . Tell me, Aiden, would you say that creature was completely constituted of energy fields?'

'That would not be possible. It must have some matter distribution for the fields to anchor themselves to, even if it is very diffuse. Dragon said it was partially gaseous.'

'Then I know how to kill it. Just as it knew precisely how to kill us. Come on.' As he walked back to the sky-bikes, Cormac pulled out his comunit. 'Sergeant, put the carrier down at our camp. Get your men down, too, and form a perimeter again.' He shut off the unit as the sergeant passed on his orders, then turned to Thorn. 'Thorn, I want you to think about this. When we went down that shaft a monster attacked us, and we fired on it.'

'Yes,' said Thorn.

'No, you see there's the rub. It may have come charging towards us, and it may have seemed intent on attack, but it did not scrap Cento nor kill Gant until we fired on it.'

'That's hard,' said Thorn.

'That's fact,' said Cormac. 'Maybe it intended to attack us – we don't know. We *do* know, however, that it was an organic machine dying from the cold.'

Cormac gestured to the bikes, and Aiden and Cento mounted them. As Thorn took the pillion behind Aiden he asked, 'What are you saying?'

'I'm saying I'm going to get to the truth of all this. You see, we've only heard one side of the story, so I want the rest of it.' He pulled his comunit as Cento took their bike into the sky. 'Mika, meet us in the carrier, will you? I'll be needing your input.'

'You'll be needing my input.'

Cormac grinned at the inferred question and turned the unit off. It could be a crippling fault, that inability to ask a direct question. He looked ahead and down, and saw the carrier landing. The diminutive figure of Mika was angrily striding across to it. The other sky-bikes were coming down in the forest around the encampment. When Cento landed, Cormac quickly hopped off and gestured to the other three.

'Come with me.'

He headed for the carrier, glanced at Mika, who was waiting beside it, then pulled open the door and stuck his head inside.

'Sergeant, if you and your man there could give us a moment?'

The sergeant and the turret gunner left the carrier with expressions of bewilderment on their faces.

'What . . . what was that thing, sir?' the sergeant asked.

'A dragon,' said Cormac, 'a real live dragon.' As soon as the others were inside, he closed the door on the sergeant's bewilderment. He looked at Stanton, still secured in place, and then gestured for the others to sit. He paced across the floor between them, his forefinger tapping his chin and a thoughtful expression on his face.

'Right . . . Aiden, I want a direct line of communication with Samarkand II. Set it up with Viridian. I want Blegg and Chaline on the other end, soonest.'

'We should be able to set up the link with this carrier's transceiver.'

'Do it, then.'

Aiden stood and moved to the front of the carrier, and was soon in contact with Viridian. Cormac turned to Thorn, Cento and Mika.

'Tell me, what are your impressions? And you, Thorn, bear in mind what I said to you.'

Thorn surprised him by replying immediately. 'Seemed to me the p-beams stung it a little, or just surprised it. It defended itself from an irritation. It was more interested in the dracomen.'

'That speaks for itself,' said Mika.

'Those two grabbed the AGC – why, do you think?' Cormac asked her.

'Judging from what I learnt about their behaviour before, I thought they were out to defend you.'

457

'That car had a roof before. I take it they ripped it off?'

'Yes, one moment they were just standing there, the next they were tearing the roof off the car. There was a weapon under the seat. Scar went straight to it. They ignored me. I was clearly not going to interfere. Anything that can tear bubble-sheet like that . . .'

Cormac looked thoughtful. 'The weapon was a laser carbine. A rather ineffectual thing to use in the circumstances, when we are thinking in terms of proton guns.'

'Perhaps they just did not realize a laser carbine would not hurt it,' said Cento.

Cormac eyed the android for a moment. 'No, I think they understood the situation perfectly. I also think we're focusing on the wrong thing. The weapon they used is not the issue. What we have to ask is why did they tear the roof off that AGC?'

'To give themselves a greater field of fire,' said Cento.

'No again, on that. They only had one target.'

It was Thorn who gave the required answer. 'So the Maker could see them,' he said.

'Right,' said Cormac. 'I think we're starting to get somewhere now. Those dracomen were here to get to the Maker. To get it defensive.' He looked at Thorn. 'Just like that thing in the tunnel . . . maybe.' Thorn looked away from him. 'I think their one purpose is that. Maybe they had another purpose, should I cease to become Dragon's best bet for killing the Maker. I guess we won't know that now.'

'We know Dragon tells lies,' said Thorn.

'Yes, but what we don't know is how many, nor how deep they are. Now, Thorn, the Maker stunned you,

Cento and Aiden. It used a different form of energy for you than for them. Aiden said it used just enough to knock him out. You said it was about stun three that hit you, which is incidentally the maximum safe limit used by ES for crowd control. It was specific, therefore it ascertained what you could take, and was careful not to kill you. Does that strike you as the action of a psychopath?'

'No, but . . .'

Cormac turned to Cento. 'Would a near speed of light collision kill that creature?'

'Yes, very likely.'

'Aiden, are you through yet?'

'Samarkand II and Blegg are ready, Chaline is a few minutes away.'

'Have you Viridian there?'

'Yes.'

'Ask it where the Maker went.'

There was a brief conversation, and then Aiden turned back from the console. 'Viridian said it moved about two hundred kilometres directly east, then went down into a system of caves there. The Thuriot caverns, before the Thuriot mountains . . . Hold on, the sergeant just said there was an AGC circling at the edge of detection range just then.'

'One thing at a time,' said Cormac. 'He knows what to do.' He scratched at his head and stared at the wall for a moment. Then he said, 'I want Pelter and this killer android off my back now. This is too critical. I think we'll head east for about a hundred and fifty kilometres, and find a suitable place to put down again.'

'Another trap?' asked Thorn.

'Perhaps. We'll see.'

'Chaline's online now,' said Aiden.

Cormac stood up, walked to the front of the carrier and took the seat next to him. Thorn looked at Mika questioningly. She shrugged and said, 'If he doesn't want to tell us, he won't.'

Thorn said, 'One minute he says the Maker isn't a killer. The next minute he says he knows how to kill it. He's an opaque chap at times.'

'He knows what he is doing,' said Cento.

'I didn't suggest otherwise.'

The three of them moved up front to listen.

'Chaline,' said Cormac. 'Is the stage-two runcible through yet?'

'It is, and it would have been set up in another ten hours if I wasn't up here on this damned ship, and if there were no other interruptions.'

Cormac grinned. 'I'm afraid there might be. Tell me, how long would it take for you to relocate the stage-one runcible?'

'What? What the hell do you want—'

'Take it as a metaphorical question for now.'

Chaline calmed down. 'Depends where you want it. The biggest time-eater is laying the s-con cables.'

'How about if you just use a microwave emitter?'

'That would be quicker, I suppose. How far away would you want it?'

'About five hundred kilometres away from all other installations.'

'Why would you want to do that?'

'Just answer the question, please.'

'OK, about thirty hours, if all available staff are on it.'

'Could the AI run it from the new installation?'

'Of course I could,' replied the voice of a bored aristocrat.

'Right, Blegg, if we bring the Maker out after us through the stage-one runcible, having destroyed the buffers after our transmission, it would likely be killed.'

Blegg said, 'Y'want Dragon to know this, of course. It should be kept informed . . .'

Cormac smiled and shook his head. How the hell had he known? 'Of course,' he said, 'and it is our prerogative to do this. It must be punished for the deaths of those on Samarkand.'

'I see. You have already encountered this Maker?'

'Yes, and I want to be there to see it destroyed. I know remote detonators could—'

Chaline interrupted. 'Are you out of your minds? Destroy another runcible?'

Blegg's voice was as smooth as a snake. 'If that is what it takes, then that is what will be done. Y'understand?'

Cormac wondered if Chaline could smell the garlic on his breath and see the flecks of gold in his eyes.

'Right,' said Chaline tightly.

Blegg had a mandate from Earth Central. He could be argued with – but it was a pointless exercise.

'Will you arrange all that, then? I want a proton weapon left in the containment sphere. You'll have to turn off any proscription device in the sphere for that. I also want a fast AGC beside the runcible, with a covered walkway leading to it. Put three coldsuits in it as well.'

'We'll contact y'when everything is ready. Dragon will be told.'

'Good, after you make contact with us, we'll be flushing the Maker out with the CTDs. That's all.' Cormac rested his fingers on his bottom lip and stared at the console until the transmission was broken. 'Dragon probably heard every word of that,' he said. 'It put a lock on the information concerning the arrival of its dracomen on Samarkand, so it has access to the grid, and I think its tracking down of this Maker to Samarkand confirms that. It will, accordingly, discover all that has happened here. Very little information will escape it.'

'Are you going to tell us what you're up to?' asked Thorn.

'I haven't quite got it all sorted myself. I am, as Blegg might say, giving myself leeway for subterfuge. I'm afraid you'll have to be content with that for now. What you heard then is all you need to know.' He centred his attention on Aiden. 'Aiden, I want you to open a channel from my comunit to Viridian. Preferably through underspace, coded and random scrambled.'

Aiden nodded. They all waited for Cormac to say more.

Thorn became impatient. 'Now?' he prompted.

'Now? Well, I haven't eaten since yesterday and I'm hungry. I suggest we eat before heading out. Pelter needs to be dealt with. I can't have an imponderable like him about while I'm dealing with . . . other things.'

27

Politics (An excerpt): Everybody knows that we
are living in a meritocracy and that those in charge
are not human. Everybody knows that AIs are
running the show. Who would trust a human planetary governor? Who would trust humans with
controlling the vast spread of human migration and
trade? Certainly not other humans. As that sublime
AI, which is referred to as 'Earth Central', once put
it, 'Humans: fast machines that serve the purpose of
slow genes.' Most right-thinking people would agree
that we are not to be trusted with our own destiny and
are glad things are the way they are. Our history
should be a salutary lesson held at the forefronts of our
minds when we consider these matters. Nowadays you
do not see such bloody resolution to events as was seen
in the past. I mean, you don't see the machines killing
each other, do you?

From *How It Is* by Gordon

The magnetic rails lifted the shuttle from the bay floor,
just like AG.

'That's it,' said Tull over the intercom. 'Now you just

ease it straight out. You'll be going out opposite to the station's rotation, so you should have no problem. Obviously, once you're out, you'll fall away at one-quarter G.'

'In what direction?'

'Depends when you get through the door. I'd suggest you do this next time Viridian comes into view.'

Great, real technical.

Jarvellis kept her eyes on the door and her hand on the slide control as she waited. Already space beyond the door was taking on a blue-green haze. Any time now, then.

When the arc of the planet slowly climbed into view, she quickly pushed the control forward. She did not really fancy hurtling directly towards the planet at one-quarter G while still trying to figure out how to operate the controls of this thing. The shuttle slowly accelerated for the door, and more and more of the planet was revealed. As it went out into space, it immediately dropped and she rose against her seat straps. A glance up showed her the station now retreating with dismaying rapidity. She moved the control column and was rewarded with a cacophonous creaking as the ion engines moved in their housings.

'All or nothing,' she said, and pressed a button marked 'Grids'. Nothing happened. There was no flare, no surge of power. She leant forward and round, so as to see the ion engines. There was a glow underneath them no more vigorous than that from a faulty toaster. Jarvellis studied the other buttons available. 'Gas feed' seemed the most likely, so she pressed it. A pump started up somewhere behind her, and there was a stuttering roar to her right. Her view of Viridian tilted, kept on tilting. The roar started to her left, but the tilt did not correct and now the horizon was dropping away. She eased the column over, corrected the tilt. How the hell did she ease off on the power, though? It took her some minutes of frantic searching before she realized her foot was flat down on a floor pedal.

'This is Viridian control calling Nix shuttle. Answer, please.'

Jarvellis ignored the radio and concentrated on flying the shuttle. She could not figure out how to get back towards the planet. The settings of the engines seemed to be designed for re-entry only. *Think!* It occurred to her then that she was thinking like someone who had lived with gravity for too long. She was thinking in terms of up and down. She moved the full column over and flipped the shuttle so that Viridian was now directly above her, and then applied some power.

'This is Viridian control calling Nix shuttle. Answer, please.'

There was the airspeed indicator, and *there* was an altimeter giving a very strange reading. Slowly Jarvellis began to understand what each of the meters and small screens signified. She had got the shuttle in a stable orbit when a completely different voice spoke from the radio.

'This is Viridian. Will the lunatic flying that antique please respond. I have no objection to you killing yourself, but you are now entering occupied airspace.'

Shit, it was the runcible AI. Jarvellis searched for a switch to turn off the radio. She found none. What she did find was a screen that folded out from the old console. The screen flickered on to give her the same view as she had out through the front screen. She pressed a button and that view flicked to one that was identified – in the bottom right-hand corner of the screen – as infrared. She clicked along the buttons and called up all sorts of interesting views, but none of them would help to prevent her spreading herself across the surface of the planet if she didn't figure out how to land this thing.

They put the carrier down in a valley in the foothills of the cave-riddled Thuriot mountains. These mountains were not like any mountains he had imagined; they were the slabbed and laminated masses he had seen from the runcible facility. Perhaps it was the case that on a heavier-gravity planet like Earth such strange formations could not exist. He sited the camp a short distance from where the blue oaks and chequer trees of the Magadar forest petered out, on level ground thick with Arctic lichens and the chewed sprouts of new trees.

'If they come on foot, they'll come from the forest,' Cormac told Thorn. 'Sergeant, I want someone at the turret gun at all times. Organize a shift if necessary. I want you in there at the command console, co-ordinating all scan input. We'll keep channels open so you can relay everything you get.'

'So too.'

'Your gunner must take out anything airborne. Anything that even hints at being a surveillance drone, I want hit. Obviously if we get any AGCs coming in without ID, I want them hit as well. Go there now. I'll relay any further orders.'

As the sergeant moved on, Thorn said, 'The other lot

came in on foot. They didn't risk coming in airborne. I doubt this Pelter chap will, either.'

'I don't believe in taking chances. Now, there are two autoguns in the carrier. Set them up in the trees and put the men either side. Between them and the trees I want weaknesses.'

'Is that a good idea?'

'We'll have Aiden and Cento in there as spotters. Anything comes through, and we'll hit it on this open ground.'

'Not much cover for us here,' said Thorn, looking speculatively at the single tilted slab behind the carrier.

'Wrong, we dig in.'

'Ah . . .'

Cormac nodded to the slab and the land beyond it. 'I want holes dug over there as well, but I don't want them occupied. I just want them to look like they are. You I want at that slab with your proton gun.' Thorn nodded to this and Cormac went on. 'When it's all set up, I want everyone to get some rest before nightfall.'

'And if there's no attack? We do have another mission.'

'The Maker can wait. We'll stay here for days if necessary. As I said, I want Pelter off my back.'

It took the rest of the morning for the defences to be set and foxholes to be dug. The ground was very stony, and a metre down was a layer of permafrost. They had an electric shear that could slice through almost anything, and EM blasts from a pulse rifle soon melted the permafrost, but in the end the men had to dig the holes with shovels. It was tiring work for men unused to it, and would perhaps not have been finished until nightfall had not Cento and Aiden lent a hand. The sergeant and his men rested in their tents afterwards, perhaps trying to remember if the ES recruiting officer had said anything about having to dig holes. Aiden and Cento moved into the trees.

Night descended and now there was nothing to do but wait. Cormac surveyed what he had wrought, then headed for the carrier.

As he reached it, Cormac spotted Thorn ferrying Stanton back inside. Even boosted men must empty their bladders sometime. He followed them inside and watched while Thorn tied the prisoner back in place. Then he sat on the bunk opposite, as Thorn nodded to him and left them, his proton gun tucked under one arm. Cormac looked round to see the sergeant was up near the front studying a screen flipped up from the control console. Mika he could hear moving about in the rear section somewhere.

'You know, John,' he said, 'you're culpable for just about every crime on the book.'

Stanton looked at him tiredly. 'I know that.'

'Why? Ever since I first met you, I kept wondering why. The way you operate, you didn't need to resort to crime. You could easily have made your fortune in the Polity. Was it the buzz? The danger?'

'Maybe,' said Stanton. 'But how many people do *you* know who made informed choices when they were young? For me, crime was a way of survival at first, then a way of life afterwards. You know what it's like beyond the Line.'

'I know.' Cormac turned away from him, then looked back. 'I don't think there's anything I can do. You've killed people and some of those people were innocent Polity citizens,' he said.

Stanton was about to reply, when Aiden spoke from Cormac's comunit, which he took from his pocket.

'What is it?'

'A message from Viridian,' came Aiden's voice. 'It may not be relevant, but a shuttle just launched from the old ring station.'

'Who's there normally?'

'Outlinkers, apparently, but Viridian tells me they don't often come down to the surface. About once every ten years ... in exoskeletons ... to buy supplies they cannot manufacture. It may be nothing.'

'All right, keep me informed.'

Cormac dropped the unit back in his pocket and looked questioningly at Stanton.

'Nothing to do with Pelter. No way of getting back up there,' Stanton told him.

Cormac stood up and moved to the door. At the door he hesitated, removed his unit from his pocket and turned it off. He then took out a little thin-gun he had been delighted to discover amongst the carrier's armament.

'You know, John, it'll be nothing less than total mind-wipe for you. Do you want that?'

'Are you making an offer?'

'I am.'

'I still have enough left in me not to want to die,' Stanton said. 'I just don't want to remember.' Cormac nodded, put the gun away, and opened the door. He turned his unit back on as he went out.

The night passed without event, and sunrise revealed heavy red blooms on the chequer trees. The air was filled with a perfume redolent of lavender, and the hum of adapted bees amongst the foliage. Underfoot, a light frost hoared the saplings and the lichens beyond the edge of the forest. Cormac sipped coffee and blew vapour into the clear air. He wished his mind was as clear. Three hours' sleep had revived him a little, but he knew he could do with a straight eight hours without interruption. With the coffee he swilled down a couple of wake-ups. He wasn't the only one doing this.

As he walked across to see how things were, soldier Tarm crawled from his tent, then paused, scratching his head and yawning. He saw Cormac and looked suddenly guilty. He reached back inside his tent for his pulse-rifle, dragged it out and hung it over his shoulder, and then stood up.

'Lovely morning, sir,' he said.

Cormac nodded and Tarm hurried off.

'They're much in awe of you.'

Cormac turned as Mika walked up behind him.

'I would rather you stayed in the carrier,' he said.

Mika looked around. 'You know, I miss the dracomen,' she said.

'I don't,' said Cormac. He turned towards the foxholes and watched Tarm dropping into one. The hole's previous occupant climbed out and trudged back towards the tents.

'Cormac.'

'Yes,' Cormac said to the unit in his pocket.

'We have an AGC coming in over the mountains,'

Aiden told him. 'I've only just picked it up. It's only two kilometres away.'

'Sergeant, you have it.'

'I do, sir. They're taking a juice harvest to Motford. The return signature I'm getting is of a transporter. Looks OK, sir.'

'Tell it to divert. If it flies over us, we hit it.'

Cormac began trotting back to the carrier. From his unit he heard a shout, then the sergeant telling someone to shut up. He opened the door of the carrier and stepped inside, with Mika close behind him. Stanton had his feet on the floor. He looked angry and he was pulling hard at his bonds.

'You must divert or you will be fired upon. This is my last warning,' the sergeant said.

'Fuck you, soldier boy. I got a harvest to get in. Some of us got to work for a living,' came the reply. Stanton fixed Cormac with a look. 'It's Svent,' he said.

'Oh God,' said the sergeant. 'Needles.'

'Take them down! Take them down now!' Cormac yelled.

Overhead the guns started up like an engine. Actinic light flashed through the windows.

'Mika, get out,' he said.

Mika immediately obeyed. The sergeant stood up from his console and looked round.

'You too,' said Cormac. As the sergeant passed him, Cormac ducked forwards and looked up at the gunner. The man's face was hidden behind a targeting mask as he operated the gun's controls. Hydraulics whined as the guns tracked across. Cormac moved to the control console and looked at the screen. Four traces, one moving slowly and erratically. The other three coming in fast. One of them disappeared while he watched. He gripped the edge of the console, his palms suddenly slick with sweat.

'Incoming,' he said. 'Anyone found not wearing a helmet will be on a charge.' He looked around and noted his own helmet on the bunk opposite Stanton.

'We're the target,' said Stanton.

'I know,' Cormac replied.

Only one of the fast traces remained. The slow and erratic trace had descended into the trees.

'Come on. Come on.'

It took Cormac a moment to realize when the last trace had disappeared. He looked around. Stanton met his look then sagged against his bonds.

'Right.' Cormac slapped the console, then headed quickly back. 'Good shooting,' he said to the soldier operating the gun. The man swung his mask away and gave him a sickly grin. Cormac grabbed up his helmet and exited the AGC. Even as he stepped out, there was a blinding flash above, and the turret guns on the carrier began to flash again like arc-welders. Cormac's visor took its time depolarizing.

'I can't see!' came someone's voice over his com.

Cormac heard the familiar vicious whir of a seeker bullet. Then a scream and a thump. He ran for the nearest foxhole and jumped in. Tarm glanced at him, then returned to the sight of his pulse-rifle.

'Where the hell did that come from? Aiden?'

There was firing in the trees. More smoke gusted. At the perimeter, one blue oak spurted flame. Then there was a concussion and a cloud of burning twigs and leaves flew into the air.

Aiden said, 'Someone got through. We missed him. He was moving very fast. I suspect it must have been the android.' Cormac was sure the Golem was as close as it could get to anger.

'Are either of you hit?'

'No. It just came in for the one shot.'

'Who was hit here?' Cormac asked, sticking his head above ground and looking around.

'Goff – took his head off . . . sir.'

Just then an amplified voice spoke from the trees. 'You next Cormac!'

'Find that!'

'We thought you might be a machine, but we were wrong. I'm glad, because at least you'll be able to feel it when I blow your guts out. We found Angelina . . .'

The voice died away with the flashing of a pulse-rifle. There was a delay, then Aiden said, 'Relay speaker. A drone must have dropped it.'

Cormac waited for what might come next. Nothing did. He gave it an hour, but nothing came up on scan and it seemed that no danger was close. He climbed from the foxhole speculating on Pelter's words. The man's anger was understandable, but Cormac had little sympathy for him. The Separatists on Cheyne III had been responsible for killing upwards of 500 civilians a year with bombs and other devices of mass destruction, and for carrying out hits on various officials and visiting dignitaries.

'Stay alert and ready. I want no one out of their holes unless absolutely necessary, and by necessary I mean pee on your boots if you have to,' he said, moving towards the forest. At the edge of the trees he crouched down by one of the autoguns. The device was tracking back and forth on its tripod. Through the trees he could see no movement. Aiden would pick up anything long before he saw it. Glancing back, he saw the sergeant and one of the men hauling a body-bag from one of the holes. He couldn't find the anger to berate them. He watched them lay the bag near the carrier. The sergeant went inside and the man returned to his hole. It seemed only a moment after that when the turret gun turned and fired a single shot into the treetops. From the white flash of impact burning leaves rained down.

'What was that?'

It was Aiden who replied. 'Another surveillance drone. I'm getting movement.'

Cormac moved back. There was a mosquito whining in the forest. The gun in front of him began stuttering. He ran for Goff's foxhole and dropped into it.

'Flares!'

The flares shot out while the turret guns on the carrier began flashing. Then he heard something else: a higher whine came from the treetops and the fire of the turret guns met it in the upper branches. Cormac saw something explode in a disc of fire. The severed half of a tree fell flaming.

'Shit! Needles again! Where the hell did he get this kind of armament?'

A silver torpedo shot from the burning treetops, turned in an erratic arc up into the sky, where the turret guns blew it to pieces. Another object shot through, and there was an explosion to Cormac's right. It happened too quickly for there to be a scream. All that was left was a burning foxhole and a few scattered pieces of gory body-armour. He looked up as the fourth missile came through and nosed overhead like a hunting pike. This one was larger. This was the one the others had made a way for. The carrier. Pulse hits crackled along the back of the missile and its flight became erratic. At the last it tumbled through the air and hit underneath the carrier. The carrier lifted on the blast, turned in flames and a cloud of falling earth, and crashed down on its roof.

'Oh fuck,' said Thorn.

Another explosion left another burning foxhole.

'Cento? Aiden?'

'I . . . tried,' came Cento's broken reply.

Two more detonations silenced the autoguns. In the trees were flashes of proton-gun fire. Something came running from the smoke and flying debris. For a moment Cormac thought it was Aiden, but even Aiden was not so tall. This figure was dressed in a long and tatty coat and had a wide-brimmed hat on its head. Mr Crane. Pulse fire hit the android from every side, but did not slow it. It came amongst them with its clothes on fire. Cormac saw it pause over a foxhole, its hand stab out. Then, all around the nearby foxholes, smoke started coiling into the air.

'Lasers!' someone yelled.

Cormac was about to ask where from, but the smoke revealed the red beams stabbing from beyond the carrier. He had miscalculated. Someone had come in at the back, using what little cover there was there. Abruptly Thorn replied to that fire. A purple line cut from the slab and there was a white detonation beyond it. The firing immediately halted. Cormac was out of his hole, reaching for his shuriken, as the android turned to him. He saw a face of polished brass. He threw. The shuriken thrummed through the air with vicious confidence. A brass hand smashed it to the ground.

The android came at Cormac.

'Hit it! Hit it!' Cormac heard the sergeant yell. Then Aiden came flashing in from the side and hit Crane with the force of an out-of-control AGC. Both of them hit the ground and slid about three metres. But even as they slid, they exchanged blows with frenetic speed. The sound of combat was like that of a log-chipping machine. Suddenly they were on their feet, apart, then slammed together again. Shreds of clothing and syntheflesh fell as they hit at each other. Cormac turned to movement at his left. Cento came from the trees at an erratic run. The syntheflesh was burnt from the upper half of his body to expose blackened metal. One of his arms was missing. He seemed to be blind and navigating on hearing alone. In a moment he leapt into the fight. Cormac saw him wrap his legs around the android and his remaining arm around its neck. Aiden proceeded to take it apart.

'As far as you go, Agent!'

Cormac turned. Pelter stepped out from behind a tree, and raised a Devcon assault rifle. Cormac reached for his thin-gun as the rifle fired. A whirring, as a steel hornet shot towards him. Slower than a normal bullet, but fast enough for Cormac to know he was dead. But in that moment, that fraction of fatal seconds, there came another whirring. An explosion rattled fragments of metal against Cormac's helmet. The seeker bullet was gone.

Shuriken hung in the air before him, flexing its chain-glass blades.

'Fuck you, Cormac!'

Pelter fired the remainder of the clip from the Devcon. Shuriken blurred through the air and took out those five seeker bullets in a chain of explosions. Pulse-fire hit the trees, but Pelter was gone, the Devcon abandoned on the smoking ground. Cormac stood where he was for a moment, too stunned yet to take in what had happened. He stared at the ground and wondered how the hell a small rubber dog came to be lying there. Then he shook himself and looked round. Cento and Aiden stood over the dismembered android. Cormac turned back to shuriken and hit the recall on its holster. Shuriken continued to bristle its chipped blades in the air for a moment, before returning to its home with a fractured hum.

'Thank you, Tenkian,' Cormac said, and headed for the trees.

Ultraviolet. A huge burst of ultraviolet. There was only one sort of weapon that kicked out that much, and Jarvellis had last seen one in the hold of the *Lyric*. If John was still alive, he would be there. If John was dead, then Pelter would be there. She tilted the ion engines of the shuttle and put her foot down. It leapt from its recent approach vector and arced towards the distant lights.

'Lunatic shuttle pilot. I suppose I would be wasting my breath in telling you that you're heading for an area that has recently become restricted to all air traffic.'

You don't have breath, Jarvellis thought, then ignored everything else the runcible AI had to say. She flicked the side screen to infrared, and saw she was getting quite a picture from that as well. Had to be them.

In the foxhole, with its only other occupant a survival suit filled with crash foam, Mika wrapped her arms across her chest and waited with grim patience. When this was all over she would have to clear up the human wreckage. There was one she knew she would be doing nothing for. The two suited killers, who had opened up with laser carbines from a spread of low scrub just beyond her, had not reckoned on Thorn being on that slab. Mika closed her eyes on the vision of one of them crouched with his carbine at his shoulder, then silhouetted in the white flash, and flying apart. His companion had let out a horrible moaning scream. He must have found some sort of cover, because Thorn did not fire again. Soon, soon it would be over. A close hissing crackle made her open her eyes. The stuffed man was smoking, a hole burnt through his back. Someone dropped into the foxhole beside her.

'Hello, pussy,' said Mennecken, resting his carbine next to the edge of the hole.

Mika did not pause for conversation. The study and saving of life was not all she had been taught on Circe. She pushed herself up with her elbows, turned, and kicked. Her foot slammed up under the mercenary's chin. Mennecken staggered back, then reached up and rubbed at his jaw. He smiled.

'Want to play?'

When he came at her he came straight into the blow

Mika hammered at his sternum. She gasped – body-armour. She chopped with her other hand at his neck, but he tilted his head and the blow caught him across the ear to seemingly no effect. His hand closed on her shirt and with casual contempt he threw her against the edge of the foxhole. She tried to come back at him, but the slap he delivered just knocked her to the ground. Next thing he was astride her and drawing a chainglass knife.

'They killed my brother, and I'll kill them,' said the mercenary. 'But there's always time to play, little pussy.'

'Playtime's over, old chap,' said another voice.

Mennecken turned his head to look, and his head disappeared in a wet detonation. Making horrible bubbling sounds the corpse dropped to one side. Mika pushed at it almost in panic and struggled away. She looked up at Thorn as he holstered his pulse-gun. The front of the Sparkind's uniform was soaked with blood.

'You injured?' he asked.

Mika shook her head.

'Very good. I'm . . . not so good,' Thorn said.

Mika climbed from the foxhole and supported him as he swayed. She looked back once at the headless corpse draining its blood into the stony earth, and then helped Thorn return to the camp.

Through the shattered window Stanton had been presented with a perfect view of the action, albeit an uncomfortable one. His wrists were still tied by the bunk – only the bunk was now above his head. He looked around inside the carrier for some way of freeing himself. Pelter was getting away! That just must not happen.

The gunner would be no help. The turret had taken full weight as the carrier had come down and the man was now folded in a tangle of metal and seat padding. The sergeant was unconscious. Stanton looked outside again. The more badly damaged of the two Golem had taken something from what remained of Mr Crane. It held that something up, before tossing it on the ground. Stanton recognized the long lozenge shape of a Golem's mind. The other drew a pulse-gun and fired. The mind shattered and the two Golem moved off. Now, that had been something Stanton was glad not to miss. He focused his attention on the scattered brassy remains and couldn't help but wonder where the suitcase was. It then occurred to him that amongst those remains lay the solution to his dilemma.

Stanton flicked the ring on his finger and twisted his right hand round so it was out and open. What was left of Crane's coat jerked into the air, and the Tenkian dagger through and away. It hit the shattered window and went straight through, turned in midair and slapped its handle into Stanton's hand. Stanton turned it and began sawing through his bonds.

'Cormac.'

Cormac turned and put his back against a tree. His comunit was still on.

'What is it, Aiden?'

'What are you doing?'

'I'm after Pelter.'

'I will be with you shortly.'

'No, you won't. You'll secure the camp and sort out the mess there. I can handle this.' There was a moment of silence before Aiden replied.

'Very well. As you order, Agent. You had best be aware then that the shuttle Viridian informed us about has landed a quarter of a kilometre in on the course you were following. It may be that this is how they intended to escape.'

'Thank you. I'll be back with you soon.'

Cormac turned the unit off, then set out again. Within minutes he found the AGC transporter, with burns all across its hull, and what remained of Dusache clinging to the wrecked missile launcher. The ground was smoking and the air acrid. Cormac approached cautiously, then crouched when he saw movement beyond the platform. A shadow flitted through the trees and the smoke ahead of him. He fired once with his thin-gun. There was a yell, and pulse-gun fire returned with startling accuracy. Cormac hit the ground and tasted leaf-mould and lichen. His sleeve was smouldering. He rolled to the side, behind an oak, as the leaf-mould and lichen caught fire. Still rolling, he fired past the other side of the tree. There was a scream, the sound of someone stumbling, then falling. A smell similar to that of roast pork wafted on the smoky breeze.

Cormac rose to his feet with his gun still pointed where he had last fired it. To one side there was a tree. From behind it he could hear someone gasping raggedly. He approached.

The man lay with his back against another tree, his pulse-gun in his hand. His body was burned from neck to groin. Cormac had hit him once through the

481

shoulder, but the wound from that was a neatly cauterized hole. These other burns were from the flare off high-energy turret-gun hits on the transport. Cormac moved in slowly and quietly. When he was less than a metre away, the man turned and attempted to bring his gun to bear. Cormac kicked it from his hand.

'Svent,' he said, 'where's Pelter?'

'Stupid . . . stupid,' said Svent.

Cormac just watched him and waited. Svent looked up.

'Should have got out. Could see that . . . when it was off.'

'What?'

'Aug . . .'

'What aug?'

'Scaly . . .'

'I'll ask again. Where's Pelter?'

'Ain't tellin' you that . . . Why should I tell you that?'

'Because if you don't, I'll kill you,' Cormac suggested.

Svent glared at him, then his glare turned into a nasty smile.

'Don't turn,' said Pelter. 'You don't know where I am, and you won't be able to turn faster than I can pull this trigger.'

It had never been Cormac's way to think too long about such situations, nor to throw himself on the mercy of any enemy. If Pelter had seen how it had been for Angelina, he would have known this and immediately shot him in the back when he had the chance. Cormac dropped to one side taking one snap shot from under his left armpit as he went. Something slammed his left biceps and he smelt burning as he rolled, then dived, snapshooting at a half-seen figure. He heard Svent scream as he reached cover behind the tree. Pelter had hit the little mercenary with his wild shooting at Cormac.

Behind the tree, Cormac inspected the burn on his arm. It was not serious, but that arm would soon be useless. Nevertheless he would wait. He stood up with his back against the tree, holding his thin-gun up beside his face. Any moment now . . .

Pelter could not believe it; you stood still when someone with a gun was demanding it. You did not run for cover in the hope they would miss. He backed up, firing single shots off at the tree while his mouth seemed to turn ceramic. The ache in his head, since Mr Crane's destruction, was growing in intensity, as if striving to fill the void left by the android's absence.

No Mr Crane now. No one left at his back. Nothing now between him and that thin-gun.

'Fucking die!' he shouted and blasted at the tree again.

Three times. Three times he'd had the agent in his sights, and three times he had failed to kill him. Maybe they had been right at the start . . . maybe Ian Cormac was some kind of android.

Pelter stopped firing and continued to back away. He kept his weapon directed towards the side of the tree where Cormac had disappeared. When the agent stepped from its other side, he stepped straight into Pelter's nightmare – straight into that vision ever imprinted on his missing eye.

The barrel of the thin-gun seemed attached to Pelter's

forehead by some invisible rod, and he seemed to feel the searing extension of that rod through his forehead and out the back of his skull. He pressed down on the trigger of his weapon and tracked fire sideways. But the time it took him to redirect his aim was not time enough. Silver light flickered in the barrel of the weapon the agent held.

Pelter saw only blackness.

With a puzzled frown, Cormac walked over and looked down to examine Pelter. Apart from the hole burnt cleanly through the Separatist's forehead, the man was already a mess: not only was the link suppurating in his head, but his clothing was ragged and filthy, and he stank. This was not the Pelter Cormac had known; this was a man ravaged by some daemon. What else could account for such lack of self-regard? Cormac wondered just what had driven Pelter to become this thing that lay before him.

He was also puzzled by the terror he had heard in the man's voice. Death was always a distinct possibility for one of Pelter's tendencies, and always something to fear. But terror? Cormac glanced down at his thin-gun, pocketed it and walked away. He guessed he would never know the answer.

28

Contra-terrene device (abbr. CTD) is one of those euphemistic labels Earth Security comes up with every now and again, normally to stick on something associated with terms like 'megadeath', 'gigadeath' and 'Oh, shit!' A forty-megaton CTD could easily be mistaken for a simple thermos flask, and there are parallels. Only, if you open one, you will not find hot coffee inside; you will find antimatter, briefly.

The antimatter is held in an s-con magnetic coil, which is also powered by a bleed-off from it. Theoretically a CTD will not explode without a complex code being keyed into its detonator. The canisters have reputedly been shock tested to a 10,000-kilometres-per-hour flat collision with case-hardened ceramal, and heat-tested to the melting point of the same. One has to wonder what the meaning of 'test' is here, because no one seems to know if the canisters survived said 'tests'. Other questions that occur are: was there anything in the canisters when they were tested – and where are the people who tested them?

From *How It Is* by Gordon

In the morning Cormac counted the cost of his single-mindedness: three men dead, one man minus his feet and one man blinded, though new feet and new eyes were no problem, Cento scrapped for the second time, and Thorn now lying on the ground beside Mika's AGC with the woman removing a lump of shrapnel from his guts. Should he let some other agent take over? He thought not.

Pelter was dead, and Cormac did not know how to feel about that. The man had obviously slipped off the far side of weird some time ago, so perhaps death was an easier place for him. Just as the Separatist had once tried to share his sister's looks, he now shared her executioner; an apposite ending, but one Cormac found uncomfortable to speculate on. He turned his thoughts away and towards the future. Now he had a mission to complete: a mission to which he was ideally suited. He must not let the death of one madman distract him. It was like being a runner in a marathon: he had just passed the pain barrier and now he must continue. With core of cold hardness, he banished what had already been done from his thoughts, and considered what must be done now.

There were things he had learnt that another agent might have missed. Another agent might not have possessed his basic distrust of Dragon, might have been more credulous, taken the easier options. Pressing his hand to the dressing on his left biceps, he walked over to Aiden.

The Golem, though not quite so damaged as Cento, had still taken a pounding. He had lost skin from the side of his face and all down one side of his body. His eye on that side was missing, his exposed metal arm-bones were bent, and his metal ribs staved in, one of them broken. Aiden moved slowly as he turned the handle on a mechanical winch. He glanced over at Cormac, and perhaps noted how he was being assessed. Small plates shifted on the exposed side of his face, while the other side grinned.

'You should see the other fella,' said the Golem with an unexpected flash of humour.

Cormac could not find it in himself to react. He looked along the winch cables to where they were attached to the carrier. 'Will it work?' he asked.

Aiden's grin switched off. 'It will have about fifty per cent AG, and one turbine is still functional,' he said, and then continued winding the winch. After a moment the carrier crashed down on its side. As Aiden went off to reattach the cables, the sergeant approached. Cormac registered his stiff expression; he was well aware that the sergeant blamed him for the deaths of his men, and was in complete agreement with that assessment. Had the men been policemen, he might have had some sympathy, but they were soldiers, and death was just part of their job.

'Any sign of Stanton?' Cormac asked.

'No sign, sir. We found the shuttle, though. Whoever brought it in must have been a lunatic. It looks like it only just made it to the surface in one piece.'

'Can't be coincidence that it landed here,' said Cormac.

'Probably zeroed in on the proton gunfire, sir. I would think that most of the planet knows something happened out here by now.'

'Yes, quite probably.'

There was a short, tense silence.

'What now?' the sergeant finally asked.

Cormac saw that Aiden had finished reattaching the cables and was coming back. He nodded towards the carrier. 'Now . . . now you take your own men, and Thorn, Cento and Mika, back to civilization in the carrier. Aiden and I continue on.'

The sergeant could not hide his relief.

'Not a chance,' came a voice from behind.

Cormac turned to see Thorn walking unsteadily towards him. Mika came out behind him.

'Should he be walking?' Cormac asked her.

'I wouldn't recommend vigorous movement, but he's all right to walk. The other two won't be walking, though. One for obvious reasons, the other because his optic nerves are burnt out. That said, they're easily enough replaced.'

Thorn was staring hard at Cormac. 'You promised me,' he said.

Cormac shook his head. 'You asked – but I promised nothing. I remember it precisely. Carn found that hole in the artefact before I could give you a reply.'

'Please,' said Thorn levelly, too proud to beg.

'You can come if you wish. But if we have to run, I won't wait for you.' Cormac turned away. Mika watched this exchange, then suddenly spoke up.

'I'm coming as well,' she said.

'If you like,' said Cormac, then turned at the sound of Aiden winding the cable in at high speed. The cable drew taut and Aiden's winding slowed. The winch, Cormac knew, had been attached to an electric motor on the front of the carrier. Strapped to the tree there was no motor to run it, and there was not a man here capable of turning the hastily fabricated handle. They all watched in silence as Aiden got the carrier up and teetering on its corner. When it crashed down level, Cormac immediately headed over to it. Shortly he returned, carrying a bulky rucksack.

'We're going now,' he said, and nodded towards Mika's AGC. The three fell in with him as he strode towards it.

In a moment they were airborne and gone.

'Goodbye,' said the sergeant, with a complete lack of sincerity. A few days before he had been eager for the chance of action. Now he just wanted to reach a safe retirement.

Cormac checked his watch after he had set the cruise-control on the AGC. 'Should be there in under an hour. Aiden, what are the precise co-ordinates of where the Maker went to ground?' Aiden told him, and Cormac flipped a map-screen from the console and checked them. 'Seems there is a cave mouth there. I'll be going in to set the CTDs. I am going alone. You, Thorn, are not capable at present, and I do not see why Mika should be exposed to the danger.'

Aiden said, 'But I see no reason why I should not accompany you.'

'You would not – and that is because you're not in possession of all the facts. You'll stay with the AGC. That's a direct order.'

There was no answer to that, so none was given.

Fifty minutes of flying brought them to a position directly above the given co-ordinates. Cormac brought the car down to twenty metres above ground level, then looked down at the cave mouth. It was a ragged rent in the side of a mountain, but easily accessible. He landed the vehicle a short distance away.

Before he left the car, Cormac reached back and said, 'Give me your thermal scanner, Aiden.'

The Golem handed it over: a grey box the shape of a soap bar, with a single screen and ball control. Cormac turned it on the three of them, and saw how little of a reading he got from Aiden. There were separate heat sources at his chest and groin, but the rest of his body was almost invisible. Mika and Thorn were statues of molten glass on the screen. Cormac moved the ball control and the area covered by the screen expanded. Positions relative to the sensors on the end of the scanner were given in metres, in three dimensions. He tilted the scanner and saw that these measurements did not change. The device was keyed to a ground level, then. He nodded with satisfaction and put the scanner in his pocket. When Aiden moved to hand over Thorn's proton gun, which lay on the back seat, Cormac held up his hand.

'I won't be needing that,' he said, and got out of the car. In silence they watched him go. He walked away with the rucksack slung over one shoulder: a tourist out for a brisk hike.

As he reached the cave mouth, Cormac ran a quick diagnostic on shuriken. It might have been damaged by the android, or by the seeker bullets. The miniscreen pointed out a slight aberration in the programming sequences, and some minimal damage to the chainglass blades. Both defects were acceptable. The blades were still more than serviceable, and he reckoned the source of the slight aberration was Tenkian himself. No way had he programmed shuriken to intercept seeker bullets, then hang in the air like a bristling terrier.

Cormac entered the cave.

A rush of creatures that he at first took to be bats fled past him. A close inspection of them showed him that they indeed had batlike wings – but seemingly no body or head. There was also something insectile about them. The cockroaches and burrowing beetles on the floor of the cave were terran, but the blue-metal centipedal creatures that seemed to be preying on them were from somewhere else entirely. Cormac trudged on through fallen bodies like dry leaves and turned on Aiden's scanner.

It indicated that there was something large about fifty metres ahead, and twenty metres further down. He advanced cautiously, wondering if he had been foolish to refuse the proton gun. He had not wanted it because shuriken seemed capable of dealing with anything the Maker might put in his way, and a proton weapon might well have brought the roof down on him. He paused for a moment and opened his rucksack. The box he took out was from Thorn's kit – he suspected it had belonged to Gant. He opened the box and took out one drone light, initiated it, then tossed it into the air. It ignited and shot off ahead of him.

The drone light bobbed down into darkness, and Cormac caught a glimpse of mirrored reflection. He halted and punched a particular attack program into his shuriken's holster, then took it out and tossed it into the air in front of him. It spun up and hung there, revolving

like a metal-saw, but with its blades moving in and out
as they had after it had destroyed the seeker bullet that
had Cormac's name on it. Cormac viewed it with suspicion: it was not supposed to do that. Tenkian, again.
No one really knew what the weapon-smith did with
his microminds, but it was often said that some of his
weapons developed minds of their own, so to speak. Just
so long as shuriken did its job, Cormac would be happy.

Twenty metres more and Cormac saw a flailing of
chrome legs – as the drone light shot to the side of the
tunnel and went out. He halted and listened at the dark.
There was no alternative. He reached down to the
holster and felt his way to the enable button. He pressed
it and listened to shuriken whir away from him.

Only a few seconds after shuriken had gone there was
a crashing from the darkness, and a familiar sound as of
an air-compressor starting. He heard a scrabbling, the
crash of a heavy body going down, then the metal-saw
whine of shuriken striking. Sparks flared in the tunnel
ahead and in their light Cormac caught a glimpse of
a nightmarish shape. The sparks went out, flared again
with a second strike, then a third, a fourth. When the
only sound he could hear was the sound of those strikes,
Cormac advanced, sending another drone light ahead of
him.

The creature that lay dismembered on the tunnel
floor resembled the one in the shaft on Samarkand only
in that it was silvered and had insectile legs. Cormac
realized immediately that the Maker had taken as its
template the same centipedal things he had previously
observed. Sure now that the creature was not going to
be getting up again, he hit the recall on shuriken. It

poised over the body with its blades going in and out, as if wondering whether to disobey and hit it again, but then it returned to its holster. Cormac plucked the drone light from the air, punched a different setting on it, and sent it out at a constant twenty metres ahead of him. A glance at the scanner showed some anomalous readings not so far ahead and a bit below: the Maker. He advanced.

Thorn stared up at the cave mouth and swore creatively, then pushed his hand against his stomach and winced. Mika had done an excellent job of knitting his intestines together, but no way was he in any condition yet to go potholing. He turned to her.

'We shouldn't have let him go alone,' he said.

'He gave orders and instructions, which amount to the same. Let me pose a question to you: would you disobey him?'

It did not sound like a question from Mika's lips, more like some sort of didactic exercise.

'I know what you mean,' said Thorn. 'He's all perfectly logical and reasonable mostly, but you know that he could quite logically and reasonably cut your throat, then wander off to find himself a cup of tea.' He turned to his other companion. 'Aiden, couldn't you follow him in at a distance.'

'He specifically ordered me to stay here. He is an agent of Earth Central Security, and we were told to put full trust in him and obey him. This was at the request of people we respect, as we otherwise have always been taught to question all orders. Cento and I did some checking and found he was gridlinked for ten years more than is normally acceptable, simply because he had become almost indispensable to Earth Central. The runcible AIs rank him not far below Horace Blegg.'

Thorn nodded. 'Blegg . . . we always used to hear about him. He's something of a legend. There's those that don't believe he exists. I wasn't so sure myself . . .'

Aiden looked at him and said, 'Perhaps I cannot impress on you enough just what it means to have that kind of approval from the runcible AIs. The records on Blegg go back beyond the first runcible AIs. It is rumoured he is over four hundred years old, which is somewhat strange, but it is certain he has now been working for Earth Central for two hundred years. Ian Cormac has only been an agent for seventy-three years, yet he too is ranked so high.'

'I guess we should stay here then,' admitted Thorn.

Mika said, 'In the Life-coven we are taught to read people. I will wait here. I will wait on Ian Cormac.'

Cormac programmed the CTD and shoved it down amongst the decaying bat-things, then he turned and watched the light retreating into the depths of the cave. He nodded his head contemplatively, then looked down at the sprawled dracoman. It was Nonscar, lying prone as if in slumber, but with its eyes open. Cormac studied it for a while, then spoke into his comunit.

'Viridian, did you get all that?'

'There was some interference. I am having trouble holding your signal through that rock.'

'Very well, I'll repeat: we go through to the stage-one runcible, and I want all information access to the containment spheres closed off. The Maker will follow us in, and there'll be a detonation at the other end. The next transmission will be to the stage-two runcible – when it's set up – but only on my signal.'

'Affirmed.'

'I'm leaving the cave now. The blast will occur in twenty-five minutes. We didn't have this conversation, so don't let it out on the grid.'

'Affirmed.'

Cormac looked down at the dracoman and clapped his hands.

Its slotted pupils flickered and it let out a hissing breath. After a moment it stood up and looked around. Cormac clapped again, then turned away. The dracoman followed him from the cave.

As soon as they were out into the light, Cormac broke into a run. The dracoman lengthened its stride to keep up, its motion bearing a strong resemblance to a running ostrich. As they came to the AGC, Cormac waved the others inside. They obeyed in silence, Mika and Thorn shuffling over to make room for the dracoman.

'Take us up immediately. We've got about twenty minutes before they blow. I want to be well away by then. Maximum speed, and step on it.'

Aiden took the car up into the sky in a steep climb. They were all thrust back into their seats as he used full AG and the boosters.

'What happened? I would have thought it would have killed them . . . the dracomen,' said Thorn in a strained voice.

'Found him unconscious, a little way inside. Scar's

dead though. Maker killed him. Don't know why this one was left unconscious.'

'Levelling . . . Three hundred kilometres per hour. Four hundred,' said Aiden.

'What speed will this thing do?' asked Cormac.

'It's restricted to five hundred on manual, a thousand on AI guidance. They don't like people breaking the sound barrier here.'

'A thousand is quite enough. You're an AI, so take us up there.'

'City ordinances restrict the—'

Cormac took his chip card from his pocket and waved it in Aiden's face. He then pushed it into a slot in the onboard computer. A sexy voice spoke from the speakers.

'Manual governors are offline. All city controls are denied. It would be inadvisable to proceed.'

The gentle ting of a bell sounded after the voice, then the voice repeated itself, only faster this time. By the third repetition that same voice had become the shriek of a hag, and the ting a discordant clank. The computer moaned and something death-rattled inside it.

'That's illegal,' said Thorn.

'So's detonating a CTD on an inhabited planet,' said Cormac.

Aiden shoved the control stick forward. In less than a minute the AGC was travelling at 1000 kilometres per hour. A quarter of an hour later they reached the runcible complex.

Aiden brought the car down in the empty AGC park, as close to the installation as he could. As they climbed from the car, Cormac glanced at the clock on the dash and then looked to the east.

'Come on, we've got to find a screen.' He ran into the complex surrounding the runcible installation. The others hurried along behind, Thorn with a little help from Aiden.

The embarkation lounge was eerily empty for a place so often busy. The people who had been here previously were well away now, and no doubt swearing about antimatter-containment fields and incompetent AIs. Cormac ran over to a bank of screens, speaking into his comunit all the while.

'Viridian, can you get it up on there? I want to see this.'

'I have surveillance drones two kilometres above the area.'

The screen flicked to a view down onto the Thuriot mountains.

'The explosions will be well contained. There may be very little evidence of them. Two minutes and counting.'

And with that a voice, softer than that of the AI, began to read off the seconds.

'One-nineteen, one-eighteen, one-seventeen . . .'

'When this hits,' said Cormac, 'we run for runcible B5, which is open right now to the stage-one runcible on Samarkand.'

Thorn asked, 'Will the detonations be enough to get it running? I mean . . . can we be sure it will run for the runcibles?'

'We can't be sure. If it doesn't run this time, we come back with greater force and do the same again.'

'I still don't see how we—'

'Hadn't you better get to the runcible now, Thorn? I don't want you dragging behind,' said Cormac, and turned and eyed the soldier coldly. Thorn returned that hard gaze for a moment, then bowed his head and moved away. Aiden went with him.

Cormac turned his attention to the dracoman. 'Nonscar, go with them.'

The dracoman moved away also.

'—eighty . . . seventy-nine . . . seventy-eight.'

While Cormac watched the screen, Mika studied him surreptitiously. The questions Thorn had been asking were pertinent in the extreme. She sensed the reason that Cormac had not answered them properly was, not because he could not, but simply because he did not want to. He knew what he was doing; that, she felt, was enough.

'Bringing the drone in lower,' said Viridian.

The view rapidly changed to one where trees and mountainsides became distinguishable. Mika was sure she was now seeing the same area they had recently quit, one mountainside appeared to be the one with the cave mouth in it.

'—twenty-one . . . twenty . . . nineteen . . . eighteen . . .'

Mika could see the tension building in Cormac's muscles. What was he seeing? What was it he wanted to see?

The seconds counted themselves out. The probe appeared to bob, but it was the mountains that shook. Dust and debris hazed everything for a moment, and then white fire jetted from the flank of one mountain, pinpointing the position of the cave mouth. Cormac glanced at the time display in one corner of the screen.

'Come on . . .'

More seconds dragged past. Then suddenly part of the mountain blew away and the incandescent Maker surfaced, jetting fire in every direction. Trees exploded into burning flinders and boulders were blown to dust. The screen whited out.

'Probe destroyed,' explained Viridian. 'I am withdrawing all other probes.'

Mika saw a fleeting quirk of a smile cross Cormac's face.

'Dramatic,' he remarked. Then said, 'Let's get the hell out of here.'

Fantastic light cut in a slow arc across the sky, and grounded at the distant runcible installation. There the finned cooling towers were haloed in St Elmo's fire. Jarvellis leant forward on the controls of the private AGC Pelter had stolen and shook her head in wonderment. After a moment the light winked out, and by contrast the day seemed unreasonably dark.

'Now, *that* you can explain in a minute,' she began. 'But first tell me about that shit Pelter.'

Stanton smiled at her. He couldn't stop smiling at her. When he'd come upon the grounded shuttle and seen her climbing out, he thought he'd finally flipped. But now, every minute, he was realizing it was true. And whether that applied to him having flipped or her actually being here he did not know, or care.

'He's dead. I think they're all dead,' he said.

'Did you *see* them die?'

'I saw Pelter – and I checked afterwards. He had that agent cold from about four metres back with a pulse-gun. Shit, I've never seen someone move so fast. I think Pelter winged him, before he freaked. He blasted away at the tree the agent ducked behind, then he seemed to lose it, and started backing off. The agent stepped out after that, calm as you like, and shot him. When he was gone I took a look. Hole right through the centre of Pelter's forehead and out the back.'

'Good. What about the others?'

'I think Mennecken and Corlackis got hit by an APW. I found some bits of Dusache stuck to the launcher, and Svent got hit in the crossfire between the agent and Pelter.'

'That's it, then,' said Jarvellis and sat back. She appeared as wasted as Stanton felt. With what she'd been through, he wasn't the least bit surprised. He looked at the flat material over her left breast.

'Now I think we get off this planet and find somewhere safe. Somewhere . . . peaceful and sunny. We'll get you that reconstructive surgery as well.'

Jarvellis looked at him tiredly. 'There'll be people hunting for us here,' she said, 'and we haven't got a ship anymore. How exactly do you think we'll get away from here?'

Stanton reached into the back of the AGC, brought a briefcase forward and laid it on his lap. The briefcase was battered, its framework showing through at the corners, and there were suspicious-looking spatters spread across it. Even so, the Norver Bank logo was still visible on it.

'I reckon we'll find a way,' he said.

At last Jarvellis managed to respond to Stanton's smile. She decided she'd give him the other news once they were somewhere safe – and when Stanton had lost any inclination to run.

29

Of course, criminals are people who have not received the correct moral education. They are people who have not enjoyed the opportunities of the rest of us. We should pity them, and as a society we should look after them. Punishment is not the answer. It only worsens an already bad situation. If we execute people, this apparently makes us just as bad as them . . . Bollocks . . . In the earlier years of the millennium this was always considered to be the case. The insanities of 'political correctness' blinded many to plain realities: if you execute a criminal, he won't do it again. Punishment of the criminal is good for the victims, if they are still alive. Why should we, as a society, look after and re-educate them when we hardly have the resources to do this for law-abiding citizens? Nowadays we have grasped these realities, so murderers and many recidivists are mind-wiped. We have not ceased to execute people because we are more 'civilized', but because that would be a waste of a perfectly useful body. And there are many personalities waiting in cyberspace (AI and uploaded human) for another crack at living in the real world.

From *How It Is* by Gordon

As Cormac stepped from the stage-one runcible on Samarkand the cold hit him like a hammer of ice. There were hastily rigged heaters in the containment sphere, but the temperature was not much above the lower limit necessary to sustain human life. Ahead of him, Aiden was half-carrying Thorn towards the exit and the covered walkway beyond. He surveyed the sphere as Mika ran past him. The proton weapon he had requested was resting on one of the heaters. He eyed it, then glanced over as his three companions hesitated at the exit.

'Get in the car. I'll be there in a minute.'

He went over to the weapon and touched it with his fingertip. It was cold, but, with conduction from the heater, not so cold as to take his skin off. He raised it, pointed it at the floor to the left of the runcible and, with the beam narrowed to pencil thickness, fired. The beam struck, diffracted through, and lit up everything underneath so that the black floor became transparent. As he traversed the beam, molten glass drained away behind it. With the hidden machinery revealed, Cormac found a duct and burnt through it. After the beam went out, fires still burnt under the glass. He looked at the resultant mess thoughtfully for a moment, then followed the others to the exit.

The AGC stood only four metres from the sphere, and the others were inside waiting for him. He reached the door of the car and ducked halfway inside. Then, estimating relative positions, he pointed the weapon at the wall of the covered walkway.

'What the hell . . .?' said Thorn.

'I've got to hit at least one of the buffers from the

outside. All I did in there was burn out some of the safety automatics.'

Cormac fired wide-beam. A section of wall, two metres long by a metre wide, disappeared in a purple flash. He could now see the edge of the buffer, and redirected the beam. Metal flashed away in seconds, exposing coils of doped superconductors and paralectric crystals. A hidden canister blew its contents and leapt into the sky on a tail of gas and flame. As Cormac shut down the beam, a fog of CO_2 vapour obscured all, then CO_2 snow began to fall. Cormac ducked into the car and slammed shut the insulated door, just before his eyes froze over.

'Out of here . . . now . . .' he managed to gasp, and began to shiver violently. He was not the only one, for the inside of the car was as cold as the inside of the containment sphere.

Aiden slammed the AGC up into Samarkand midnight, not bothering to disconnect from the walkway. The walkway held for a moment, then broke and fell away like a snake that has just missed its prey. From the windows of the AGC they could see one of the runcible buffers glowing with the colours of magma.

'OK . . . Aiden, no airspeed restrictions here. What's it capable of?'

'Fourteen hundred kilometres per hour, in safety; any faster than that and I might lose it.'

'Fast enough,' said Cormac. 'Fast enough.'

He leant back in his seat next to Mika and looked across at the dracoman, then he glared out through the window. Poised in the sky, like a watching moon: Dragon.

'I knew it wouldn't miss this. Gloating bastard.'

Mika turned to him questioningly, but he offered up no further comment, for just then Aiden applied full acceleration. They were all thrust back in their seats so hard they had not the breath to speak anyway. Only when the AGC was streaking along at its maximum speed did the pressure relax. Cormac looked at the clock set into the dash. It was on solstan time, permanently updated by a signal from Samarkand II.

'I wonder when it will come through,' said Thorn carefully.

'Any time now, I should imagine,' said Cormac flatly. 'Could be right this . . . second.'

At that moment Samarkand experienced a premature day. The light was hard and white: an ungentle light that lasted for twenty seconds and seemed to find and burn away every shadow. When it went out, they looked back at a growing sphere of yellow fire, cut through with sheetlike flashes of lightning.

'One unmade Maker,' commented Cormac.

Thorn looked at him in exasperation, about to say something. Cormac gave a fractional shake of his head, and flicked his eyes at the dracoman.

'How long till we reach the complex?' he asked Aiden.

'Not long: quarter of an hour.'

Thorn turned to face forwards. He asked no more questions.

'I think you can slow up now,' said Cormac, and closed his watering eyes.

It was difficult getting their coldsuits on in the confinement of the AGC, so they had only managed to get fully clothed by the time Aiden was bringing them in to land. With his body temperature rising, Cormac began to feel the coldburn on his face and the backs of his hands. When the temperature reached its optimum, he felt in some pain, and did not relish the prospect of pulling off his gloves.

Aiden set them down at the edge of the complex and, as they left the car, three suited figures came out to meet them. The dracoman began shivering, but this was the only effect the extreme cold had on it. It otherwise walked along as if taking a stroll on a mildly wintry day. Aiden walked likewise.

'Y' made it then,' came Blegg's voice over the com.

'Yes, and the Maker has paid for its crimes,' replied Cormac.

'And a perfectly good stage-one runcible obliterated,' muttered Chaline.

Cormac did not reply to that. 'Let's get inside,' he said, 'I want to see how much skin I've lost.'

The building they entered was a recent addition to the complex. They passed through a cold lock to get inside, and had to wait for a few minutes while their suits and the air around them was heated. Beyond this was an unsuiting room, with its lockers for the suits, showers and blow dryers, a machine for dispensing hot drinks, and lockers containing fresh clothing. Mika and Thorn were quickly out of their suits and soon drinking cups of hot soup. The other three – Blegg, Chaline and surprisingly, Carn – got unsuited just as quickly. Cormac took his time, leaving his gloves for last.

'Ow! Shit!'

Patches of skin lifted off the backs of his hands and his

fingers. His face was not a lot better. Chaline reached into a nearby locker, took out an aerosol and approached him.

'Synthiskin – it will seal the burns and kill the pain. It's good that it hurts. If there had been no pain, you'd then have had cause to worry.'

He held out his hands, and as she sprayed them they went gloriously numb. She did the same for his face, holding her finger over each of his eyelids in turn to prevent them becoming sealed shut.

'Thorn? Mika?' She turned to them next.

Both of them had a redness to face and hands, but neither had caught the brunt of it like Cormac.

'I'm fine, just a little coldburn,' said Thorn.

Mika held up her hand when Chaline turned to her queryingly, and continued sipping at her soup.

During all this, Blegg had stood silently to one side.

Cormac eventually addressed him: 'I want to get back to *Hubris*.'

'More?' wondered Blegg.

'More,' Cormac confirmed.

Chaline looked from one of them to the other. 'What's—'

Cormac interrupted. 'You can stay here and get on with setting up the stage-two runcible. Ten hours, didn't you say?'

'Less now, we've already been working on it,' she said.

'Good . . . Good.' He turned back to Blegg. 'Any communication from Dragon while we were on Viridian?'

'Nothing of any consequence . . .'

507

Cormac shot a question at Chaline. 'What condition is *Hubris* in now?'

'Pretty good,' said Chaline, eyeing him warily.

'Is there a shuttle ready to leave *now*?'

Blegg said, 'One hour. You can wait that long.'

Cormac looked about to argue, then said, 'Yes, I'll take a shower, I think.'

It was the heavy-lifter they boarded after that tense one hour. Cormac had been unable to relax. He toyed with his food and drank lots of coffee. He even wished he had picked up the smoking habit from Gant. Now would have been a good time to use it. Halfway through that same hour, Mika came with some instruments to run tests on the dracoman.

'I would like to find out what—'

'No,' said Cormac.

Mika looked at him in surprise.

'No tests, none at all.'

He stared at her levelly. She met his gaze, then packed away her instruments. They continued waiting.

The lifter was empty of cargo, and on its last trip before being re-stored. It had been used to bring down the old engine casings for transmission to Minostra; even damaged, they were too valuable to scrap. This had now been done, and the lifter was ready to return.

As Cormac settled in his seat, he said, 'When we board I want all communication channels to Dragon closed down. Should it try to contact us, we ignore it.'

'Why?' asked Thorn. 'Surely you can—'

'I'm giving orders, not making suggestions. Just listen – and shut up,' said Cormac.

Thorn went suddenly still, icy. Blegg leant across and caught hold of his arm. Thorn turned in cold irritation to look straight into those flecked eyes. No words were spoken out loud, but Thorn jerked away as if he had been snarled at. He stared at Blegg in amazement, then relaxed back in his seat with a nod. Blegg released his arm.

Mika stared at Blegg in perplexity for a moment, then turned her attention to Cormac. 'There's something else as well,' she said.

'Yes, the dracoman goes straight into Isolation. *Total* isolation. That means no probes, no testing, no scanning.'

Mika nodded.

Cormac checked the viewing screens nervously. One of them revealed the distant mote of Dragon on a far horizon. When he spotted it, Cormac's face hardened and he then watched it constantly.

Hubris opened for the lifter and accepted it back into its bright-lit guts. Before they stepped out into the bay, there was a delay as clamps took hold of the vehicle and pulled it into place against banks of shock absorbers. They exited across a long ramp that crossed the chasm in which the lifter nestled. As they stepped from this ramp, huge floors and walls began to turn and shift like the wheels in some giant clock as *Hubris* locked the huge vehicle away.

'*Hubris*,' said Cormac, as he stepped from the drop-shaft that had wafted him up to the living quarters, 'I want you to secure for impact, and clear the area around Isolation once Mika has delivered the dracoman. All communication channels with Dragon are to be closed.

The dracoman is to be sealed in; weld the unit shut if you have to.'

'Proceeding as directed.' Lights began to flash in the corridors as Cormac headed for Downlink Com.

Hubris announced, 'Proton guns charging.'

Cormac came to an abrupt halt, his hands clenched into fists. He looked at Blegg and then Thorn. After a moment he said, 'There will be no need for those. Charge them down.'

'Ship's safety is my first priority. Dragon is trying all channels. The indications are that there will be another attack. I cannot charge down proton guns without a direct order from agent Prime.'

Cormac looked at Blegg. '*You* have the authority now. I want you to order *Hubris* to charge down the proton guns. They were damaged in the previous attack so are unsafe to use,' he said carefully.

'Y'heard that. Close 'em down,' said Blegg.

'Proton guns charging down.'

Cormac continued walking. 'I also want all information systems closed off. All access is to be denied. If it looks like unauthorized access can get through at any time, I want those information banks dumped or destroyed.'

'I cannot initiate this without a direct order from agent Prime,' said *Hubris* stubbornly.

'Y'got my order,' said Blegg.

'Initiated.'

'You want Dragon to—' began Thorn.

'Yes, yes,' said Cormac irritably. 'But everything we say or do is recorded somewhere, and therefore possible to access. So keep it to yourself.'

This time there was no one in Downlink Com. Cormac dropped in a chair before the communications console, and called up a view of Dragon.

'At least this time we won't be shutting down Chaline's operation. Samarkand II will be operating everything down there. I think she's had about as much as she can take of my interference.'

'Nothing is more important than runcibles to her,' Thorn observed, as he pulled up a chair.

'Very shortsighted of her,' replied Cormac. Then he said, '*Hubris*, prepare for a major breach. Get everyone out of the areas on the route of Dragon's previous attack, then close all blast and security doors. Stand by with seals and foam.'

'Initiated.'

Cormac looked at Blegg and Thorn. 'Patience,' he said.

'Oh, I've always had that,' said Blegg. Thorn just appeared uncomfortable.

'Attempts to open a communication channel have ceased,' said *Hubris*. 'Dragon accelerating.'

'Pull away in close orbit. That should slow it,' said Cormac.

'Secure for impact. Secure for impact. All personnel to emergency modules.'

Cormac closed his eyes and began to breathe deeply and evenly, his brow beaded with sweat. The three of them could feel the vibration through *Hubris* as it accelerated away, and the slight pull to one side as the ship's gravity did not quite compensate for the vector of its course.

'Impact in three minutes twenty seconds. Mark . . . Impact in three minutes ten seconds. Mark.'

At that moment Mika entered Downlink Com. Cormac watched her frantically trying to read the situation, and lick her lips as she prepared herself for a question. He glanced past her to the door which had a flashing yellow-and-black-striped light above it.

'I see you got through just before the main doors closed,' he observed.

She nodded, staring at him.

'We'd best get ready then,' he said.

They locked down all the chairs in Com and any instruments that were loose. Then they went through to the emergency module; a circular room with twenty acceleration couches secured all round. This module, like many others scattered throughout the ship, contained its own separate life-support, and theoretically could withstand the break-up of the entire ship. The four of them lay down on couches and strapped themselves in.

'Impact in one minute ten seconds. Mark . . . Impact in one minute. Mark.'

It was not particularly reassuring to see the piped-in image of Dragon's all-too-rapid approach. It grew on the screen until they could see the pseudopods breaking from its surface.

'Impact imminent! Impact imminent!'

It was not as bad as the first time. The ship boomed, but did not seem to be breaking. Cormac still wondered how many people he might have killed. As the shuddering stilled, he unstrapped himself and exited the emergency module.

'Unauthorised information access at external port. I am isolating all systems . . . Shuttle-bay doors opening.'

'It knows the ship better this time,' said Mika.

Cormac glanced at her, then turned back to watch the pseudopods flooding into the shuttle bay, and squirming across the floor to the drop-shaft.

'Intruder-defence systems online.'

'Take them offline until my order,' said Cormac.

'Unauthorized access . . . all consoles and ports closed down in shuttle-bay area. Stress readings at drop-shaft doors.'

They watched, as for the second time, the safety doors buckled and crashed into the drop-shaft, and the pseudopods flooded down it.

'Vocal communication from Dragon.'

'No reply, but let's hear it,' said Cormac.

'Cormac! Cormac!' screamed the speaker. Only then did Cormac see the pterosaur head amongst the pseudopods. It rose out of them and came up against the camera.

'Cormac!' it screamed again, spraying the lens with milky saliva.

'Sounds pissed off,' said Thorn.

'Yes, and scared,' said Cormac.

Mika looked at him sharply, then returned her attention to the screen.

'Give me what is mine!' shrieked Dragon.

'Wants the dracoman,' said Mika.

'Do you wish Isolation unsealed?' asked *Hubris*.

'No, keep it sealed. If it wants its dracoman, then it'll have to take the whole chamber.'

'There will be extreme damage to the interior of the ship.'

The Dragon head appeared next in Isolation. 'Open! Open!' it shrieked.

Cormac began to rattle his fingers on the console. He was humming a tune and chewing his lip at the same time. After a moment he said, 'Then prepare for extreme damage to the interior of the ship . . . Tell me, what could the intruder-defence systems do now?'

'Specific nerve gases, low-intensity lasers, EM pulse-guns, evacuation of sealed areas—'

'Use low-intensity lasers and the EM guns.'

'Beton-twelve nerve gas—'

'Just! . . . as I said.'

Over the intercom they heard the high-speed crackling of the pulse-guns. Pseudopods began to fly apart and become charcoaled with black lines; but where one pseudopod was destroyed, another took its place. The ship convulsed.

'Charge up proton guns.'

'Charging. Stress readings all round Isolation Chamber One. Stress reading along all corridors to drop-shaft. Stress readings in drop-shaft.'

The screen showed walls and struts being torn away in Isolation, wads of insulation falling, pipes bursting and snaking through the air on jets of vapour, then it showed walls buckling and being pushed back into the corridors. One scene flickered out as a camera was destroyed. The screen then showed the whole of Isolation Chamber One peeled down to its armour, and being shifted by the pseudopods.

'Cormac! Cormac!' screamed the Dragon head.

'Target that head.'

The head was suddenly latticed with black lines, and then EM pulses began to blow pieces of it away. It shrieked and drew back out of Isolation. The chamber was dragged along after it, tearing walls, folding out ceilings. Sparks rained down, and cameras went out one after another.

'Isolation chamber in drop-shaft. Stress readings at drop-shaft doors. Ventilation seals breached, closing secondary seals.'

Just then there came into the room a smell of burning flesh and metal, and another smell – so strong it was almost a taste – of cloves.

'How long until proton guns enable?'

'Forty seconds. Mark.'

Suddenly the scene revealed was of the shuttle bay. The mutilated Dragon came on-camera. Its jaws opened and slammed forwards. The camera went out.

'Not too happy, I would say,' said Thorn.

'General idea,' muttered Blegg.

'Dragon has isolation chamber. Detaching. Flooding drop-shaft with crash-foam. Massive air loss. Crash-foam not holding. Closing shuttle-bay doors.'

The screen showed the shuttle bay from another angle. The bay doors were labouring to close against a hailstorm of crash-foam and wreckage. The debris was hurtling out into the vacuum.

'Pull away, maximum acceleration. Fire proton guns when ready.'

Dragon receded from the doors. A purple flash ignited space and a charred hole fifty metres across appeared in its scaled hide. Cormac watched for a moment, then removed a black cylinder-section from his pocket, with a miniconsole on it. He poised his finger over a flashing touch-plate.

'That's a—' began Thorn.

'Remote detonator, yes,' said Cormac impatiently, then asked, 'Distance, *Hubris*?'

'One kilometre. Mark. One and one half kilometres . . .'

The proton guns fired again, but this time the purple flare was not on Dragon's surface. It ignited over an invisible membrane and did no damage.

'Dragon preparing to return fire.'

They could all see the ripples crossing its surface.

'Distance?'

'Three kilometres. Mark. Four and a half. Mark. Six kilo— Fire imminent! Fire imminent!'

Cormac pressed his finger down. Everything under that membrane turned to light. The membrane broke and the screens whited out. *Hubris* bucked and they were flung to the floor.

Epilogue

The bleak sun inched above the horizon and a new day fell across the ruination that surrounded the complex. Above the corroded-bronze sky Samarkand was gaining yet another feature; a spreading orbital cloud of frozen gobbets of flesh, pieces of bone and metal . . . Dragon remains. *Hubris,* poised geostationary above the complex, watched this cloud spread with an aesthetic appreciation only available to AIs having the full spectrum of senses it possessed. With another fraction of its sensorium it listened in through the computer of the departing mini-shuttle. In a completely disconnected way it knew that it too was being used in this way, by a mind as many orders of magnitude greater than it, than it was of the computer.

'It woulda looked at everything y'said and did,' said Blegg, then he chugged down a large cup of whisky and grinned wickedly.

With his own cup resting on his knee, Cormac stared down at the floor of the shuttle with the unseeing gaze of exhaustion. He was finding it difficult to grasp that his plans had paid off.

Eventually he spoke. 'I guess it's a case of knowing who your enemies are.'

Blegg looked at the bottom of his cup in annoyance, took out his flask, shook it, and then smiled benevolently. Cormac had never known anyone like him. He probably knew exactly what had happened, yet managed to appear completely unconcerned. A strange man was Blegg. He rested his head back and closed his eyes.

It seemed only a minute had passed before Blegg was shaking him awake. He looked up at the screen and saw that the shuttle was coming down on the edge of the complex, in a storm of CO_2 crystals. He waited until he felt it touch down before he spoke.

'Aiden, ask Samarkand II how the stage-two runcible's coming along.'

The Golem got up from his pilot's chair as if he had not heard. Samarkand II answered the question over the shuttle's speakers.

'The stage-two runcible is undergoing rough alignment. This will take approximately fifteen minutes. I will fine-tune it in one tenth of a second.'

If ever an AI had been guilty of conceit, Samarkand II was that one, thought Cormac. He moved to the door of the shuttle as a covered walkway attached itself like a lamprey. As he waited at the door for the air beyond to heat up, he turned back to Blegg.

'You know, they have a carrying pouch inside them. Dragon knew everything that was going on here. It just grabbed them to make sure they were internally clear of the mycelium. It didn't want us finding that.'

'Y'not wrong. That where the CTD went?'

'Yeah, but it had to cut away some material to get it in.'

The door thumped open like the door to a fridge, and they entered the walkway. Soon they were passing by the milling technicians, and Samarkand II's voice droned over the speakers.

'Stage-two runcible alignment test commencing . . . Test complete. Still too far out for insertion of five-D cusp.'

The larger containment sphere of the stage-two runcible now rested under a large dome with floorspace all around. The open door to the containment sphere was big enough for heavy transport sleds. Cormac recognized the familiar figure of Chaline next to the door. He walked up to her and saw she was directing the adjustment of machinery under the black glass floor inside: the same kind of machinery as he had destroyed in the stage-one runcible. Dislodged floor panels were resting up against the wall of the sphere.

'Much longer?' he asked.

She watched him suspiciously for a moment, and then relented. 'A few minutes.' She gestured at the work going on. 'This is only cosmetic. One more test and the spoon'll be in.'

Cormac left her to it and walked back to Blegg. The Japanese was refilling his flask from a drinks dispenser. How he managed that, Cormac had no idea; the dispensers here did not normally dispense alcohol. When the flask was full they turned and watched as esoteric adjustments were made and Samarkand II gave notice of the next test. Inside the sphere they saw rainbows shimmering between the wide-apart horns of the runcible. They climbed to the roof of the sphere, penetrated it, then to the roof of the dome and through that. It was a beautiful sight. Cormac remembered the first time he had seen this with the stage-one runcible: the tower of rainbows reaching into the sky. It still did not fail to impress him.

'Spoon's in. All yours, Samarkand II,' said Chaline with glee.

Cormac said, 'Samarkand II, inform Viridian that access is now allowable from there.'

'Viridian has already been informed.'

'You mistake me. Inform Viridian that Cormac says access from there is now allowable.'

There was a pause, and when Samarkand II spoke again it sounded as surprised as an AI could be. 'Viridian tells me your message is affirmed . . . Transmission coming through.'

At that moment the runcible flickered and Cento stepped through. He had been rebuilt, partially. His missing arm had been replaced with one the colour of brass. He held it up and grinned triumphantly as he approached. Aiden greeted him with a perfect emulation of human happiness. The Golem came over to join Cormac and Blegg.

'Transmission coming through: energy anomalies,' Samarkand II announced.

The cusp of the runcible flared with light, and a glass dragon stepped through. There were screams of surprise, some screams of fear. The dome seemed full of light.

'There is no need for panic,' said Samarkand II – and those who had screamed felt a little foolish, perhaps.

The Maker came down from the dais on limbs of fire, scanning the place with its three glass eyes. It seemed to Cormac it should dwell in that tower of rainbows he had seen. It seemed wholly mythical.

'Now, I didn't expect to see *him*,' he said.

He pointed to the blackly silhouetted dracoman walking before the alien, like a slave – or its tamer. Soon the Maker reached them, and now they could see the workings of its body, like a glassy display of flasks and tubes in a chemistry laboratory. It spoke, and its voice seemed to draw sound from every direction and precipitate it out in gusting words.

'Cormac,' it said, and its terrifying head bowed down to peer at him.

'I thought you were going to use Scar for the blast,' said Cormac.

The voice came again, its elements seemingly drawn from the people who were gathering round to watch, to gawp. One brave soul reached out to touch, then snatched his hand back before it was burnt, or before he touched something ineffable.

'Scar is an advantage,' said the Maker.

Staring into light, Cormac suddenly felt even more tired. He looked round at Blegg, but the Japanese seemed preoccupied, his expression opaque.

Through Samarkand II and through *Hubris*, Earth Central watched the culmination of events with small facets of itself. Eventually it opened a communication channel that it still did not wholly understand.

CONCLUSION: SATISFACTORY?

Within certain limitations, Hal.
Explain.
Dragon died here, but Dragon still lives.

—Dragon dialogues—
DELAY.
DELAY.
DELAY.
Satisfactory conclusion deferred — projection.

The AI closed off that odd channel and once again focused all its attention through *Hubris*. The ship AI continued to watch the spreading cloud, fascinated by the pattern of its dispersal, and analysing it continuously. The remains of Dragon stretched out and out, and still following the creature's original course, they drew a glittering ring around the planet. Some of this debris fell into atmosphere. *Hubris* detected strange proteins and exotic metals. Some of these substances had been made to withstand extremes of heat and force, so certain fragments were not burning up on re-entry.

On Samarkand it was raining Dragon scales.